Dangerous Obsession

Maria Barrett

WARNER BOOKS

Dangerous
Obsession

A *Warner* Book

First published in Great Britain in 1994
by Warner Books

A CIP catalogue record for this book
is available from the British Library.

ISBN 0 7515 0693 1

Typeset by M Rules
Printed and bound in Great Britain by
Clays Ltd, St Ives plc

Warner Books
A Division of
Little, Brown and Company (UK) Limited
Brettenham House
Lancaster Place
London WC2E 7EN

Prologue

THE WIND WAS FIERCE.

It blew across the southern Italian hillside in icy gusts, pulling back the fragile, stripped branches of the olive trees, sleeting the rain against the desiccated landscape. It whipped through the graveyard of the church of San Nicola, crushing the early spring flowers and making the small group of mourners shiver painfully.

'Eternal rest grant to them, oh Lord, and let perpetual light shine upon them.'

The small crowd bowed their heads as the coffin was lowered into the grave. 'May they rest in peace.'

They did the same as the tiny olive-wood box was laid alongside it. The little girl began to cry.

'In the name of the Father, the Son and the Holy Spirit.'

Each person blessed himself and in the respectful silence that followed, the child's small, wracking sobs rang out on the hillside as the wind carried them through the air; an aching, pitiful sound. 'Amen.'

'Amen.'

'Leno, come away now, we are waiting.'

The elderly priest touched the young man's arm and felt him flinch at the contact.

'Please, Leno.'

But he continued to stare at the open grave and the two coffins splattered with sodden earth.

The priest glanced back at the little girl, standing alone

1

by the church: her bare legs red and sore where the hard sleet had chapped painfully against the skin, her slight frame trembling in the force of the wind. He pulled the long black skirt of his cassock around him.

'Leno, Francesca is waiting. Please. Leave Elizabeth now, let her go. Come with me to Francesca.'

He touched him again, pulling gently on his arm.

'Don't touch me, you . . .!' The young man swung round and the priest caught the full force of his anger.

'Take Francesca! . . . Go! . . . Just go, leave me alone with my wife.' He moved aggressively away from the priest, face into the freezing, harsh wind.

'But Elizabeth is dead, Leno, please. Come away from the grave.'

'Dead!' The young man turned back and spat the word out. 'No, Elizabeth is not dead, not to me, never!' He watched the priest's face closely, as if waiting for disagreement, then he saw him glance over his shoulder at the little girl.

'Her!' he shouted. '*She* is dead! Take her out of my sight!' He started violently towards her, his face contorted with anger.

'Leno! Stop there!' The priest's voice was clear and sharp. The young man stopped. 'In God's name! What are you doing, Leno?'

He looked back at the priest, suddenly confused.

'I . . .' His pain and grief were open and raw and he hung his head.

'Leno.' The priest moved towards him. 'Francesca is your daughter. Please, you have been so hard on her. She is only a child, a blameless child, and she needs you, she has no one else.' He looked into the face of the young man.

'Please, Leno.'

'Father . . .' The young man clenched his fist. 'I cannot . . .' He turned away. 'She killed my wife, my son . . .'

His voice was cold. 'I . . . cannot love her.'

'Leno!' The priest was angry suddenly. 'A virus killed Elizabeth! Your son lived only a few days, but it is not Francesca's fault – all children are ill! God chooses who he takes. In the name of Christ, what has happened to you?'

'It was Francesca's virus.' The voice was bitter now, uncompromising.

'Oh, Leno.' The priest hung his head. It was always the same argument, the same ending. It was Leno's final word and Father Angelo knew it.

He shook his head, blessed himself and asked silently for God's help. He had made a promise to the dying woman, several promises, in fact, and he did not know how he was going to keep them. The young man burned with anger; what if the flame never went out? He was too old to carry such a burden.

He looked back at the little girl, silent now in her anguish, and sighed heavily. He would have to try, for her sake, to comfort her as best he could, soften her life. What a life, he thought sadly, God help her.

Then, shivering in the wind, he turned and walked hopelessly back to Francesca and left Leno Niccoli bitter in his grief, a tall, dark figure, alone on the hillside, in the sleeting, raging wind.

The woman stood away from the gathering, a tall figure in her black cashmere coat and silk headscarf, her head covered against the soft Irish rain. She held her hands in her pockets and looked at no one. Her young brother stood at her side and as the people moved away, she remained, dry-eyed, looking down at the open grave. Finally, when the churchyard had cleared, she turned to leave.

'Maggie?'

She took in the well-dressed middle-aged man who had

placed his hand on her arm, then glanced at her brother. 'Will you wait for me in the car, Paddy?'

'Yes, of course.' Her brother looked inquiringly at her but her face was blank. Slowly he walked away.

'I didn't think you'd come, Maggie.' The man spoke with the soft brogue of the south. 'Thought your old da would have been an embarrassment to you.'

'I came.'

'Ah, I'm glad you did. You look good, Maggie me girl. And the boy's done well. Was that a Trinity College scarf I saw him wearin'?'

'Yes.' Maggie did not want to speak. She stood with her face turned away.

The man tightened his grip on her arm. 'Will you be staying long?'

'No!' She made to pull away from him.

'What's the matter, Maggie? Don't be so cold with me now, girl! You never used to be.'

Her anger flared instantly and she turned towards him. 'That's because . . .' She stopped, suddenly.

'Because you had to be, eh?' The man released her arm. 'You're a beautiful woman, Maggie. You've done well for yourself, I admire that. But then I knew you had guts, I knew that right from the first time.' He moved closer to her and lowered his voice. 'I would have looked after you, you know. If you hadn't gone off to London like that.'

She shook her head slowly. 'Would you?'

'Ay, I would.' He shrugged. 'But that's in the past now, and it's more the present I was after talking about.'

'Oh yes?'

'Your father was a gambler, Maggie, a true risker to the last.'

She looked away again. 'How much did he owe you?' she asked coldly.

The man just smiled. 'It wasn't really the money I was after. I remember that you always knew how to pay off your old da's debts, didn't you, Maggie?'

She moved back a pace, suddenly shocked. She stared at his face and a look of loathing came over her own. 'Tell me how much he owed you, Michael, and I will see to it that you're paid.' She made to walk past him.

'Got a bit above yourself, have you, Maggie?' His voice sank to a hiss. 'You'll end up like all the Devlins, you will, with nothing but grief! You're good for nothing, the lot of you!'

'Don't you believe it, Michael Finney,' she said defiantly. 'You just wait and see what happens to the Devlin family!' She held her head up and walked past him, through the gate and away from the church.

'Wait and see, eh, Maggie?' he called after her. 'Wait and see? Oh, I'll do that, don't you worry! But I won't get nothing for me pains. I know that, Maggie, along with the rest of County Clare!' And against the hushed patter of the rain, he began to laugh. A taunting, ridiculing laugh.

Part I

Francesca – 1989

CHAPTER
One

FRANCESCA WOKE AT SIX, AS she always did, to the pale morning light creeping into the room through the uneven slats in the old wooden shutters. She climbed quickly out of bed, pulled on a tatty, faded cardigan against the chill of the dawn and crossed to the window. She threw open the shutters.

The sky outside was a wide, bleached blue, but the narrow streets of Mitanova were cool and cloaked in shadow, shivering, waiting for the warm spring sunshine. She breathed in the fresh, sharp smell of the new day and stood, perfectly still for a few moments, listening for sounds of movement from her father's room next door. There was nothing.

Hastily, she washed her face and hands in icy water from the bowl on the table, splashed her chest and arms, then dressed, trembling from the cold and damp on her skin. She bent to fasten her sandals.

Dressed and ready, she walked silently to the door, eased it open and walked into the small living room she and her father shared above the print shop. Again, she stood perfectly still and listened for sounds from her father's room: silence.

She crossed quickly to the stove, shovelled more coal into it and filled the coffee pot with water. Then she tiptoed to the door of her father's room and inched it open. He was not there. Turning back, she began to sing, a high, joyful tune that she had heard in church, but she sang it quietly, under her breath, afraid to let it out.

She carried on singing as she swept the small room, made her coffee, and washed the floor. The light from the sun, low in the deepening blue sky, fell in a slant across the room and illuminated her as she worked. She hurried through her tasks, careful, but eager to be out, before the sun flooded the sky and brought Mitanova to life.

Finally, she was satisfied: the room was scrupulously clean and tidy. She gathered up her bag, her books, her cardigan and some bread for breakfast, then crossed silently to the door. She pulled it open, stepped out onto the top of the stairs – then heard the painful crack of her father's body as he stumbled and fell heavily against the door. She froze.

Trying to think quickly, she edged back a pace to look for somewhere to hide, but he had seen her already. He was at the foot of the stairs and he shouted up at her drunkenly, swaying and lunging his fist in the air. She could feel his violence from twenty yards away and her fear rose.

Easing her body along the wall, she managed to slide into the room, pressing herself into a corner. She closed her eyes, listened to his footsteps, and waited for the blow.

Stumbling appallingly, her father struggled into the room, knocking over a small table and a bowl of fruit. He didn't even see her. He cursed and kicked an apple viciously across the room, then staggered blindly to his bedroom, banged open the door and fell onto the bed, wine-stained and dishevelled, reeking of urine and alcohol.

Francesca watched him for a moment, then picked up her bag, hugged it to her chest and ran down the stairs, out of the print shop, into the cool morning air. She sprinted, as fast as she could go, not daring to slow, not until she was streets and streets away from her home.

By the time she reached the church square, Francesca had forgotten her fear. The sun had climbed in the sky and the

shadows had begun to disappear, leaving the square warm and filled with light. She took off her cardigan and sat on the bench in front of the church for a few minutes, enjoying the warmth on her bare arms, tilting her face up to the sun. Then she heard the church clock chime the half-hour and, hurrying across the square to the Presbytery, she lifted the latch on the door and let herself in. Father Angelo called out to her.

'Ah! Francesca! Is that you, my child?'

She walked along the darkened passage to the old priest's study and pushed open the half-closed door.

'Yes, Father, it's me.' She crossed to him and kissed him lightly on the cheek as he sat reading the paper.

He patted her hand and looked up at her. Her long dark hair fell over her shoulders, thick and glossy, and she smiled at him with her funny half-smile, slightly reserved, self-contained. She smelled of the morning air and at seventeen, she was so young and fresh and beautiful that just the sight of her made him feel good.

'And how are you this morning, Francesca? Have you brought your books to read to me?'

'I'm fine, Father.' She frowned. 'And yes, I have brought my books.'

'Good girl.' He shook his finger at her. 'There's no point in frowning, little one, you must practise your English every day, or it goes bad. Every day, you understand?'

She nodded. 'Every day.' Then she smiled, opened up her bag and put the books on the desk. They went through the same ritual every morning.

'What time is the boy coming in to lay out Communion?'

'Half past eight. Terrible child that he is. I will have to do it all myself after he has finished, but . . .' Father Angelo shrugged and looked down at his watch. 'That will give us an hour until then. Come.' He pulled up a chair alongside

13

him. 'Come and sit here and let me hear your beautiful English voice.'

Francesca laughed.

'Ah, you are so like your mother, Francesca. You are more English than Italian, I tell you, a rose. You are·a rose.'

He kissed his fingers and she turned to him, the light in her sharp green eyes clear and bright. She was indeed like her mother, he thought, so much the same it was little wonder Leno resented her. Ah, pity she didn't have her mother's influence too, maybe she might have been able to rid the brute of some of his shameful, drunken violence.

'What shall I read, Father?'

Father Angelo looked up from his thoughts. 'Oh, er, you choose, my child.'

'Christina Rossetti then,' she said, and picked up the leather-bound book, opening it at the first page. Elizabeth Cameron, she read quietly to herself, the inscription on the inside leaf, in her mother's hand. Elizabeth Cameron.

> *'Love, strong as Death, is dead.*
> *Come, let us make his bed*
> *Among the dying flowers . . .'*

Almost an hour later, Father Angelo looked across at Francesca and waited for her to finish the last poem in the book of verse. Her English was near perfect, and he smiled at the precise diction.

Old Mrs Mcbride was a thorough teacher, he thought, God rest her soul, and his mind wandered off over their years of friendship as Francesca read on. Daphne Mcbride had been a good ally to him; a knowing confidante to an old priest tired of his responsibilities to the cloth. And she'd taught the girl well. No, more than that, she had taught her brilliantly; just the sound of Francesca's voice made him

picture England and the pale watercolours on Daphne's walls. These things were important. After all, Francesca was half English.

'Father? You're not listening to me!'

He focused back on the room again; his mind wandered too often recently.

'Oh, Francesca my child, I am sorry. What did you say to me?'

'Shall I make us some coffee?'

'Yes, yes, coffee, that would be nice. I had better go over to the church and check on that boy, see if he's remembered to wake up in time. You go on into the kitchen, child, I'll be with you in a few moments.'

Francesca tucked the slim volume of verse, along with the other books, into her bag. She stood up and helped Father Angelo to his feet.

'Mind the kitchen now, Francesca, you know that Signora Franelli doesn't like anyone in her office!' He smiled and held up his hands.

'*Dio mio*, give me strength, that woman!'

Francesca smiled and accompanied the elderly priest to the door. She could just picture the gnarled old spinster bullying Father Angelo in his own home.

'You love her really, Father,' she said, laughing.

'Yes, yes, of course I do.' He rolled his eyes. 'See you in a minute.'

And, waving briefly, he disappeared out into the square, a small, dark figure in the sunlight, the long black skirts of his cassock sweeping over the stones as he hurried across to the church.

Francesca carried on down the darkened, musty passage to the kitchen at the back of the house and began to make the coffee.

*

It was just after nine when Francesca left the Presbytery. Father Angelo had already left for Mass but she stayed behind to clear away their coffee cups and tidy his study. She wanted to save him the wrath of Signora Franelli.

She heard the last of the hourly chimes from the church clock as she crossed the square and looked up at the belfry as the bells began to ring for the first Mass of the day. A small crowd of old women moved together inside the church, huddled and whispering, shrouded in black, then the square was deserted.

She listened for the silence of the beginning of the Mass, then slung her bag over her shoulder and strode across the square, away from the church, down towards the coastal road and the blue, glistening sea.

The steep rocky slope was still in shadow when Francesca climbed down from the road onto it. The coarse grass at the top of the rocks was damp and slippery but she was slow and precise in her footing – she knew her way perfectly.

Below her she could see the white of the sand and the deep blue of the sea, the sunlight dancing in diamond patterns on the water; her heart quickened. This was her beach, her secret place, undiscovered and unseen. These were her stolen moments of peace.

Jumping down lightly onto the sand, she left hardly a footprint. She bent and unfastened her sandals, enjoying the warm, soft sand between her toes, and then stood, surveying the land. The light from the sun was reflected off the water, warming the air, and she could taste the salt of the sea on her lips.

Quickly she crossed to a rock and began to undress, neatly folding her clothes, laying her sandals on top of the little pile. She crossed her arms over her naked breasts and walked slowly down to the edge of the water.

Looking out to sea, with the whole sky, the sun and the clear blue water entirely hers, she stood for a moment, then laughed with the joy of it, and ran headlong into the waves.

From a ridge on the cliffs, hidden above the beach, Vincenzo Mondello watched. Lying on his stomach, the ache in his groin almost painful in its intensity, he watched, his eyes scanning the water for the shape of her as she dived down under the surface of the water and came up gasping for air.

He watched as she swam to a shallow part of the beach and stood up, waist high in the sea, laughing as the waves washed over her naked, lithe body, her long, dark hair wet and clinging in heavy strands to the shape of her breasts. She ran out of the surf along the beach, her long strides sending the sea foam high up into the air, and he rolled over onto his back, shielding his eyes from the sun, his mind dark and writhing with images of her.

She was like a child, innocent and unashamed, as natural in her beauty as the sea and the sky, alive and free. She was the most beautiful thing Vincenzo had ever seen.

As he moved his hand down his body, he listened to the sound of her running through the waves, and the moment he touched himself he knew once again that he could not wait any longer. It was always the same, for years it had been the same.

'Francesca,' he murmured. The images came thick and fast as he began to release the power inside him and his head swam with every exquisite stroke of his hand. She belonged to him, he took her and controlled her, and in the depths of his soul and the darkness of his mind, her beauty and spirit were all entirely his.

As Francesca walked slowly back to her clothes, letting the warm breeze dry the salt water on her skin, she heard the

cry of a gull overhead. The boats were in with the catch, and she had to go home. Dressing quickly, she picked up her bag and her shoes and carried them to the edge of the rocks. She looked back at her beach, but it seemed less inviting now. The fear of going home tainted everything. Slipping on her sandals, she secured her bag across her body, then began to climb up the steep rocky cliff, back to the coastal road.

With a heavy heart, she reached the top, looked around to make sure she had not been seen, then wandered slowly off towards the village, to another hard and lonely day.

Only Enzo Mondello watched her go.

CHAPTER

Two

FROM THE COASTAL ROAD, AS he climbed up towards the estate, Vincenzo Mondello could see the expanse of land that belonged to his family.

The hillside that rose up steeply to the small town of Mitanova was cut by the road and layered with grapevines raised high on arbours, the fruit of the land, the Mondello wealth.

His eye followed the land up, to the whitewashed and clustered buildings of the town, sheltered away from the sweep of the wind as it blew in off the Adriatic. Then up again to the further hills of vines, inland, to the bulk of his family's land: the vintage grapes. He loved to look as far as his eye could see, to think of that land as his, and to pretend that he was master of all he surveyed.

But as he began the trudge up to the small winding road that would lead him home, he thought grudgingly of the day ahead, of his labour out in the sun with the other workers, of their coarse conversation and laughter. He thought about the sweat, the rank smell of it, mixed with the heavy odour of the earth and the acid sap of the vines, and he thought about the pain in his back, the cuts on his hands.

The reality was harsh. None of it was his. He was the middle brother of three and, at twenty-two, he was master of nothing.

Approaching the house, he could see Giovanni, his older brother, in the courtyard in front of it. He was drinking a

glass of wine with his coffee and chewing noisily on a crust of bread.

'Eh! Enzo! Where've you been?' Giovanni called out to him, throwing the remains of his bread down on the ground and kicking it away. 'It's late, you should have been out helping in the fields hours ago!'

Enzo shrugged. As he came closer he could smell his brother: he was still drunk from last night.

'Ah, you've been out all night too, eh?' Giovanni slapped Enzo hard on the back and laughed. 'Go and change, Enzo, get out to the vines – it should take your mind off your cock for a while, huh?' He laughed again and poured the last of his wine out on the ground.

'It's piss, that stuff!' He spat on the red stain by his feet. 'Absolute piss! Vadala thinks he's got a good grape. Ha!' He looked across at his younger brother. 'Hurry up, Enzo, for God's sake!' Then he turned and went back into the house, calling for the housekeeper to make him more coffee.

Enzo stood where he was and watched his brother disappear into the darkened interior of the house. He could hear the slur of his words, his drunkenness barely concealed, and his face twisted suddenly with anger.

'Pig!' he spat, and went inside to change.

The morning was long and the heat intense for a spring day. By the time the foreman called lunch, Enzo was red and sweating, the skin on his lean, muscled forearms sore from the sun as it burned, darkening it to a deep, olive brown. He stood straight and looked down at the vine he was working on. The tips of his fingers bled where the wood had cut into the flesh so he sucked them, cleaning out the cuts.

Picking up his jacket, he made his way to the end of the row and spoke briefly to the foreman. Lunch would take

several hours, out of the heat of the midday sun. He was thirsty and hungry and he wanted to be home, in the privacy of his own room. He wanted to think about Francesca.

The walk back to the house took Enzo some time. The air was uncomfortably warm and dry and he could feel the sweat on his skin, irritating him. In the courtyard in front of the big stone farmhouse he saw Giuseppe, his younger brother, sitting on the doorstep, washing grapes for lunch.

'Enzo, look what I got in the village!' Beppe held up a small bunch of imported grapes for Enzo to see, and laughed.

Enzo smiled distractedly, his mind full of Francesca. 'Good lad, Beppe!' he said, going to step past him. 'Make sure they're really clean now, won't you?'

But Beppe laughed delightedly and held up the fruit again. 'They're nearly clean already, Enzo! See!'

Enzo bent to inspect the grapes as Giovanni came up behind him. He suddenly felt the sharp point of his brother's boot in his back. 'Hey!' But he fell forward and the grapes were knocked out of his hand. Beppe scrabbled on the floor to retrieve them, gritty and dusty from the ground.

Enzo spun round. 'Giovanni, there's no need . . . ' He stopped. Giovanni had already gone into the cool of the house: any pandering to Beppe made him sick. The youngest Mondello brother was a small and beautiful boy of eighteen, with the mind of a six-year-old.

Beppe dropped the grapes back into the bowl of water and put his face in his hands, and as Enzo ruffled his hair comfortingly, he let out a low, frustrated cry. Enzo shook his head and followed Giovanni inside.

*

The rooms in the house were cool and dark, the blinds drawn against the sun. The dining room was set for lunch, its table heavy with food. Enzo took a chunk of bread from the basket and wandered upstairs to his room. He wanted quiet, he wanted to be alone with his image of Francesca.

'Hey, Enzo!'

Enzo stopped at the top of the stairs and looked back at Giovanni. 'Come down here!' his brother shouted. 'You spend too much time sulking on your own! Lunch is ready.'

So Enzo turned, angry and resentful, and made his way down to the dining room. Giovanni had seated himself and poured a tumbler of wine from a bottle on the table. He slopped it onto the white tablecloth as he overfilled the glass.

'Have a seat, brother,' he said, a peculiar smile on his face. Enzo took his place. 'I have some business in the village this afternoon, and I'd like you to stay around the house and watch the office for me. All right?' Enzo nodded and Giovanni stood up, crossing to the door and shouting out, 'Beppe! Lunch!'

Then he sat back down again, unfolded his napkin, and tucked it into the neck of his shirt, his large belly only half covered by it. He took a chunk of bread and scooped some pickle onto it, chewing with his mouth open.

'I thought you might be interested in my business, Enzo.' He spat some of the crumbs from his mouthful as he spoke. 'After all, it's you who's always telling me I need a wife.' He laughed loudly as Enzo's surprise registered. 'There! Interested you now, haven't I?'

But Enzo turned his face away. 'I promise you, Giovanni,' he answered coldly, 'Whoever you might be able to get for a wife would not interest me in the slightest.'

'Really?' Giovanni continued to smile.

'Yes, really!' Enzo retorted.

Giovanni put down his fork and looked across at his brother. Enzo's habitual coldness irritated him but he was feeling too self-satisfied today to rise to the bait.

'Well, why don't you just wait and see, little brother?' he taunted, and reached for the wine. 'I think you might be interested in this one!' And then he laughed at Enzo's stony face as the housekeeper shuffled into the room, followed by Beppe.

'It has the atmosphere of death in here!' she remarked, placing a heavy bowl of steaming pasta on the table and settling Beppe into his seat. She tutted irritably when neither of the brothers stood to help her but she was used to their rudeness, and without further comment, she began to serve the food. The meal was finished in silent hostility.

Giovanni went upstairs to his bedroom after lunch. Usually he would sleep off his lunchtime excesses in the cool comfort of his room before he tackled the afternoon's work, but today he had important business. He had a visit to make.

Sweating heavily and full from his lunch, he changed out of his overalls into his Sunday suit, pulling the tight, uncomfortable nylon of his shirt over the swell of his belly and forcing the zip and button on his fly. He belched loudly, and then, his stomach settled, he tugged on his jacket and slipped his feet into imitation leather loafers. He wouldn't bother with a tie, his neck was too fat for his collar and he doubted if he could get it done up.

Almost ready, he glanced at himself in the mirror, spat in his palms to slick back his hair and picked a bit of meat out of his teeth with his thumbnail. He turned, buttoned through his jacket and left the room.

Enzo was counting stock when he heard the sound of the diesel engine on the Mercedes starting up. Unable to

contain his curiosity, he walked across to the door of the storeroom and glanced through a gap in the wood. Giovanni was inside the car.

He watched his brother, red in the face and sweating, yank the gears into reverse and manoeuvre the car out of the wooden shed. Moments later, he yanked again, and shifted the car into first. He held up his hand in a half-wave to Enzo and the sleeve of his Sunday suit was clearly visible. Enzo was puzzled. Giovanni pulled the wheel of the battered old Mercedes round and the car chugged off down the sweep of the drive. Enzo turned away, resentful of his own interest.

In Mitanova, Giovanni parked the car in a small alleyway close to the Niccoli print shop and climbed out. He smoothed the crumpled fabric of his suit and again wiped his brow on his handkerchief. He was unused to wearing a suit and he was sweating profusely in it. Self-conscious and uncomfortable, he made his way up to the print shop, entering quietly and standing for several minutes before coughing to attract Francesca's attention.

Francesca was working on the portrait of a small child in the village when she heard Giovanni's guttural sound. She was deep in concentration and she looked up startled, not aware that anyone had come in. She placed the worked plate on the table and stood up, going through to the front of the shop.

'Can I help you?' she asked, looking briefly at Giovanni, before turning to busy herself with a stack of Easter cards on display. Her father had told her never to appear too anxious to serve and this fierce instruction, coupled with her shyness, had made her uneasy with people in the shop. She fiddled nervously.

'Yes, actually, you can.' Giovanni stared at the back of

her, the fullness of her body just apparent under the blue cotton of her dress. He swallowed hard, feeling his excitement rise.

He cleared his throat. 'Your father said that I could come in today to see you. I have something to ask you.'

She turned back, surprised. 'Me?'

'Yes, you.' He moved forward. 'Your father has given me permission to ask you to come out with me.' Giovanni tried to smile but he was unused to pleasantries and the smile was false and lewd. 'So I've come to ask you to come out to dinner with me, tomorrow evening.'

Francesca stood where she was and looked incredulously across at the young man in front of her. Giovanni Mondello. She knew him by sight, knew of his reputation in the village, and of Father Angelo's opinion, but she had never spoken to him before; the idea repulsed her. She shook her head and turned away from his intrusive gaze.

'I'm sure you must be mistaken,' she said quietly. 'My father never . . . I'm sure you must be mistaken.'

Giovanni smiled again, this time openly, a conceited grin. 'No, I'm not mistaken.' Then he laughed and, unable to find his handkerchief, wiped his face on the sleeve of his jacket. 'Your father did give me permission, but he was drunk last night. I bet he forgot to tell you! Probably hasn't even rolled out of bed yet? Ha!' He inched closer to Francesca. 'He'll remember our words, though.' Giovanni knew that Leno's debt was far too high this time for him to forget them. He leaned forward. 'He gave me his blessing, Francesca.'

She could smell the stale wine on his breath.

'I'm really not sure if . . .'

Giovanni touched her cheek with a hot, damp finger.

'Of course you're not, pretty one, I wouldn't like it any other way.' He pinched the flesh on her face and then let his

25

hand drop down to his side, brushing past her breast. She moved back a pace, repulsed.

'You ask your father, Francesca, check up on me if you like, and I will call for you tomorrow night at seven.' He turned towards the door and she saw the faint dark line of sweat on the back of his jacket. He opened the door.

'Tomorrow then, at seven.'

She looked at him blank-faced, unable to answer. Moments later, he was gone.

Running to the door, she fastened it after him and turned, sinking back against the glass. She felt sick with apprehension. Her father had never let her go out with anyone. But Giovanni Mondello? He was disgusting, a fat, clumsy thug, a drinker and a gambler. She rubbed at the patch of skin on her face where he had touched her and shivered. She couldn't believe it, it made no sense.

But, as she heard the heavy creak of her father's footsteps on the floor overhead, and waited for the harsh sound of his voice, she knew that very little made sense in her life. She jumped when he shouted.

'Francesca! Francesca?'

'Yes, Papa?' She hurried towards the stairs.

'Has Mondello been yet?'

She swallowed. 'Yes . . .' her voice came out as a whisper and she saw the dark shadow of her father's bulk at the top of the stairs.

'What did you say?' He held onto the wall and swayed slightly.

'Yes, he . . .' She cleared her throat. 'He was here a few minutes ago . . .' She stopped. 'He said I was to go out with him . . . tomorrow.'

'Good!' Leno Niccoli turned back into the little room. 'That's what you'll do,' he said over his shoulder. He couldn't bear the sight of his daughter, so earnest and hum-

ble; she nauseated him. He shut the door to the stairs on her and the small passage was suddenly in darkness. Francesca backed away into the shop. She leaned against the desk for support and closed her eyes. The thought of Mondello revolted her, but fear of her father was stronger than any other feeling.

CHAPTER
Three

THE SQUARE WAS STILL WARM at five. Leno Niccoli crossed it to the small café opposite the church, the late afternoon sun on his back and the light reflected off the pale stone underfoot in his eyes. His head hurt and he resented the spring heat; there was no joy in it for him. He walked silently past the small group of old men sitting out in the sun and entered the café. He went quickly up to the bar. His mouth was dry and he needed a drink.

'Leno.' The owner of the café greeted him bluntly. He was not welcome here and he knew it; that made it all the more satisfying.

'A bottle of brandy, please.'

The owner looked at him and shook his head.

'Sorry, Leno, I'm not serving you.' He moved back slightly. Leno Niccoli made him nervous: he was trouble, violent trouble.

Leno shrugged. He took out a wad of lire from his pocket and placed it on the bar.

'How much do I owe you, Marotta?'

The bar owner glanced down at the money.

'One hundred and twenty thousand lire.' He watched the money, as if he expected it to vanish any minute. 'That yours, Niccoli?'

Leno nodded. He took several notes from the stack and placed them on the bar.

'A bottle of brandy, please.' He walked across to a side table and sat down. He had paid his debt here now; Marotta

could bring it over. It was time he was treated with a little respect.

Alone for a while, Francesca sat in her room by the open window and listened to the vibrant sounds of the street below. She loved them: they made up for the silence in her life. The last of the light lingered, falling across the bare wooden floor in a thin slice, its warmth comforting in the dull, shabby room.

On her lap she held a small blue box tied with a white ribbon, and she ran her finger over and over the smooth marbled card of it as if touching something precious. She took off the lid and took out the mementoes of her mother.

The collection was small and worn, a few black-and-white snaps, a letter, and a tiny pencil sketch drawn by her father, a portrait of her mother. It was exquisite. She took it out of the box and looked down at it, the fine, sensitive lines of it, the beauty of the face so obviously drawn with intense love. She read the inscription and closed her eyes.

'For Elizabeth on the birth of our darling daughter, Francesca. I love you both, Leno.'

She whispered the words over and over; she wanted so much to believe in them. For years she had kept them close to her heart, desperate, in the hard, violent face of the truth, to have something to give her hope. Her father had once loved her, and blindly she went on trusting that somehow, in some way, he still did.

She placed the drawing back in the box and took out the photographs, torn and tattered, black and white, smiling, laughing faces. Her father, painting in his studio in Rome; the new print shop in Mitanova; her mother, tall, fair and English, serene and lovely, cool, even in the heat of the southern Italian sun. She saw herself, a child, loved and adored, and it made no sense to her at all. She ached at the

loss of it all. Then suddenly, looking up, she heard the noise of her father's footsteps in the street below. Her heart stopped.

He staggered and must have fallen because she heard a crashing and then shouting, the shrill, angry cry of a woman's voice. He swore and spat and again she heard the shouting. Minutes later, the door of the shop opened and he stumbled inside. She panicked, jumped up suddenly and the box fell to the floor, its contents scattering. She knelt to pick them up but she was not quick enough.

'Francesca! Francesca! Where the hell are you?' Her father flung open the door of her room and stood, dark and menacing, glowering down at her.

'What in Christ's name are you . . .?' He caught a glimpse of the portrait on the floor. 'What's this . . .?' He crossed the room in a flash and bent, seizing Francesca's wrist. She cried out in pain.

'Give that here!' He wrenched her arm, twisting it. 'Give it! What is it?'

She held the portrait tight in her fist, wincing at the pain. As he twisted her arm, he leaned down towards her and she could smell the brandy on his breath.

'Give it to me, you little bitch!' At last he pulled it free, ripping the corner. Francesca cried out helplessly. 'Where did you get this, you thief?' He pushed her away and looked down at the floor. 'What else have you stolen from me?' He had begun to shout. 'Show me! What else is there?'

Trembling, she collected the small pile of things together and handed them over. She hung her head, afraid to look at him.

And then suddenly he hit her, hard across the cheek, and she fell back. The pain in his face was ghastly.

'How dare you touch these things? How dare you! Get up!' He dragged her to her feet. 'Get up and get dressed!' He

pulled her towards the door and she stumbled. Still holding her possessions, he hauled her out of her room.

'Here! Here's where these belong!' He opened the lid of the stove and held the photographs over the fire.

'Papa! No!' Francesca lunged forward but Leno held her arm painfully. 'Please, Papa! Please don't!' He threw the things into the stove.

'Oh, Papa!' She tried to hold back the tears.

A bright flame licked the opening of the stove and her fragile memories burned.

'See, Francesca – they're my memories, they don't belong to you and I . . .' He had begun to shake. 'I . . . I can't stand the sight of them!' He dropped her arm. 'Now get dressed. Get ready for Mondello.' He looked across at her, his eyes hard and dark. 'Wear that dress I left out for you, and try to make yourself look attractive. You're a mess, you don't even look your age.' He stared at her for a moment, and then he walked through to his room and slammed the door. She heard him slump down on his bed and then the loud, droning noise of the television.

Determined not to cry, she took a jug of water from the side and went through to change.

At exactly seven that evening, Giovanni Mondello rang the bell of the print shop and stood outside, smoothing the crumpled front of his jacket down over his swelling belly. He looked up at the scruffy building and felt a smug sense of satisfaction: any girl would be pleased to swap this for his house; Francesca had a lot to be grateful for.

He waited for a couple of minutes and then rang again, more insistently this time. He was impatient, a Mondello was never kept waiting. And besides, he was doing Niccoli a big favour: he was due some consideration.

A few moments later, he heard light footsteps on the

stairs and wiped his oily forehead quickly with the palm of his hand. He saw Francesca through the plate glass as she hurried across to the door to unlock it and smiled at her through the window. She nodded in reply.

'Hello, Giovanni.' She pulled open the door and he stepped inside.

'Good evening, Francesca.' He bowed, in what he considered to be a gesture of infinite grace, and glanced down at her bare legs below the short hem of her skirt.

Francesca pulled her dress down shyly and moved away. He made her feel very uncomfortable. 'If you don't mind waiting, I'll just go and get my bag,' she said, trying to cover the dress with her bare arms, pulling them tight around her. She turned towards the stairs.

'There's no need,' Giovanni said sharply. 'I'll pay for everything.' She glanced back and saw him look long and hard at the full curve of her breasts above the tight low neckline of the dress.

He moved towards her, his excitement high, and put his sweaty hand on the bare skin of her shoulder. 'Come on, let's not waste any more time,' he said. He smiled and opened the door, waiting for her to pass close to him. 'The evening is all ours,' he commented, the heat of his breath touching her cheek. 'And I'm hoping we can really get to know each other.' Francesca nodded and shuddered in the cool night air.

It took nearly an hour to drive to Barletta. It was the first main town they came to along the coast and Giovanni knew it well – he gambled there. He drove to the Via Sipontina and swung the Mercedes carelessly up onto the pavement, tooting his horn at some children, frightening them out of the way. He had booked a table at Bacca's. Leaning over Francesca, he opened her door for her, brushing his body

up against her, and then clambered out of the car, pulling his jacket over the seat of his trousers, which was shiny from sweat and wear.

'This restaurant is the best, Francesca,' he said. 'I know my way around the menu like an expert. Come, it's over here.'

She followed him, pulling down her dress and tucking her arms around her to hide her appearance. She had never been to a restaurant and her nerves flared, making her seem gauche and ill at ease. She stood behind Giovanni as he spoke to the patron and then trailed him to their table. She felt wrong, wrong and embarrassed.

When they arrived at their table Giovanni called loudly across the restaurant. 'Waiter! Waiter!' Several heads turned to see the commotion and the waiter came straight over.

'Signore?'

'This table is too open, waiter, we'd like something more intimate.' Giovanni smiled knowingly and the waiter glanced at Francesca, took in the tight red dress, then smiled back.

'Of course, signore,' he said. 'Follow me, please.' He led the way across the floor to a table hidden away in a small dark corner.

'Perfect,' Giovanni said. He slipped ten thousand lire into the waiter's top pocket and winked. 'A bottle of your house wine, please, and some water for Signorina Niccoli.'

The waiter moved off.

'Oh, and we'll call you when we're ready.' He glanced at Francesca. 'We'd like to be left alone, we have some important things to discuss.' The waiter nodded knowingly and Francesca glanced down, embarrassed.

'Sit here, Francesca,' Giovanni said, pointing to the tight space in the corner. He sat himself down without waiting for her.

33

'Move a little closer.' He picked up his napkin and wiped his face with it while he waited for her to adjust her seat. 'That's better.'

His close proximity heightened her anxiety. He smelled faintly unpleasant and she could see the sweat on his forehead.

'Now, Francesca, I know that you're impressed by this place but I don't want you to think that I come to restaurants every night of the week. Oh no! I do have money, admittedly, quite a bit of money, but I'm not a spendthrift. No, tonight is special. I have something to tell you that I thought deserved the right setting. Something important.' He placed his hand over hers on the table.

'So, I might as well get down to business before the meal arrives – I like to concentrate on eating when the food comes, you know.' He ran his tongue over his teeth under his lip, clearing the spit from his mouth.

'Francesca, your father has assured me that you are a good girl, you work hard and you cook well. This I'm pleased about, I like my food, you see.' He smiled, patting his belly. 'And you're pretty too, I wasn't expecting that. Not that I'd have any old dog. No, no, don't get me wrong, I'm as fussy as the next man, but you have . . .' he rubbed his thumb over her hand and pinched the flesh, 'certain attributes that surprised me.' His hand crept up her arm and she looked down at it, horrified. She pulled away from him.

'Modest, too. I like that!' He laughed and dropped his hand.

'Francesca, I've offered your father eight million lire for your hand in marriage and he has accepted. He is somewhat in debt to me at the moment and I've also agreed to cancel the outstanding sums. In fact, I've already made him an advance payment.' He looked across at Francesca's face. She was staring at him with open shock.

'Now, Francesca, I know it's a lot of money, but I think that you will be worth it in the long run. Look here . . .' He took a notebook out of his pocket and opened it at a page full of calculations. He began to run his finger down a column of figures.

'NO!' Francesca stood up. 'This is impossible! It can't be true!' She looked down at Giovanni, fat and repulsive, and began to tremble.

'No, you've made a mistake, Signore Mondello! You must have!' She started to move away from the table. 'I must go home, I must speak to my father!'

People in the restaurant had begun to stare as she spoke. Her voice was high and shrill, full of panic.

'Sit down and shut up!' Giovanni snarled, grabbing her arm.

She did as she was told. She recognised the violence in his voice and it chilled her to the core.

'Now listen to me, Francesca! The deal is made, your father owes me a hell of a lot of money and he can't pay it, it's as simple as that. We agreed on a price and he's already taken half the money. As far as I'm concerned, that's as good as a contract and if he breaks that contract, I'll come down on him like a ton of bricks. You do understand that, don't you?' He still held her arm and she felt the pressure of his nails dig into her flesh.

'You wouldn't want your father to get into trouble, would you? Or yourself, for that matter?'

Silently she shook her head; she was trapped. She felt his fingers relax their grip and stroke where they'd hurt. She couldn't bear to look at him.

'Good girl.' He pressed his leg against hers and his other hand moved under the table to her thigh. 'Now you just sit here quietly and enjoy your meal. We have a lot of things to talk about, Francesca.'

She felt his hot, sweaty fingers on her bare skin and choked back the tears. She felt sick.

'That's more like it.' He smiled as the tip of his thumb stroked the edge of her panties.

'Your father said you were a good girl.'

It was after midnight when Francesca rang the bell of the shop and waited for her father to let her in. There was a sharp chill in the night air and she shivered in the red dress, rubbing her arms to keep warm. She was weary and wretched; she felt defeated, lost.

On her shoulder there was the beginnings of a small bruise where Giovanni had held her down as he kissed her; the strap of her dress was torn and her hair dishevelled. She slumped against the shop front, her whole body heavy and numb, aching with misery.

She heard her father stumble down the stairs and the lights in the shop came on. She shuddered in the glare, not wanting to be seen. As he opened the door, she tried to slip past him, her head hanging down, her arms wrapped round her body, shivering and pathetic.

'Francesca!' He caught her as she went past. He seemed to want to look at her, to further her humiliation.

'So Mondello got what he wanted then.' He flicked her shoulder with his finger and she winced at the pain.

'What do you think of your future husband then? Huh? You like him, I think.' He ran his hand over her tangled hair. 'Judging by this. Eh?' He looked down at her face and for a moment he softened. 'You will make a good wife, Francesca,' he said quietly.

And suddenly she broke down. It was his softness that shattered her.

'Oh Papa!' she cried. 'Please, please say it's not true, please.' All her strength had dissolved and she began to

weep, tears streaming down her face.

'I cannot marry this man, please, Papa, I cannot love him!' She reached out to touch her father. 'Please don't make me marry him, Papa, Please! Say it's not true!'

But as she looked up at him, her hand outstretched, she saw a look of such violent hatred in his face that she started physically and moved back.

'It's true, Francesca,' he said, his voice harsh. 'I care nothing for you, I might as well be rid of you. At least I got a good price!' He moved towards her and she cowered under his height.

'What good are you to me, eh?' He caught her hair. 'Why should I be reminded, every minute of every day, what you did to me, how you killed the only two things I ever loved!' He pulled her hair and she cried out.

'Why?' He leaned close to her and spat the question. 'Why? Tell me!'

'Don't say that to me, Papa!' she cried. 'Don't!'

'Why not? I hate you!' He yanked her hair back so that he could see her face. 'Your eyes, your skin, even the smell of you reminds me of her, of what you murdered!'

'No, Papa, please!'

He let her go suddenly and she slumped to the floor.

'Get out of my sight!' he shouted. 'I hate you, I can't wait to be rid of you! Marry Mondello, do something for once, to atone for your terrible crime!'

And, turning his back on her, he walked across to the stairs and left her weeping bitterly on the floor.

CHAPTER
Four

FATHER ANGELO HURRIED ALONG THE street, head down,
the long black skirts of his cassock billowing out behind
him. It was mid-morning in Mitanova. The sun was warm
and the women of the village were outside their houses,
washing and chattering, preparing food. He hardly saw anything. He merely nodded in reply to greetings called out to
him as he rushed towards the Via Diomede.

Finally reaching the print shop, halfway along the street,
he rang the bell loudly and called out for Francesca. He had
no fear of Leno's rage this morning; his concern was too
great to consider Niccoli. Something had happened to
Francesca and he had to know what it was.

He waited for several minutes and then he called again.
The rooms above the shop were dark and closed and his
anxiety increased.

'Francesca! Are you there?' He tried the door of the shop,
rattling the handle noisily, and found that it swung open
under his touch. He went inside.

'Francesca!'

Slowly, he crossed to the stairs and began to make his
way up. The passage was dark but the door at the top was
half open and he could see the faint glow of an electric
light. He carried on, calling out quietly to Francesca as he
climbed.

At the top, he pushed open the door and stepped into
the small living room. It was empty of people, everything in
its place, scrupulously clean and tidy. The light came from

Francesca's room and he walked across and knocked lightly on the door. He waited for an answer but none came, so, carefully and noiselessly, he eased the door open and peered inside.

There he saw Francesca.

She was kneeling on the floor, folding her few items of clothing and packing them into a small cardboard box. She looked small and frail; her body seemed without form, as if she had no life left inside her.

'Francesca?'

She turned her face and Father Angelo saw the red, ugly swelling of her weeping, the pain in her eyes. She looked at him helplessly for a few moments and then turned back to her task. He walked across to her and placed his hand on her head, gently stroking her hair.

'My poor child, I had prayed it wasn't true.' He felt her tremble and he bent and pulled her to her feet. He held her and she wept silently, the sobs strangled in her throat, a testimony to all her years of hidden sorrow.

When she was quiet, he led her to the chair and sat her down. He faced her, and held out his handkerchief.

'Can you tell me why, Francesca? Why?'

She hung her head, twisting the handkerchief between her fingers.

'When Mondello came this morning, I knew something had happened to you. I knew that you could not accept such a man of your own free will.' He knelt and took her hands in his own, stilling them.

'Tell me, child, what is it? Why have you agreed to marry Mondello?'

Finally she looked up.

'Why not?' she asked quietly.

Father Angelo stood straight. He walked to the window and threw open the shutters, letting the harsh morning

light flood into the room. Francesca put her hand up to shield her face.

'Everything!' He answered. 'A whole life ahead of you! Look at the day, Francesca, bright and new! What about all that? What about your drawing, all your beautiful work, your dreams to go to England? And the language, all that Mrs Mcbride taught you, all those lessons? You've learned so much!' He faced her but he could see that she was not listening to him. 'Francesca?'

She glanced up. She was looking at him but her eyes were strangely withdrawn, as if the girl he knew had retreated, had somehow ceased to exist. 'You always knew, didn't you?' she said. 'That's why you have looked after me, because you knew about it, you tried to stop it hurting me.'

He was confused. 'What do you mean? What is "it"?'

'I thought it was the drink that did it, I thought . . .'

'What is "it"? What do you mean?'

'His hatred of me,' she said. It was a statement of fact, without resentment or self-pity. 'He has hated me all my life.'

'Oh, Francesca!' Father Angelo wanted to go to her, to touch her, but as he moved forward she flinched and he stopped dead.

'It is grief, not hatred,' he whispered.

'No,' she said calmly. 'It is hatred. I have seen it, and I have felt it.' She rubbed at the mark on her wrist. 'You know, I always believed that he never meant it when he hurt me. It didn't matter, you see, the bruises and the pain, not if he loved me. They were bearable if he loved me, even just a scrap.'

Father Angelo looked away. To hear her speak like this was beyond bearing.

'Francesca, please. Don't say such things, please.'

'I am not afraid of the truth, Father, and I am not afraid

of Mondello.' She shrugged. 'Why should I care? I have nothing here, he even destroyed my photographs, my memories. What can Giovanni Mondello do that has not been done to me already?'

'Oh, my dear, sweet child.' He felt helpless, she was like a small puppy that had been kicked so often that it had not the strength to get up. It just lay and waited for the next blow.

'Francesca, will you promise me something?' He crossed to her and placed his hand on her shoulder, looking down at her face. She avoided his gaze.

'Please. Promise me that if ever you want anything, anything at all, you will come to me.' He tilted her chin up and forced her to look at him. Her eyes were blank and he could see his own reflection in them.

'Promise me.'

She closed her eyes and for a moment he thought she would break. But she sat perfectly still, hardly breathing, and then she said, 'I promise.'

It was late in the morning when Giovanni returned to the house, in his cheap Sunday suit, crumpled and baggy from the previous two days' wear. He had been to see the priest and then to the bank. He parked the Mercedes carelessly in the courtyard and climbed out, calling loudly for the housekeeper. He was flushed with the heat of his excitement.

'Signora?' He took off his jacket and wiped his palm under his armpits to dry off some of the sweat.

'Signora? Helloo! Signora!' He wandered into the house and continued calling for her.

Enzo watched him from behind the door of the side barn. He had not been to work that morning, he had been waiting for Giovanni. His brother was up to something and he wanted to find out what it was. He pulled open the door

and walked out into the sunshine. He could hear Giovanni laughing in the house and suspicious envy flooded his mind. He followed his brother inside.

'Ah! Enzo!'

Giovanni had just finished his telephone call and he swallowed the last gulp of his brandy as he put the receiver down. 'You're back early.'

Enzo shrugged. He didn't see why he had to make excuses to his brother.

Unexpectedly, Giovanni smiled.

'Oh, well, couldn't wait to congratulate me, huh?' He watched the confusion on Enzo's face with delight.

'I am getting married, little brother!' he announced, and slapped Enzo hard on the back. He began to laugh. 'I thought that would surprise you! Pleased for me, are you, eh?' He pinched Enzo. 'Eh? Little brother, . . . eh? . . . eh?'

Enzo pulled back abruptly. 'Get off!' he shouted. He rubbed his arm.

'Oh, in a bad temper again, are we?' Giovanni had stopped smiling. 'You'd better learn some manners, Enzo, for my new bride.' He walked away, through to the dining room, and poured himself another brandy. Enzo followed. He didn't want to ask, but he couldn't stop himself.

'Who is it then?' He watched Giovanni turn and waited for the answer. He saw a slow, leering smile come over his brother's lips. It was a moment that he would remember all his life.

'Francesca Niccoli,' Giovanni replied.

For a split second Enzo saw nothing. His mind filled with a deep, dark, red as the shock and anger washed over him. And then, he saw Francesca.

Her naked body was in front of him, so close and so real that he almost reached out to touch her, his excitement instant and powerful. But she laughed at him, ridiculing

him, making him feel small and then suddenly, she disappeared. Giovanni stood before him, fat and repulsive, laughing and sneering.

'What's the matter, little brother? A touch of jealousy, maybe?' He poked Enzo hard in the ribs. 'You've seen my future wife then, have you?' He turned to walk away, still laughing.

'How?' The shout came from deep within Enzo as he lunged forward and grabbed Giovanni from behind. He pulled him back. 'How could she marry someone like you?' he shouted. 'How? Tell me! How?' He was shaking Giovanni, his rage out of control.

But the blow was quick, hard and vicious. It knocked him sideways.

'How . . .? How . . .?' Giovanni towered over him, his hand raised. He paused, and in that instant his violence died. His hand dropped to his side. 'Get up!' he growled.

Enzo scrambled to his feet.

'Don't you ever . . .' Giovanni stopped and took a breath. 'Don't you ever insult me like that again! D'you understand?' He stared at Enzo. 'Do you understand?' He moved towards his brother and Enzo nodded. It wasn't the first time Giovanni had hit him. He knew better than to argue back.

'Good.' Giovanni stepped back a pace. 'Now get out of my sight!'

Enzo turned to go.

'Oh, and Enzo?'

'Enzo looked back, trying to conceal a sudden surge of hatred.

'I own this vineyard. Just you remember that!'

Five

AT SEVEN-THIRTY ON THE FOLLOWING Friday morning, Giovanni barged into his brother's room. He crossed to the window, opened the shutters, squinting at the glare, and then turned towards Enzo's bed.

'Get up!' he ordered. 'Now!'

Enzo rolled over and put his hand up to his eyes to keep out the sunlight. He saw Giovanni.

'What the hell . . .?'

'I said, get up!' Giovanni stood looking down at him and scowled.

'Why should I?' Enzo closed his eyes. 'I told you, I'm not coming.' He turned onto his side, away from Giovanni.

'Yes you are.' Giovanni walked over to the bed and pulled off the covers. 'Now, get up. Father Angelo just rang me and told me Leno Niccoli has disappeared.'

Enzo still lay there. 'So?'

'So you're coming to my wedding, whether you like it or not. Francesca has no one else. She needs to be collected and brought to the church and she needs someone to give her away. You!' He poked Enzo in the back. 'Got it?'

Enzo sat up. He looked up at Giovanni and enjoyed the look of panic he saw. 'What if I refuse?'

Giovanni shook his head. 'It's a question of family honour, Enzo,' he said coldly. 'I'm not going to be made a fool of by that swine. You won't refuse. Understand?' And then he turned and crossed the room. He glanced back from the door. 'Look, can't you be pleasant, eh? Just for one day? It is my wedding day.'

44

Enzo felt a piercing stab of jealousy and hatred. 'Yeah, all right,' he answered as evenly as he could, but his heart raged with bitterness.

Giovanni left the room and Enzo listened to his clumsy, heavy footsteps along the passage. Moments later, he hurled the glass from his bedside violently at the wall and watched as it smashed and shattered into a thousand tiny pieces.

The print shop on the Via Diomede was empty and closed up when Enzo arrived at ten that morning. He glanced up at the building and saw just one light on, in a room at the front. The rest of the place looked deserted.

Knocking loudly, he called up at the lighted window and waited. Edgily, he turned away from the building to look down the street and began to whistle. When he turned back, several minutes later, Francesca was standing inside the shop, silently waiting. She made him jump.

Unlocking the door, she pulled it open and stepped outside. Close up to her, in the bright morning sunshine, Enzo saw how her hair gleamed and her skin flushed with embarrassment and nervousness. The pale blue starched cotton of her dress smelled fresh and clean and her bare legs and arms were covered in fine pale hair. She looked like a child to him, more innocent and more beautiful than he had ever imagined her.

They looked at each other for a moment, without speaking, and then he held out his arm for her.

'My brother is waiting for you,' he said quietly. The touch of her hand on his arm filled him with confusion and he felt unsteady. The excitement of her pulsed powerfully through him, its intensity making him nauseous.

'Are . . .' His voice failed him and he cleared his throat painfully. 'Are you ready?'

She nodded.

'Where are your things?'

'At Father Angelo's.'

He glanced behind him at the shop, wanting to prolong the moment, not knowing what to do. Then he saw that she was watching him uneasily.

'We should go,' he said.

'Yes.' She seemed cold and emotionless. Only her trembling hands gave her away.

He tucked her arm in his and finally they moved off down the street. Several of the women watched them go from the open front doors and the balcony windows in the Via Diomede, but none of them called out their congratulations.

Francesca Niccoli went to her own wedding sad and alone and the people of Mitanova watched on in perverse silence.

When the dusk of the evening came, Francesca was relieved: the day had been almost unbearable. She sat on the front step of the house with Beppe and watched the sun drop in the sky, taking with it the heat, and leaving the air cool and thin. The light gradually faded and the darkness spread, pressing the land into shadows. She listened to the hush all around her and wished it was in her heart. She could not still the fear Giovanni aroused inside her.

The farmhouse behind her was dark and lifeless. Her husband had been gone for hours and she waited, as she had been told to do, not knowing where he was or why he had gone. The meal that had been prepared for them lay cold and uneaten on the dining-room table and her small, tatty pile of things sat, still unpacked, in the hall. He had simply brought her back after the wedding, taken her luggage into the house and then driven off with Enzo.

Laughing, he had told her to be ready for him when he returned, but the thought of it terrified and repulsed her. So she just sat where she was; afraid, but strangely resolute. She knew that despite what she had to face, even if her courage failed her, her will would not.

It was nearly midnight. The surrounding silence had lulled her and when she heard the noise of the Mercedes' diesel engine, Francesca started.

Giovanni swung the big black car carelessly into the courtyard and yanked on the handbrake. The car shuddered to a halt. Unsteadily, he climbed out and slammed the door shut, looking over at Francesca.

'What are you doing still up?' He moved forward and his shadow in the moonlight loomed over her, menacingly huge. 'I told you to be ready for me.'

Francesca glanced across at him. He was drunk, but he held it well. 'I . . . I didn't know what you meant,' she lied.

Giovanni smiled. 'Go upstairs and get yourself ready for bed,' he answered. 'I'll be up in a few minutes.'

But she sat where she was, too frightened to move.

'Go on!' he persisted. 'Beppe will show you where to go; I've moved us into Mamma's old room, the bed is bigger.' He touched her cheek with his hot, fat finger and his hands smelled stale. She recoiled and he saw her repulsion and fear. His good humour vanished.

'Get up and go with Beppe! Go on, before I lose my patience.'

She scrambled to her feet, moving back, away from him. He reached out and took hold of her shoulder.

'Francesca!' He squeezed it and leaned close. 'Relax!' His eyes were hard and glazed and she saw a harsh excitement in them. His hand moved up to her neck and stroked the

skin beneath her hair; his quickened breath touched her cheek.

'Now, go.' He dropped his hand down to his crotch. 'Go on.' He fiddled with his fly. 'I won't be long.'

She struggled with her disgust for several moments and then she looked towards Beppe, who was inside the hall. She was blocked between the two. Turning towards the house, she took a deep breath and struggled to control her trembling.

'Hurry up!' he growled.

She stepped inside the dark, empty house and followed Beppe up the stairs.

Enzo walked up the long drive, nearing the house, his solitary figure weaving amongst the shadows of the trees. He had left Giovanni to walk back alone, unable to stand the thought of seeing Francesca, of watching her go up to her wedding night with his brother. Unable to bear his intense and writhing jealousy.

He listened to the dark silence as he walked. It calmed him and filled his mind. Yes, the silence was good; it was all around him, clear and sharp, making his footsteps and even his breathing an intrusion. Enzo felt like the only person alive in the night.

And then suddenly, he heard the cry.

It rang out into the clear air, painful and echoing, an eerie, almost animal sound, shocked and desperate. He stopped and listened hard. Moments later, it came again. Only this time it was weaker, defeated, and in an instant he knew what it was. He covered his face with his hands and tried to block out the terrible images of Francesca that ran through his mind. He sank to the ground.

Curling himself up against the pain, he rocked back and forth, his voice humming one tone, his head buried in his

arms. She was his, she belonged to him. But still he could hear it. The quiet sobbing went on and on, driving him insane. There was no escape from it.

On it went, until it overwhelmed him and filled him with a rage so suffocating that he struggled for breath. On and on, until it existed only in his head, where it would remain forever, shattering all his rational thought, and controlling his life.

CHAPTER
Six

THE WARMTH OF APRIL CONTINUED into May and the days in Apulia grew longer and hotter. Already the soil was beginning to crack, dry and hard underfoot, and the vines needed constant attention. The fatigue of the unexpectedly hot weather began to take its toll and patience weakened.

Leno Niccoli was found, washed up on the beach, bloated and half eaten away by the sea, a bottle of brandy in his pocket, almost empty. The village gossiped for a while and speculation fuelled the interest, but an inquest decided he had fallen from the cliffs, drunk and incapable. A death by drowning.

To Francesca, the weary tolerance of it all was natural. She was bitterly unhappy but she was resigned to this; she was frightened and alone but she had never known anything else. She accepted a life that she could not change; she had no other choice. And going about her daily tasks silently and carefully, she watched her husband meticulously and charted the course of her life through his violent mood swings and bouts of drinking. She managed all right, escaped some of the humiliation, and she found a friend in Beppe.

In the space of one short month, Francesca Mondello grew up .

It was dinner time and Giovanni sat at the head of the table, looking across at his wife as she collected the soup bowls, her head bent and silent, hardly glancing at him. He

watched her, resenting the droop of her shoulders, the cool, wary expression in her eyes and the thin line of her mouth. She never smiled, never laughed, she was tense and rigid under him and she flinched at his touch. She tried to hide it but he knew; he knew her type.

She was useless, dull and frigid, she was worth only the money he had saved on the housekeeper. She was a disappointment to him. He had hardly touched her the past month. It wasn't worth the bother. It infuriated him, every time he saw her pitiful expression, that he still had to pay for any decent pleasure. He took a gulp of his wine and called across the table to her. She looked up nervously.

'Hurry up with the food, will you?' He saw her glance sidelong at Beppe, who jumped up and took the bowls from her, carrying them out to the kitchen. Their silent communication angered him. They were always at it, talking, whispering together. She paid more attention to that dimwit of a boy than she did to her husband, but he noticed, oh yes, he noticed.

'Francesca! Come here!'

She turned from the door and hesitated. 'The dinner . . . I . . .'

'Come here, I said.' He put down his glass and moved his chair back. His belly hung over the belt of his trousers and his shirt was sweat-stained. He held out his arms.

She crossed the room and stood before him. She could not bring herself to move forward into his embrace. She had to wait for him to pull her; it was the only way. She stared down at the ground, fighting back the revulsion that rose in her throat.

'Francesca . . .' He put one hand up to her breast and cupped it, squeezing roughly, then pulled her close with his other hand. He wanted a little affection; he was entitled to it. She swallowed hard and bit the inside of her lip.

'Jesus! Can't you at least show a little pleasure?' Giovanni pushed her back roughly and she cracked her hip on the side of the table. She cried out briefly but he lifted his hand threateningly.

'What the hell . . .?' Enzo stood in the door and glared at his brother. Francesca edged back as Giovanni looked over her shoulder and instantly dropped his hand. Enzo came into the room. 'Can't you leave the poor girl alone for five minutes?' He took Francesca's arm and she buckled slightly under his touch. He could feel her pulse just beneath the surface of her skin and the sudden contact with her inflamed him.

'Leave her!' Giovanni hated the sight of her weakness; his anger suddenly erupted. 'You! Get on with the dinner!' he shouted, 'And you, Enzo, can mind your own business!'

Francesca turned quickly towards the kitchen and met Enzo's stare fleetingly; he saw the relief in her eyes and perceived in that moment a world of communication between them.

'Look, Giovanni . . . I . . .' Enzo moved only fractionally as she went past and the touch of her body was so close that it was almost a caress. He felt it, she had wanted him to feel it!

'You what?' Giovanni said icily and Enzo glanced up quickly at his brother. Giovanni's face had hardened with resentment.

He shrugged. 'Nothing,' he said quietly. 'Nothing.' He took his place at the table and waited for Francesca to come back in with the dinner. He ached to see her face again, to see her eyes; he had to know that what he had just experienced was right.

'Where the hell is that stupid boy?' Giovanni couldn't sit still; he stood and crossed to the door. 'Beppe! For Christ's sake, Beppe! Come back to the table!' His lip curled as

Beppe came running from the kitchen and he smacked him hard across the head. Beppe whimpered and began to cry. 'They're always together,' Giovanni muttered, 'Always! Whispering in corners . . . laughing at me . . .' His voice trailed away.

'Hey! Giovanni, I don't think . . .'

But Giovanni cut him short. 'You don't think what?' he snarled. 'How the hell would you know anyway?'

Enzo looked away before answering and saw Francesca come into the room. Again she met his eye and he was sure he saw the briefest flicker of a smile. He kept quiet. A smile, it was a private communication between them. A smile! So what he had perceived earlier was right! Maybe Giovanni's jealous ranting wasn't so stupid after all?

An idea began to form in his head, the smallest flicker of hope. Could he have Francesca? Had she begun to want him, to need him, the one person who truly loved her amongst the tangle of violence and abuse? He hardly dared think of it, but . . .

He watched her as she served the food, then looked around the table at Beppe, merely a child, a useless, snivelling child, and then at the fat, grotesque shape of Giovanni. Was it really so impossible? He had seen the look of revulsion in her eyes for Giovanni; he had seen her flinch at his touch. And tonight he had felt her body, felt the warmth of it, the beating of her pulse, quickened at his touch. And why shouldn't it be so? The flicker of hope flared and a small flame began to burn.

He had wanted her for so long that the feelings raged in his body; they made him ache and cry out in the night. Why shouldn't she feel the same? These things happened. Love does not choose indiscriminately, he thought, there is a purpose in everything we do. He watched Francesca closely for as long as he dared. She seemed to speak to him

with every movement, with every breath: it was as if her body silently communed with his.

It wasn't the first time, either, oh no, he had noticed it before, whenever he helped her, whenever he was close to her. He had sensed it, felt it deep inside him, thinking that maybe it was him, all him. But perhaps it wasn't, perhaps tonight she wanted him to see how it really was? She had given him a sign; she had needed him to know. And now he did, he could see it all. Tonight, all of it finally began to make sense.

Giovanni spoke to him and he started. 'My wife would like to know what you want to eat,' he said, his voice drawling nastily over the word wife.

Enzo saw Francesca shudder and his heart soared. 'Not much,' he answered; 'I'm not hungry, I'll help myself.' How could he eat? He was too churned up to eat.

'No you won't.' Giovanni prodded Francesca. 'Give him meat and potatoes, and some aubergine. Beppe, give Enzo the bread.'

'But I told you, I'm not hungry.'

'This is my house, Enzo, and if I say you'll eat, you'll eat! Understand?' Enzo bit back his retort and nodded. From now on he would have to be careful.

'Good,' Giovanni said. 'I work hard to put food on this table and I want it finished. Now eat!' He smiled, a conceited, triumphant smile, pleased with his own power, and Enzo bent his head to the plate of food in front of him.

Smile all you want, Giovanni, he thought, because tonight I just discovered I have more than you think. Little Enzo is not so small in someone else's eyes. Silently, he began to eat.

Later that night Enzo sat out in the courtyard for a long time after dinner. The air was humid and warm and Giovanni

was asleep in the front room, the heavy slumber of a surfeit of food and drink making him snore, his body lifeless and spent in greed. He was unconscious to Enzo's waiting.

The sounds of Francesca in the kitchen ceased after ten. She had washed and tidied, prepared for the morning, and now she crept out by the back door of the house for a moment's peace and to look up at the sky with its thick blanket of stars. Enzo came round the side of the house and up behind her without making a noise.

'Francesca . . .' He placed his hand on her shoulder and she jumped, spinning round.

'Oh! I . . .' She looked away for a moment. 'I thought you were Giovanni.' Her heart throbbed in her chest and she took a breath to try and dispel her dread.

Enzo saw it and said, 'You're scared of him, aren't you?' He could feel that she longed for him to know it, to be there to calm the fear. Only she was too frightened to say. She didn't answer him and he knew that she was scared to. He pressed his fingers down into the flesh of her shoulder. He had to ask, he needed to know. 'Why don't you leave him?' He heard her catch her breath and his spirits soared. She was waiting for him, if only she would just turn to him. 'You could, you know, if . . .' But he didn't finish his sentence.

She moved away from him, as frightened of him as she was of Giovanni, sickened by the whole thing. She couldn't answer, she didn't have the strength. 'Enzo, please . . .' She turned her back on him completely and he couldn't see the revulsion in her eyes. He thought that he had spoken too soon; she needed time to work it out. He heard the weakness of her voice, though, and in his mind he heard a plea, a need, and he imagined it as intense as his own.

'But . . . Francesca . . .' He stopped again, only this time because he heard a movement from inside the house. He

backed away from her and stared for a last moment at the droop of her shoulders. There was no time to say any more. He had sensed her want; that was enough. He knew now what to do. Seconds later, just before Giovanni appeared, he was gone.

'What are you doing?' Giovanni stood in the kitchen, looking out.

'Nothing . . .'

He stepped forward. 'Well, come inside. I want to go to bed and I have to lock up.'

Francesca scurried past him and headed off towards the stairs.

'Make sure you're ready for me,' Giovanni called after her.

She didn't answer. She ran up, fear and loathing foremost in her mind, and he stayed to lock the door and switch off the lights in the kitchen, then followed her silently up the stairs.

CHAPTER
Seven

GIOVANNI STOOD AT THE EDGE of the field that Enzo was working in and wiped the sweat off his brow onto his shirt-sleeve. It was hot, midday, and the sun burned high in the sky. The ground seemed to have shrunk; the earth was like dust, grey ash. He wondered how much longer the heat could last.

It had been the driest April for years, the hottest May. He glanced up at the sky. No sign of rain, absolutely nothing. Everywhere was barren, his sky, his land, his wife. Just the thought of her filled him with anger – frigid bitch. He kicked a lump of soil by his foot and it dispersed into sand, dry, useless, barren sand.

Putting his arm up to shield his eyes from the sun, he looked across at Enzo as he worked on the land. He was bent double, working on the vines, the bare skin on his back burned dark brown by the sun, the sweat of his labour visible as a dirty film clinging to his body. He worked hard and Giovanni was pleased.

Enzo had changed, he reckoned; in the past few weeks he had calmed, he was even friendly. He seemed to under-stand Giovanni's problems, his work, his marriage. He was like a brother should be – he listened, took stock; he helped out. Perhaps he's beginning to grow up, Giovanni thought, making his way across the field. Perhaps.

Enzo looked up and saw Giovanni as he came towards him. He lumbered heavily in the heat and on the uneven

ground and it satisfied Enzo to see him as such, uncomfortable, ill at ease. He stood straight and waved at his brother.

'Eh! Giovanni! What are you doing out here, in this heat?'

Giovanni reached him sweating and short of breath. 'Everyone has to chip in,' he said and looked down at the new vine Enzo had been working on. 'It's bad, eh?'

Enzo patted him on the back. 'Not too bad.' He followed Giovanni's gaze. 'We need rain.' He shrugged. 'We'll manage.' He could sense his brother's worry. The more he worried, the more he took it out on Francesca. She would turn away soon, she had to. 'You wanna eat?' Enzo's glance indicated a basket in the shadow of one of the bigger vines and Giovanni looked up, surprised. It wasn't like Enzo to offer.

He nodded. 'Yeah, I'd like that.'

'Good.' Enzo wiped his hands on a piece of rag and picked up the basket of food. He carried it over to the end of the row of vines, with Giovanni following, and found a patch of shade. He sat down. Everything he did and said was carefully measured, thought out. He couldn't let Giovanni suspect.

'Your wife makes a good lunch.' He uncovered the food and began to spread it out. 'She's a good wife, eh?'

Giovanni said nothing. He picked up the bottle of wine and took a swig, then wiped his mouth on his sleeve. Enzo watched him out of the corner of his eye, seeing Giovanni tense and aggressive. He decided to test the ground.

'You're happy, eh? A married man! And Francesca has settled well; she seems content.'

Giovanni nodded and started on the food. He didn't want to talk – he had nothing good to say. But Enzo felt perversely triumphant. He enjoyed Giovanni's misery – he'd had enough of it himself over the years – and he wanted to

go on; he couldn't help himself. 'It's a relief she takes good care of Beppe, eh? They understand each other!' But the moment it was out he saw Giovanni's face change. A sharp needle point of spite had gone in, it was patently visible in the older man's expression, and for the first time in his life, Enzo experienced the thrill of malice.

'Beppe?' Giovanni stopped chewing. 'What do you mean, they understand each other?' He sat perfectly still and waited for Enzo to speak.

'I mean . . .' Enzo stopped. Ordinarily he would have simply corrected the comment but something in Giovanni's response prevented him. If he suspected Beppe, then why not use that? Jealousy was a powerful tool, he knew that only too well. Glancing away for a minute, Enzo made his decision, although he really had no choice. He was too far gone in his obsession for Francesca now to do anything else. The thought of having her had begun to control his every waking moment.

'Nothing,' he said eventually. He saw Giovanni's face settle into resentment and still he kept quiet.

'You think they're close?' Giovanni snapped. Enzo shrugged. 'Jesus!' Giovanni took another gulp from the bottle of wine and stood up.

'Hey! Where're you going? What about lunch?' Enzo looked up at the huge, menacing bulk of his brother and felt strangely unthreatened.

'I'm not hungry,' Giovanni said. He held onto the bottle and turned towards the fields. 'I'll see you for dinner tonight – don't be late!' And without another word, he strode off.

The sun rose in southern Italy at five. It came up from out of the sea, a globe of deep orange, and as it rose in the sky it changed to gold, and then to a brilliant burning yellow,

washing the sea and the sky and the land with its bright, radiant light.

Francesca woke early, nearly always before Giovanni, who drank so heavily before he came to bed that invariably he slept on, long after she had risen and dressed. And it was in these early hours, on her own, that she liked to think, not about who she was or how she lived, but about who she could be, about a life and a world that had never existed for her but was still as real and as believable as if it had.

She drew it all, this fantasy, in dazzling colour and perfect line on the pages of her small private book. She created images for the pain and anger she felt, and she tried to make beauty out of the ugliness of her life. She poured light into her work from an existence that was lived in darkness and she found her escape from the terrible harsh reality that was really hers. She thought about her father often, about his disappearance, but not as the cowardly, pathetic running away that it was, but as a gesture of great courage: a whole fantastic story woven around him that helped her accept that she was so finally and totally alone.

Her life was desperate and painful but she lived it by believing in something else, in something better, in something that, sadly, could exist only inside her head.

Sunday morning, and Francesca woke early and looked across at the window and the sky outside, trying to let her mind drift, to let her imagination take over and to blot out any memory of the previous night.

She failed.

In the past week, every day her escape had slipped further and further away from her, as Giovanni became more aggressive and she became more frightened and confused. She did not know what to do.

Moving slightly in the bed, she attempted to relieve the

pressure on her thigh and on her spine. They ached painfully where she had stumbled under Giovanni's blows and she felt it through her whole body. She put her arm outside the covers to loosen them, shifting across. It was bruised from the wrist to the shoulder. The movement woke Giovanni and she froze.

'What the . . .?' He opened his eyes, looking blearily over at his wife. 'For God's sake, go back to sleep, can't you?' He turned away from her onto his side.

'And keep still,' he mumbled. 'Or I'll . . .'

She heard his breathing slow and thicken, and, as carefully as she could, she eased herself out of bed and began to cross the room to her clothes. He stirred and she jumped. But within seconds he was snoring, so she was momentarily safe.

Dressing silently, she crept to the wardrobe and peered inside for the book she kept hidden in amongst her clothes, then she padded to the bedroom door and inched it open. She slipped noiselessly out onto the landing and made her way along to the stairs. She was eager to get as far away from him as she could, to be alone and to find her own private world.

She descended quickly, walked through to the back of the house and unbolted the kitchen door. She welcomed the cool morning air on her face and stepped outside, hurrying off in the direction of the fields.

Francesca had been walking for some distance before she realised she was being followed. She had been trying to daydream, half thinking herself into another world, when she heard the tiniest crack of a dry twig as it snapped. It made her jump and she spun round. She stood still and listened hard. Nothing.

She walked on a bit further, trying to pull together the threads of her fantasy, but now she was tense, the image

would not work, and her mind settled into its habitual wary state.

She strained to listen, telling herself she was a fool as she did so, but she could hear nothing, just the quickened beat of her own heart. She attempted to hum but she could remember no tunes: since she had married it seemed that all song had left her body. She walked on in nervous silence.

Then suddenly she heard the footstep. It was loud and heavy and she stopped dead, holding her breath. Someone was behind her. Very slowly, she turned her head, fists clenched at her side, ready to hit out. Suddenly she screamed.

There was nothing there.

Turning back, she looked ahead, and moments later, she started to run, her hair streaming out behind her and her arms and legs moving together as she sprinted, with all her energy, down to the road and back towards the precarious safety of the farmhouse.

Giovanni watched her go and swore at his own ineptitude. Where she had been headed he would never know now, but she was going somewhere, that was for certain. The bitch. Next time he would . . . He snapped the branch off a vine. The next time he would find out where it was and go after her. She would have no secrets from him. She was his wife and she owed him respect!

He looked at his watch and saw that it was just after six. It was too early to start the day and he was too wound up to go back to bed. He felt in his trouser pocket for his wallet. If he walked cross country, he could be in Mitanova in half an hour and he knew from experience that at least one of the girls would still be up with a client. It was worth a try. It was about time he got a little decent pleasure, even if he did have to pay for it.

*

Francesca was in the kitchen preparing the Sunday meal when Giovanni returned to the house. It was near one o'clock. She heard him enter and go up to their room, his steps heavy on the stairs. She cared little where he had been but the sound of his tread unnerved her, it was all too familiar.

She continued what she was doing and listened to him upstairs, her whole body tense. She knew the noise of his step; she knew she had heard it that morning. She stood still, shocked and afraid. Why should Giovanni follow her? Why? Minutes later, the floor above her was silent.

Moving across to the oven, she opened it and bent to take out a steaming dish of baked pasta. She needed to be busy, to put the fear from her mind. The dish bubbled and the heat of it came through the cloth she was holding. Her fingers burned.

'Francesca?'

The voice caught her by surprise. She jumped and spun round, and as she did so, the cloth slipped and she lost her footing. The boiling plate of pasta fell from her hands and smashed to the floor. It spilt out over her foot, scalding the bare skin under her sandals. She screamed.

'Christ! What the hell . . .?'

Giovanni leaped back, away from the mess, and his hand went up automatically in the air. He hit her across the face.

'You stupid, clumsy bitch!' He moved forward to hit her again, but then stopped mid-motion.

She had fallen back against the side, her face white with the shock of the burn, and she was shaking violently.

'Beppe! Quick! Come here!' Giovanni was suddenly frightened by the course of his own actions. He shouted behind him to his brother and moved to Francesca to hold her up. Beppe appeared at the back door.

'Beppe, take hold of Francesca. Quickly!'

Giovanni passed her over and rushed to the sink, filling a bowl with cold water. He took it to Francesca and bent to bathe her foot.

'Hold your leg up,' he commanded. 'Come on, I can't help you unless you let me.' His voice was sharp and hard. Beppe, holding Francesca's hand, began to cry.

'For God's sake, shut up Beppe! It's not you that's hurt!' Giovanni looked up. He saw Francesca's head on his young brother's shoulder and the way Beppe stroked her hand. He looked down again, sick with jealousy. He handled Francesca's foot more roughly than he should have and she flinched.

'Keep still!'

Minutes later, he was finished. The jealousy burned in his mind. He took some ointment out of the drawer and threw it on the table.

'Here! Beppe, you can put this on. It seems my wife prefers your touch.'

Francesca glanced up. Giovanni's face was cold and angry and the feeling of fear and confusion deepened. She started to say something, to explain, but her voice failed her.

Her silence angered him further. Without another word, Giovanni stormed out of the kitchen.

'Hey! Giovanni!' Enzo was crossing the courtyard to the house when he saw his brother.

'Enzo. Where've you been?' Giovanni stopped. He could not think straight; he was dizzy with the intensity of his emotion.

Enzo shrugged. 'Just out, that's all.'

'Well, you should tell me when you're just out!' Giovanni began to walk away. 'I deserve a little respect round here!'

'Whoa! Giovanni! Wait!' Enzo caught his brother's arm.

Something had happened; he had to know what. 'What's up? This isn't like you!'

Giovanni shook his head, as if trying to clear it.

'Beppe,' he said. 'And Francesca. I . . .' He broke off and looked away. For the second time in ten days Enzo had the chance to stop what he could plainly see was happening. He ignored it. 'Look, Giovanni,' he said, 'I . . .' But he paused, for just long enough to spur Giovanni on.

'You *what*?' Giovanni faced him. 'You what, Enzo?'

'Nothing, nothing!' Enzo held his hands up in a gesture of despair. 'Calm down, Giovanni, stop jumping to conclusions!' He shook his head in disbelief and all the time he was thinking, this is my chance, this is what I've waited so long for. I can turn her against him, I know I can. It was a chance he just had to take. 'That's what I said last night to some people in the café,' he lied. 'They're friends, I said, a brother and sister relationship, that's all.'

Giovanni rose instantly to the bait. 'What d'you mean, you said to some people?'

Enzo shifted on his feet uncomfortably. 'Last night . . . it's nothing, really.'

'What d'you mean?' Giovanni demanded. 'Tell me, Enzo, what people? What have they been saying about me?'

'They said . . .' Enzo stopped. He was on the verge of something truly destructive but he couldn't stop. 'Look, it's just gossip, idle gossip.'

'I don't care! Tell me what's been said!'

'OK, OK! Some of the village have seen Francesca and Beppe together – they talk, that's all!' He knew the power of intimation. 'Stupid talk, tongues wagging. I told them as much and I put them right. That's it! OK?' He looked straight at Giovanni. 'OK?'

But Giovanni seemed not to have heard.

'Giovanni! OK?'

Giovanni started. 'What? Oh, yeah, I suppose so.' He looked away into the distance, his mind in chaos. What talk, he kept thinking, whose tongues wagging? He couldn't think clearly; all he could see were the faces of the villagers, laughing, sneering. He moved off towards the fields.

'Hey! Giovanni!' Enzo called after him. 'What about lunch?' But he continued on, away from the house, as far away from her as he could get. The very thought of her made him feel sick.

'Hey! Giovanni!' Enzo called again. But it was pointless; his brother didn't even hear. Giovanni had taken the last step towards jealousy, the step that would finally take him right over the edge.

CHAPTER
Eight

IT WAS EARLY IN THE morning, mid-week, and the weather was oppressively hot, even now at the beginning of the day. Giovanni was unable to sleep. Watching the light, he listened to his wife's gentle breathing beside him and resented her peace – his own mind was in turmoil. He decided to get up.

Reaching over, he pushed Francesca roughly in the back before he climbed out of bed.

'I'm getting up,' he said. 'I'll need some breakfast.'

She lay on her side as he started to dress, not wanting to look at him. He crossed back to the bed and pushed her again. 'Did you hear me?'

'Yes.' She waited until he had gone to the bathroom and then she rose, dressed quickly and hurried downstairs, out of his sight.

Several minutes later, he joined her in the kitchen. She handed him a coffee and busied herself cutting bread.

'What are you doing today?'

She looked up. He had never asked her before what she was going to do. He sounded suspicious.

'Nothing . . . I . . . I have to make some sauce . . . clean . . .' She did not know how to answer.

He finished his coffee. 'I'll be out all day. Is my lunch ready?'

She hurried to the fridge and took out a few final things and placed them in the basket. She held it out to him.

'Here.'

He took it and looked at her. She immediately looked away; even his eyes frightened her recently. Without another word, he picked up his bottle of wine and walked out of the house.

Enzo saw him go. He had been hanging round outside for hours, careful not to be seen: he didn't want to arouse suspicion. He walked into the house and through to the kitchen where he knew Francesca would be working. She saw him come in and stopped what she was doing.

'Hello, Enzo.' She was edgy in his presence but he couldn't see it. He mistook it for excitement. She glanced nervously at the door. 'You just missed Giovanni,' she told him.

'Did I?' He walked further into the room. He had planned it all so meticulously, but if it was to work he had to appear casual. He picked up an orange from the bowl and sat on the edge of the table to peel it.

'Yes.' She hated his close proximity. 'He . . . he would have liked to see you.'

'Oh, well, never mind.' He stopped what he was doing and glanced up at her. 'Look, Francesca, could you do me a favour today?' He put the fruit down. 'It's just that I need some things from the village and I haven't time to go myself.' He avoided her eye at this point. He was so desperate for her to agree that he dared not look at her. She had to agree. Giovanni had to see her with Beppe; it would finish their marriage for good, he knew it would. 'Could you go for me?'

'I'm . . . not . . .' There was something aggressive in his manner, something that unnerved her. 'I don't know . . .'

'I could give you some money to buy Beppe a drink. He'd like that!' Enzo dug in his pocket. 'Here, I've got a list.' He held a piece of paper out to her and some lire. 'Please? I've so much work to do.'

Grudgingly she took them and turned away. 'All right,' she answered.

'Great! Thanks a lot!' He jumped down off the table and headed towards the door. 'You ought to go before it gets too hot,' he said over his shoulder. She nodded.

'Thanks again then.' He smiled. It was probably the first time ever he had openly smiled at her and it made her uneasy. Moments later, he had gone.

Francesca took Beppe's hand as they climbed down off the bus and crossed the main street in the village. He was easily led and he liked to have his hand held, especially by Francesca. They went into the shop to buy the things for Enzo and several minutes later came out with a small package which Francesca let Beppe carry. They headed off towards the church square and the café to buy the drink that Enzo had promised them.

They were halfway across the square when Father Angelo saw them. He hardly recognised Francesca. It was Beppe he saw first, then, looking closely with his glasses on, he saw that Francesca was with the boy. He jumped up and called to them from the open window of his study. They stopped and he hurried out to meet them.

'Francesca! Francesca!' He embraced her. She felt stiff and tense. '*Dio mio!* And Beppe too! You've grown, young man!' Father Angelo turned his attention to Beppe but he could see Francesca out of the corner of his eye. She was pulling the sleeve of her cardigan down to cover the bruises on her forearm and she fiddled nervously. He turned back to her.

'And how are you, little one?' He was smiling but the shock of her state had hit him hard. She was pale and thin, and her eyes were dull and sad. He reached out to touch her arm but she moved away, as if frightened of contact.

'I'm fine, Father,' she said. 'Fine.' She tried to force a smile.

'I haven't seen you for a long time. Your husband doesn't come to Mass.'

She looked down. 'No.'

'Ah, well.' He did not want to chastise her. He changed the subject. 'And Beppe, how do you like having my Francesca as a sister?'

Beppe blushed. 'I . . . I love Francesca . . . But . . . but she's not yours,' he blurted out.

Father Angelo began to laugh. 'Of course she's not,' he answered. 'Of course she's not.' And Francesca finally smiled. Father Angelo seized the opportunity to speak. 'Are you sure you're all right, Francesca? You look so . . . so – unhappy.' It was a mistake, she clammed up.

'I'm fine, really. Just a bit tired, that's all.' She took Beppe's hand. 'We have to go, I'm afraid. I promised Beppe a drink at the café and we can't be late back. It was nice to see you.'

'Yes, yes, of course, you must go.' He had been too intrusive. 'If ever you . . .' He hesitated. Unable to stop himself, he put his arms round her and hugged her close. He expected her to pull away, but she clung to him and he wished to God he was not so helpless.

'If ever you need me,' he said quietly. He released her and looked at Beppe. 'Enjoy your drink now, young man.'

He stood and watched them walk off towards the café and thought that despite Mondello's insistence that his wife be left to settle in, he would wander up to the estate at the end of the week. A bit of interference never did a bully any harm.

Enzo saw Giovanni working long before he let himself be seen. He had waited back at the house until he saw Francesca leave for the village, then he'd set off for the fields

and Giovanni. He reckoned they'd be there by now so he stood and thought carefully about what he was going to say, how to phrase it, then called out to the foreman for instructions, knowing that Giovanni would look up at the sound of his voice. He was right.

'Enzo! Where've you been?' Giovanni was in ill humour, having to work out in the intense heat. 'I thought you were working the other side of the hill?'

'I was, earlier, but I forgot my lunch. I had to go back for it and I reckoned it'd be better if I worked here before lunch – I'd only waste time walking back over the hill.'

'Yeah, you're right. Jesus, this heat is killing!'

'It is. I could have done without the bloody walk back to the house, and it was locked up when I got there!'

Giovanni stopped working. He looked up. 'Locked?'

'Yeah, I think Francesca took Beppe into town.'

In that moment Giovanni's face changed. He made no attempt to veil the irritation in his eyes and his lip curled with resentment. 'She never said she was going.'

'Oh? Perhaps she didn't think,' Enzo answered. He hesitated for a split second before adding, 'They often go, or so people say. It's no big deal.' He shrugged and began to turn away.

'What the hell do you mean?' Giovanni grabbed him suddenly by the shoulder. 'How often? When?' He had begun to shout but he didn't realise. 'All the time I'm working out here! Working in this fucking heat and she's out and . . .' He stopped, breathing hard. Then he let Enzo go and dropped his tool down onto the ground. He started to walk away.

'Giovanni!' Enzo ran after him. 'Where are you going? Hey! Wait!' But he knew exactly where his brother was going – any attempt to stop him was merely pretence. He dropped back after struggling to keep up and stood watching

Giovanni's great bulk stride over the hard, dry ground. He allowed himself the smallest feeling of satisfaction. Not long to wait now, he thought, not long at all.

The café was busy. It was nearing midday and several people had stopped in for a drink on their way home for lunch. Francesca and Beppe sat outside, watching the small crowd come and go, a drink in front of each of them, and they sipped slowly, enjoying the treat of being out.

Every so often Francesca would look across at Beppe, as he sipped and then checked carefully the level of his drink. He was a beautiful young boy, she thought, more so for his simple, childish mind and gentle ways. She smiled across at him and he caught her eye and grinned.

'I've nearly finished my whole drink, Francesca.' He held the glass up for her to see.

'I know,' she said gently. 'You're a good boy.' She reached out to pat him on the arm, leaning across the table.

It was then that Giovanni grabbed her from behind. Wrenching her arm back, he heard her scream but it did not register. 'Go on! Try to touch him now, you conniving little bitch!' He was breathing hard and fast and the blood roared in his ears. He yanked her to her feet where he could see her properly, see the deceit on her face. Then he hit her full force across the mouth, knocking her down to the ground.

Again he yanked her to her feet, pulling her roughly as she stumbled. He hit her once more, this time hard across the face, a face he had come to hate and suspect, and she fell back against the table. He lunged forward and seized her shoulders, shaking her violently and knocking her spine against the hard edge of the table.

'Tell me!' he shouted. 'Tell me the truth!'

She was crying but she would not answer him. Her silence enraged him. He raised his arm and flung it at her, fist

72

clenched, and she staggered back under the force of it, hit the edge of the table and fell heavily to the ground. Somewhere in her vague consciousness, she could hear shouting and Beppe's terrible childlike screaming. She looked up fiercely at Giovanni and the hate blazed in her eyes. The last thing she remembered was the force of his foot as he kicked her in the stomach and the frightening, searing pain.

'For Christ's sake! What are you doing?' Father Angelo's voice roared from thirty feet away, all the wrath of God in his anger. 'Get off her!' he shouted. 'Get away from her! Now!' He ran across the square, shoving Giovanni, a man twice his size, out of the way, and bent to Francesca as she began to come round.

Giovanni stood motionless, momentarily dazed and confused by his violence.

'Get some towels!' The priest looked up at the small crowd from the bar. 'Don't just stand there like idiots, go! Get some water! Towels!'

People began to hurry into the bar, one of the men stepped forward and knelt next to Father Angelo. 'It's a bit late now!' he said sharply. He lifted Francesca's head and cradled it in his lap. 'You should have helped her five minutes ago.' He took a towel from one of the women and dipped it in cold water. He held it against the gash on Francesca's shoulder.

'Leave her be.'

He looked up.

Giovanni towered over him, blocking out the light. His eyes were hard and unrepentant. 'Leave her,' he said again. 'I'll deal with her.'

'Don't be stupid, man! She needs help!' Father Angelo continued to bathe the cut.

Giovanni moved forward a pace. 'I said leave her' His

voice was harsh and controlled. 'She is my wife and I'll help her if she needs it.'

Father Angelo stopped what he was doing. He was not afraid of Mondello, but he knew that Francesca would suffer for his interference. He looked down at her and touched her hair.

'Are you all right, *bambina*?' he whispered.

She answered him with her eyes. He had to do as Mondello said; it was what she wanted. Gently he helped her to sit up and then called across to Beppe. 'Help me to get her to her feet.'

Beppe hesitated, glancing nervously at his brother.

'Help him,' Giovanni ordered.

He ran across to Francesca and helped Father Angelo lift her up. She stood unsteadily and her courage made Father Angelo want to weep.

'Thank you, Father,' Giovanni said. 'My wife is fine now.' He did not look at the old priest as he spoke, but turned away from the scene and looked across the square.

'Beppe, help Francesca to the car.' He glanced back. He felt no pity, no remorse, and still no peace of mind. Just the jealousy. It raged on.

He began to walk away and Father Angelo watched helpless as Francesca, propped up by Beppe, struggled to follow him, her head held high and the brutality of her humiliation covered by pride.

It was dark when she woke. The shutters were open and she could see the night sky outside, a cold dark blue, fathomless and endless.

She moved, and felt the painful tear of her skin where the dried blood from her cut had stuck to the sheet. She eased herself gently up the bed and sat back against the headboard, touching the wound with her fingers and winc-

ing at the pain. She had to bathe it, clean it. It could become infected in the heat.

Slowly she shifted her legs to the edge of the bed and let them dangle for a moment to gather the strength to lift herself up. Every part of her hurt, but her mind was numb. She remembered very little, just the crawling into bed and the inescapable ache that seeped through her whole body.

She put her feet down onto the ground and stood, gripping the bed for support, dizzy and faint. She sat until it passed and minutes later tried to stand again. Finally, she made it to the bathroom.

Once there, she sat on the edge of the bath and filled the small sink with warm water. She took off her slip and, shivering, she bent to the basin and began to wipe the gash with a wet towel. She caught a glimpse of herself in the mirror as she did so and saw a tired and desperate face, and she knew then that she no longer cared. She had nothing left, no imagination, no escape and no strength to live.

Enzo approached the house unseen from the fields. The night was unusually black but he stepped deftly through the shadows. He knew his way.

Entering the courtyard, he saw to his surprise that the lights in the house were out. It was peculiarly silent and as he called out he got no reply. Alarmed, he went through the open front door and called again.

Beppe appeared from the darkness of the kitchen. It was obvious he had been crying.

'Beppe?' Enzo took hold of his shoulders. 'What is it? has something happened?' He began to feel afraid.

Beppe snivelled. 'Francesca . . . Giovanni, he hit her, she's . . .' His tears started again.

'She's what?' Enzo's voice was high with panic. 'She's what, Beppe? What?'

But Beppe, confused and frightened, could not answer. Enzo dropped his shoulders and ran to the stairs. His fear escalated. He could see a light on up there and he called out to Francesca. No reply. He shouted out again and started to run up.

He found her in the bathroom.

'Oh my God!' He stood in the doorway and looked down at her. The shock hit him and he was unable to move. 'What has he . . .?' His voice broke.

Her body was discoloured, covered with angry red welts and ugly swollen bruises; the gash on her shoulder was raw and open. He moved into the room and put his hand out to her.

'Don't . . . touch me, please . . .' She did not look at him.

He stepped back. He could see her eyes in the mirror, dull and blank except for the fear, which lurked dark and desperate behind the veil. The fear and the hatred. He felt tears of anger and shame in the back of his throat.

'Francesca . . . I . . .' He could not speak. He covered his face with his hands. 'Oh, God I . . .' He had never, in all his wild scheming manipulation, thought that Giovanni would do this. Never!

At last, Francesca looked up. She did not care what he felt, what he saw. 'Get Beppe for me, please,' she said quietly. She needed help.

He stood for a moment, paralysed by the terrible sight of her. And then he turned, her image seared on his memory, and he ran, guilty and afraid, along the passage, down the stairs, calling out to Beppe, and finally into the black, night air, desperate for the darkness to hide his misery and shame.

He was still running when he saw the headlights of the car. He stopped, breathing hard, and listened for the sound of

an engine, his heart pounding so hard in his chest that his whole body seemed to throb. Moments later, he recognised it. Giovanni! He saw a fleeting image of Francesca and Beppe in his mind's eye and then he turned round and sprinted, as fast as his body would go, back to the house and back to Francesca.

Beppe touched the bruising on Francesca's back gently and carefully with the ointment and she flinched. He drew back. He was so frightened by the state of her that she had to talk to him every second, telling him over and over what to do. Again she reassured him and he continued but she did not know if she had the strength to keep on. She dropped her head forward and closed her eyes, exhausted by the pain.

It was then that she heard it.

The car swung into the courtyard and screeched to a halt. The door slammed. She froze, Beppe's hand on her naked back, and waited for another sound. There was nothing, silence. Frightening, deafening silence.

Suddenly Giovanni smashed into the room.

The noise was terrible and the massive, terrifying bulk of him filled her vision. She screamed. It all happened in a few blurred seconds.

He pushed Beppe away, and she saw him fall, knocking his head on the cistern. She tried to move but she was paralysed. She caught sight of Giovanni for a moment before she felt his hands round her neck. His face swam before her eyes as she struggled to pull him off. The breath caught in her throat and she heard the shrill roaring of blood in her ears. Her lungs burned and the pain in her chest seemed to take her over. She could see herself, quite clearly, about to die, and she was vaguely conscious that she felt nothing, nothing except relief. She closed her eyes.

A split second later, she felt warmth.

The pain had gone and a strange warmth washed over her, wet and flowing, like bath water. The grip around her throat loosened and she wondered briefly if she had died.

She opened her eyes.

And then she started to scream.

The full weight of her husband fell onto her and she staggered back as the blood washed over her, pouring torrent-like from the slit in his throat. His eyes were open, glassy and unseeing as they stared at her, inches away from her face, and she could smell his blood, taste it on her lips. It was everywhere, a sea of warm, pungent red. She could hear someone screaming but she did not know it was her.

A hand covered her mouth.

'Stop it! Francesca! Stop it!'

The body was pulled away from her and slumped to the ground. She stared wild-eyed down at it, the blood still pouring from the slit. The hand forced her mouth closed and the screams died in her throat.

'Francesca!' She tore her eyes away from the dead body and Enzo looked at her, his eyes fierce.

'Francesca, listen! You've got to listen to me!'

She was shaking uncontrollably and she could not register Enzo's face. He slapped her cheek.

'Francesca! Look at me! Listen!' He took his hand away and gripped her shoulders. She looked up at him.

'Was that all you were wearing in here?' He indicated the slip, soaked in deep, red blood.

She nodded.

'OK.' He turned and took a towel from the rail, moving towards her. 'Now listen to me, Francesca. You've got to do as I say. You're in a lot of trouble and you must listen to me. Do you understand?'

She shook her head, confused.

'Giovanni's dead.' He glanced down at the knife by her

feet. 'We've got to protect you. Now, you must listen and do what I say. Please, Francesca. Is that clear?'

This time she nodded. She was too shocked to think.

'Good.' He opened the towel and wrapped it round her. He lifted her up, across Giovanni's body and into his arms. Tucking the towel round her to stop any blood dripping from her, he turned and carried her out of the bathroom and into the passage.

'Beppe!' She looked back and saw Beppe on the floor, covered in blood. She struggled.

'Leave Beppe!' Enzo held her tighter and carried on to the stairs. 'There isn't time.' Carefully, he descended and walked through the house to the back. The door was open and he stepped out into the night, taking her round the side of the house and into the dark empty storeroom.

He switched on the electric light.

Placing her on the ground, he crossed to an old tin bath in the corner of the barn and dragged it over to where she was standing, next to the cold water tap. He turned on the tap and began to fill the bath.

'Stand in it,' he said quietly. He reached for the towel and gently pulled it away from her body. 'Come on, we need to wash you.'

She did as she was told and Enzo bent and filled a small bowl with water. He held it up and poured it over Francesca's bloodstained chest. She started at the cold and looked away, embarrassed, as Enzo ran his hands over her breasts to clean them. The shape and feel of her was just as he had always imagined. He saw no blood and no bruises or marks; he saw his Francesca, naked and wet, and he bathed her with an almost chaste reverence.

When he was finished, he wrapped her in his jacket and lifted her into his arms again. She was dazed and numb. He carried her back to the house and up to her room, passing

the bathroom and covering her view. He laid her down on the bed and released her.

'Francesca, I want you to stay here, and not come out. Do you understand?'

She nodded blankly.

'You must try and sleep and, whatever you do, you must stay here.' He bent and kissed her mouth.

She felt nothing.

He stood and crossed to the door, glancing back at her. She had turned onto her side and lay, curled up, her eyes closed, like a child, vulnerable and exposed.

Only a few more hours, he thought, gazing down at her, and she would be his. He turned and closed the door behind him, turning the key in the lock. Only a few more hours to wait.

CHAPTER
Nine

FRANCESCA DRIFTED IN AND OUT of consciousness for some time before she properly woke. She could see light – it flashed, a strange blue-white brilliance – and she could hear voices, but they made no sense. Everything in her mind was covered in a dark red film; nothing was clear. She was frightened.

And then finally, the knocking brought her round. She opened her eyes and sat bolt upright. The reality hit her.

'Signora Mondello? Signora Mondello?' The voices behind the door were loud and insistent, calling, banging. She could hear urgent whispering.

'Signora? Are you all right? Are you in there?' She pressed herself against the headboard, unable to move, willing them to disappear. Then she heard Enzo's voice.

'Francesca, it's me, Enzo.' She started. 'Francesca, open the door for us, please. Don't be afraid, come on now, open the door.'

She closed her eyes to try and blank out the voice but the image behind them was so terrifying that she blinked them open instantly.

'Enzo?' She remembered the knife at her feet, the blood, so much blood. 'Enzo, what's happ—' Her voice broke and she began to cry. What had he done?

'It's all right, Francesca. There's been an accident. Beppe and . . . and Giovanni.'

Beppe? Beppe? Once more she heard the loud, urgent whispering. She was confused, afraid. Enzo started to speak again and she stopped weeping and strained to listen.

'Please, Francesca, just open the door. The police are here, they need to see that you're all right.'

She recognised the command in his voice. She had heard it before, earlier that night, and automatically she responded to it.

Slowly, she eased herself out of bed and reached painfully for her dressing gown, pulling it tight around her to cover her bruising. She crossed to the door and bent to pick up the key from the floor, where it had been pushed under the gap. She turned it in the lock and pulled open the door.

'Enzo? I . . .'

All the lights in the hall and on the landing blazed and the glare knocked her back. The place was full of people. She put her hand up to shield her eyes and several of the officers tutted as the neck of her dressing gown gaped open and the ugly, painful gash on her shoulder became visible.

Enzo stepped forward and put his arm round her.

'I told you she was in a bit of a state. Beppe was there when it happened, that's all I know.' He hugged her to him. 'And then I found him . . .' His voice broke.

Francesca had begun to shake.

'What? And then you found him what . . .?' She looked up at Enzo in panic. One of the officers shook his head.

'Signora Mondello, there's been a terrible accident.' He moved to her and took her arm, leading her back into the bedroom. Enzo hung his head, too upset to speak.

The officer helped her to a chair and then knelt in front of her. 'I'm sorry, Signora, but your husband . . .' He stopped and swallowed hard. 'Your husband is dead. His brother found him in the bathroom, earlier tonight.'

'But . . .' She shook her head, dazed. 'No . . . that's not right . . . It can't be . . . It . . .' She broke off. This made no sense; she couldn't think straight. But she glanced up and

saw Enzo's face over the young officer's shoulder. His eyes burned into hers for a split second and then he turned away. She had been silenced.

'It seems,' the officer went on quietly, 'that Signore Mondello's youngest brother Giuseppe is responsible.' He held her hands to try to comfort her. 'He was found at the scene of death, confused and crying . . . He . . . he was holding the knife.'

Francesca hung her head. What had he done? What had Enzo done to Beppe? Poor, childish Beppe? She felt the grip of Enzo's hand on her shoulder as the young officer stood up.

'I'm so sorry, Signora . . .' He did not know what to say in such a difficult situation. 'What a terrible night this is,' he murmured and moved away.

Enzo increased the pressure on Francesca with his fingertips and she nodded silently.

'Signora, I'm afraid that you will have to speak to my superior, just to answer a few questions. It's a mere formality, you understand?' Again she nodded.

She seemed broken, he thought, by her grief and the shock of it all. 'It won't take long.' He glanced at Enzo before turning towards the door. 'You have already seen Detective Sergeant Lagana, haven't you, Signore Mondello?'

'Yes, I spoke to him earlier.'

'Good. Then there is nothing further you can do, except wait.' He glanced once more at Francesca. She looked so frail and ill . . .

'Is there anyone you can telephone?' he asked. 'Someone to come over, maybe, and help Signora Mondello for a few days, until you get over the worst of it?'

'No!' Enzo shrugged quickly; he had spoken too abruptly. 'I mean . . . we would rather be left alone, I think, at a time like this.' He covered himself well.

'Of course, of course.' The young officer finally turned away and, not knowing what else to do, moved out into the corridor and left them alone.

Enzo bent to Francesca's ear.

'Not long now,' he whispered, insistently. 'And you will be mine.' His grip tightened and the warmth of his breath touched her neck. Despite the heat of the night, she hugged her arms around her and pulled her dressing gown in closer. She heard the echo of his words in her mind and shivered.

It was nearly light by the time the house was cleared and the remainder of the police had gone. Enzo stood out in the courtyard and watched the night fade as the last car left and the silence of the estate was restored. He looked up at the dawning of the new day and felt triumphant. He felt as if he controlled it, the end and the beginning, all of it, it was all within his grasp. He knew that after what he had done tonight, the waiting was finally over. Francesca was his. And allowing himself a small smile, he turned and walked back inside the house.

Francesca heard him from her room. She sat in the same chair she had sat in for the past three hours and she listened to his footsteps on the stairs, along the corridor and finally outside her door. She looked up at him as he entered. She knew what was about to happen and she neither thought nor cared. She just waited.

Silently, he moved across to her and lifted her to her feet. She made no attempt to resist. He slipped his hands down to the tie on her robe and loosened it, his arms encircling her naked body underneath and his hands running the length of her. He pulled her close to him, caressing her back, and bent his head to her neck, kissing her, his lips hungry for her skin. He moved his mouth down to her

breasts and his hands round onto her hips, to her thighs, his fingers eager, excited. He pushed the robe from her body and lifted her, carrying her naked to the bed, Giovanni's bed, and laid her down, gazing at her as her long dark hair fanned out over the crumpled white sheet. She closed her eyes in numb anticipation.

Unfastening his trousers, he moved over her, parting her with his knees, and holding himself above her so that he could look down at her face and see his dreams, a thousand times dreamed, lived out, made real, and felt in his blood and in the heat of his loins.

He entered Francesca and saw her eyelids flutter momentarily as she felt a vague warmth and relief that he had not hurt her, before her mind closed off to him and an all-consuming emptiness swamped her.

The day was full when she woke. The light streamed into the room and Enzo lay beside her, looking at her, his eyes dark and possessive, his body hot and close. She inched away from him.

'Francesca?' She turned. 'Come here.' He put his hand on her bare shoulder and stroked her neck with his fingertips. He bent and kissed her. 'Do you know how long I've wanted you?' He felt powerful this morning; he wanted her to know the extent of his passion.

'For years,' he said. 'For years, I've wanted you, thought about having you.' He smiled briefly. His fingers slid up to her face and then her mouth as he stroked. 'I did it all for you, you know, all of it.'

She started. 'What do you mean?'

'I mean everything.' He bent and kissed the side of her face. 'Giovanni should never have had you – you belonged to me.' He looked into the deep green of her eyes. 'You always belonged to me, even when he . . . when you . . .'

Then suddenly, he pulled her to him and buried his face in her hair. 'Oh, my darling,' he whispered fiercely. 'You are mine now, completely mine. I did it all for you, all the lies, all of it!'

But she pulled away. A feeling of suffocating panic rose in her chest. 'Did what Enzo? Did what?'

The light swiftly left his eyes and his expression hardened. He was suddenly defensive. 'Did what I had to, to get you away from him.'

She watched his face, a terrible idea forming. 'Did you make Giovanni hate me?' she asked slowly. But he didn't have to answer, she saw a fleeting look of triumph pass over his face and in that instant she knew. She backed away from him, shocked and confused.

'I told you,' he said, holding onto her arm. 'I did what I had to.'

'But you made Giovanni hate me,' she repeated. 'You, you did this to me?' It was just a murmur; the truth was so appalling that she hardly dared speak it. Then the memory flooded her mind, bright and clear. 'You killed him,' she whispered.

But Enzo grabbed her wrist in panic. 'You'll never prove that!' he spat. 'You weren't there, remember. Think what you told the police!'

She looked at him for a moment, the pain in her wrist hardly registering, then she looked down at her battered and bruised body. 'It was you – you did this to me, you killed him,' she murmured, over and over. 'It was you . . . you . . . you!' And then she began to tremble, but not with fear. For the first time in years she shook with anger, a bitter, burning rage. She swung her legs over the side of the bed, broke free of him and stood up.

'How could you?' Her eyes were wild, the green in them burning angry and defiant. She brought her arms down on

him and hit out, with all her energy and force. 'How could you!' she screamed, flaying at him savagely with her fists. 'You bastard! How—'

But Enzo lunged forward and grabbed her round the waist, dragging her back down to the bed. The fire in her inflamed him even though she struggled wildly, screaming abuse at him. He held her in his grip, filled with a deep excitement, and pinned her writhing body down with his legs. He moved his hands up to her face to hold it steady and then closed his mouth over hers, forcing his tongue inside it. Moments later he felt her yield, her mouth opened and she was his. His triumph was complete.

A short time later, Francesca lay under him and felt his heartbeat against her chest; it had slowed and his body was limp, spent. She stayed still, she let him stroke her hair and silently she burned. She burned with an indignation and rage so fierce that it almost took her breath away. It was a fire deep down in the pit of her belly and its flames licked her inside. At last she knew – she knew that no matter how hard Enzo tried to control her, the fire had started, she was alive again, and the fear was dead.

Enzo was obsessed, he was mad, desperate to control her beyond all reason, and Francesca knew one thing as she lay there – she knew that she had to get away from him. His obsession would destroy her if she stayed. Its evil had already destroyed him; it would ruin all that he touched. There was no other choice: it was the only way out and she prayed for the courage to succeed.

After a while Enzo lifted himself up and looked down at her. He could see a light in her eyes that had not burned there before and he smiled, a lazy, sardonic smile. 'So, you liked it, my Francesca. I knew that you would.' He rolled

off her and sat up. She covered herself with the sheet.

'Don't.' He tugged it away again. 'I like to look at you.' She let it drop. She would play his games, only for as long as it took. 'That's better.' He moved over and stood up. 'Francesca, I have to go out this morning, up the coast to see about Giovanni's funeral arrangements.'

She lay perfectly still and held her breath, afraid that if he turned and looked at her he would see the sudden flash of excitement in her eyes. She could hardly believe that her chance had come so quickly. He began to dress with his back to her, and she watched him, all the time the throb of freedom pounding in her chest.

'Will you be all right?' He looked over his shoulder.

'Yes, fine.' She avoided his eye, not wanting him to see how she felt. 'How long will you be gone?' she asked.

'I don't know, several hours, maybe even the whole morning. You just can't tell how long these things take.' He shrugged. 'Bureaucracy!' Crossing back to the bed, he bent his head to her chest and kissed her breast. She tried not to flinch. 'You'll miss me,' he said arrogantly.

She remained inert, repulsed by his touch.

'I can tell.' He straightened. 'I'll see you later, my darling. I'll be as quick as I can.'

She nodded as he walked to the door, not looking at him, so frightened that he would change his mind. He opened the door, looked back at her and then stepped out into the passage, closing it firmly behind him. She listened to the click of it and breathed a sigh of relief. He turned the key in the lock.

Minutes later, she jumped out of bed and ran to the window, peering out onto the courtyard from behind a gap in the shutter. Her body was still stiff and sore but the pain didn't matter: her fear and her excitement dulled it, made it

bearable. She watched Enzo climb into the Mercedes, start it up and move off, down the drive and to the entrance of the estate.

She watched the long black shape of the car as it moved onto the coastal road and finally disappeared from view into the dazzling, intense sunshine. She heard the sound of the diesel engine fade into the distance and then she threw open the shutters and ran back to the bed. She had only a few hours.

Opening the drawer in the bedside table, she rummaged around, looking for Giovanni's wallet. She found it and took all there was in it: two hundred thousand lire. She moved across to the wardrobe and surveyed her small collection of clothes that hung in a row beside Giovanni's Sunday suit, tatty and pathetic. She took the dress, her trousers and one of Giovanni's thick sweaters, bundling them all into a small plastic bag. She found her book and turned back to the bed.

Pulling on a skirt and shirt, she located her sandals and fastened them. She had begun to feel faint and sick, so she sat for a minute and took a deep breath, the panic still coursing through her veins. Moments later she stood up; there was no time to waste.

Picking up her bag, she went across to the window that looked out over the courtyard. The small flat roof of the front bay window was directly below. She yanked the window wide open, dropped her bag out and watched it fall heavily to the ground. It landed hard on the stone, but she had no time to worry about that.

Easing her leg outside, she sat on the window-ledge and got a feel of the height. She swung the other leg over, wincing at the pain of stretching, and let both legs dangle for a moment while she gathered her courage. It was a twelve-foot drop down onto the roof below. Then slowly she turned herself round, gripping the ledge with her fingers,

and finally let herself drop, her arms straightening with the weight and her body dangling six foot above the small roof. Seconds later, she let go.

She landed painfully and fell back, crying out in pain. Momentarily stunned, she struggled to stand, holding onto the wall. The image of Enzo's body, his face twisted in orgasm, came into her mind and she fought back the panic. She had to go on.

Moving to the edge of the small roof, she glanced down at the final drop and saw her freedom. It was so close. She sat down, let her legs drop onto the window-ledge and eased her body down, gripping with only one arm. Finally, she jumped to the ground.

She was safe.

Running over to her bag, she gathered it up and slung it over her good shoulder, supporting the sore one with her free hand. She turned towards the fields, empty of workers as a mark of respect to Giovanni, and saw her way clear.

Careless of the pain, she ran. The taste of liberty was so sweet and so strong, the feeling of it so exhilarating and the anger so terrible at what she was leaving behind, that she sprinted up over the hot and sweltering hillside, as fast as her legs could carry her, through the vineyards, down into the valley and on towards the village.

She ran for her life. And she knew, with the knowledge of one condemned, that this was her only chance.

Father Angelo was in the cool of his study, the blinds drawn against the bright morning sunlight. He was on the telephone to the Police Commissioner.

The situation was better than he had expected. Beppe could not be tried for murder due to diminished responsibility and the worst that could happen would be a corrective institution. Better than Mondello looking after

him, he thought – he had always argued that the boy needed proper care.

He was anxious to get the Commissioner off the phone. All he could think about was Francesca. He was exhausted – he'd been up since the early hours with Beppe at the station – but he could not rest, not until he'd seen Francesca. He drummed his fingertips lightly on the desk, waiting for the man to finish his lengthy sentence.

He heard a tap on his study door.

'Come, come,' he called out. 'Excuse me a moment, Commissioner, there's someone at the door of my study.' He placed his hand over the mouthpiece and called out again. 'Come in!'

Francesca opened the door and stepped into the study.

'*Dio mio*,' he whispered. 'My dear child!' He held out his hand to her. 'Come, quickly, come and sit.' He went back to the Commissioner on the line.

'Commissioner, I'm afraid I must go. One of my elderly parishioners has just come in for confession. I do apologise. I will ring you later this afternoon. Yes, yes, I'll do that. Thank you for your help. Goodbye now.'

He finished hurriedly and replaced the receiver. Standing up, he moved to Francesca, and embraced her. She came into his arms, stiff and tense. She felt so thin and frail that he was afraid she might snap.

She pulled back and looked up at his face. 'Father, I . . .' She did not know what to say. She had been so brave and strong and now she was afraid that all her courage would fail her. She began to panic.

He watched her face and her eyes for a moment and then he said: 'Do you have something to tell me, child, something about Giovanni's death?' He could sense her fear and confusion and guilt. He had seen it all his life, the expression of guilt, and he knew it at first glance. 'What is

it?' he asked softly. 'Tell me and I will try to help.'

Moments later, she started to cry. The fear, the shock and the terrible violence took hold of her, and she could not stop. She wept, great wracking sobs, tears she had kept inside her for far too long.

As she cried she told him about Giovanni, about the murder and about Enzo – she couldn't stop herself. She talked fearfully of his control and his obsession, knowing that it was this that terrified her more than anything.

'Francesca.' She had quietened and Father Angelo stroked her hair. 'Francesca, I understand, and you are right.' He looked down at her face. 'You must leave, and you must go now, before he comes back. You will go secretly, so that he will never, ever find you.'

He released her and crossed to his desk. 'Now, dry your eyes and go upstairs and wash your face.' She looked edgy. 'It's all right, Signora Franelli is not here, she has gone to the market.' He pulled open the drawer and took out a key. 'Go on!' he said. 'Hurry, I have things to sort out here if we are to get you away. Go, we may not have much time.'

She turned and hurried out of the room and up the stairs.

Glancing quickly across at the door, he took the key and went over to the bureau against the wall, pulling it away, and bending to the small safe he had hidden behind there. He turned the key in the lock.

Taking out a leather wallet, he closed the safe, secured the bureau back in its place and carried the wallet over to his desk. He opened it and looked down at the papers, the things he had kept for so many years, the promises he had made to Elizabeth. They were Francesca's heritage, her escape.

He began to go through them, to check they were in order, and then he picked up the telephone and dialled the

number of a friend down the coast at Taranto. A friend who sent a twice-weekly delivery to Venice which travelled up the Adriatic coast. He made the connection, found there was a lorry that had just left Bari and asked his friend to contact the driver on his radio. He waited, listening to the blur of voices over the CB in the background, and several minutes later he was told that the driver would stop for them on the road just past Mitanova. They had little over an hour. Father Angelo hung up and blessed himself: Francesca was on her way.

Next he went to a painting of the Madonna that hung behind his desk. He removed it from the wall and laid it flat, slipping his paperknife around the edge and easing the back of the painting off. In between the back and the canvas there was a brown envelope. He took it out and opened it, counting the notes inside. There was just enough to pay for a sea crossing. Again he blessed himself and hurriedly replaced the painting. God was on his side.

He picked up the telephone once more and, leafing through his address book, he found the number he wanted in Chiavenna, high up in the mountains, near the Swiss border. He dialled, then waited patiently while the line rang, knowing that the Sisters of Clare rarely received calls and would take a long time to answer.

Finally he was through. He spoke to Mother Superior and arrangements were made, with few questions asked. He knew that Francesca would be safe there: he would trust the order with his heart. Indeed, that was what he was doing. From Chiavenna, she could travel into Switzerland, down to France and finally go across to England. He glanced at his watch and went to the door of his study.

'Francesca!' He kept his voice down to a loud whisper. 'Francesca, hurry! Everything is ready, you have to leave soon.'

She appeared at the top of the stairs. She seemed merely a shadow of the girl he had known three months ago. Her face was drawn and sad, the bruising on it ugly and sore; she was stooped, as if the weight of the burden she carried had defeated her. But as she came down towards him, he saw that her eyes were alive – they burned, almost emerald green, and the fear he had so often seen had left them.

'Francesca, we must talk, I must explain some things to you.' He held out his hand and led her back to the study.

Seating her at his desk, he gave her the wallet and she took out a small, dark blue book with a gold Royal coat of arms on it, a British passport.

'Francesca, that is yours,' he said. 'Your mother applied for it just before she died, she wanted you to have British citizenship, it was important to her. As your guardian, I have kept it in order. It entitles you to go to England to live.'

'You're my guardian?' She glanced up. 'I never knew.'

'No, your mother was dying, she asked me to sign the papers in confidence, she . . . she did not want your father to know.'

Francesca swallowed hard. 'Did he hate me even then?' she whispered.

'No! No, it's not that, it's just that your mother wanted to keep it between ourselves . . . She . . .' He stopped. She was right and he did not know what to say.

'I see.'

'She asked me to find someone to teach you English and to keep your things in order. She hoped you might want to go to England one day.'

Francesca looked down at the passport. 'Why haven't you told me any of this before?'

'Because I promised your mother that I would wait until you came to me. She wanted you to settle here, Francesca, with your father, she didn't want me to interfere with that.'

He shrugged. 'I had thought of telling you many times, but your mother had no relations that I knew of, only her parents, and they died shortly before her. I didn't know what it would achieve to tell you.'

She held the passport in her fingers. 'And what will happen to me now, if I go to England?'

'I have someone there I can contact, someone who I'm sure will help you. He's a good man, I've met him. He's the nephew of the late Mrs Mcbride.' He blessed himself and murmured, 'God rest her soul.'

'I see.' She looked up again. 'Father, I don't know what to say. I'm scared and . . . and I'm not even sure I'm doing the right thing . . . and then, then I think of Beppe . . . and . . . Enzo . . .' She broke off, as if just saying his name frightened her.

'Think of no one, Francesca! Think of yourself!' He moved across to her and took her hands. 'Beppe will be safe, I promise you that, but you, you must go. You must escape Enzo, you must!' He dropped her hands as the church clock struck the half-hour.

'Francesca, John Mcbride will look after you, I know he will. Your English is near perfect, and you have a British passport.' He stood up and took the envelope from the desk. 'It is a good chance, little one, you have to take it!' He hurried over to the window. 'Now we must go! There is no time left and we must be there when the lorry arrives.'

Peering round the blinds, he looked out onto the church square and saw a small crowd of people. It was not safe.

'We will have to go out the back way,' he said. 'Then no one will see us. We can go cross country to the coast road.' He glanced across at her. 'Are you ready?'

She nodded. 'Yes, I'm ready.'

'Good. I'll explain the rest of my arrangements on the

way.' He saw her gaze around his study, taking in every last detail. 'It may not be forever,' he said quietly.

She shrugged and smiled, a sad, half-smile. 'No, it may not.' But neither of them believed what they said. It was forever, of course it was forever. He took her hand and led her out of the room. Francesca Mondello had ceased to exist and Francesca Cameron was now in her place.

It was dark when Enzo finally came out of the house, a suffocating, thick blackness that felt as if it was choking him. Hot and close. He walked into the courtyard and looked out over the Mondello land: acres and acres of vines, all his, every last clump of dry, hard, burned earth, and then he slumped down onto his knees and buried his head in his hands. It was nothing, it meant nothing. She had gone.

'Francesca!' he cried out. 'Where are you?' His whole body ached for her, a desperate, searing pain. 'Where? In God's name, where?' And then he began to cry. Harsh, dry sobs that came up from the pit of his stomach as if he were retching on his own grief. 'I will find you!' he screamed into the silence. His face twisted in agony and he fell forward. 'I will find you,' he moaned, seeing her body writhing in the dark space of his mind. 'I will find you!'

CHAPTER
Ten

Motcom Park, Motcom, North Yorkshire

LADY MARGARET SMITH-COLYNE MOVED her thigh an inch or so to the right – it allowed Richard better access. She was lying on her stomach, her head resting on her folded arms, and tilted to the side. Her eyes were closed, and her long red hair, bright and glossy in the soft glow of the lamp, fell slightly over her face. She had raised her bottom, its white, almost translucent skin turning pink as Richard worked away at it, gently kissing and nibbling the round curve of her cheek, edging his mouth provocatively down to where he knew she liked it best. She moaned softly and wriggled a little higher.

'Hmmm, darling that's . . .' She sighed. 'Ohhhh . . .'

She had moved up onto all fours and knelt forward, holding onto the pole of the four-poster bed for support.

'Oh, Richard darling . . . hmmmm . . . yes . . .'

Suddenly he stopped.

'Richard . . .?'

She glanced behind her and smiled at what she saw.

'Hmmm . . . Darling . . .' He was ready. Reaching back, she touched him and guided him towards her, hearing the quickness of his breath and the short sharp moan. She gripped the pole with both hands now and closed her eyes as his fingers found the heavy, warm flesh of her breasts.

'Oh, darling . . . yes . . .' she murmured, and slowly the bed began to shake.

*

'God, darling, that was wonderful!' Lady Margaret rolled away from him and reached to the bedside table for her cigarettes. She put two between her lips and lit them both, handing one to Richard. She turned onto her back and lay against the pillows, holding the cigarette, and Richard, at arm's length.

He lay on his side and watched her.

She was large and voluptuous, her skin pinkish white, Irish in its fairness, and her curves full and heavy. She was beautiful in a haughty, rather grand way and her public face gave no hint of the abandonment she enjoyed from her pleasures.

Lady Margaret Smith-Colyne was a tough and arrogant character in society but she loved to be dominated in bed. She was like a different person between the sheets, and it was this that excited Richard Brachen more than anything he had known for years.

He trailed a finger over her thigh.

'No, Richard. Not again, not now.' Lady Margaret leaned over and stubbed out her cigarette in the ashtray by her side. 'Later, perhaps.' She swung her long legs over the side of the bed and stood up. 'John said he would call and let me know when he is due to arrive back tomorrow. I must be up and around when he does.' She smiled. 'Anyway, don't be such a greedy boy!'

He reached a hand out and slapped her bottom. The flesh wobbled.

'Ouch!'

'John, John, John,' he teased. 'You live in constant fear of Mcbride, but he's only your husband's man.' He reached out again but she moved away quickly. 'God! We worry more about being caught by him than we do Henry!'

She looked at him from across the room. He had a splendid physique, strong and lean, a deep ridge of muscle

running the length of his torso, ending at his pelvis. She glanced down at his amazing size. She was using him for his contacts – politics was a cliquey world – but the fact that he was so good in bed was quite a bonus!

'I wouldn't mind, but John is such an unpleasant bugger, the dour old Scot!' he went on. 'I really don't know why you can't persuade old Henry to get rid of him.' He looked up and saw her staring at him. 'We could have as much of this as we wanted then.' He knelt up, glanced down at his rapidly increasing size and grinned.

'Come over here and see what fun we could have.' He took himself in his hands and watched her face. Seconds later, she padded across the room and bent, the soft warmth of her mouth closing over him.

'See,' he said, running his hand through her hair. 'Who needs dull old John?'

It was an hour before Lady Margaret made it to the shower: Richard was practically insatiable. When finally he'd had his fill, she lay back to get her breath, flushed and perspiring, and took a long, satisfied drag of the cigarette he passed to her.

'You don't really have to get up, do you, Margaret?' Richard was comfortable in the big four-poster bed; he could have stayed there all afternoon.

'Hmmm, sorry.' She passed him back the cigarette and stood up.

He rolled over petulantly. 'Bloody John!'

She smiled. 'It's all about appearances, Richard. Besides, if John found out, he's so puritanical, he'd probably tell Henry and that would be it.' She clicked her fingers. 'Goodbye, Lady Margaret Smith-Colyne.' She crossed to the dressing table and picked up her silver-backed brush, gently stroking it through her hair.

'How would you like a new wife?' She glanced at him over her shoulder in the mirror. 'Exactly!' She started to laugh. 'The thought terrifies you as much as it does me!' She put the brush down. 'Anyway, at the end of the week, we'll be in Scotland, you in your house and me in mine. All I'll have is one hired little nanny to help with the girls and you'll have your dear old couple who turn a blind eye to all your rude comings and goings.'

Bending her head forward to twist her hair into a knot, she gave him a perfect view of her well-curved bottom.

'You can have me as much as you want then,' she said through a mouthful of pins. Then she stood straight and walked across to the bathroom.

'If you can cope, that is.' She wiggled her hips and went through to shower, leaving the echo of her laughter behind her.

John Mcbride stood in a line of people waiting for passengers to disembark from the ferry and held his name board up nervously with both hands. He was waiting for Francesca Cameron.

In the top pocket of his jacket, he had a letter from Father Angelo, a letter he had read so many times in the week since he received it, that he knew it off by heart. It was a letter that still caused him distress, even though he had done what he could in the circumstances, given that he was a middle-aged man in service, and in no position to take on that kind of responsibility. He had sorted it out, quickly and efficiently, with the minimum of fuss.

He had organised the girl somewhere to live, with friends in Newcastle, arranged for some money to be transferred from his deposit account to tide her over until she found a job and taken time off work to settle her in. He had done everything he could think of, and yet, he didn't feel quite

right about it. He was unable to say why, but he was not quite comfortable with his impeccable arrangements.

However, he tried not to think about it. He was not a sentimental man and the sooner everything was sorted out, and he was on his way back to Yorkshire, the better. He just wanted to be done with it.

Looking up, he saw a trickle of foot passengers start to disembark and he held his board up a little higher, scanning the crowd for his ward. He had no idea what to expect so he concentrated hard, peering through his glasses at the sea of faces.

A few moments later, he spotted her. He put his hand up to wave and called out to attract her attention. She turned towards him and recognised her name. She was the most haunting young girl he had ever seen.

She smiled shyly and began to walk towards him. He watched her, tall and thin, her hair cropped short, her clothes a drab collection of cast-offs that hung shapelessly from her frame, and he thought she was beautiful. He could not see how, really, but he simply could not take his eyes from her face. She looked lost and alone, broken almost, and yet as she drew nearer, he could see her eyes: they were sharp and green, the sort of green that Indian emeralds were, solid and intense. They were bright and trusting and full of hope.

'Francesca Cameron?'

'Yes.'

They stood facing each other for several moments, John unsure of what to do next. Her eyes, he thought – there was nothing veiled in them, he could see every emotion reflected. Then he saw the anxiety. It flickered briefly in the green and he remembered that she was only just a young woman, a child at heart. He stepped forward and, a little clumsy from lack of experience, he hugged her close.

'Welcome to England, Francesca,' he said. 'I am so pleased that you are here.'

She drew back and looked up at him, uncertain.

'Are you, are you really?'

He swallowed hard. Newcastle, the place to live, the money; they all began to slip away from him. She was vulnerable and she needed him; he had to respond.

'Yes, yes I am,' he said. And suddenly he smiled, a warm, genuine smile, surprising himself with it. 'Very,' he added. Then, picking up her bag, he placed his arm protectively around her shoulder and without another thought, led her off towards the car. His decision had been made.

However, driving up the A1, back to Yorkshire, John began to wonder just what he was going to do next. He had never made an impulsive decision in his life before and although he did not regret it, he hadn't a clue how to progress. He had nothing worked out, and for a military man who lived by strategic planning, this was quite extraordinary. He was not a man to leave things to chance but, in the circumstances, he could not see what else he could do. The idea worried him incessantly as he drove.

'John?'

Francesca had been silent for most of the journey and he jumped at the sound of her voice. He had almost forgotten she was there. He turned and glanced quickly at her.

'Hmmm?'

'You know, Father Angelo, he promised me that you would look after me.' Francesca spoke quietly, tripping slightly over her accent. She stole a look at John's profile and then she went on. 'But I wasn't so sure, I mean . . .' She stopped and looked down at her hands. She held the bruised wrist, now only faintly discoloured, with her fingers

wrapped tightly round it. 'I mean, I never thought . . . after all that's happened . . .' Again she stopped. She was struggling with her English and her shyness and she did not know how to explain her thanks. 'Well, it's that . . . I never believed that you would, really.'

John dared not look at her. Her words touched him in a way he did not understand and he was nervous of that. He knew very little about her, except that she had suffered and that Father Angelo trusted him to take care of her. He was not at all sure why this meant so much to him.

'You are very kind, John.'

He coughed uncomfortably. He was unused to sentiment and it embarrassed him.

'No,' he said. 'Not really, I . . .' He coughed again to clear his throat. 'I just want everything to turn out for the best, that's all.' He reached over and patted her hand, a little self-consciously. He was drawn to her, he wanted to touch her, to reassure her, but his lack of experience overwhelmed him and he kept his distance.

'I will not let you down,' she said quietly.

He saw her out of the corner of his eye, staring straight ahead, her face set and her hands clasped tightly together in her lap. She was so determined, and so sad, that his heart went out to her.

'No, of course you won't,' he answered. Nor I you, he thought, though he did not have the courage to say it.

And they drove on in silence, stopping only once to call Lady Margaret and the friends they would not be going to see in Newcastle.

Lady Margaret sat in the drawing room at Motcomb Park in an extremely foul temper. She smoked a cigarette and stared out of the window, kicking the toe of her Kurt Geiger court shoe against the leg of Lord Henry's favourite Sheraton side

table. She flicked her ash into a small Royal Doulton dish that she balanced on her knee.

'Bloody John,' she muttered under her breath. 'Bloody Milly.' She took a long drag of the cigarette and blew the smoke slowly out of the side of her mouth.

As if John's phone call earlier wasn't enough, she thought angrily, she now had Milly on her way home, sent back from a friend's house with wretched chickenpox, and to top it all, Mrs bloody Brown on the phone to the agency, blowing the whole thing, apparently by mistake!

Lady Margaret stubbed the cigarette out, grinding it into the saucer. She had not been expecting John until tomorrow morning, and his extraordinary change of plan was really most inconvenient. The dinner with Richard had had to be cancelled – she had ushered him out of the house in five minutes flat and her one night, tonight, of glorious nonstop sex had been indefinitely postponed. She needed it too; she wanted Richard pliable by the time they got to the Highlands, if they ever got to the bloody Highlands.

'Bloody Milly,' she said again. She stood and walked over to the window. Why in God's name did the child have to develop the pox this week? She could at least have waited until they got to Scotland, then the agency girl could have done absolutely nothing about it.

It had been raining all day, a dull, grey drizzle, and Lady Margaret looked out at the gardens, sodden and miserable. After tea, she decided, she would ring round some other agencies and see if she couldn't replace the girl. She just had to go to Scotland; she had been planning it for weeks. Besides, she deserved a fortnight alone with Richard; what with the children, Henry and dour old John snooping round the place, it was about time she had a little fun.

John turned off the A1 at Bedale and drove cross country in

the direction of the A19 and the Vale of Pickering. The village of Motcom, where they were headed, lay nestled into the Hambleton Hills. With its houses of grey York stone, weatherworn and covered in lichen, it swept gently up to the edge of the Smith-Colyne estate and the entrance to Motcom Park.

It was a small place, one of a group of villages clustered together within a ten-mile radius of each other. It had a post office, with a shop attached, a bed and breakfast for the summer trade and two pubs, each at separate ends of the village. People kept themselves to themselves in Motcom: they noticed the comings and goings but little was said. It was rural and private and for Lady Margaret Smith-Colyne, deadly boring.

Lady Margaret was down in the village at the post office when she saw John's car drive past, on his way back to the estate. She had been talking to the Post Mistress, explaining her dilemma in great and exaggerated detail. She had rather hoped that the daughter of the establishment, just turned sixteen, would be offered for employment, but was disgruntled to find that she had already gone to France on a school exchange trip.

The post office had been Lady Margaret's last resort and she took the disappointment badly. She couldn't help commenting, out of sheer frustration and anger of course, that French seemed hardly necessary for a girl who would probably never leave Motcom. But the Post Mistress just folded her arms and nodded; her fit of pique was ignored.

Driving the Range Rover back up to the estate, she wondered what had brought John back so early to Motcom. He rarely changed his plans once made, in fact, she had never known him to do so before. She smiled to herself as she drove through the gates and up towards the house. Perhaps there is a woman involved, she thought, swinging the car to

a halt in front of the house. Doubtful, though, she decided, climbing out of the driver's seat and jumping down, doubtful in the extreme. Still, now he was back, she could at least hand the whole problem of the girl's nanny over to him. Dull and boring he might be, but when it came to it, he was bloody efficient.

John parked his immaculate 1963 Austin Rover in the small courtyard at the back of the house, reversing perfectly into his space, and turned to Francesca.

'Well, here we are.' He smiled.

She nodded.

'Let's get your things out then and we'll take you through to the kitchen to meet Mrs Brown.'

She sat where she was, looking round her at the extensive outbuildings that housed the kitchen, utility room and office, along with the small apartments for John and Mrs Brown. They were all one storey high, attached to the side of the house, and in the same warm grey stone. Above them she could see the roof and the back facade of Motcom Park, an imposing eighteenth-century Georgian hall, built by Bourchier and set in two hundred acres of parkland. It was simply the most splendid thing she had ever set eyes on.

'But who lives here?' she murmured.

John smiled at her awe.

'Lord and Lady Smith-Colyne, it's their family home.' He had forgotten, having lived there for so long, just how beautiful the building was.

'Come on, there'll be plenty of chance to look round later.' He was eager to go in, to get the introduction to Mrs Brown over with and to face Lady Margaret. He hated to prolong uncertainties.

Francesca unfastened her seat belt and began to climb

out of the car. John came round immediately to help her.

'Thank you,' she said, surprised. She was so unused to kindness that for a moment just the offer of his hand overwhelmed her and she hesitated, feeling gauche and inexperienced. She took it and struggled clumsily out of the car, painfully shy of him. He looked down, embarrassed, catching sight of the faint bruising on her arms, and thought: What in God's name happened to her? She's so young, just a child, to be damaged in this way. He stared, shocked at the bruised, marked skin, and Francesca hurriedly pulled down the sleeve of her cardigan. She dropped his hand and moved away. He had stood too close to her, she needed the distance.

Whatever it was, he thought sadly, it was obviously still painful to her and she did not want him to know. He shrugged and reached into the car for her bag.

'Come on,' he said quietly, and silently they went inside the house.

'John!'

Dora Brown had glanced up from her pudding basin on hearing a noise at the door and was amazed to see John walk into her kitchen. 'My goodness me! What a surprise! What on earth are you doing back from . . .?' He was followed in by Francesca and Dora stopped mid-sentence.

'Dora, let me introduce you to my ward,' John said quickly. 'The young girl I was telling you about. Remember?'

Dora wiped her floury hands on her apron and Francesca stepped forward. She could plainly see John's discomfort and the girl was trembling with nerves.

'Oh yes, yes of course!' She moved over to Francesca and covered her surprise, taking her hand and holding it warmly. Something had definitely gone awry, she thought,

but John would explain it all later. The girl was a strange-looking thing, obviously shy, and so thin you could feel her bones. Perhaps John would explain that as well.

'So Lady Margaret didn't tell you I'd rung then, Dora?'

'Did she heck!' Dora had crossed to the sink and was filling the kettle. John ushered Francesca to a chair at the table.

'Her Ladyship has one of the worst tempers I've seen on 'er for years!' She spoke to them over her shoulder.

'Milly's gone down with the chickenpox and when I came in this afternoon, from me morning off, I'm greeted with this news and told she's on her way home from her friend's because of it and could I make sure her room's ready!' She plugged the kettle in and switched it on, tutting irritably. 'As if it ever isn't, I ask you,' she muttered. Turning, she gave them her full attention and folded her arms across her ample bosom.

'Anyway, then the agency rings, you know, the one she's using for the trip to Scotland. They wanted to send a girl over today to meet Milly and Sophie and I told them not to because Milly had the pox and it's very catching in the first week.' The kettle boiled and she reached up for the teapot.

'So, then they ring back and say that they can't send a girl to Scotland, in light of the illness, and they'll refund the money. Quite right too, in my opinion, but Lady M. throws a wobbly! Goes right over the top, if you ask me. The agency's got a right to protect them girls – they shouldn't be exposed to children with catching illnesses!' Dora stopped her monologue to finish making the tea. She brought the pot over to the table while John fetched the cups and milk.

'So, what is Lady Margaret going to do?'

'Gawd knows! She isn't speaking to me, so I certainly won't!' She snorted and began to pour.

John's discomfort deepened. He had always found Lady

Margaret difficult, even in the best of moods. 'I suppose I'd better go through and tell her that Francesca will be staying with us for a while.'

Dora raised an eyebrow, then she glanced across at Francesca who had flushed deep red with embarrassment. 'She'll be cream itself, John, don't you worry!' Dora patted Francesca's hand. She looked so nervous that Dora thought she might cry. 'She'll ask you to find her a nanny and you're to say that you'll do everything you can. She won't utter a whisper.'

John smiled. 'Mrs Brown, you're a cunning old devil! And where do you suppose I'm going to get a nanny from?'

'Who cares, so long as you look as if you're trying!'

She stood up and bustled over to the fridge. She was a large woman whose skirt and nylon slip rustled when she walked. She pulled open the door and bent to take out a joint of gammon.

'And while you're gone, I'm going to make Francesca a nice ham sandwich.' She glanced over her shoulder. 'Would that suit, lovie?'

'Yes, please.'

'Thought so.' Dora threw John a withering look. 'I bet you never even stopped for a bite to eat on the way, did you?'

'Of course not, Dora!' John said irritably, turning towards the door. 'You know how I hate to waste time!'

Dora smiled. This was more like her John. She waited until he'd disappeared out into the main house and then carried the gammon over to the table.

'Men!' she said conspiratorially to Francesca, and began to slice the meat.

'Ah! John! Come in, come in!' Lady Margaret was flicking through a copy of *Harpers & Queen* and had just spotted a

photograph of herself in Jennifer's Diary. It put her in better humour.

'A change of plan then, John?' She dropped the magazine down onto the sofa beside her, while John stood uneasily just inside the room. 'You're back much earlier than expected.'

'Yes, yes I am. Things didn't quite work out the way I had thought they might.'

'I know the feeling! I suppose Mrs Brown has already told you that I am now minus my help for the trip to Scotland?'

'Yes, she did mention . . .'

'I bet she did! I tore her off a strip, I have to confess, but I'm bloody furious and the girls will be bitterly disappointed if they can't go on Friday. I just don't see how I can manage on my own at Lairbeck.' She shrugged. 'Of course Lord Henry will be very upset; he knows how much we were all looking forward to it. Still . . .'

John waited patiently for the next comment, knowing she was building up to it. He watched her fiddle with the magazine for a few moments and then she said, a little too casually, 'I don't suppose there's anything you might be able to do, is there, John?' She looked directly at him, for the first time since he had come into the room. 'I know how marvellous you are at fixing things, and I really would be most awfully grateful.'

She was an attractive woman, he thought, particularly when she smiled. Shame it wasn't very often.

'I'm sure I can try, Lady Margaret. I can't promise anything, but I'll put my mind to it.'

'Oh, John, would you really? How sweet of you.' She picked up her cigarettes and drew one out of the packet, tapping the end lightly on the box, a habit John found ridiculous with filtered cigarettes. She lit it and inhaled

deeply. 'Is there anything else, John?' She had picked up the magazine and held it on her lap, waiting to open it.

'Yes, there is actually. I wanted to let you know that I have a guest staying, and to check that's all right with you and Lord Henry.'

'Well, I can't vouch for my husband,' she paused strategically. All part of letting me know my place, thought John. Then she added: 'But I'm quite happy for you to have a guest. A relation is it?'

'No, not exactly.'

She raised an eyebrow.

'I have been asked to take care of a young woman from Italy, a ward I suppose you would call her.'

'I see.' She waited for more information but she wasn't going to get it. She had given permission and that was all John needed.

'Right, well, if that's all, Lady Margaret?' He shifted impatiently from one foot to the other.

'Oh, yes John, of course.'

He turned towards the door.

'Er, by the way, how old is this girl?' she called after him and he swung round.

'About seventeen or eighteen, I think.'

'Does she speak English?'

'Oh, yes, she'll not be any trouble, she speaks perfect English.'

'Good. Thank you, John.'

'Lady Margaret.' He nodded and before she could ask him anything further, quickly left the room.

John headed back to the kitchen, irritated, with himself and with Lady Margaret. She was never overtly rude to him but she was so superior, and it annoyed him even further that he stood there and took it. He should have said something years ago, made his position clear with her when she

first arrived. It was too late now – she dominated the place and he was getting on. He couldn't take the chance of offending her, his whole life was Motcom Park. So he just put his head down and ignored her, never answered back – it wasn't worth the aggravation. But more fool you, a little voice in the back of his head cried, more fool you.

Opening the door to the part of the house that was his own, John breathed in the warmth and the smells of a living, working kitchen and felt better. He made his way towards the women and heard the echo of girlish laughter along the passage, something he hadn't heard for a very long while. He pushed open the door and Dora looked up at him from across the room, her eyes streaming from laughter.

'Oh, John! Come and have a look at this!' She put her handkerchief up to the corner of her eye and wiped away a tear. Her large, ruddy face was round and creased with smiling and the laughter still glistened in her eyes.

He bent his head and saw Francesca giggling and kneeling on the floor with the string of Dora's apron in her hand, and the fat, lazy, old black cat chasing it as she wiggled it, threw it up in the air, trailed it out and then drew it back in before he had a chance to claw it. His portly, overindulged body flopped heavily as he tried to prance, his belly hitting the floor before any other part of him. He behaved like a kitten half his weight and twice his energy and the two women giggled mercilessly at every undignified movement.

John started to laugh. Just the sight of Francesca, her sadness abandoned for the moment, was enough to fill him with pleasure, but the sound of her happiness as well suddenly dissolved all his doubts and uncertainties. For the first time in years, he felt as if he'd done something worthwhile.

The feeling was good.

She looked up at him and her eyes flashed, a bright, vibrant green. Her whole face changed when she laughed: it softened, all the features fell into place and she was beautiful, the sort of beautiful that was complex, difficult to describe. He remembered that on the quayside he had wondered why he found her so lovely. He could see it now, and he was proud. That feeling too, was good.

He caught Dora's eye. The addition of youth and laughter to our lives is a good thing, her glance told him and he smiled in reply. She was right, he thought, even a dour old Scot could see that.

And, a short while later, when Francesca had gone through to the spare room to unpack her things, Dora said as much to John. They had lived together as friends for nearly ten years. Their relationship was easy but not communicative: John was a man who kept his feelings close; quiet and unassuming, he rarely spoke about himself. Now, he felt the need to share something with Dora, to explain, as if talking it through with her would help him to understand it himself.

They sat over another pot of tea and he told her about Father Angelo, his kindness to John's aunt, and his trust in John to help someone he had described as a 'lost child'.

'I had it all planned out you see, Dora,' he said. 'You know, like I told you. I'd arranged with that friend of mine from the regiment and his wife, Tom and Grace, that is, to take Francesca in for a couple of months, see to it that she was all right, help her get a job. Tom's very good like that, very caring.' He drank the last of his tea and Dora mechanically poured him another cup.

'I thought, Newcastle is a big city.' He took a gulp. 'Not too far away, she'll be fine.' He stopped. 'But when I saw her, Dora, well, I just knew that I couldn't leave her on her own.

She was so lost and alone, so vulnerable.' He paused thoughtfully. 'Yes, vulnerable, that's the word, and I thought, this girl needs some help, she really does. Simple as that, I suppose.'

Dora nodded but kept quiet. She didn't know what to say.

'You know, Dora, when I saw her come off the boat, she looked so brave, shoulders up, head high. She had this bright smile fixed on her face, and yet I could see the fear, I could feel it. It's like her sadness; it's an aura, it's all around her and . . . I don't know, it makes me want to hug her in close, you know? To make it go away.'

Dora glanced down at her red, chapped hands in her lap. This was the most John had ever said to her in years and although she wasn't surprised at his sensitivity, having always suspected it was there, she did wonder why he'd kept it so tightly bottled up all these years.

'That's a good feeling to have, John,' she said simply.

'Is it?'

'Yes. She needs you, it's only right you should help.' She drank the last of her tea. What else can I say, she thought, the girl's obviously had trouble and who am I to give her any more?

'You think I've done the right thing then?' He needed her reassurance.

'Yes, I do,' she said firmly and then smiled. 'Besides, a bit of young laughter around the place will do us old fogies the world of good.'

He smiled back. 'Yes, perhaps you're right there, Dora.'

'Right about what?' Lady Margaret stood in the doorway of the kitchen and smiled. Both employees looked up, startled by the intrusion; Lady Margaret never came into the kitchen. 'Oh, I am sorry,' she said pointedly. 'Have I interrupted something?'

'No, of course not, Lady Margaret.' John stood up quickly. 'Come in, if you'd like to. Can we offer you some tea?'

'No, thank you, John.' She acted as if Mrs Brown was not in the room. 'I wondered if I might have a word?'

'Of course.' He held his ground: he was not going to scurry after her into the main house, not this time. 'What is it you want?'

'Well . . .' She paused for a moment. 'That girl you mentioned, your "ward"?'

'Yes?'

'I've been on the phone to Lord Henry, and he's come up with the most splendid idea! I, well he really, thought that, if she was agreeable, your girl could come up to Scotland with me on Friday. It would be the most perfect solution to our problem!'

'Well now, I don't think that Francesca—'

'You did say she spoke English?'

'Yes.'

'And she's over sixteen?'

'Yes, but—'

'I don't see there's any problem then, John.' She spoke a little more sharply than she intended. John was such an old woman, it really irritated her. 'As Lord Henry said, she might as well make herself useful if she's going to be staying. If I have to feed and look after her, I can just as easily do that in Scotland as down here in Yorkshire. Wouldn't you agree?'

John saw Dora out of the corner of his eye. She was looking up at the ceiling with exasperation and it gave him an unexpected courage.

'No, actually, Lady Margaret, I wouldn't agree.' He caught the full force of her icy glare and his courage momentarily faltered. 'You see, Francesca, that's my ward, she's very shy

and not terribly experienced.' He spoke quickly, unused to disagreeing. 'She's come from a remote part of Italy, you see, and I just don't think she's up to going off on her own. I don't think she has the confidence and—'

'What nonsense, John!' Lady Margaret could see the answer to her dilemma slipping away from her. 'Do be brief! We're talking about a family holiday to Scotland here, not a round-the-world trip!'

'I know, Lady Margaret, but it's just that—'

'Oh, for goodness' sake, John! Why don't you just ask Francesca whether she would like to go or not?' She folded her arms and stood, feet slightly apart, balanced and ready to do battle. 'I'll wait while you call her. It would be nice to be introduced, after all.'

'Yes, of course.' He coughed but he wasn't put off; for the first time in years he'd argued back. Well, he did have Francesca to think of. 'I'll go and find her,' he said. But, he thought, if she doesn't want to go, and the decision is entirely hers, then I'm sure as hell not going to make her. Francesca has suffered enough, he decided with a wry touch of humour, without two weeks on her own with Lady Smith-Colyne.

Minutes later, he reappeared, followed by Francesca, and Lady Margaret administered an enormous smile, the sort she kept for people she wanted to please. Uh-oh, thought Dora, the poor, unsuspecting mite doesn't stand a chance.

'Oh, Francesca!' Lady Margaret stepped forward. 'How nice to meet you. John has told me so much about you and we are delighted to have you as his guest at Motcom.' She took Francesca's hand and shook it warmly, the honey dripping off her words. 'Have you been unpacking? You probably don't have any of the right kinds of clothes for this beastly climate, you poor thing!' She led Francesca over to the table.

'Now, my dear, come and sit down because I have something to ask you, a small favour that would practically save my life!' She ignored John's scowl and sat Francesca opposite her. Francesca had not spoken a word.

What a funny-looking thing, she thought briefly, before launching into her next sentence; so quiet and shy, a real waif and stray. Where on earth did John find her?

'Francesca, I wanted to ask you to help me out. As I said, it's a small favour and I feel sure that you'll be only too happy to do so once you know what's involved, and how much it means to all of us, of course.' She dazzled momentarily with her smile and then continued to speak, addressing herself to the spot slightly above Francesca's head. 'Briefly, without boring you with too many details, myself and the girls, Sophie and Milly, are due to go up to Scotland at the end of the week for our annual holiday. We were meant to have a young girl with us to look after the children and generally help me out, but, unfortunately, she is unable to come, and . . .'

Dora glanced at John.

'Did you mention that Milly has the chickenpox?' he asked. 'That's one of the details and it's infectious, of course, Francesca.'

'Yes, thank you, John, you're quite right, it is slightly infectious.' Lady Margaret glared at him.

'So, you would like me to come to Scotland with you and help you to look after the children. Is that right?' Everyone suddenly looked at Francesca. It was the first time she had spoken and they had almost forgotten she was there.

'Yes, that's right!' Lady Margaret sensed victory. Of course the girl wanted to go. John was such an old fusspot, he knew nothing about young people. 'It's just a month, and Lord Henry and I thought that you might enjoy seeing

something of Scotland while you have the chance. It's a beautiful country.'

Francesca glanced up at John. She could feel the undercurrents of tension in the room and she did not know what to do. Did he want her to go? She was, after all, being asked by his employer. She hesitated for a moment. He must want to please Lady Margaret and he had seemed edgy when she asked – perhaps he was afraid that Francesca would refuse. She caught his eye.

'Of course it is entirely up to you, Francesca,' he said. 'If you don't feel ready to go off on your own, then you must say so.' He kept his voice level, when really he wanted to shout: Oh! For goodness' sake, Lady Margaret, think of someone other than yourself for once!

Francesca nodded. John wanted her to go, she could tell by the tone of his voice, as if he were warning her somehow. I must do as he wants, she thought. I am used to my own company, it will not be so bad.

'Lady Margaret, I will be happy to go with you to Scotland,' she said quickly.

'Are you sure, Francesca?' John moved across to the table, surprised.

'Of course she's sure!' Lady Margaret answered abruptly and then smiled instantly to cover her rudeness. 'The girl's not an idiot, John!' she laughed.

'No, no of course not.' He was embarrassed by her and she knew it. She rose and smiled down at Francesca. 'We leave early Friday morning, Francesca. I'm so pleased you've agreed to join us and I'm sure you'll have a lovely time.'

'Like heck she will,' Dora muttered under her breath.

'I beg your pardon, Mrs Brown?'

'I said, I bet she will, ma'am. Scotland's a beautiful country.'

'Yes, quite right, Mrs Brown.' Lady Margaret knew exactly what Dora had said, but was in no position to cause a scene in front of the girl. She must not be put off.

'If you'd like to come through when the girls come home, Francesca, I'll introduce you. Milly will be straight upstairs to bed, of course, but I'm sure you can spend some time with her there, reading or something.' She turned to Dora. 'The room is ready, Mrs Brown?'

'Yes, Lady Margaret.' Dora bit her tongue.

'Good! See you later then, Francesca. John, you'll bring her through, will you?'

He nodded. And with a flutter of her hand, Lady Margaret bade them goodbye and disappeared through to the main part of the house.

'That's that then,' said Dora and stood to clear away the tea things. 'She always gets her own way in the end.'

CHAPTER
Eleven

FRIDAY MORNING CAME BEFORE ANY of them knew it, except for John. Milly had been in bed since she was sent home from her friend Kitty Larson's house. She knew very little about the preparations for Scotland, her days passed in a sickly blur. For the other members of the household, there were things to be packed, remembered, organised and sorted, and for Lady Margaret there was a hurried trip to London while Lord Henry was in Geneva on business, to purchase some exotic essentials that would make her illicit two weeks with Richard all the more memorable.

John watched it all with a sinking heart. He took Francesca to be kitted out at his gentleman's outfitters in York with thick sweaters and corduroy trousers, walking boots and a Barbour. He noticed that Lady Margaret had left off her list anything that might make the girl look feminine or attractive.

He was not happy about the trip to Scotland. He knew that Francesca would be too much on her own and it worried him. She had been happy enough at Motcom the past few days – he had been watching her closely. But every now and then, he would catch a glimpse of pain and fear in her eyes, emotion raw and exposed, as if it lay so close to the surface that even the merest scratch could bring it through. When he saw it, he wanted to hold her like a child and soothe it away. It was a strange feeling for him: he was needed and that made it all the more difficult for him to let her go. She looked to him for guidance, needing his reas-

surance and his confidence, and it brought out the best in him. To be wanted had been sorely missing in his life.

But Friday morning arrived and John was up early, as the light crept over the estate and the dew lay thick on the ground. He could not sleep and he had a great number of things to do; at least that was what he told himself. He made tea and sat at the kitchen table by the warmth of the Aga and began to go through the list Lady Margaret had prepared for him; she liked to leave all the final details to someone else.

He was checking off the luggage he had packed the night before when he heard the door quietly open. He looked up and Francesca stood at the door, dressed and ready to go.

'Francesca! What are you doing up so early?'

'I could not sleep.' She shrugged and came into the room. 'I think that I am nervous.'

John smiled. Her English was so good that often he almost forgot she was Italian, and then, like now, her words would trip over a sentence and she would sound so funny, out of character, as if she was joking.

'Come and sit down. I'll make you some tea.'

She pulled a face and again he smiled.

'Oh, sorry, coffee then.' He walked over to the kettle and filled it at the sink. 'Those clothes look a little big on you, I think, Francesca.' The sweater he had chosen for her was the smallest the outfitters stocked but it still swamped her. She pulled it up and he saw that the corduroy trousers she wore were gathered in and secured with a big brown belt – they were at least three sizes too big.

'Oh my!' John exclaimed and then typically said: 'Still, I suppose you will always grow into them.'

And suddenly they both started to laugh. It was one of those moments when two people unexpectedly realise they are friends and this friendship is sealed with laughter.

*

'So then, John, it'll be just the two of us for a while, eh?'

John was standing looking at the packed car when a strong voice interrupted his thoughts. He looked up as Dora's footsteps clicked on the stone of the courtyard. She carried a huge basket stuffed with food and brought it round to the passenger door of the Range Rover, handing it over so he could slot it in behind the seat.

'Just the two of us,' he agreed. He looked at his handiwork: everything was neatly packed away into the car.

'I'll miss the girl,' she remarked and John nodded. Since that first day he had not spoken to her again about his feelings, but she had seen a change in him so sudden and so noticeable that it took her aback. The warming of the stone, she thought, the girl's done that. He had softened, smiled more, and once or twice she had even heard him laughing. Just once or twice.

'What's so funny?' He untied the green cotton apron he wore, folded it into a neat square and glanced at Dora, who stood, arms folded across her ample bosom, grinning in a private, knowing way.

'Was I smiling? I didn't realise.'

'Yes, you were,' John said peevishly.

'Sorry.' She shrugged and began to make her way back to the kitchen.

'I'll get Francesca,' she called. 'Her Royal Highness will want to leave soon.'

'You do that.' He watched her go and found himself refolding the apron, over and over into a tiny creased square. Now the car was packed, he wasn't sure what to do with himself next. Normally he would have got on with the day's tasks, let the family depart under their own steam, but not this morning – he didn't want to miss anything this morning.

Dora called to him from the kitchen doorway. She had

seen him standing by the car fiddling with his apron. 'I think I might go round the front to see them off, John.'

He raised a quizzical eyebrow.

'Not for her Ladyship's sake!' she laughed. 'Don't be daft! I want to wave Francesca off.'

And in the back of his mind, the familiar retort came to him: 'We don't want to be wasting time now, Dora.' But he didn't say it, instead he just smiled and answered: 'I think I'll join you.'

Now there's a change, she thought, and she smiled again to herself before turning back into the kitchen. There's a change indeed!

Francesca was settled in the front seat, Milly directly behind her within reach, in case she threw up. To compound the misery of the chickenpox, the poor child now seemed to have developed an upset stomach as well.

'I can't stop every time the child feels sick!' Lady Margaret had said and handed Francesca a clump of plastic bags. She had told Richard she would be there for dinner and she had no intention of cancelling the arrangement this time.

'Do you have everything you might want on a long journey now, Francesca?' Dora leaned into the Range Rover behind Francesca and tucked Milly's blanket tighter round her, ruffling her hair affectionately.

'Of course she does, Mrs Brown! It's only Scotland, for God's sake!' Lady Margaret climbed into the driver's seat and reached for her seat belt. Her manner quite plainly indicated that Dora had not yet been forgiven.

'Thank you, Dora,' Francesca said quietly. She caught Mrs Brown's eye and they smiled at each other. John came round to the front of the car.

'Well, that's just about everything in now, Lady Margaret. You're all ready for the off.'

'Thank you, John.' She switched on the engine.

'Perhaps you'd ring us when you get there,' he said to Francesca. She nodded and he heard Lady Margaret sigh irritably. He stood back and went to slam the door shut.

'John?'

He stopped.

Francesca put her hand out and touched his arm: it was the first time she had done so. She smiled and was about to say something when Lady Margaret switched on the wind-screen wipers and squirted the screen with soapy water. She tested the horn loudly.

'Right then, we're ready,' she said.

'Oh, yes, right.' John jumped back, and, embarrassed, closed the door without looking further at Francesca. He walked across to Dora and stood by her side to wave the family off.

'Cheerio then!' Lady Margaret called out of the window as she put the car into gear and the wheels crunched on the gravel. 'Cheerio!'

John and Dora watched the Range Rover as it travelled down to the gates and disappeared out onto the main road. They could just see Francesca turn and wave and Lady Margaret's leather-gloved hand raised in salute out of the driver's side window, then, moments later, the car had gone.

'Well, that's us on our tod for now.' Dora dropped her hand down into the pocket of her apron. 'We've got so used to her, I don't know what we'll say to each other.'

'Nonsense, Dora!' John spoke abruptly and turned towards the house. 'There's plenty of work to be done; we've no time for sentimentality.'

'Course not,' she answered. But she knew John Mcbride better than that. He'll miss her more than I will, she thought, the dry old stick.

*

Lairbeck House, between Duiar and Cromdale in the Grampian region, was the Scottish home of the Smith-Colyne family. An ugly, grey granite building in Gothic style, it lay tucked in amongst the natural woodland of the Spey Valley and had views over acres and acres of prime sporting land: the Smith-Colyne Scottish estate.

The surrounding country possessed a rare and subtle charm, spreading from the mild, open pastures in the valley of the River Spey, out into the Cromdale Hills and the Grampian Mountains, and a wilder, more majestic scenery of snowy hilltops disappearing into bands of sweeping cloud. It was an area of huge sporting estates owned by rich, absentee landlords and run by their Scottish employees.

Lairbeck House was reached via a small road that turned off the A95 and led up towards the Cromdale Hills. It could be seen from here, its cold, grey bulk and two towers rising up against a backdrop of hills that, deceiving to the eye, looked as if they lay directly behind. In front, woolly sheep grazed the open land that ran into natural woodland and a few trees hid most of the building's facade, a tribute to Pugin's fervour for the Gothic style.

Lady Margaret made the turning off the main road and heaved an enormous sigh of relief. She had been driving for near on seven hours with only one short break in Aberdeen, to eat the lunch Dora had packed and to let Francesca dispose of three full plastic bags.

She drove the two miles along the borders of the Smith-Colyne estate and finally turned into the grounds of the house. It was just after five pm and the northern light was still cold and clear.

'This is Lairbeck, Francesca,' Lady Margaret announced as they approached the house, and slowed the car so that they could gaze fully on the size and dimensions of it. In all

honesty, she hated the place. It was draughty and cold, the plumbing was archaic and the comfort minimal, but she liked to show it off – it was another testimony to her wealth and position.

'I'm sure you'll be very comfortable here.' A blatant lie, but a necessary one. She swung the car into the wide stone drive in front of the house and stopped, yanking on the handbrake.

'Well, girls! Here we are!' She turned in her seat and looked behind her at Sophie and Milly. 'Come on now, let's get our things together, shall we?' Unclipping the seat belt, she jumped down from the car and stretched her long limbs. God, she needed a bath, and a drink, and later, one of Richard's long, slow screws. She glanced down at the swell of her breasts as she stretched her arms over her head. 'Come on, girls!' she shouted. 'We haven't got all day!'

Francesca helped the girls out of the car while Lady Margaret went across to talk to an elderly couple who had just come out of the house. Milly stood forlornly, a blanket wrapped round her, a pillow in her hand, and waited for her mother to remember she was ill. Francesca put her hand on the little girl's shoulder and gave it a squeeze.

'Oh, girls! Francesca! Come over here and say hello to Mr and Mrs Mackenzie, will you, please?'

Francesca led the girls over.

'Milly, Sophie, you remember Mr and Mrs Mackenzie, don't you?' They both nodded. 'And this is Francesca, my help. Mr and Mrs Mackenzie look after the house for us, Francesca. They will be here over the next month taking care of things.' Francesca shook hands but neither one smiled.

'Right. well, if you could take the girls in, Francesca, Mrs Mackenzie will show you their rooms.' Lady Margaret turned away from the small group on the steps of the house

and looked towards the car. 'I'd like to get unpacked as quickly as possible please, Mr Mackenzie. I have an invitation for dinner this evening.' She turned back. 'I should be leaving about seven, so Francesca, you can either eat with the girls or Mrs Mackenzie will leave you something cold to have later. Is that all right with you, Mrs Mackenzie?'

The elderly woman nodded.

'Good! Let's get going then.' She smiled and led the way into the house. 'Oh, by the way,' she said from the doorway to the drawing room. 'When you've done the girls' tea, you and Mr Mackenzie can take the rest of the evening off, Mrs M. And don't bother to make a fire just for Francesca, I'm sure she'll be warm enough.' Glancing over at Francesca, she asked: 'Won't you, dear?' And without waiting for an answer, disappeared into the drawing room to pour herself a large glass of Strathspey malt.

Later that evening, Francesca heard Lady Margaret call to her from the oak-panelled hallway, on her way out to dinner. She hurried from Milly's room down the passage to the stairs, hoping to catch her employer, but she was too late. All she caught was the lingering scent of Guerlain, heavy in the air, and the echo of light, expectant footsteps across the drive to the Range Rover. The car engine was started and the Range Rover gone before she even had a chance to descend the stairs.

'Damn!' She stood looking down at the huge, draughty hallway and caught the glass eye of one of the stag's heads stuffed and mounted on the wall. 'I don't know what you're looking at,' she said irritably and drew her arms in around her. Even in the thick Shetland wool sweater she wore she felt cold and she thought she could see her breath in the damp, chilled air.

Coming downstairs, she peered into the drawing room

on her way through to the kitchen. It was an enormous room, high-ceilinged and stuffed with heavy furniture. There was none of the Georgian grace of Motcom; the feel was masculine and somewhat functional. Thick tapestry drapes hung at the windows, a large, worn Bijar Persian carpet covered the stone floor and the sofas were draped with heavy tartan blankets and big tapestry cushions. It was a comfortable room but still it felt cold. She picked Lady Margaret's empty whisky glass off the side table and took it with her through to the kitchen.

Making herself a coffee, Francesca listened to the echo of her movements in the ancient stone silence, every sound seeming louder than it really was in the empty stillness of the house. She could see the shadow of the mountains as the sun sank and disappeared behind them, leaving the sky the colour of dying embers edged with ash. She could feel the isolation: it was everywhere, around her and inside her, it was in the echo of her footsteps and in the plaintive howl of the wind outside.

She was alone and was glad of it. There was nothing new in solitude, she had known it all her life, only now there was no fear, no dread, or pain. It was a blank loneliness, her memories locked securely away and her emotions hidden. All she felt was an overwhelming sense of numbness and relief. She had closed herself up and withdrawn from the world.

CHAPTER
Twelve

LADY MARGARET WOKE EARLY. SHE lay under the warmth of the quilt and looked around at her bedroom. It had taken years, years of subtle bullying to get it the way she wanted it. 'The house is a hunting lodge,' Lord Henry had said time and time again. 'I'll not have it fancified.' 'Then I won't come,' she had answered finally and promptly withdrew her favours. The following month builders were called in from Aberdeen and it had been modelled to her specifications. It was the only truly comfortable room in the house.

She stretched lazily. The cold, north light was warmed by the apricot of the drapes as it filtered into the room. Her whole body felt good, it tingled with remembered pleasure and the faint traces of Richard's mouth on her skin. Two weeks, she thought, two weeks of being made love to by a man ten years my junior, two weeks of moaning for him to stop. Delicious! And something to show at the end of it, the beginnings of a political career for Patrick maybe? Or if not, at least a few well-earned connections.

She wondered briefly if the Italian girl would make a nuisance of herself – she might have some archaic Catholic views on morality. Unlikely, she decided. Francesca can hardly answer me without blushing and quaking in those ridiculous boots John bought her, let alone interfere with my private life. She had nothing to worry about there, and the dear old Mackenzie couple were so silent as to be practically struck dumb. So, she was quite safe from their verbal interference or from any gossip to Henry.

And with that settled in her mind, and the glorious prospect of thirteen more nights of glorious sex before Henry arrived in Scotland, she climbed out of bed and went through to shower and dress for a day's stalking on Richard's estate.

Francesca was already up and dressed when Lady Margaret came in to see the girls. She had run a bath, waited fifteen minutes for it to fill and than lacked the courage to get into it, the water being lukewarm and the bathroom freezing. In the end, she had splashed herself clean and hurriedly dressed, pulling on two sweaters and an extra tee shirt underneath her Viyella shirt. She still felt icy.

Once ready, she walked briskly along the passage to the girls' room, knowing that Mrs Mackenzie had put a small electric heater in there to keep the chill off Milly. She opened the door and breathed in the warm air with relief.

Sophie was already up, standing at the window in her nightie and counting the sheep in the field. At just five, she could only count up to ten, and so kept starting from one every time she got stuck.

'Francesca!' She turned from the window and ran across the room, hugging Francesca's knees.

'Can we go out to see the sheep today? Can we? Can we?'

Francesca removed her short arms and held her hands. 'Well . . .' Sophie's face fell and she laughed. 'Of course we can, Sophie. But we have to make sure Milly is all right before we do. OK?' She crossed to the seven-year-old's bed and felt her forehead. 'Hello, Milly, how are you feeling this morning?' she said softly and bent to kiss Milly's cheek.

'All right. I suppose.'

'She'll be much better off if we don't fuss!' Lady Margaret walked straight into the room and made them all jump. She crossed to the window and flung it open. 'God, it's like

an oven in here!' She turned and looked down at Milly. 'You won't get better if you don't get some fresh air you know.' Then she glanced at Francesca. 'Children hate fuss, Francesca. They don't like to be mollycoddled.'

She came and sat on the edge of Milly's bed.

'Now, I am off early this morning for a day's stalking, and I am leaving you two girls completely in the charge of Francesca.' She looked sternly at Sophie and Milly. 'I want you to be good, d'you understand? I don't want to hear tonight that you've been playing up.' She smiled. 'But I'm sure I won't.'

Leaning forward, she brushed Milly's forehead with her lips and then stood. 'So, be sweet for Francesca, and I'll see you tonight.' Sophie held her arms out and Lady Margaret bent to give her a quick hug. 'Don't mess Mummy's hair now, darling.' She kissed her and let her go. 'Francesca, could I have a word outside please?' Glancing briefly over her shoulder, she blew a kiss. 'Bye-bye, girls. Be good.' Francesca followed her out of the room.

'Now, Francesca, I'm not at all sure what time I'll be back tonight. I didn't want to say in front of the girls, but I might not be in till very late, it all just depends.' She smoothed her tweed skirt down over her hips. 'So if you'd feed them and put them to bed, then Mrs Mackenzie won't have to bother to come back this evening. All right?'

Francesca nodded.

'Good.' Lady Margaret peered closely at her face. 'You should get out today, dear. It's a nice day, for Scotland anyway, the air would do you good.'

'Yes, thank you.'

'Not at all. Look, I must be off.' She started towards the stairs. 'See you tonight,' she called over her shoulder, and holding onto the banister, ran lightly down the stairs, picked up her keys from the hall table and threw her jacket

over her shoulders. She was gone and Francesca hadn't even said goodbye.

The morning flew by. Lady Margaret was right, the day was fine, the clouds swept over a pale blue sky and the sun shone in between them. Everything was green, shades and shades of varying green, from the dark brownish-green lowlands of the mountains, to the blue-green of the gorse and the bright, verdant green of the fields. Strathspey basked in the fickle sunshine and Francesca was surprised at its beauty.

She looked out at the land from the window in the girls' room and watched the patterns made by the ever changing sky, clouds chased by the wind across the sun, diffusing the light and scattering the shadows. It was constantly altering – the light, the colour, the movement of the trees – the land seemed to have a life of its own; it mesmerised her. Then suddenly she felt Sophie tug on her arm.

'Francesca, you've been sitting there for ages, why don't you come and play with us?' Sophie pulled her shirt. 'Come on, come and buy something in our shop.'

Francesca blinked, turning away from the glare and took a few moments to clear her vision.

'I'm sorry, Sophie, I was dreaming. What did you say?' She glanced down at her watch. 'Oh my goodness! It's almost lunch-time!' She had completely lost track of time. 'I must have been sitting here for hours!'

'Told you.' Sophie took her hand. 'I'm starving,' she announced, and then. 'Guess what!'

Francesca shrugged.

'Milly's been sick!'

Mrs Mackenzie was down in the kitchen when Francesca went for a bowl and some water. She moved silently around the room in her floral housecoat, grey hair scraped severely

off her face into a bun, the line of her mouth grimly set and her house shoes shuffling over the stone floor.

'Yae'll be wantin' fud then, Missie?'

Francesca turned from the sink. It took her several seconds to interpret the question. Mrs Mackenzie held up the knife she was using to chop with. 'Oh, yes please, and something for Sophie.' She filled the bowl and looked around for a cloth. 'I don't think Milly will eat, she has been sick again.'

'That darn't surprise me. The bairn should have the doctor out, she looks reet poorly ta mae.'

'Yes.' Francesca found a cloth and made for the door. She hadn't understood a word of Mrs Mackenzies's observation.

'I've a note from Lady Margrit. She tells mae ta leave some fud for yae this evenin', is that reet?'

Francesca stopped and turned. She held her breath and decided she had two options: to shake her head or to nod. She nodded.

'Will I pripare a wee pot for yae or wud yae rather do yaeself something?'

Again she nodded, she was completely lost.

'What, leave it for yaeself?'

'Yes.'

'Reet yae are.' Mrs Mackenzie went back to the chopping and Francesca heaved a sigh of relief. She was painfully embarrassed and it was solace to her that Mrs Mackenzie was not a woman of great conversation.

The mess cleared up and the children fed, an hour later Mrs Mackenzie sat down on an easy chair in the kitchen and Francesca went upstairs to the girls. Sophie was boisterous – she had been inside too long and she needed to run around. Francesca decided to take her out; the weather was still fine and they both needed air.

'Milly, will you be all right if we leave you for a while?'

'Suppose so.' Milly felt rotten. She wanted to say, 'No, stay here with me!' but her mother had taught her never to make a fuss. 'I think I need a sleep,' she added more kindly. Francesca was the nicest nanny they had ever had, and far nicer than Mummy was most of the time.

'OK. Mrs Mackenzie is downstairs in case you need anything. She'll come up in a little while to check you're all right. I'll run down and fetch some water for you and then we'll be off. We won't be gone for long – we'll be back before you open your eyes again!'

Milly almost smiled. Well, she would have done if she wasn't feeling so sick again.

Francesca went for the water and minutes later reappeared and placed it beside Milly's bed. She bent, kissed her forehead and crossed to the window to draw the blind.

'See you in a while, Milly,' she whispered, and taking Sophie by the hand, she led her tiptoeing to the door and outside into the passage.

Together they padded down the stairs to the hall where Francesca found Sophie's coat, fastened her into it, tying her scarf, and pulled on her own jacket. Then, before the sunshine disappeared, they rushed outside and ran across the fields, out towards the hills with the warm sun on their faces and the wind in their hair.

They walked, holding hands, Sophie surprisingly quick on her feet, and said hello to the sheep. Then they headed onwards and upwards, lured by the thought of being high up and able to survey everything around them. They sang, Francesca told rhymes in Italian and Sophie counted from one to ten over and over as she numbered the bright purple flowers of the thistles in their path. Before long, they were some way from the house, the gradient had steepened and they could look down on the sheep, small, grubby blobs

scattered over the field. The wind was stronger up higher – it whipped their cheeks and flailed the long strands of Sophie's hair around her face. She stood, her tiny frame head-on into the breeze, arms out wide, and laughed joyously as the full force of the wind swept over her, pushing her backwards and into Francesca's arms.

They had been out for an hour, but the time went with the speed of the wind. Francesca was conscious of Milly and knew they could not be out too long. It had grown cooler, the clouds had massed together and blocked out the sun and the wind became sharper without the sunshine behind it. She told Sophie that they should start to head back.

It took longer to walk down from the hillside than it had to walk up, or it felt that way. The sky had darkened quite suddenly and it seemed to get lower, to close in on them, the air thickening with moisture and the wind increasing. It was no longer fun; it blew hard and fierce against them and made walking difficult.

Francesca began to feel panic. She was unused to the swift change of the elements; they overwhelmed her and frightened her. She glanced down at Sophie, stalwart in her determination to be brave, and saw that her little hands were white from clenching her fists.

Then it started to rain.

A huge bolt of lightning ripped through the sky, everything cruelly lit for a split second with its weird electric light, and moments later, thunder tore down from the mountain, roaring, as if the earth had a voice, an angry, violent voice. Francesca jumped and Sophie screamed. A torrent of water followed.

'Sophie! Here! Quickly!' Francesca bent to the child and picked her up. She was small and light for five. Her arms went around Francesca's neck and she clung on, burying her face and gripping with all the force of her small, childish

hands. Heavy, painful sheets of rain battered down from the dark, menacing sky and drenched them in minutes. The thunder roared again.

'It's all right, Sophie,' Francesca murmured. 'Hold on to me, don't worry, little one.' She could feel the child shaking. 'Hold on tight!' And then she started to run, hugging Sophie in close to her with the rain pouring down in leaden, icy blasts, making her face and hands sting terribly as she ran headlong into it.

Patrick Devlin stood at the kitchen window of Lairbeck and looked out at the wide expanse of land behind the house that led up towards the hills and their wild, rocky scenery. It was feral and terrifying in the ravages of the thunderstorm and he scanned the scene, searching anxiously for two figures. The rain pelted down, banging against the glass, and the wind howled, the chill of it coming in off the window. At last he spotted them.

They came out of the cover of the trees, a tall, thin young girl, carrying Sophie and running, scared and unsteady, headlong into the elements, racing towards the house. He rushed to the door, unbolted it and pulled it open, sprinting across the back fields and up towards the hills, calling out to them and waving his arms to attract their attention.

Francesca saw him some while before she heard him: his voice was helpless against the noise of the storm. She looked up from watching her footing to see how far they had to go and caught sight of a figure coming towards them, shouting, his words dying on the wind, and waving his arms. Peering through the sluicing rain, she ran on, startled and confused by his appearance, and then, not concentrating, she lost her footing. Her ankle went over and the pain shot through her leg. She stumbled for several yards, des-

perately trying to regain her balance, holding onto Sophie with all her might, but she was unable to control her body. She fell forwards, turning sideways to protect Sophie from the impact and closing her eyes in grim expectation of the pain.

Patrick caught her just as she toppled.

'Whoa!' He held onto her tightly, surprised at her lightness, and stopped her fall. She slumped against him and he pulled Sophie from her arms, letting her collapse forward and taking her weight. He propped Sophie up onto his hip, held her secure with one arm, and with the other, he tucked Francesca under his shoulder and supported her, trying to help her to walk. But against the beating wind and rain, it was virtually impossible.

He stopped and faced her. 'Are you all right? Can you walk?'

Her face was white with shock and pain. She shook her head.

'OK. Wait here!' Hurriedly, he put Sophie down on the ground and pulled off his Barbour, wrapping it round Francesca. 'I'll run home with Sophie,' he shouted. 'And come back for you. Just stay here, all right? Cover yourself up and wait for me.' He picked Sophie up again and began to run. She watched him, moving easily and athletically down the slope towards the house, and tucked her arms around her, sinking to the ground because her legs could no longer hold her up.

It seemed like forever on the side of the hill in the sleeting rain, but it was actually only a few minutes. Patrick deposited Sophie in the warmth of the kitchen and, without stopping, ran out again into the storm for Francesca. When he reached her, he bent, scooped her up, holding her across his arms, and turned back to the house. He held her tightly and ran, his grip firm but gentle, his head bent forward over

her, to try to shield her face from the terrible wind and rain.

Within minutes they were back into the warm, dry safety of the kitchen.

'My God! What a storm!' Patrick, breathing heavily, carried Francesca over to a chair by the Aga and lowered her gently onto it. He raised her leg and placed it on another chair, slipping a cushion under the ankle. She was shivering, drenched through, and she dripped a pool of water slowly onto the stone floor.

'Sophie?' He turned to his niece. 'Come here, sweetheart.' He picked her up and hugged her, taking a couple of minutes to get his breath. Then he said:

'I'm going to take Sophie up and get her into a hot bath. Will you be all right here for a while? I really ought to see to that ankle of yours before you start moving around on it.'

Francesca nodded.

'Good.' He reached for a towel drying on the stove and passed it to her. 'Here!' he said. 'You're dripping!' And then he smiled. It was the most charming smile Francesca had ever seen.

'See you in a few minutes,' he said, and stopped at the door. He knew who she was – Milly had told him – but he realised she must have no idea about him.

'Oh, by the way,' he said. 'I'm Patrick Devlin, Lady Margaret's brother.' He laughed. 'You'd never know though, would you?' And leaving the warmth of this behind, he left the room and Francesca heard him talking quietly and kindly to Sophie all the way up the stairs.

When Sophie was warm and dressed, Patrick brought her back down to the kitchen and sat her on the edge of the table.

'Milly is delighted with the story of the storm rescue,' he said to Francesca as he filled a towel with ice from the freezer. 'She wants you to go up and show her your swollen ankle.'

Francesca smiled.

'Gruesome child!' He carried the ice-pack across and knelt to unfasten Francesca's boot. 'Very elegant footwear!' He heaved the heavy leather walking shoe off as gently as he could and peeled away her sock. The ankle was badly swollen and he was surprised at her courage.

'Here, this will hurt for a moment.' He placed the ice on the swelling and she gasped. 'Told you.' Holding it in position, he glanced up at her face for the first time.

What a startling-looking girl, he thought, studying her features. She was beautiful, but he couldn't quite see how. Her eyes were lovely, bright sharp green, framed with the longest black lashes he had ever seen. It must be her eyes, he decided, or maybe the shape of her face, he just wasn't sure. Looking down at her foot once more, he removed the ice-pack and checked the swelling.

'It seems to have eased a little. D'you think you can stand on it?'

She nodded.

'Good. If I help you up the stairs and run a bath for you, can you manage to get in and out on your own?'

She sat silently for a few moments and then said shyly: 'I do not think I need a bath, I am warm enough now.'

'Nonsense!' He was surprised at her voice – it was not at all what he had expected. Milly had said she was Italian but her voice had only a trace of an accent, the merest soft lilt. 'You must have a bath,' he said. 'You'll never get properly warm if you don't.'

'No, really, I do not need one.' She turned away from his gaze, flushing at its intensity.

'Hang on a minute!' He stood. 'What room has Maggie, I mean, my sister put you in?'

'The room on the side of the house, under the tower.' She looked up. 'Why?'

'With that crusty old bathroom down the corridor? No bloody wonder you don't want to have a bath! It's freezing up there!' He looked down at her and shook his head. Suddenly they both smiled.

'Tell you what, I'll help you upstairs and you can use the bathroom next to the room I'm in. It's the most comfortable bathroom by far.'

'Thank you.' Again she blushed, this time at his kindness.

'And later on, if you pack your things up, I'll move them down to the first floor just along from me and find you a heater for the room.'

'But . . .'

'But nothing! You can't possibly spend the next few weeks freezing up there! Besides, we'll tell Lady Margaret there was no alternative – you can't climb the stairs, it's as simple as that.' He held a hand out for her and she took it, easing herself with his help out of the chair. She hopped precariously on one leg, trying to balance, and then he picked her up and held her in his arms.

'Come on, Soph, look sharp! Open the door for us please.' Sophie jumped down and ran across to the door. She held it and her uncle passed through carrying Francesca, who looked both embarrassed and alarmed at her extraordinary predicament.

Some time later, feeling warm for the first time since she had arrived in Scotland, Francesca made her way slowly down to the study, holding tightly onto the banister and hobbling as best she could. She knocked on the door and

Patrick jumped up to open it for her, helping her to a big old leather sofa and settling her next to Milly who sat, wrapped in blankets and looking the most cheerful Francesca had seen her for days.

'You should have shouted for me,' he said, finding her a footstool. He lifted her ankle onto it and pulled up the hem of her trousers to see the injury. 'I think we'll bandage that with some anti-inflammatory cream on first.' He smiled at the alarmed look on Francesca's face. 'Trust me,' he said quietly, and both girls suddenly chorused: 'I'M A DOCTOR!' and broke into peals of hysterical laughter.

Once her foot was bandaged, Francesca lay back against the padded comfort of the sofa and relaxed. The study was warm, a fire blazed in the grate and the reds and golds in the room held the heat, glowing in the soft light of the table lamps. The atmosphere between Patrick and his nieces was one of childish frivolity, telling jokes and swapping vastly exaggerated stories, in between bouts of excited girlish laughter. Francesca sat and watched it all. She was not confident enough to join in, but was happy to be on the edge of such a scene.

Yet every now and then she would find Patrick staring at her, when the girls were talking and didn't need his attention. It unnerved her. He seemed to be searching her face for something, something that puzzled him, and each time she caught his glance she would turn away, frightened of his scrutiny. She did not want to be fathomed, she had too much to hide.

Patrick could see her distance, he could see her sadness, so well covered. There was something poignant about her, something wise and knowing and complicated, and yet she was fresh, as fresh and as innocent as a child. It fascinated him, that and her extraordinary beauty. He felt as if he could not leave her alone, could not stop looking at her

nor wanting to talk to her. She hardly answered him, blushing and tripping over her words, but that only made her more charming, more elusive – and that made Patrick more eager.

He listened to the girls, joined in the fun but his mind was on Francesca. He was enchanted by her. The time passed in a kind of blur. He found he was conscious of nothing but the room and his gaze, curiously drawn, time and time again, to the young girl with the intense green eyes.

And so the remainder of the afternoon slipped away. Warm and comfortable, the girls became sleepy, the jokes died down and the laughter faded. Patrick talked less and an intimate silence descended. Milly dozed, Sophie looked through a much-loved picture book and Francesca watched the flames in the fire. There was no noise save the cry of the wind and the constant tap of the rain against the window.

'Well I never! What on earth is going on here?' Lady Margaret walked into the study, switching on the overhead light, and the room was suddenly flooded with a bright electric glare. Everyone visibly jumped.

'Good Lord! Patrick! What the hell are you doing here?' She stood in the entrance to the room and looked across at her younger brother. Then she smiled. She always did at the sight of Patrick. 'Why didn't you tell me you were coming? How did you get here – your car's not outside?'

'Hey! One question at a time, please!' He stood and she crossed the room to him, embracing him and then standing back to look at his face. 'You look well, a bit tired maybe, but quite well.'

He laughed at her maternal tone. 'Thank you, and so do you.'

She laughed and kissed him, then she turned away.

'Well, girls, I might have known who'd have Milly out of

bed and the pair of you drinking whisky in Daddy's study!' They giggled. 'Come on now,' she said. 'I think it's time you went up.'

'Oh no, let us stay up a bit longer, pleeeease,' Milly whined.

'Well, you certainly seem better!' Lady Margaret crossed to her eldest daughter and bent to kiss her forehead. 'I'll tell you what, girls, if Francesca takes you up and you get ready for bed, then your uncle can bring you both a tray up and read you a story.' She looked at Sophie. 'How does that sound?'

But both girls were disappointed; they had been fine until their mother came home. Lady Margaret clapped her hands. 'Come on now! Up, up!'

Francesca moved her foot off the stool and eased herself up, holding onto the sofa. She put her bandaged foot down and found it was not as painful as she had expected.

'Oh, my dear!' Lady Margaret cried. 'What have you done?' She spoke a little sharply – the last thing she needed was a crippled nanny.

'It's a sprained ankle, Maggie,' Patrick said quickly. 'Done in the call of duty.'

Francesca stood. 'It is fine, thank you. Nothing at all.'

Relieved it was manageable, Lady Margaret allowed Francesca some sympathy. 'Oh, you poor thing!' she murmured. 'However will you cope?' It was, of course, a rhetorical question. Patrick stepped forward.

'Can I help?'

'No, no thank you.' Francesca flushed. 'Come on, Sophie, Milly.'

Both girls stood up at her request and trailed behind her to the door. 'Do we have to . . .?' Milly asked.

'Yes.' Lady Margaret would stand no nonsense. 'Go on, chop-chop!'

And grudgingly, they followed Francesca out into the hall and slowly up the stairs to their room.

'Phew! Children!' Lady Margaret crossed to the door and clicked it firmly shut. She turned towards Patrick.

'I don't know, Maggs,' he said. 'You're very lucky – they're lovely girls.'

'Yes, I suppose so.' She sighed. 'Drink?'

'Hmm, yes please.'

'There's some of Henry's Islay Jura here, somewhere.' She had bent and was rummaging through a collection of bottles in the cabinet. Patrick noticed the label on her jersey showing.

'Who's the latest then, Maggie?'

She stopped and looked at him over her shoulder. 'I don't know what you mean!'

'Come on, your sweater's on inside out.'

'Oh Lord!'

'Exactly.'

She stood straight, holding a bottle of whisky. 'Richard Brachen,' she said and walked across to the side table to pour them both a glass.

Patrick remained silent: they had argued about this too many times in the past, he was weary of it.

'As long as you know what you're doing, Margaret.'

She turned from the table. 'Don't I always?' He shrugged. 'Anyway,' she said, coming over with his drink, 'it's not serious, it's very discreet and no one will get hurt. All right?' Again he shrugged. 'Well, at least that saves me giving you any blarney about dinner tonight. I won't be in, but Mrs M. has left lots in the larder. You don't mind, do you?'

'No.' Actually he was relieved. It would give him time to think about Francesca.

'So, how long are you staying?' Lady Margaret plonked

herself down on the sofa and looked at him. 'You can stay as long as you like, you know that.'

'Yes, thanks Maggie. I'm not really sure at the moment. I've taken three weeks' leave from the hospital, and I might go to Edinburgh to see some friends for a few days. I think I'll just wait and see.'

'Fine. Henry's not up until the middle of the month, for the glorious twelfth, of course!' She smiled. 'Come and go as you please, there's plenty of sport here or on Richard's estate.'

'Great, thanks.'

'Look, darling bro, I must go and get myself changed. It absolutely pissed down this afternoon and we got caught. I smell like an old mutton and I can't sit here drinking with this pong!' She snorted. 'I'll take my drink up, I think. See you later maybe?'

'I don't know, I might get an early night.'

'OK. Whatever.' She stood and blew him a kiss. 'Cheerio, darling. Eat and sleep well; you know where the cellar is.' And with a brief wave, she crossed the room and left.

He splayed his legs out, cradled his whisky in his hands and lay back in the warmth of the fire.

He had been there some while when he woke. He heard vague noises in the back of the house from the kitchen, adjacent to the study, and stood up to go and investigate. He had no idea of the time – his watch had got wet bathing Sophie – but the sky outside had darkened completely and he guessed it was well into the evening. Crossing to the window, he drew the drapes and then went through to the hall, along the passage and into the back of the house. He followed the noises to the kitchen.

'Hello.' He had cheated. Creaking open the door to the kitchen, he had stood for several minutes watching

Francesca as she moved around the room preparing food. She was humming, very low, barely audibly, and her movements were easy and graceful. Unwatched, even with a bad ankle, she had a natural poise.

She spun round; he had startled her.

'Oh! Hello.' Stopping what she was doing, it took her a few moments to control the fear in her heart: Enzo's legacy.

'I'm sorry, I made you jump.'

'Yes.'

He came into the room and pulled out a chair at the long, scrubbed oak refectory table. 'Are you all right?'

'Yes.'

'What time is it? I must have fallen asleep.'

Francesca glanced up at the station clock on the opposite wall. He followed her gaze.

'God! I must have gone out like a light!' It was nine o'clock. 'What happened to the girls' story and supper?'

'I took it up and I told them that you were asleep.'

'Thank you.' He was surprised, he could not remember anyone so undemanding. 'Were they awful about it?'

She smiled and he saw how it lit up her whole face. She was lovely, so gentle and unassuming.

'No, I told them that if you slept now, you would wake earlier tomorrow and they would have longer to play with you then.'

He laughed. 'Did they buy that?'

'Oh yes, they are very fair children.'

'Yes, they are.' He watched her as she went back to her task. 'What are you cooking?'

'A . . .' She stopped. 'I cannot remember the word for it. In Italian, *brasato di manzo*. Meat, with vegetables.'

'Ah! A stew.' He could see as she moved that her ankle was sore. He went over and stood beside her.

'You know, this is something that I rarely tell people, but

my speciality is stews.' He smiled and watched her face change as she understood and smiled back. 'So, why don't you go and rest that ankle of yours and talk me through cooking the dinner?' She was not sure that he wasn't teasing her, so she stayed where she was, not wanting to make a fool of herself if he was.

'Go on,' he said. 'And don't try to pretend that your ankle is perfectly all right. I know these things—'

'I'm a doctor,' she interrupted and they both laughed. She moved across to the table and sat. He was right, her ankle had really started to hurt.

'So, Francesca,' he said as he began to chop. 'Tell me all about yourself, and Italy and what you are doing with my sister's children in Scotland. I want to know absolutely everything.'

But, later, after they had eaten, he realised that in fact he knew absolutely nothing. He had done all of the talking and found, in the relaxed warmth of her company, that he had spoken in a way he would never usually have done. He had told her about his childhood in Ireland, about his father and the old man's slow death from alcohol. He had explained how much he owed Lady Margaret, how she had always looked after him, paid for his education and been more like a mother to him than a sister. Then he had gone on about his days at medical school, about his hopes and dreams, and she had listened to it all, content to let him tell her as little or as much as he wanted to. She wanted nothing from him. At thirty-three, with dark Irish looks, an innate charm, connections and a future, that was something quite different for a man like Patrick Devlin.

He was used to rich, vapid beauties, interested in what he could give and in taking all they could get. He took as

well, it wasn't all one-sided, but he never seemed left with much at the end.

Looking across at Francesca, tracing the grooves of wood in the table with her finger, Patrick wondered just what it was about her that intrigued him. She was tired, he could see that, she had stayed up to listen to him and her face was white and drawn. She was still lovely, though. He reached out and stopped the movement of her finger with his hand. The sudden physical contact made her jump.

'Sorry.' He looked away, embarrassed. 'You look tired,' he said. 'You should go to bed, your room's ready.'

'It's OK. I must clear first.'

'No.' he stood. 'I'll clear, you go to bed.' Standing above her, he could see her fierce determination to stay awake and she looked like a child to him. 'Go on! You've done quite enough tonight, listening to me drone on for hours!' Then he smiled. 'Honestly, go.'

Francesca stared up at him; she had never met anyone like him. 'Really? It's all right to leave this?'

'Yes.'

She did not know what to say. It was so rare that anyone had done anything for her that she felt strange, at a loss to know what to do or say. She looked down at her hands in her lap, feeling painfully shy and ill at ease, and then she stood, murmured her thanks and hobbled across the room to the door. Within seconds she had gone.

Patrick watched her close the door quietly behind her, went back to his clearing and found himself curiously disappointed to be finally alone.

CHAPTER
Thirteen

IT WAS SEVEN AM, THE air was sharp, but the sky was the clearest palest blue and the sun was high, already warm and beginning to dry the fresh morning dew on the fields. It promised to be a glorious summer day.

As quietly as she could, Lady Margaret opened the back door at Lairbeck and crept into the house. She eased her shoes off by the step and walked in stockinged feet through the kitchen and silently out into the hall. She slipped her headscarf off and left it in its usual place over the banister, then she stole up the stairs and along the carpeted passage to her room, gently clicking the door open and closing it just as quietly behind her. She crossed to the bed, dropped her shoes down on the floor and slipped off her coat. She was completely naked underneath.

Walking over to the mirror, she looked at her reflection and trailed her hand down from her breast to her hips and then her thighs. She ran her fingers where Richard's had been just an hour ago and felt the same wonderful flush of excitement. She had been up all night. They had talked and made love continuously; they had swum naked together in the freezing water of the river, clinging onto each other in the icy flow. He took her on the wet grass, the hard, cold ground under her making her climax sudden and quick. And then he had told her about his house party, and her final orgasm had been her best.

She turned away from the mirror and reached for a hair tie from her dressing table. She fastened it in her hair and

padded through to the bathroom, picking up a thick white towel from the rail and flinging it over the top of the shower cubicle. Turning on the hot water, she stepped into the shower and let it course down over her body, gently soaping herself and thinking about how to proceed, as cleverly and as carefully as she could.

By the time she had dried herself and smoothed a liberal amount of Guerlain body lotion into her skin, she had decided on the best way forward.

It would have to be a dinner at the house, there was no other option, and preferably on the weekend of Henry's arrival, to add a bit of aristocratic clout. She would only invite the most influential members of Richard's house party, of course, and maybe a couple of close family friends.

She was taking a chance, she knew that, inviting Richard to Lairbeck when Henry was present. He liked to take risks, silly, dangerous risks. But she also knew that she would never get Patrick onto the Brachen estate. Two cabinet ministers and a leading Tory MP were an opportunity she could not afford to pass up. Not if she was going to eventually get what she wanted.

And why else, she thought, spraying Guerlain scent over her breasts, apart from a big cock and enormous staying power, would I put up with an arsehole like Richard Brachen? There's more to life than sex. Being married to Lord Henry Smith-Colyne, a man twenty years her senior, and worth more than the national debt, she knew this only too well.

Patrick heard the faint click of his bedroom door and smelled her before he opened his eyes. She crept across to the window and reached up to open the drapes.

'Don't you dare!' He called gruffly from under the covers.

She turned and laughed. 'I knew you were awake – I

wouldn't have attempted to open the curtains if you were asleep, my darling Patrick!'

'Liar!' He pulled the covers down to his nose and smiled. 'Phew! What a whiff! It's a bit early for perfume, isn't it?'

'A lady always wears scent, Paddy!' Lady Margaret came to the edge of his bed and sat herself down. 'Anyway, don't be grumpy, I've hardly seen you for days.'

'Whose fault is that?'

'Mine. Point taken. I have rather neglected you, haven't I? I hope the girls haven't been too much of a nuisance.'

He smiled. 'No, of course not. I love 'em dearly, you know that.'

'Hmmm. You should get married and have a family of your own, Patrick, instead of stealing mine every time you're here.'

Funnily enough, for the first time in his life, Patrick had begun to think the same thing the past few days. He pulled himself up the bed and his sister handed him a couple of pillows. He propped them behind him and lay back to look at her.

'So, to what do I owe this pleasure, Maggie? Early morning visiting is not your usual thing.'

'No, you're quite right, there was something I wanted to talk to you about.'

He folded his arms behind his head and settled himself. 'OK, my dear, fire away. I'm listening.'

But, as his sister began to talk, Patrick was not listening. He was not yet fully awake and his mind drifted lazily back over the past ten days and the hours and hours he had spent with Francesca. Francesca, Francesca. Even her name was wonderful to him, it was like a whisper, a murmur on his breath.

She was the strangest, most captivating girl he had ever met. She was so natural and free, laughing and roaming

across the fields in the wind and the rain, like a child, full of
joy at the beauty of the sky and the land. He loved that part
of her and envied it: it was everything he wanted to be
himself. He loved to watch her draw as well – her exquisite
tiny sketches of him and the girls, capturing in five minutes
the essence of their characters, making them all laugh with
her frown of concentration and the lower half of her lip
stuck out petulantly as she worked. The patterns too: the
colour and life in them were like the colour and life she
made him feel; their exuberance was his and it was as if she
was able somehow to put down on paper all that was wonderful in the world around them. It amazed him and it
filled him with inspiration.

And then suddenly, just when he thought he knew her,
just when it all seemed so wonderful, she would close up,
her abandonment to joy would disappear and she would
become dark and silent, withdrawn and alone. He could see
the pain in her eyes but had no idea why, he could only
guess at the turmoil inside her. It was weird, difficult and
complicated, something secret and unknown, a part of her
he couldn't have, might never have, and that fascinated
him. He was used to having it all.

'Paddy!' Lady Margaret poked him hard in the ribs.
'Paddy, did you hear me?'

'What?' He looked blankly at his sister.

'I asked you if you think it's a good idea?'

'What is?'

'Oh God!' She cuffed him on the top of the head. 'Henry
and I are thinking of giving a large dinner a week on
Saturday for a few people who're up for the shooting. I
asked you if you thought it was a good idea.'

'Yes, whatever you want, Maggie.'

'Good! You will still be around, I take it, I'll need you to
liven things up a bit.' She fiddled with the edge of his blan-

ket as she spoke, and he noticed. It was a sure sign she was not being entirely honest.

'That the only reason you want me there, Maggie? I might go to Edinburgh then, you see.'

'No, Paddy! You can't go then!'

'Ah, thought there was something else.'

'Actually,' she said quietly, unsure of his reaction, 'I'm going to invite a few people who are staying at Richard's – Charles Hewitt and John Anderson are there at the moment.'

Patrick moved his hands from behind his head, altering his relaxed attitude. 'Any other cabinet ministers up your sleeve, Margaret?' he said sarcastically.

'Look, Paddy, there's no need to be like that! These people could be useful to you, I'm only trying to help!'

'Oh?' He climbed out of bed and strode across the room in his shorts, pulling on his towelling robe. He was angry with her for interfering again but he couldn't keep down his excitement at the mention of such political power. He turned. 'Margaret, I've told you before, if I do this, I want to do it on my own! A career in politics is too important to me just to end up as "jobs for the boys"!'

She watched him carefully. He was cool but she could see the excitement underneath.

'Who's interfering?' she asked. 'All you have to do is meet these people.' She stood. 'You never know, Paddy, when you might come across them again. A previous introduction is always useful.'

'OK, Maggie.' He sighed. 'If you think it's important, I'll come.' He crossed back to the bed. 'But that's all, right? I don't want any favours doing. The only person who will decide on a political career for me, Margaret, is me. Do I make myself clear?'

She smiled, she couldn't help herself. At least she'd got

him in the right place at the right time. He hadn't got a clue, of course, that the whole world was run on favours. 'You make yourself quite clear, Patrick darling,' she said. 'But I do wish you wouldn't be so damn grumpy about it!' She reached up and kissed his cheek. 'Spoiled child!'

He smiled back. She was incorrigible, she always got her own way.

'Well, now that's settled, I'll leave you to go back to bed.'

'Hardly! I have to be up anyway, we're taking the girls on a picnic today.'

She raised an eyebrow. 'We?'

'Yes, we. Francesca and me. Francesca is the Italian girl you brought up here to look after Milly and Sophie, remember?'

'OK. There's no need to be sarcastic.' She eyed him suspiciously for a few moments. No, she decided quickly, he couldn't possibly be interested in the nanny, she was far too skinny, a real waif and stray and not his type at all. 'Well, have a nice day then,' she said and turned towards the door. 'I may see you later, I'm not sure.'

'OK.'

She blew him a kiss. 'Bye darling.' And wafting her scent in the air with her hand, she disappeared out into the passage and along to the stairs, humming merrily as she went.

By the time Patrick had dressed, the morning was well underway. The sun had climbed, the blue of the sky deepened and the dew evaporated into the warm, dry air. He looked out, delighted at the day for their picnic, and grabbed his things from the chair, stuffing them into a small rucksack and making his way downstairs.

Francesca was already in the kitchen. She sat at the table in a pair of white cotton shorts he had lent her, pulled in tight with her old brown leather belt, and an oversize white

tee shirt on top. Her long, tanned legs were tucked up under her and she was carefully placing the things Mrs Mackenzie had made for their lunch into a huge wicker basket. She looked up as he came in.

'Hi!'

'Good morning.' He walked over to the sink to fill the kettle and touched her lightly on the shoulder as he passed. She smiled. She liked him to touch her: she felt no threat from his physicality, just warmth and comfort, the feelings of friendship.

'I have made you some coffee,' she said. She glanced back at him. 'It is on the stove. Here!' She stood and reached for the pot on top of the Aga. As she uncurled, she reminded Patrick of a long, sleek cat. 'You want milk?'

He took the cup she handed to him and sat down opposite her. 'Has Mrs M. made us anything nice?' He rifled in the basket and looked at a couple of things, lifting lids off containers and dipping his finger into one to taste the contents.

'Don't!' She laughed and moved the basket away.

He pulled a face. 'Oh, by the way, where are the girls?' Much as he loved Sophie and Milly, Patrick had found that the past couple of days he'd almost forgotten they were there. He looked across at Francesca as she rolled the cutlery into napkins, her dark head bent, and he thought how quiet and still she was, how serene. She glanced up and flushed at his stare.

'They are outside,' she said quickly. 'Getting their fishing nets and buckets.' She bent her head again to avoid his gaze.

Damn, he thought, I've embarrassed her. I should leave her alone. 'Well, I'd better go and jolly them along,' he said and stood, draining his coffee cup. 'Hmmmm, delicious coffee.' He saw her smile. She was like the rarest, most delicate

flower – she reacted to warmth with the tiniest unfurling of her bud, almost imperceptible, except to someone who . . . He stopped his mind right there. He was being foolish, unrealistic.

'Is everything ready?'

'Yes, a few more minutes.'

'OK. I'll bring them in once we've sorted their equipment.' He smiled, crossed to the door and then stopped. 'Is your foot all right this morning?' He still worried about her injury, suspecting that it probably hurt more than she admitted to.

'Yes.' She finally looked up. He was so kind. 'It is fine,' she said. 'Thank you.' And the bud opened out a tiny bit further.

The spot by the river was perfect. Patrick had forged on ahead to choose it while the girls walked slowly behind with Francesca, Sophie too small to go any faster and Milly not strong enough yet. He carried most of their things and had looked so funny by the time they had loaded him up, with basket, rugs, rucksack, buckets, nets, spare clothes and drink, that the girls fell about giggling and kept calling him donkey. As he lumbered ahead of them he would Eeeh-Aw every now and then and send all three into fits of uncontrollable laughter.

Laying out the rugs, Patrick organised a shady spot for Milly under a tree and found a nook in the river-bank where he could safely lay the drinks to cool them in the water. He placed the basket at the base of the tree out of the sun, lined the nets and buckets up at the water's edge and had it all ready by the time the girls reached him.

'Mademoiselles, votre picnic!' he announced.

'It's brilliant, Uncle Paddy!' Milly said and followed Sophie over to the edge of the river.

Francesca sat down on one of the rugs and crossed her long legs. Patrick watched her. She looked extraordinary in the sun: tanned and dappled with light, her skin seemed golden, the colour of honey. He turned away from her to the water and reached for a bottle. He was staring again, he had to stop it.

'Would you like a drink?' he asked. She nodded and he found a beaker to pour the lemonade. 'Here.'

She took the drink and smiled up at him. 'Thank you,' she murmured. Everything was perfect. No, she thought, it was more than that, it was better than anything she had ever known before. She was happy, and it filled her mind, her heart and her soul. It was new for her, thrilling, and consuming, and it was the first time she could ever remember being glad she was alive.

The rest of the morning turned out better than they had hoped. The wind dropped to a faint breeze, the sun took the temperature up into the seventies and everyone languished in the warm summer air. Lunch was eaten in the shade, all the home-made lemonade drunk and Mrs Mackenzie's food gobbled down. Milly fell asleep and Patrick lay and watched Francesca on the slope of the riverbank with Sophie as they fished things out of the waters of the Spey.

She tried to explain each new treasure that went into the bucket and he found himself smiling as she struggled to find the English for the obscure collection of things Sophie would insist on keeping.

Patrick was happy. Really happy, though, like he was when he was a boy. It was a complete and uncomplicated happiness and it made him feel young, as if he had his whole life to look forward to, and not that he had lived too much of it already. He had forgotten his pain, the pain he

had carried around with him for years, the pain of his father's alcoholism and his slow, agonising death. He could not remember a time in his life like this. It was as if Scotland had seeped some magic into his soul, a magic he saw all around him, in the land and the sky and in the vibrant green of Francesca's eyes.

'Uncle Paddy! Uncle Paddy!' Sophie ran across to him and held a dripping bucket out for him to see what she had. The icy water dripped on his bare arms.

'Look, Uncle Paddy! I've got a whole load of things to take back and put in the bath.'

'Gosh, lucky you, Soph!' He glanced at Francesca and they both laughed.

Running back to the water, Sophie edged down the slope to where she had been standing, holding the bucket high and squatting to see what else she could find. Francesca moved away and sat down on the grassy bank.

'You look tired,' he called and she turned towards him, putting her hand up to shield the glare.

'Eeeeeek! I've seen a fishie!' Sophie shrieked delightedly. 'Oh, Chesca! Look!' Sophie had edged nearer the river's edge and was peering down into the water, one arm out-stretched with her bucket, the other pointing at what she had seen. Francesca looked back momentarily. 'I wonder if I can . . .'

She disappeared.

'Oh my God! Sophie?' Francesca jumped up and ran down the slope. Sophie was screaming, her arms and legs flailing, her head only just above the freezing water. The river's current swept swiftly downstream, pulling the small child with it.

'Oh God! Sophie! KEEP YOUR HEAD UP!' Francesca shouted. 'DON'T PANIC!' Seconds later, she dived in.

The water was even more icy than she had expected.

She gasped and the breath caught in the back of her throat. The pull was strong and her body was dragged several yards before she recovered enough to resist, then she started to swim.

'SOPHIE! SWIM!' she shouted. She was closer now, within reach, and she could see Sophie's face, deathly white with panic. 'SWIM!' She put her hand out and felt for Sophie's leg. 'Come on now, Sophie, try and come towards me,' she encouraged. 'Come on.' But she had no idea if Sophie could hear her – she was splashing and fighting wildly to stay above water, blind with fear.

In the background, Francesca was conscious of Patrick's voice. He seemed to be shouting something but she had no idea what. She was swimming so hard against the current and reaching with all her might for the child that she could focus on nothing else. Finally, using the last of her strength, she pushed herself forward and managed to reach Sophie.

'Sophie! It's me, don't panic! Come on, relax towards me.' She pulled her close, held her chin up out of the water and started to swim for the bank. 'It's all right,' she murmured over and over. 'It's all right now.'

Patrick was at the water's edge when she reached the bank. He bent down and grabbed her arm, heaving her and Sophie out of the water in one go. He hugged them both to him for a moment and then Sophie began to cry, great howling sobs that racked her tiny frame.

'Ssssh, come on Soph, it's all right,' he whispered. 'You're safe now. Come on, don't cry.' She held out her arms for him and he took her from Francesca, holding her head into his chest and smoothing her wet hair with his hand.

'Here!' He bent, still holding Sophie, and lifted a blanket from the ground, placing it round Francesca's shoulders. She was shaking.

'I'll dry Sophie off.' He moved across to the rug and sat

down, cradling Sophie in his arms. Glancing up at Francesca he asked softly: 'Are you OK?' She nodded. 'Thank God,' he murmured, and turning away from him, Francesca dropped her head down and silently started to cry.

When Sophie was quiet, he managed to get her out of her wet things and into a dry tee shirt and knickers. He wrapped a rug round her, making her feel important, and looked towards Francesca. She was sitting on the river-bank, turned away from him and shivering, despite the sun's warmth. He stood and crossed to her.

'You're frozen.' He touched her cheek with his fingertip and the skin was damp and cold. 'Come on, you need to get out of those wet clothes. I've got a spare pair of swimming shorts in my bag.' He went to the rucksack and took out his shorts, then he pulled his tee shirt over his head and handed them both to her. 'Change quickly now, before you get chilled.'

She held the clothes and avoided his gaze. She did not want him to see her tear-stained face. 'Thank you,' she mumbled and stood, dropping the blanket down onto the ground.

And as she did so, Patrick caught the grace and beauty of her whole body, perfectly visible through the transparent wet cotton of her clothes. He could see the full, round curve of her breasts through the fabric of her bra, the dark circle of her nipples and the taut line of her stomach down to her hips. He swallowed hard and turned away. His excitement was so intense and so sudden that it took him by surprise. He walked over to the rug and sat down, acutely aware of Francesca changing behind him.

'Uncle Paddy, is Chesca all right?' Sophie was sleepy, after the shock. He stroked her forehead.

'Yes, of course she is.' Absentmindedly, he looked behind

him as he spoke and it was then that he saw the marks. Francesca had lifted her teeshirt over her head and she had her back to him, a back covered with the remains of some vicious bruising and a gash that ran down from her shoulder. She had been beaten, violently, and Patrick turned away in disgust.

Why? He sat stunned for several minutes, unable to think clearly. Why would anyone . . .? The idea of violence to her filled him with an overpowering nausea and the shock of it left him cold. He struggled with his feelings, not sure what he felt, or why, and then suddenly he realised that he was angry, angry that he knew nothing about her, angry that she could be hurt. He was angry at his own helplessness and he wanted to protect her.

When she had finished dressing, Francesca came back to the rugs and sat down. Milly and Sophie had fallen asleep, exhausted after the excitement. Francesca curled her knees up and hugged them, still cold, and then rested her head on them, looking at Patrick. He was picking at the grass and she could watch his face without him knowing. She had done this often the past few days, going over every tiny detail: the colour of his eyes, the line of his jaw, each fine wrinkle on his skin. She had memorised his face and she could bring it to mind any time, in perfect and exact formation. Now she saw that his face was sombre.

'What is the matter?' she asked.

'Nothing, I'm fine.' He didn't look up at her and she looked away. It was one of the things he loved about her, she never kept on, she would accept his answer and leave it at that. Simple, and undemanding.

'Francesca?'

She turned back.

He had to ask her, he couldn't leave it, it was important. 'What are the marks on your back from? What happened to

you before you came to England?' But as soon as he said it he knew he should not have. Her face altered, no, not really her face, he thought later, but her eyes. The colour in them died somehow and he saw the pain. Raw and open, like a wound, and then the veil came down, a blank, empty veil smothering the green, and finally he saw nothing, nothing but his own reflection. She said not a word.

'Francesca?' He reached out to her but she flinched. 'Please, tell me, what is it?'

But she felt betrayed. A part of her that she had to keep private had been trespassed. It was her secret and she would never let it out. Never.

'Francesca?'

She ignored him.

'For Christ's sake, Francesca! Answer me!'

'No!' She stood. 'Leave me alone!'

He stared at her back and thought: this is ludicrous, why am I so upset? What is happening? I am a grown man acting like a child. Then he knew he would have to get away from her, sort himself out. He suddenly just wanted to be away from her to escape the feelings she had evoked in him. He said: 'Look, Francesca, I'm sorry.' He didn't know what else to say, but she shrugged and kept her back to him.

'I think I should get away for a few days,' he continued, more to himself than to her. 'I need some time alone, a bit of space.' I'll go to Edinburgh, he concluded in his mind.

She turned back. 'Yes,' she said quietly. 'If that is what you want.' But her mind was in turmoil; the thought of him leaving was like a physical blow.

'Yeah, I'll leave tonight.' He reached out and touched Sophie on the shoulder to wake her and then Milly. 'Come on girls,' he said gently. 'It's time to head back.' He looked up at Francesca but she had already started to collect the things together. He sighed wearily, feeling foolish and con-

fused. How had all this come out of one beautiful, sunny afternoon? He had no idea: it was something that he was unable to work out. Patrick Devlin, paediatric consultant, was an expert on all kinds of emotion and pain, but sadly, not his own. He had never been in love before.

'Are you ready, Francesca?' He could not look at her, although he longed to.

'Yes.'

The spot by the river looked less idyllic now and he wondered why they had stopped there. 'Come on then, girls,' he said, picking up the bundle of things to carry back. 'The picnic is over.'

But as he said it, he wished he hadn't. The words seemed to mean so much more than just a plain statement of fact.

Fourteen

IT WAS THURSDAY AND PATRICK had been gone for two days. He had telephoned from Edinburgh and Francesca had heard the call, but Lady Margaret passed on no message. Not that she expected one, but she did wonder about him, and she thought about him, involuntarily, whenever her mind was free to wander.

She missed him, and that was natural, she told herself — he had been her constant companion for the past ten days. But she knew her heart was heavier and the time seemed longer, more wearing. She hardly noticed the sun and the pale blue sky; she heard the chant of the breeze through the leafy branches of the trees but it was no longer magical, unique; it was merely a noise.

And the girls felt it too. Sensitive to moods, they had blossomed in the warmth of Patrick's affection for Francesca, unaware that they were part of something special. Now he had gone, they were fractious and argumentative and Francesca was less patient. The sparkle had gone from their holiday, and they missed the enchantment of love.

Francesca had left the girls to play in the long, lawned garden of the house, while she wandered through to the kitchen to arrange some food for their lunch with Mrs Mackenzie. The day was warm and the three of them had been out all morning, at the far end of the garden, where the cultivated met the wild, looking for toadstools, and fairies underneath.

Walking into the hot, bread-scented kitchen, she saw Lady Margaret seated at the table with Mrs Mackenzie. Surrounded by a pile of glossy-looking cookery books, she was busily writing a list. Francesca was surprised: this was the first time she had seen Lady Margaret at home during the day.

'Ah, Francesca!' Lady Margaret looked up and smiled. Lord Henry was due up at Lairbeck that evening and she needed to put things onto a more familiar footing with her nanny. It had to look as if she had spent much of her time at home and Francesca was a key element in achieving that. 'You look well,' she said. 'I do believe the Scottish air suits you.' Again she smiled, while Mrs Mackenzie sat beside her completely straight-faced.

'Come on in. I'm compiling a menu for Saturday night, with Mrs Mackenzie's help.'

Francesca nodded and crossed to the table. As she pulled out a chair and sat down, Mrs Mackenzie gave her a look which was the closest she ever got to a smile.

'Them bairns'll want fud then, hinny?'

'Yes please, Mrs Mackenzie.' Francesca only understood half the sentence but it was enough. Patrick had painstakingly taught her some of the dialect and, recognising one or two words, she could make out the gist of what was being said.

'The girls can wait five minutes, Mrs Mackenzie,' Lady Margaret said shortly. 'We must organise this menu so that I can order the food at the shop.'

'Yes, ma'am.'

Francesca listened to the conversation for a few minutes and felt embarrassed, just watching and listening. She was ignored and felt intrusive.

'I think I will come back in a few minutes,' she said quietly and stood to leave.

Lady Margaret looked up a second time. 'Oh no, dear!' she said quickly. 'Don't leave yet!' She could sense Francesca's embarrassment in her presence and knew it had to be relieved. Henry would notice straight away: he was very perceptive.

Francesca hesitated. She was uncomfortable and she wanted to be outside with the children.

'You might find it interesting,' Lady Margaret continued. 'And you'll know what to expect. You will be one of the guests, after all.' Damn! She hadn't planned to invite the girl, in desperation it just slipped out. Oh, well, she thought, it should make Francesca warm to her and it would certainly show Henry how considerate she was.

But a slow and painful blush spread over Francesca's face, from her neck to the roots of her hair. She was silent for a few moments and then, her voice wavering with emotion, she said: 'Oh no, Lady Margaret, I couldn't possibly!'

Lady Margaret sighed irritably. She was losing patience with trying to be nice. She couldn't believe the girl would have the nerve to refuse. 'Nonsense!' she said brusquely. 'Of course you can. Don't fuss, dear, everyone will love you.'

She couldn't care less, frankly, if they did or didn't, as long as her presence reflected well on Lady Margaret. She went to open another recipe book and noticed Francesca's agonised face.

'What is the matter?' she asked none too kindly.

'I . . .' Francesca found it difficult to speak. 'I, er . . . really don't think I can come . . . I, er . . .'

'Come on, spit it out!'

'Well, I don't have anything to wear, you see, not to a party.' She looked down at her hands.

Lady Margaret felt momentarily ashamed of herself. 'Oh dear, I am sorry, I never thought.' She tapped her fingertips lightly on the open pages of the book, then she suddenly

had an idea. 'I tell you what!' she said, warming to her flash of inspiration. 'There are a few old things of mine up in one of the cupboards upstairs. You could try a couple of dresses and we could get the lady in the village to take one in.' She smiled triumphantly. 'How does that sound?'

'I . . . er . . . it is very kind of you.'

'Nonsense, it's the least I can do.' That much was true. Delighted with her generosity, she knew that once Henry saw how much trouble she had gone to he would automatically assume the best. The reward far surpassed the effort.

'While we're at it,' she continued, quite taken with her own kindness, 'I could make an appointment with the hairdresser for you.'

'Oh no, I—'

'Don't be silly! It'll be fun.'

Francesca blushed again and put her hand up to her hair. She had hardly touched or looked at it since the day in the convent when they had cropped it short. She had watched her beautiful, long, dark hair fall to the floor in great clumps and thought, I must not care, it is vain to care. But she had kept a strand and held it in the dark solitude of her cell, weeping for the loss of it.

'You'd look nice if they restyled your hair,' Lady Margaret said, implying quite obviously that she didn't already.

'Yes, I—'

'Good! That's settled then. Once I've done the menu with Mrs Mackenzie, I'll go up and sort through some dresses, then call the hairdresser.' She made a note of it on her list. 'All right, Francesca?'

'Oh yes, thank you.'

'Good. You needn't stay if you don't want to.' Now she had the girl's confidence no further effort need be made. 'I'm sure Milly and Sophie will need pacifying if their lunch is to be late.'

'Yes.'

'Quite.'

There was a momentary, uncomfortable silence as Francesca struggled to find the right words to convey her thanks, until Lady Margaret put her out of her misery. 'I won't keep you then.'

'No.' Embarrassed, Francesca hurried out of the kitchen.

Patrick drove the Range Rover along the A9 towards Strathspey with only half his attention on the road. The drive from Edinburgh had taken the whole afternoon and he was tired. His mind had become clouded the closer he got to Lairbeck, and his concentration had dwindled. All he could think about was Francesca.

The past four days away from her had been dull and motionless, as if he only half existed. He kept apologising to his friends for his lack of form. He had desperately wanted to get away from her and yet as soon as he had left, he could not wait to get back. But he was no clearer in his mind about her.

He told himself time and time again that he was tired and lonely and that Lairbeck was a sanctuary for him. All his feelings for Francesca were connected to this. He had felt better over the ten days he had shared with her than he had done for years but he convinced himself that it was the complete rest and the tranquillity of Scotland that had done it.

And yet, as he approached the road to Lairbeck, she filled his mind; his whole body seemed more alive at the thought of her. Of course I am going to think about her, he argued reasonably to calm his feelings, I've spent more time with her than I have with anybody in the past few years. Of course I will be pleased to see her. But somewhere locked away in his heart was the feeling it was more than that,

much, much more, only he was much too afraid to admit it. She was young, a girl from out of nowhere, and he knew that the opposition to how he felt would almost be greater than the feeling itself.

He tried to put her out of his mind as he drove on and to think about the dinner that Margaret had arranged. But, as he watched the sky over the hills with the light slowly seeping out of it, he felt a strange intensity of emotion and a curious elation at the glory of the sun sinking down behind the wild and craggy backdrop. He felt all the colour and wild euphoria of love; he just didn't know it.

Finally, Patrick pulled up in front of Lairbeck House. He switched off the engine and sat for a few moments, leaning back in the seat and stretching his arms above his head. He could feel the impact of the drive in his legs and his spine but his tiredness had suddenly disappeared. He was excited, relieved, happy and filled with an unusual boyish delight at being back. He unclipped his seat belt and looked up at the ugly, grey granite building just as the door burst open and Milly came running out, fast followed by Sophie, both shouting and waving in a race across to the car.

'Whoa!' He swung open the door and they both clambered up to hug him. 'Watch it, girls!' He laughed. 'You'll suffocate me.'

'Uncle Paddy, guess what? Guess what?'

'You said I could tell him, Milly!' Sophie pulled at Milly's sleeve. 'You promised!'

'Hey! Let me out of here!' The girls had started to struggle, both trying to get close to him. He swung his legs out and climbed out of the car. 'Tell me what?'

He reached across for his bag from the passenger seat.

'Go on then, Sophie. If you *must*!' Milly pulled a face and tucked her hands on her hips.

'Uncle Paddy, Francesca is at the hairdresser's,' Sophie blurted out. 'Mummy took her there and she has a lovely white dress that she showed us and . . . OUCH! . . . That hurt!'

Milly withdrew her fingers and saw the nasty red mark she had left on Sophie's arm. 'That was my bit,' she said. 'I was supposed to say that!'

Patrick dropped his bag down and took Sophie's arm, kissing the sore spot. 'Don't pinch, Milly,' he said. 'It's not nice.' Then he took both girls' hands. 'How about you tell me all the details then, Milly, now I know the storyline?' And together, all three of them walked into the house, Milly exaggerating wildly on the details of their information as they went.

'Patrick! Come on in, old boy!' Lord Henry was at the side table in the study pouring himself a malt when Patrick came into the hall. He left the drinks and came across, taking Patrick's hand and shaking it warmly. 'You look well, quite tanned in fact. Ha! Wouldn't think it was Scotland, eh? You look as if you've been to the old Costa Brava!' He laughed loudly and looked over Patrick's shoulder at his daughters.

'Come in, girls! No mischief out there in the hall, I want you where I can see you.' He went back to the decanter and poured Patrick a glass. 'Margaret's gawn and left me in charge.' He laughed again. 'Means they'll get away with murder.' Sophie had crossed to him and he put an arm around her. 'Doesn't it, Soph? Eh?'

Patrick smiled and took the drink Lord Henry held out for him. 'Thanks, Henry.' He was fond of his brother-in-law, sometimes more so than of his sister.

'Margaret's taken the Italian girl, what's her name?'

'Francesca.' Just saying her name felt good.

'Yes, that's it, Francesca. Well, Margaret's taken her down

to the hairdresser's. Seems they've become quite friendly over the past ten days or so. Bit of a softie at heart, your sister.'

'Hmmm.'

'Well, she seems to have taken the girl under her wing anyway. She's coming to the dinner tonight.'

'Oh really?' This was a surprise. Patrick knew it was very unusual for his sister to act entirely out of charity.

'Oh yes! You know Margaret, once she takes to someone, that's it! I gather the girl's become almost one of the family.'

'Oh, yes, of course.' Patrick wondered just what his sister was up to.

'Hardly surprising, really. It's lonely for Margaret up here with only the girls for company. Seems to have done her the world of good having someone young about the place. She hasn't been bored at all this time round.'

Patrick nodded and sipped his whisky silently. So that was what she was up to – Francesca was the perfect alibi. He dared not say another word, he was too angry to keep it to himself. Sometimes, he thought coldly, just sometimes, Lady Margaret Smith-Colyne, his darling sister, was just a little too clever for her own good.

Francesca stood in her room and listened to the sound of Patrick's footsteps on the stairs as he went down. She was dressed and ready but her nerve failed her and she was unable to call out to him as he passed her door.

Turning back to the window, she looked down at the light that shone out over the lawn from the windows of the drawing room and dining room. She could see shadows pass across it as people moved in and out and she wished she could watch it all from there, behind the glass, safe and alone.

She started as someone knocked on her door.

Hurrying across the room, she glanced in the mirror above the washbasin and stopped for a moment as she caught her reflection: it was the first time she had looked at herself since getting ready. Her hair had been cut properly and styled to suit her. It was still short but the rough, blunt shape of it had gone and it shone, dark and soft around her face.

Lady Margaret had insisted on make-up, just a little, to take away the plainness of the dress, she said. But she had no idea that when Francesca put it on, the cream silk dress would fall perfectly to the curves of her body, its long line emphasising her lithe, slim form and the pale, creamy white making her lightly tanned, olive skin look translucent, glowing. She had no idea that the make-up would heighten the extraordinary beauty that was naturally there and turn Francesca from the scrawny child she always saw her as into the woman who appeared that night. That shock was yet to come.

The knock came again and startled Francesca. She put her hand up to her hair, to reassure herself it was real, and then continued to the door. Shyly she pulled it open and there she saw Patrick, standing smiling in the passage, waiting to take her downstairs to the party.

But his smile froze as she pulled the door wide and he took in the whole of the image before him. He felt his heart stop and all the blood in his veins stand still for the briefest snatch of a second. And then he realised, with the full force of someone who has never, ever felt anything like it before, that he loved this girl, and that he loved her with an all-consuming passion, a passion that was in his mind, his heart and deep, deep down in his soul.

They stood for several moments and then he moved forward and put his hands on her shoulders. He bent his head and kissed her. It was easy and natural and she tasted sweet,

of toothpaste. Her lips were soft and full and when he stood back and looked at her face he saw that the green in her eyes burned bright and intense, the colour of emeralds.

'We should go down.'

They smiled at each other but stood where they were, neither wanting to break the spell. Lady Margaret called up the stairs: 'Patrick, is Francesca ready?'

He rolled his eyes and turned towards the stairs. 'Yes,' he called back and bent to kiss her again.

'Come on,' he said quietly, and, tucking her hand in his, he walked with her to the stairs and then separated as they went down.

The room was full, and although there were only twenty-six for dinner, to Francesca it seemed like a huge crowd. She stood at the edge of the drawing room and watched Patrick across a sea of faces as Lady Margaret introduced him to a small group of people. She saw him smile, politely and formally, not like the way he smiled at her, and she watched the way his skin crinkled around the eyes, and thought how strong and sensitive his face was. She had missed him, she knew that now, she had missed him more than anything ever before and now, the mere sight of him across the room filled her with joy.

'Francesca, you look lovely!'

She started from her reverie and turned. Lord Henry smiled at her. He was sincere in his compliment, she did indeed look lovely. He had seen her walk in and thought, that girl has something special, and it made him feel young just to look at her. 'I hardly recognised you out of those baggy shorts,' he said. 'And that enormous brown belt you wear to keep them up!'

She smiled.

Yes, he thought again, she definitely has something

special. When she smiles it makes her whole face change. 'What do you think of Scotland then?' He motioned to the waiter to refill their glasses. 'It's rather beautiful, eh?'

'Yes, it is really beautiful, especially when the sun shines.'

'Doesn't happen very often I'm afraid, me dear.' He took a gulp of champagne. 'That's the only problem. But not all bad, though – means the grockles don't come up here in their droves looking for fish and chips and a deck chair on the side of the road. Eh?' He laughed and she did too, knowing that was polite, although she didn't quite understand the joke: she was beginning to get to grips with Mrs Mackenzie's impenetrable dialect, but Lord Henry's vernacular posed a new set of problems.

'Well, I suppose it's time for dinner, the gong'll go any minute.' He pulled the cuff of his evening shirt up to look at his Rolex. 'Thank God. I'm starving!'

'I wonder where I am sitting.' Francesca glanced nervously round the unfamiliar faces. Lord Henry touched her arm.

'That is where being the host really comes into its own, my dear,' he said. 'I have cleverly arranged it so that you are sitting next to me!'

She looked up, surprised.

He winked. 'But ssssh! I did it rather surreptitiously, moving name cards around and stuff. You won't tell anyone, will you?'

She took the arm he offered. 'No, I won't tell anyone,' she answered, and smiling, caught Patrick's eye across the room. She was so very good at keeping secrets.

'Well! My darling Patrick, you never cease to surprise me!' Lady Margaret came back into the drawing room from the hall in her stockinged feet, carrying her Bruno Magli gold strappy shoes in one hand and holding the hem of her dress

up with the other. 'Thank God those beastly people have gone! Now I can find out exactly what you said to Charles.'

She slumped down on the sofa in front of the fire and wriggled her toes in the warmth. There were just the two of them left and she was dying to know what he'd said to the eminent cabinet minister. She had been out of earshot and had been bursting with curiosity ever since.

'So?' She looked pointedly at her brother. She had a right to know.

'So what, Maggie?' Patrick drained his glass and placed it on the floor by his feet. 'I'm tired, I think I'll go up.'

'Oh no you don't!' She reached a foot across to him and ran her toe up his lower leg. 'Come on, tell me what you said. From what I could gather, he was bloody impressed! I never knew you had such strong views on the NHS!'

Patrick held her foot. 'It's hard not to when you work for the organisation, Maggie.' He was tired, it was true, but he was also bored with politics – they had dominated the evening. And, from the moment she had left, all he could think about was Francesca. He just wanted to be alone, to let his mind run free with images and dreams of her.

'Oh, you are a bore, little brother!' Lady Margaret stood up. Patrick had already done exactly as she'd wanted tonight; she did not want to push him too far. 'I know you in this mood, I won't be able to get a thing out of you! I suppose it'll have to wait until the morning then.' She sighed theatrically and bent to kiss the top of his head.

'If you weren't so good-looking, Paddy, I could get really quite pissed off.' She smiled and, leaving her shoes where they were, walked noiselessly across the room and out into the hall. He heard her double-check the big front door was locked and then climb the stairs to bed.

For a long time he sat and stared at the fire. He could hear the slow tick of the clock on the mantelpiece but was

unaware of time. He watched the flames, smoked a cigarette and felt as if time was suspended and that he was waiting, waiting for the world to start turning again.

And when finally he heard a noise, he knew it was her. He stood and quietly made his way to the kitchen, aware that events had moved beyond his control, that it was all just meant to be. 'Francesca?'

She stood by the window looking out at the lightening sky and half turned when he whispered her name. She knew. Moving across to her, he turned her to him and gently stroked her cheek with his fingertip. Her face was wet and he bent to kiss away the salty tears. He could feel the frantic beat of her heart and thought that he had never been so close to anyone. Carefully, he picked her up and carried her, her head against his chest, out of the kitchen and back to the drawing room. 'Here.' He placed her on her feet in front of the fire. She had begun to shake.

'Francesca, don't.' He wrapped his arms around her to stop the shivering. 'Please, don't.' He held her for some time and then finally drew back, tilting her face up so as to see her eyes.

'My darling Francesca,' he murmured. He touched her lips with his own, lightly, gently and felt her sigh. Then he saw her eyes, for one singular moment, burning with a bright, green fire and he was lost. His passion consumed him and his love overwhelmed him.

Hungrily he sought her lips again, this time to taste her, opening her mouth with his tongue, wanting to be inside her, part of her. And she met him, her own passion surprising her, filling her, overtaking her. He pulled her to the floor.

Moving over her, Patrick ran his mouth down her neck to her shoulder and kissed the warm, scented skin. She was naked underneath her robe and he eased it open, look-

ıng down at her body before he bent his head to caress her. He felt the silk of her thighs, the small swell of her belly and then her breasts, hearing her moan softly as his fingers traced the curve of them to her nipple.

He pulled back and knelt up, watching her face as she unfastened his shirt and moved her hands to his groin. She touched him and he groaned out loud. He wanted her, wanted to be part of her body – so much that he could wait no longer.

Moments later, they were skin to skin and he could feel the heat of her. Rolling over, he lifted her up onto him, holding her hips with his hands and sensing her whole body shudder as she cried out. He put his hands up to her face, traced the outline of it and closed his eyes. It was the most perfect moment and he wanted to seal it in his memory forever.

When it was over, he held her. She leaned her head down onto his chest and he stroked her back, tracing the outline of her spine with his fingers. He could feel her breath on his neck and her heartbeat next to his own.

'Are you all right?' he whispered.

'Yes.'

He could hardly hear her and he wondered if it was all real. 'I love you,' he said. He stroked her hair. 'I have never felt like this before.' And he meant it. 'I—'

But she put her finger up to his lips to quieten him. It was too much, she did not understand half of it and she did not want to try. Not now, not yet. Just the relief of being able to feel was sufficient. He had banished the dark fear inside her and that was all she needed. She had never been loved before and she had no reason to think there should be anything more. It was everything, for now at least.

'You're cold,' he said after a while; she was trembling. He

moved very slightly and reached for his shirt to wrap around her. 'That better?'

She nodded and uncurled her body from him, lying in his arms, the shirt around her. The fire was warm and she could smell his skin, his hair; it was a strong masculine smell and it surrounded her, filled her senses, excited her. She was safe with him, warm and secure, and she knew, looking down at the flush of love over her body, that she was finally complete.

CHAPTER
Fifteen

THE NEXT WEEK PASSED IN A blur for Francesca and Patrick. And later, when he thought back on it, all he could remember was a feeling of completeness, a sense of all-consuming happiness. Yet he knew he had to go back to London.

He had booked three weeks off from the hospital but had never thought he would stay in Scotland that long. The days with Francesca just seemed to slip away. The realisation and consummation of their love made time seem unreal, as if it had no boundaries or had ceased to exist. Even the weather had an eerie calmness: the days were settled and warm, the sun high in the sky. Complete happiness made them blind, and when they finally looked up, there were only three days left.

From the night of the party they had spent every moment together. It was no different to before, except that now they had a freedom with each other that came from the security of being loved. They talked and laughed, ran with the children in the glorious sunshine and shared the secrets of their hearts and minds. All except one.

Behind the warmth and joy of loving, Francesca carried her dark and frightening past locked away in her soul, and her pain shut deep down in her heart. That, she was unable to tell him. He loved her and had opened her up in a way she would never have believed possible but she could not unburden herself to him. She just could not do it. She was so afraid of it, so ashamed of it that she could not see how anyone could accept it, even someone who loved her. So it

stayed in her heart and it lurked, like an evil shadow, one pace back from the radiance of their love.

She tried to let love fill her days and light up her soul, and hoped silently that one day it would banish the darkness. She glowed with a rare feeling of happiness and of being loved and for now, nothing else mattered.

And in a way she was right. The wide, open lands gave Francesca and Patrick a heady liberty and Lady Smith-Colyne was far too preoccupied with her husband to notice anything around her. She left her brother to his own devices, as she had done all through his stay. It was impossible for her to imagine that he could fall in love – she had never seen Francesca as anything other than 'the help' and Lady Margaret was arrogant and foolish enough to think that she and her brother Patrick were in a station far above the realms of ordinary people. She had forgotten her own past and she had forgotten that love crosses all boundaries.

It was a warm, cloudy afternoon, the first without sunshine for some time. The cloud was heavy; it seemed to press down, locking in the warmth and moisture, making the atmosphere close and almost oppressive. The lowland hills of Cromdale had changed in the greyer light, their colours becoming muted, duller, more brown and earthy. The higher climbs were darker in the distance, more forbidding. They overshadowed everything.

Patrick and Francesca walked together across the foothills of the mountains. The girls had run on ahead and they walked close, not touching but within inches of each other. Every now and then as they talked, he would touch her arm or tap her jokingly, pull her to him for a couple of seconds. Any kind of contact was good, just the proximity of her made him feel whole. He couldn't bear the thought of leaving her.

And yet he couldn't tell her this. He had worked it all out in his mind, that their separation would be only for a few weeks and after that he would send for her to come and live with him in London. But he found it almost impossible to say.

The days and nights drifted by and the intensity of their love seemed to him unreal, something way beyond the mundaneness of plans and decisions. He was naive enough to think that nothing could go wrong and for the moment he was so bewitched by being in love that he was unable to break the spell. He said nothing to Francesca, except that he loved her, and he thought that this was enough.

That same night, the weather broke. The wind howled across the land, bringing with it a torrent of rain that beat against the windows and flooded the dry, hard ground. The warmth vanished and everything became cold and damp, dark and dismal, the grey granite chilled and clammy to the touch.

Patrick made a huge fire in the drawing room. He and Francesca were alone and once the girls had gone to bed, he laid a pile of cushions in front of it on a bed of thick tartan blankets and drew the curtains, closing out the cold.

The change in the weather had unnerved him. It signified the end of his time in Scotland, but it seemed more than that: its sudden harshness and violence was eerie, like a strange, foreboding sign.

He turned away from the window and listened to the whip of the wind in the trees outside, a painful, horrible sound. It sounded as if the branches were screaming.

'Patrick, are you all right?'

He started. Francesca walked into the room and stood at the edge. It was a habit she had – she always waited to be

sure before she came fully into a room. He looked across at her and thought how lovely she was.

'Yes, I'm fine,' he answered and then crossed to her. There was something about her reticence that made him want to take her in his arms, to hold her. He hugged her close to him and stroked the length of her back.

'You're cold,' he whispered, moving his face back so that he could see her eyes. 'But you're happy.' The green was dark and velvety and the lashes were black against the colour. 'Here.' He bent to kiss her face and warm her skin with his breath. 'Don't be cold, come to me.'

She smiled and he knew that she felt as he did, he could feel it. He had to talk to her, to tell her, tonight. He had to warn her that it would be hard, that there would be much opposition and that they would need to be strong, to stand together, to face it together. He wanted to say that sometimes it scared him, that he wasn't sure he had the strength to do it even, but he knew he couldn't. She would never understand the hold Margaret had over him and he wasn't even sure if he understood it himself.

'Francesca, I've got something to tell you. We need to talk . . .' She stopped his words with her mouth. He broke free. 'Please, Francesca, I have to say . . .'

But again she silenced him. Placing a finger on his lips, she stood back a pace and looked up at his face. She had never known anything like this before: it was as if the energy of life flowed between them, as if they were the world. There was nothing else that existed except this, this moment of pure love. Slowly she unbuttoned her shirt and he watched, a sudden and powerful excitement rising in him.

She slipped the shirt off her shoulders and unfastened her trousers, letting them drop to the floor and stepping away from them. She wore nothing underneath. Her body

was so beautiful, long and lithe, her breasts full and high. He reached a hand out and touched the tawny skin.

'Oh, Francesca, you are so . . .' But he didn't finish. She stepped towards him and kissed his mouth, her body an inch away from him. She slipped her hands down to him and her fingers found his response. Moments later, he pulled her hard towards him and found her tongue with his own. His need of her was deeper and more intense than he had ever felt and it burned inside him. He held her face and kissed her as all the time she pressed her hips into him, moving against him, her body on fire.

Finally, he freed himself and picked her up, drawing her legs up and around his body, holding her underneath. She clasped her hands around his neck, tilting her head back and pushing her hips forward. Slowly, as he stood and held her, they began to move together, their bodies locked and their passionate, united image reflected in the soft light of the mirror above the fireplace.

Later, as they lay together, naked in the warmth of the fire, Patrick knew that tonight had been different from other nights: there had been an abandoned and fierce passion in Francesca, and in himself. There was an emotion there that had shocked him in its power and strength, an emotion that had almost frightened him. He loved her, more than anything he had ever loved before, and the very idea of that filled him with awe and trepidation.

But for Francesca, loving Patrick was simple and complete. Her experience had only ever been of fear and pain and now the joy of his love, and her happiness in it, filled her. It was so new and so incredible that she had no thought to question it.

Turning towards her, Patrick touched the scar on her shoulder, lightly, with his fingertip. He had always wanted

to know, right from the beginning. He bent his head and kissed it. 'What is it?' he asked gently. He wanted all of her, even the secrets of her heart. 'Whatever it is, you can tell me, I promise.' He pulled back to look at her. 'Explain to me,' he whispered. 'Please.'

Francesca met his eyes: they were clear and loving. She could no longer hide it from him. He could see into her soul; he possessed her completely. She had to tell him the truth – there could be nothing but the truth between them, not now, not after tonight. She would trust him with her life; indeed, that was what she was doing. 'It's a scar from my husband,' she said quietly. 'He beat me.' She felt Patrick's body tense for a moment and she held her breath. He was still, silent for some time and then he moved away from her and rolled onto his side. He sat up and looked down at her. She could see the shock in his eyes.

'I think you had better tell me,' he said. 'Everything.' He had never imagined she was married, never dreamed, never thought . . . He looked away; he hardly knew her at all. Glancing back, he saw that she too had sat up and she wrapped the rug round her shoulders, her long bare legs tucked up under her. He could see the warm orange light of the fire on her skin, it made it glow. Her face was in shadow, sculpted by the light and dark. 'Francesca.' He reached out to touch the beautiful tawny skin and she looked at him. Nothing had changed, whatever her past, nothing could change the way he felt. He would have to try to understand, that was what loving someone was all about, wasn't it? A momentary spark of doubt ignited in his mind and then extinguished itself. He moved over to her and eased her closer. 'I will understand,' he put his arms around her, 'if you tell me the truth.'

She closed her eyes, warm and secure in his embrace. Of course he would understand. 'All right,' she whispered.

And slowly, the words painful to speak, she told him the story of her bloody and violent past.

It was late when finally she was quiet, and the fire had begun to die in the grate. Patrick was tired. He felt the burden of what she had told him heavy in his heart and he needed to sleep, to put it out of his head, to think about it tomorrow. 'Let's go up,' he said quietly. He did not want to leave her; he wanted to be wrapped in the sheets with her, to comfort her and for her to comfort him.

She moved away from him. 'You go up,' she answered wearily. 'I'll stay and tidy.' She was always conscious of Lady Margaret, of not being caught. She would not sleep with him.

'No, not tonight, leave it. Come up with me.' He leaned forward and kissed the hollow of her neck. 'Please Francesca, come to bed with me, I want to wake up with you.' He had wanted to say 'I can't bear to be alone, not if I have to face what you have just told me,' but he didn't. He just said 'Please' once again and she rolled towards him, unable to refuse him anything. He ran his hand the length of her body and caressed her back. 'Come on then,' he murmured. His excitement rose suddenly and he knelt up and pulled her up with him. 'To bed.' He wrapped a rug round her and picked her up, kissing her as he did so. 'To bed,' he whispered once more and she shivered, despite the sudden rush of heat through her body.

It was seven am and Lady Margaret was in a deep, dreamless sleep. It had been a late night – she and Lord Henry had been out until one – and she had fallen exhausted into bed. The interruption in her slumber took some time to penetrate and when finally she heard the shrill ring of the telephone by the side of her bed, she woke foggy and

confused, fumbling in the dark for the receiver and swearing loudly when she dropped it.

'Hello!' Her voice was slurred and hoarse with sleep.

'Lady Margaret Smith-Colyne?'

'Yes, speaking.' She didn't recognise the voice.

·'Hello, sorry to wake you so early. This is Charles Hewitt.'

Lady Margaret sat up instantly. 'Charles!' A call from a cabinet minister deserved a little charm, even in the middle of the night. 'How nice! What on earth is the time?' She switched on the bedside lamp and looked down at her watch, blinking at the light. 'My God! It must be something important!' She laughed and then thought to keep her voice down – she did not want to wake Lord Henry in the next room.

'It is quite important. Can I be frank with you, Lady Margaret?'

'Yes, of course. I'm on my own. What's the problem?'

'Not really a problem, at least not from your point of view anyway. You mentioned to me when we last met that your brother, Patrick, was interested in a political career? Is that right?'

'Yes, yes it is!' She felt a shock of excitement in the pit of her stomach.

'Excellent! I'll be brief then, Lady Margaret. One of our better known members has been involved in somewhat of a scandal with young boys. His career is over, of course, and we need to find a strong and sympathetic candidate to replace him. It's a safe seat, naturally, but the story's about to break in the national press and I want someone lined up ready, someone squeaky clean, and someone on the right side of the fence.'

'I see.' She was trying to sound calm but she could hardly think straight. Was he suggesting Patrick?

'Good! With the current lack of confidence in the

government's NHS policies, we thought a medical man would just fit the bill. I've taken the liberty of already mentioning your brother's name to one or two of my colleagues. They're impressed, Lady Margaret, and we'd like to see him in London this afternoon; that's why I'm telephoning so early. I hope that's going to be possible?'

Lady Margaret swallowed. 'Yes, yes of course that's possible. He can fly down this morning.'

'Good!' She heard him talk over his shoulder to someone and the blood thundered in her veins. She could virtually hear the thud of her heart in her chest. 'You say it's a safe seat? And you want Patrick for it?' She wanted to hear him say it, to be quite certain.

'Yes, that's correct. He'll have to stand for selection, of course, but that's pretty much a foregone conclusion, I'm glad to say. The job's there, it's really just picking the right man for it and we want someone young and dynamic, someone with a future. It's a good seat from which to build a career, Lady Margaret, for the right candidate. That is what you were interested in, was it not?'

'Yes, I was.' She could hardly believe she had come this close. She could sense her triumph, smell it.

'Good. I think you and I understand each other quite well, Lady Margaret, don't you?' The implication of this sentence was quite clear. A favour is never given freely. She smiled. 'Actually, Charles, I do.'

'Perhaps we might have lunch the next time you're in London? You must come down to visit your brother?'

'Hmmm.' She stretched her arms over her head and glanced down at the heavy curve of her breasts. Her nipples had hardened. 'Lunch would be delightful,' she said softly. Power turned her on, more so than money these days.

'It's a date then. I'll await your call.'

'Yes, of course.'

'Good. I will tell my colleagues to expect Patrick this afternoon at the House . . . around what time?'

'I should think by four, Charles, allowing for travel delays.'

'By four then. I'm sorry to have woken you, Lady Margaret.'

'Please, don't worry.' She dropped her voice a note. 'I'm glad you did.' And without a goodbye, she replaced the receiver and lay back against the headboard for a few moments to let the flush of excitement spread through her entire body.

Minutes later, she swung her legs over the side of the bed and stood up. She was now wide awake. She would have to go and tell Patrick, get him up, discuss the whole thing. This was an opportunity not to be taken lightly. She would have to work on him, she knew that, but she couldn't foresee any real problem. Not once he knew he was really in with a chance, that it was his for the taking.

She crossed the room and threw her silk wrap on, tying it loosely. Finding her mules, she slipped them on and quietly clicked her bedroom door open, then stepped out into the passage. She did not want to wake Henry – this was between her and Patrick, a family thing. Noiselessly, she walked along to the small flight of stairs that separated her and Henry's rooms from the rest of the house and made her way down to the next floor. She hurried to Patrick's room, silently eased the door open and walked halfway across to his bed. She stopped dead in her tracks.

The curtains were open and the morning light struggled into the room through the heavy blanket of cloud across the sky. It was just enough to see the two figures, their bodies curled together in sleep, their fingers entwined. Francesca was tucked into the curve of Patrick's body and slept like a

child, content and at peace. Patrick held her, even in sleep, as he would something precious.

Lady Margaret's breath caught in the back of her throat and she put her hand up to her mouth. It was not the sight of their nakedness or sex that shocked her but the terrible truth of their love. It was so obvious that it made her feel physically sick and she felt the shattering of a thousand dreams. Her anger broke.

'Patrick! What the bloody heck do you think you are doing?' she shouted. She couldn't stop herself.

Patrick woke in a panic. He heard her voice and then he opened his eyes to see his sister, her face twisted with rage.

'Oh Jesus!' He sat up instantly, covering Francesca with the sheet, trying to shield her. 'What the hell are you doing in here?' He lost his temper. 'Get out, Margaret! Go on, get out!'

But she stood where she was. Her initial anger had turned and she was suddenly calm, in control.

'This is my house, remember, Patrick. If anyone should get out it will be you, not me.'

Francesca had woken and sat up, confused and frightened.

'Don't worry, it's all right,' he murmured.

'No it bloody well isn't all right!' Lady Margaret said icily. 'I suggest you get up, Patrick. NOW. I came in here to speak to you about something important, and I would like to see you downstairs.' Still she stood across the room, glaring at them. 'Did you hear me, Patrick?'

'For Christ's sake, Margaret! Of course I bloody heard you! Who do you think you are?'

'I am your sister and this girl's employer.' Her lower lip curled slightly in a sneer. 'So get up, Paddy. I won't ask you again.' She turned to the door. 'I will see you in the drawing room in five minutes.' And with that, she walked out of the

room, leaving the door open behind her so that they could hear her footsteps along the passage and all the way down the stairs.

Patrick looked down at Francesca. Her face was white with tension and for a moment he hated his sister for that.

'Look, I'd better go.' He bent and kissed her forehead. 'I won't be long, I promise.'

She nodded and watched him as he climbed out of bed and pulled on some clothes.

'This is all I damn well need, a bloody great row with Margaret!' He buttoned his shirt and crossed to the door, muttering more to himself than to Francesca. 'Christ, what a fiasco!' And forgetting even to glance at her again, he left the room and hurried down the stairs, still only half awake and seething with anger.

Lady Margaret stood at the window in the drawing room and looked out at the lawns behind the house. They were sodden, a dull, dark green, under a rolling grey sky. She smoked a cigarette, inhaling deeply, letting the smoke fill her lungs, and then blowing it out again in a thin trail that curled up and over the top of her head.

She turned when Patrick entered the room.

'Come in and sit down, Paddy.' Her tone was icy, the anger tightly controlled.

'I'm not a child, Maggie.'

'Really?'

He came in and stood by the fireplace. 'So, what did you have to say to me that was so important?'

'First things first, Paddy.' She stubbed her cigarette out into the small ashtray she was holding. 'I'd like to know what the hell you think you are doing?'

'I don't think that's any of your business.' His reply was sharp and angry.

'Oh, for God's sake! Grow up!' She came across the room.

'I happen to think that you fucking my staff *is* my business! It's *my* house and that young girl is *my* employee!'

'Not for much longer, she isn't!'

'What the hell is that supposed to mean?'

He sighed, suddenly weary. He didn't have the stomach for this, it was too early and it was too damn personal.

'Look, can't we drop it? I'm sorry I upset you but I really don't want to discuss it. Not now.' He reached for one of her cigarettes and lit it, throwing the match into the fire grate. 'What did you want to talk to me about?'

Lady Margaret looked at her brother's face. It was closed, his expression blank. She wondered if she had pushed him too far. Picking up her cigarettes, she lit another and sat on the edge of the sofa. She couldn't afford to waste time.

'I had a call this morning from Charles Hewitt,' she said. 'He told me that there is a safe seat coming up for re-election and he wants you to stand.' She flicked her ash and looked up at Patrick. 'He'd like you to go down to London today to be interviewed, although apparently it's a pretty sure thing.' She took a long drag and then added: 'I told him you'd be there.'

Patrick stared at her for several moments. She was so arrogant, he thought briefly, poised on the edge of the sofa in her silk, smoking and talking about his life with such assurance.

'I said you'd fly down from Aberdeen this morning,' she finished.

'You did *what*?' His mouth was a thin, tight, angry line. 'Don't you think you should have asked me first if that was convenient?'

'Isn't it?' Her tone was openly sarcastic. 'What else did you have planned?'

'That's none of your business!'

'Oh, grow up, Paddy! I've worked damn hard to make this happen and you think it's about as important as fucking some teenage tart! Spare me, please!'

'How dare you talk about Francesca like that!' He had begun to shout now, too wound up to stop himself. 'And what the hell do you mean, you've "worked damn hard to make this happen"? I thought I told you I didn't want any favours!'

'No favours!' she cried. 'How else do you think you'd get a seat? By magic?'

'So you fixed the whole thing?' He was incredulous.

'More or less. Is that a problem? It's never been one before!'

'Jesus! That's it! I don't have to stay and listen to this!' He strode over to the door.

'Stay right where you are!' She shouted so loud that he stopped dead. Slowly he turned.

'You are going down to London this morning, Patrick! I have said that you will be there and damn it, you will!'

He stared at her open-mouthed. 'Oh no! You can forget it!' he said coldly. 'I told you, I will not be bullied!'

'You are going!' She stood and walked over to the fire-place. 'You know the score, Paddy,' she said icily. 'You always have.' Her voice was hard, matter-of-fact. 'I've never made any secret of my ambitions for you – I've always made it quite clear what's expected of you.' She looked at him. 'You want this political career as much as I do, Paddy. And you owe it to me.'

'I owe it to you?' He could not believe he had heard her right. 'What do I owe?' He came back into the room, feeling confused, disorientated.

'I have paid for everything, Paddy, everything! Your education, your degree, your flat in London while you were at Charing Cross. Everything! And I've always made it quite

clear – all the way through I said I wanted you to go into politics.'

'Yes, but when I was ready. I thought—'

'You thought what? Did you think that I should just do it? For the love of Patrick? That I could wait forever?'

'No! I thought . . .'

She snorted. 'Thought that I would marry a man twenty years my senior in order to finance you and just sit around lovingly, waiting until you were ready to play politics? Or not, as the case may be? That I'd watch you turn down any opportunity on a whim? On a good fuck?' She almost smiled. 'Come on, Patrick!' But her voice was bitter now and he winced at what he could hear in it. He hung his head.

'I cannot be exactly what you want me to be, Margaret,' he said quietly. 'I have to be myself.'

'You can be anything you want to be, Patrick. You are a Devlin and it's up to you to prove that the family is worth something!'

'Oh God! Good old Irish family pride, eh, Maggie?' His sadness was touched with cynicism. It all seemed so ridiculous. 'Does it really mean that much to you?'

'Oh yes,' she murmured. 'It means that much to me.' She suddenly remembered all her father's debts and the only way she had known how to discharge them. She remembered the contempt on the men's faces, nameless faces, when they handed over the money to her for their pleasure. She shuddered and took a breath.

'Of course, you do realise who owns the leasehold on your flat in Holland Park, don't you, Paddy? And the estate in Ireland? Preserved at the great expense of my husband for your children. How much does a consultant in the NHS earn nowadays?'

'Margaret,' he said coldly. 'If I didn't know you better, I'd take that as some kind of threat.'

'It will only be a threat if it has to be, Patrick!' And he saw the hard, cold determination in her eyes. Finally he snapped.

'Oh no!' he roared. 'You have no right to do this to me! I couldn't give a shit about the flat or the estate. And I won't be blackmailed, Margaret!' He headed towards the door. 'I'm getting out of here now! Before I do something I regret! Oh, and find yourself another nanny as well – Francesca is coming with me.'

But Lady Margaret lunged forward and grabbed him by the arm. 'You're going nowhere, Paddy!' She gripped his shirt and her fingers pinched his skin hard. 'You will leave that little tart alone!' I order you to do as I say! If you don't I will ruin her. God damn it! I will make you and her suffer!' He started to move to the door. 'Did you hear me? Stay here! I order you to—'

'*Order* me?' Her words incensed him and he lost control. Blindly, he raised his right hand and pushed his sister back with all his might. He had to break free, to get away from her. He watched motionless as she fell and crashed heavily into the edge of the sofa. She slumped to the floor.

'What the hell? . . . MARGARET!' Lord Henry ran into the room and bent over his wife. He looked up at Patrick. 'Get out of my house! NOW! Get out!'

Patrick stood, terrified by his own actions, and then turned and rushed out into the hall, pulling open the heavy oak door and slamming it hard behind him. Lady Margaret cried out but he was gone.

Still seething, he strode across the fields beside the house and out onto the open land towards the mountains. He could think of nothing – his mind was blank save for the pain and anger and the deep shame at striking his sister.

Lady Margaret lay where she was for several minutes while

Lord Henry went to get her some water. She was not hurt, just shocked and, for the first time in her life, afraid that she was about to fail, to fail in the only thing that had ever really mattered to her.

I have not done all this to let him walk out now, she thought, I will not let go. Pulling herself up, she slumped back on the sofa and waited for Lord Henry to come back. She needed him, she could not do it without him.

Francesca would have to go, she knew that, and she would have to go now, before Patrick came back. If she was out of the way then at least he would be easier to handle. Lady Margaret reached for her third cigarette of the morning and lit it quickly, snapping her lighter shut.

'Margaret! Are you all right, darling?' Lord Henry carried the water across to her and placed it by her side. She nodded weakly.

'It's more shock than anything,' she murmured. 'I've never seen Patrick behave that way before.'

He took her hand and comforted her. 'What on earth was it all about?'

She sucked in her breath and a small sob escaped her.

'Take it easy, darling, don't upset yourself.' He was trying his hardest to comfort her but to his horror she started to cry. The tears came easily and freely – she was well practised. 'She will have to go, Henry,' she sobbed. 'I can't have it going on in front of the children. I just don't know how he could have let it happen.'

Lord Henry patted his wife's hand uncomfortably. He abhorred scenes and the sight of her tears threw him right off balance.

'Who has let what happen? Now, Margaret, take it easy and try to explain to me exactly what has been going on.'

'Patrick has been sleeping with the nanny!' she said. Shock tactics always worked best with Henry.

'Good God!'

'Under our roof!' she continued. 'And in front of the girls!' He shook his head. 'I don't believe it!' he muttered.

'Oh, you should believe it, Henry!' Her tears turned instantly to anger; she knew exactly how to play him. 'I saw them myself this morning. It was disgusting!' She shuddered.

'God damn it, you're right! She'll have to go!' Lord Henry stood. 'I shall go up right now and tell her that she must be out by the end of the week. No excuses! She's out!'

But Lady Margaret restrained him, her hand on his arm. She had other plans. She looked up at him and shook her head. 'She has to go now, Henry. I'm sorry, but I really can't tolerate this kind of thing.'

'Margaret, I know you're upset but I can't turn the poor girl out at seven-thirty in the morning, whatever she's done.' He took her hand and held it in his own. 'Come now, let's be reasonable—'

'*Reasonable!*' She pulled her hand away and willed on a fresh bout of tears. 'Really Henry, if you'd seen them! Just think of the girls!'

Lord Henry felt his strength ebb away with the flow of his wife's tears. 'Margaret, I really don't think—'

'No, Henry! She really must go *now*, she has to!'

He could see her hysteria rising again and he just hadn't the stomach for it.

'All right, Margaret,' he said wearily. 'If you say so.'

'Yes! I do say so!' Then she softened. 'She could catch a train from Aberdeen, Henry. You wouldn't mind driving her there, would you?' She stood and faced him, fingering the edge of his dressing gown. 'Please,' she murmured.

'No, my love, of course not.' He put his arms around her and kissed her cheek. Anything for peace. 'I'll go and speak to her now,' he said.

She looked lovingly at him. 'Why don't you go and dress and I'll speak to her?'

He raised an eyebrow. 'You wouldn't mind?' The idea of dismissals unnerved him – he would much rather his wife did it.

She shook her head. 'I know you hate scenes,' she said. 'Anyway, I feel much better now.' She kissed her finger and held it to his lips. 'You're so sweet to me, Henry. Thank you.'

He shrugged and moved towards the door. 'Tell her I'll be ready in ten minutes,' he said.

She nodded, and smiling briefly, collected up her cigarette and followed her husband out of the room.

Francesca was dressed and seated by the window in her room when she heard the knock at the door. She called out and was not surprised to see Lady Margaret step into the room – she had been expecting some kind of reprisal.

She stood immediately, her hands trembling, and faced her employer.

'Francesca, I am afraid that you will have to leave our employment.' Lady Margaret was brutally short. 'The sooner this happens the better. Lord Henry will be ready to drive you to Aberdeen in ten minutes. I'd like you to be packed and out of here by then.' She stood, steely-mouthed, and looked at Francesca. Little slut, she thought, and it showed in her face.

Francesca saw the look and felt the shock of the words hit the pit of her stomach. She caught her breath.

'Leave . . .?' Her voice was just a whisper.

'Yes, now. I'm sorry, but it is no more than you deserve.'

'But . . . Pa—'

Lady Margaret cut her off mid-sentence. 'You can forget that right now!' she snapped. 'My brother has already left.

He is highly embarrassed and has asked me to deal with the situation.'

Francesca put her hand up to her mouth. 'No . . . I . . .' She didn't believe it, it wasn't true.

'Look! I'm sorry, but there is very little I can say, I'm afraid. It is not the first time this sort of thing has happened, unfortunately. My brother is very irresponsible in his relationships.'

Francesca felt her throat constrict and she had to struggle to breathe. Her hands were trembling so badly that she clenched them by her side. Lady Margaret was lying, she had to be. He loved her, he had told her he did.

'I'm sorry, Francesca, but I shall have to ask you to pack right away. If you don't mind, I'll stand here while you do.' Time was moving on. Lady Margaret had no idea how long Patrick would be gone.

'But please . . . I . . .' It couldn't be true, it couldn't be. Francesca clung helplessly to her hope.

Lady Margaret lost patience. 'You what, dear girl? You surely didn't think that my brother took you seriously, did you? Come now, do let's be reasonable. Patrick has his career to think of. He is moving into politics and he knows as well as I do that he needs the right sort of person beside him. You surely didn't expect . . .' Lady Margaret's eyes were as hard as cut ice. 'My dear, we know absolutely nothing about you! Nothing. You have no background, no money, and no prospects. God knows where you came from . . .' She stared hard. 'Or what violence and ugliness you left behind!'

Francesca's hand went automatically to her shoulder. She felt naked, exposed. She had told him everything, everything!

'Yes, I have seen the bruises,' Lady Margaret said. 'We all have.' Then she turned to the drawer and pulled it open.

'Francesca, please, get on with your packing. Lord Henry does not like to be kept waiting, and there is really very little more to say on the matter. Patrick has been foolish and he has led you on. I'm sorry, but that's the hard fact of it. It's not the first time and I'm sure it won't be the last!' And she stood, her arms folded, and waited for Francesca to begin her packing.

Racked with a terrible humiliation, Francesca moved slowly and silently round the room, collecting her meagre things and placing them in her small brown leather bag. It took only minutes, and as she did it, she was almost blind with the pain. She saw nothing, her mind and body completely numb.

'Good.' Lady Margaret waited for the click of the bag being shut before she opened the door. 'If you're ready now, we'll go.' She held it open for Francesca and turned away as she passed. She could see the tight control of grief on the young girl's face and she did not want to confront it up close. She followed Francesca down the stairs to Lord Henry waiting in the hall and all the time her heart hammered hard in her chest lest Patrick should suddenly walk in.

She stood on the bottom stair and watched her husband take Francesca's pitiful little bag from her and open the front door.

Francesca turned as Lord Henry walked out of the house.

'May I say goodbye to the children?' Her voice was strong but Lady Margaret glimpsed her tears. They angered her.

'No,' she said coldly. 'I'm sorry.'

Francesca turned back, picked up her coat and, head held high, walked outside to the car. Minutes later, she was gone.

It was only fierce pride that had stopped her from

breaking down and begging to be allowed to stay. She sat in the car and gripped her bag on her lap, the pain and shame so intense that she thought she might faint. She looked out at Scotland as they headed up over the Cromdale hills and scattered her sacred and happy memories out over the wet and weeping landscape. She was too shocked to speak. It was over, and so, she felt at this moment, was her life.

Lady Margaret sat down on the stairs and rubbed her hands wearily over her face. She heard the noise of the car engine as it disappeared up the drive, out onto the main road and away from the house. Gradually it faded and there was nothing, nothing but the sound of her heartbeat finally beginning to slow. She looked up.

Half of it was over; half of that morning's terror had gone. She had removed the threat. Now she had to convince Patrick, make him see what could be achieved, make him want what she wanted. She was almost there.

And for as long as she could remember she had wanted it, wanted Patrick to be someone, wanted the power attached to that, the glory. It would make up for the past, she knew that, for the shame of her father and for the things she had had to do for money. It was her vengeance, to be above recrimination, to be powerful enough not to care. And she would have it, she had come this far, she was not going to stop now.

Patrick walked slowly back to the house. He had been gone for several hours. The walk had done him good but he still didn't understand his actions. He was confused, ashamed of himself, but he was angry too, and shocked. He had lost control, something that had never happened before, and the humiliation of that was crippling.

Entering the house, he silently crossed the hall and made

his way to the stairs. He needed to see Francesca; he needed her support.

'Patrick!'

He turned and his sister came out of the drawing room. There was an angry red mark on the side of her face where he had struck her and her eye had swollen. Patrick flinched at the sight of her.

'Margaret, I'm sorry,' he said dismally, 'I should never have struck you.' He could not look at her, he was too ashamed, and he turned round to continue up the stairs.

'Patrick, she's gone, if that's where you're headed.'

He stopped. 'Gone?' Slowly he looked round. 'What do you mean, gone?'

'Francesca left several hours ago with Henry. She's gone back to Motcom Park. From there, I don't know where she'll go.' She put her hand up and painfully touched her wound, reminding him, making him suffer for it.

He stared long and hard at her and then he slumped down and put his head in his hands. 'Oh, Margaret,' he murmured. 'What have you done?'

'I have done what is best for you, Patrick, like I always have.' She walked over and knelt in front of him. 'I love you, Paddy, you know that,' she said quietly.

'No, not like this you don't.' He swallowed back his pain. 'I'll ring John, ask him to keep her there until I arrive.'

'No,' she said. 'You won't ring John.' She put her hand over his. 'You will go down to London to see Charles Hewitt.'

'Maggie . . . please, don't do this to me.' He closed his eyes but all he could see was Margaret's face and the terrible mark of his violence against her. He felt weak and confused.

She stood and wrapped her arms around him, cradling him to her. 'Oh, Paddy, you are such a fool,' she whispered.

'Don't you see? That girl is just a child, a mixed-up, helpless child. You wanted to protect her, to look after her. You have always been the same.'

'No! I . . .'

'You are . . .' She paused. 'So kind and so loving.' She kissed the top of his head. 'She knew that, and so do I. How old is she, Paddy? No more than sixteen? Seventeen? And where does she come from? Can you take the burden of what violence she left behind? Can you?'

He drew back and looked up at her. He remembered the shock of last night, all that Francesca had told him.

'A child,' she said again. 'Please, don't ruin your life for a romantic notion. How long have you known her? What — two weeks, three? It's infatuation, Patrick, can't you see it?'

He shook his head. 'No, it's more than that, Maggie.'

'Is it? You forget, I know you, sometimes better than you know yourself. You are not in love, Patrick, trust me. You were vulnerable, that's all, you needed affection, you always have done. It was a weakness, an unguarded moment. Daddy was weak too — he let his infatuation with drink ruin our lives. You know that, don't you?' And all the time she spoke, her voice soothed him, her hands gently stroked his hair.

'Paddy, have I not always looked after you?' There was a soft Irish lilt to her voice and he was reminded of his childhood. 'Haven't I?'

He nodded.

'Then go to London today. Do it for me, Paddy, will you? Please.'

He felt as if he had no strength left; he was powerless in her hands. She had always been there, all his life, shaping, moulding, making things right for him. Could he stand alone? Did he have the courage? He just didn't know.

'What if I don't?' he asked quietly.

'But you will, Paddy, you will.' She touched her face again, once more reminding him of what she had suffered today and always, for him. 'You'll do it for me, and for yourself.'

He looked across at her. 'Margaret, I don't know, I . . .' He tried to think. What if he did go? Could he have this opportunity and Francesca too? He could ring her from London, tell her to wait for him, explain it all.

'Maggie . . . I . . .' He stopped as she put a finger to his lips.

'Please, Paddy. Go for me today, just this once more, trust me.' Her voice was so soft that he felt the caress of it, the warm, safe caress of it. He was confused, walking a thin line way up above the rocks. He didn't know what love was, he had always been balanced, on the ground. What if he fell? She had moved her finger and gently stroked his cheek, as she used to when he was a boy. He looked up at her face. 'Oh, Maggie,' he murmured. What else could he do? He desperately wanted this chance, he just didn't want to have to make a choice.

A few moments later he answered Margaret. 'All right,' he said, 'I'll go.' And, as he did so, he swallowed back an aching sense of loss, still unsure of what he was doing, and hoped to God that Francesca would understand. He had never had the strength to fight Margaret, and especially not now, not when what she offered him was so enticing.

THE TRAIN AT YORK WAS late. John sat in his car in a limited waiting-time space and kept careful watch on the time. He would go and check developments in five minutes.

Drumming his fingers on the dashboard, he thought constantly about the telephone call from Lady Margaret and tried to puzzle out what on earth had gone wrong. She had been curt, almost to the point of rudeness, on the line, but that was something he was used to. He was pretty sure it was more than that: she had sounded panicked and secretive, as if she was doing something underhand, had something to hide. Not that he had ever trusted her. John knew full well what she got up to, he was just too much of a gentleman ever to mention it, to anyone.

What on earth induced me to take all this on? he thought. I should have stuck to my original plan, I should never have got involved. Irate telephone calls and angry dismissals, now probably pain and embarrassment at having to ask the girl to leave Motcom. Oh dear, he sighed, what a mess!

But just as he thought this, he also looked down at his watch and realised with a jolt that he had been sitting there for over twenty minutes. He climbed hurriedly out of the car and dashed back into the station, jogging along to the platform where her train was due. He hated the idea that she might have come in with no one to meet her.

Francesca was waiting for the train to pull to a halt. She

stood by the doors in the carriage and gripped her small leather bag with both hands. It stopped them from trembling. She had no idea what to expect, but she braced herself for the worst.

She was pale and exhausted, having cried all the way from Aberdeen to Edinburgh. She had locked herself into the small lavatory, sat down with her head in her hands and sobbed, the shame and bitter grief wracking her body. When finally she looked up, her face was red and swollen, she was relieved, but the pain was still there. She had wept nothing away.

Now, as she stood, her mind was blank but a terrible fear was lodged in the pit of her stomach, the fear that she had been punished for what she had done, for Giovanni's soul. If she was castigated now by John, sent away, she would have to face it, but the loneliness suddenly seemed unbearable after the happiness of the past few weeks.

Finally, the train stopped and Francesca stepped down onto the platform, pivoting to close the door behind her and holding the bag with one hand. She felt physically sick with nerves. Turning back, she looked up and saw John.

'Hello, Francesca,' he said quietly. Then he leaned forward and took her bag, placing it on the ground beside him. He saw her face and gently put his arms around her.

'Oh, my dear, what has been happening?' he whispered as he held her. 'Come on now, child, there's no reason to cry.' And in the middle of platform three, amidst the bustle of crowds rushing for trains, he stood and hugged her and felt her pain as a father would have done.

In the car, heading back onto the motorway, Francesca was silent and withdrawn, peering out of the window, mindlessly watching the passing scenes. 'I am sorry,' was all she had said to him. 'I did not understand.'

And John hadn't the heart to question her further. He felt that all the anguish she had carried with her since she arrived in England had suddenly come to the surface and that if he bent her, in any way at all, she would break.

So they drove on in silence and he tried to quiet the questions that rose in his mind. He would have to ask her at some point, he knew that, but now was not the time. Now, he would just have to comfort her; she needed him far too much for him to let her down.

Much later, when they were back at the house, John knew he could no longer put off what needed to be asked. There were decisions to be made and the phone calls from Lady Margaret and Lord Henry worried him. There was too much insistence that she should go for him to be able to ignore it further. He had to act – he hated himself for doing so but there was no other choice.

He went to Francesca's room and called her, then went back to the kitchen to wait for her. She appeared a few minutes later and he asked her to sit with him at the table.

He watched her face for a few moments and then looked down. 'I have had another call from Scotland, Francesca, from Lord Henry.' He stopped. 'He has once again said that you must leave Motcom and . . .' He paused a second time. 'Well, I feel that I have to ask you why. I'm sorry, but I must know what has happened.' He looked up at her. 'Please, try and explain.'

Francesca sat motionless and stared down at her hands. She could still see the faint shadows of the bruising on her wrist and traced the marks with her fingertip. Her past. She was silent, not knowing where to start, wrought by the confusion of it all. Finally, she swallowed hard and stilled her hands. 'I have never known, you see,' she whispered, 'What it was like . . . to be happy.' She stopped and glanced

up at him, the pain in her eyes raw. 'No one ever loved me before,' she said simply. 'That is why I was so foolish. It overwhelmed me, I had no idea that . . .' She stopped again. She had no idea that love could be as painful as hate and violence; worse, because the pain was from the inside. To be loved had been so incredible, so honest and complete that she had never dreamed it could deceive and hurt with lies and shame. 'I have always been alone,' she said and put her hand on her heart. 'Alone here.' And then, in a muddled and distressed way, she began to tell him the truth. Everything, the whole truth. She had nothing left to lose; she could not be hurt any more.

For a long time afterwards, John sat alone in the dark and thought about what she had said. The enormity of her burden was almost too great for him to comprehend, the violence and misery of her life too terrible. He thought about that bastard Devlin leading her on, using her, and the whole thing made him sick. If he ever got hold of the little shit he'd knock the bloody daylights out of him.

He swore silently and stood up from the table to go to bed. He was tired, and he was shocked – it was all too much to take in. He had no idea what to do. He would have to put off any decision until the morning. Crossing to the sink, he rinsed his coffee cup and turned to look for the towel to dry it, but as he did so, he heard the door click open and he twisted round, trying to make out the figure in the dark.

'Francesca!' He was relieved – the noise had unnerved him. He walked towards her and then stopped halfway. She stood by the door in the clothes she had arrived in and held the old, battered bag containing her meagre possessions. She was dressed and ready to leave.

'Francesca, where are you going?' he asked quietly. He

stepped a pace forward and saw her face. It was ashen, her eyes dark and swollen. 'Please,' he said sadly. 'Don't leave without talking to me.' And he reached for her bag, taking it and placing it on the table. Silently she began to cry again. For one so strong all her life, it seemed now love had broken her she would never, never mend again.

'Oh, Francesca.' For the second time that day he put his arms round her and hugged her close. The feel of her body against him, a child, desperate and needing him, made his heart ache. He knew in that moment what he had to do. She is so sad and lost, he thought, as he soothed her weeping, she must have someone to take care of her.

And it was then that he really made up his mind, and once he had, he knew there would be no turning back. It has to be me, he thought, stroking her hair and listening to the sound of her pitiful, painful sobs. I must help her, she has no one else but me. This poor child has suffered too much already; without me she may never recover. He glanced down at her. The feeling of being so essential to her and of being so needed was like a warmth in his veins – it dulled the fear of such an enormous, unexpected decision and it gave him hope. His decision was so clear and so final that he knew in his heart it had to be right.

When Dora came back from her three days with her sister in Harrogate, John met her at the local station in the next village to Motcom. He was there on the platform when her train pulled in and she knew immediately that something was wrong. It was a totally uncustomary gesture on his part.

'You shouldn't have bothered, John,' she said when she saw him. 'I could have easily caught a taxi.' She was prickly with him; his appearance unnerved her.

'No bother, Dora.' He carried her bag for her and stored it in the boot of the car before opening the door for her.

She climbed in, fastened her seat belt and then came straight to the point as John got in beside her. 'It's all right, I know something's wrong. You might as well tell me now, John, get it over with.' She folded her hands in her lap and waited for him to speak.

He smiled. 'You're a canny woman, Dora.'

'Don't change the subject.'

'All right then.' He turned to face her. 'I've decided to leave Motcom Park, to go on my own.'

'Oh, I see.' She stared straight ahead. They had been at Motcom together too many years for her to be able to take the news lightly. She took a breath. 'Is this something to do with the girl, John, with Francesca?'

'Yes, as a matter of fact it is.'

She continued to gaze away from him. 'I thought so.'

John placed his hand on her arm. 'Please, Dora, this wasn't an easy decision to make.'

She dropped her eyes down to her hands in her lap. 'No, I'm sure it wasn't.' Then she fumbled in her pocket for a handkerchief. 'I'm sorry, John—' She blew her nose, struggling to compose herself. 'It's just so unexpected . . . I—' She stopped and John sat uncomfortably for a few moments, not knowing what to say.

'Well!' After a minute or so, Dora blew her nose again. She had regained control of herself and she sniffed, dabbing at her eyes. 'It's quite a shock you know!' She smiled, covering her embarrassment.

'Yes, I know. I'm sorry.'

Then she faced him for the first time. 'Do you know what you're doing, John?'

'Yes I do. Believe me, I've given it a lot of thought.' He shook his head. He had done nothing but think about it over the last twenty-four hours – he was exhausted from thinking about it.

'Well, I suppose you'd better tell me why, then, if you've made up your mind, that is.'

'Yes.' He turned to her and she thought: he has changed, even in a few days he has changed, he looks tired and . . . She searched her mind for the right word. He looks more of a person, as if the polish has been worn off, the veneer stripped. He looks real, she thought and – happy. Yes, that was it, he looked happy! For the first time, since she had known him, John was content, and, for the briefest moment, she envied him that.

'Francesca has been asked to leave Motcom,' he said. 'And I've decided to go with her. There was some sort of thing with Lady Margaret's brother in Scotland, a minor indiscretion by all accounts, but they want her out. I can't let her go alone. So I've decided to take early retirement and try to set up on my own.'

'Oh, John! That sounds terribly rash to me. Are you quite sure this is the right thing to do?' Dora's voice was shocked and hurt. 'Perhaps you should take some time to think it over properly, a week at least.'

'My mind's made up, Dora. Besides, I've already informed Lord Henry. He's coming down at the weekend to speak to me and to finalise the details.'

'He's happy to let you go?' She was incredulous. 'Surely not?'

'Of course, Dora. I am only an employee.'

'But John—' Dora put her hand on his arm. 'Your whole life has been Motcom. Why now, why with this girl?'

John hesitated before he spoke. He was not sure that Dora would understand and he had always found it impossible to explain his feelings. He cleared his throat.

'She needs me, Dora. After all the years of working for the family, of picking up the discarded pieces of their lives, now I've a chance to find a life of my own. Oh, I'm not kid-

ding myself, it could all go wrong and I could end up far worse off than I am now, but at least I'll have tried. I'll have done what I thought was right. Francesca just won't survive on her own – she's no more than a child and she desperately needs someone to look after her. For the first time in my life, I'm really important to someone, I have a sense of purpose, a responsibility.' He shrugged. 'That probably sounds very foolish, but it means a hell of a lot to me.' He looked at her and Dora could see the hope in his eyes. 'She needs me, Dora,' he said again. 'I can't let her down. You do understand that, don't you?'

And Dora thought about her own life, how lonely she sometimes felt and how she missed being loved.

'Oh yes, my dear John, I understand.' Then she bent towards him and kissed his cheek. It was the only time she had ever done so in their ten years of friendship. 'And I'm glad for you,' she said. 'I wish you all the luck in the world.' There was nothing more she could add.

Seventeen

MANY YEARS LATER, WHEN FRANCESCA looked back on it, she was unable to recall any of the details of her last few days at Motcom Park. All she remembered was a numbness, and a terrible crushing grief that drained her body of every last bit of strength and life. She had loved, with all her heart, and she had trusted, trusted in Patrick and believed completely in the happiness he brought to her life. He had let her down, dropped her from an appalling height, knowing all the time that she was not good enough for him and leaving his sister to tell her the truth.

She had no idea that he had rung, that he had tried to contact her, to at least lessen the pain. But John had been dismissive, angry and defiant. 'She doesn't want to speak to you,' he had said coldly. 'Leave her alone! Haven't you done enough already?' And Patrick had hung up, afraid of his own emotions, and guilty that he was letting his sister dominate his life.

So Francesca clung to John in those days, when the night seemed endless, just interminable darkness, and the sins of the past haunted her. She never left him, needing his physical presence, his constant reassurance. He was her anchor to sanity.

And John knew. He knew the burden she had carried for so long and he knew that she had finally broken under the strain. She had broken because of love and he was filled with a seething, burning anger on her behalf. He would

gladly have killed Patrick Devlin, if he thought that it would give his child some peace.

His child. He had come to look upon her as his child, as someone so close and precious to him that he felt as if she were his blood, a part of him. And, as he moved quickly and surely, creating a new life for them, he realised that he did it with the fierce determination that an animal has to protect its own. To protect and survive.

So the days passed quickly as John drove to and from Newcastle, where he had decided to settle, and searched for a small house for them to live in. He packed up his things and made arrangements for them to be moved, saw to the financial details and finally ended his life at Motcom Park with an abrupt interview in Lord Henry's study.

'So you've made up your mind then, have you, John?' Lord Henry took no pains to cover his disapproval. 'You think this is the way forward, do you?'

John shrugged. 'It is the best solution as far as I can see it,' he answered.

'Well, who am I to argue then?' He stood at the fireplace and looked across at his man. He was bloody furious about the whole business if the truth be known. 'Nothing I can do to change your mind?' He knew what John's answer would be, bloody fool.

'No, sir. I'm sorry.'

'All right. No point in wasting any more time then. It's just the matter of your pension that we have to sort out.'

'Yes.'

And that was it. Twenty years of service with Lord Henry Smith-Colyne over in five minutes. John knew he should have expected it, but it was worse than he could have imagined.

Lord Henry crossed to his desk and took out his cheque

book. He wrote a cheque, signed it with his usual flourish and walked round to hand it over. John took it and folded it away.

'Look, John, I er . . .' Lord Henry put his hands in his pockets rather embarrassed, and leaned back against the edge of the desk. 'I shall miss you,' he said and cleared his throat. 'I'm er – sorry about all this bloody business. If you ever need advice, help of any kind, please, you will let me know?'

John nodded.

Lord Henry held out his hand. 'You know I don't approve of what you're doing, John. I won't pretend to think it's a good idea, but good luck anyway, I wish you well.'

John smiled, for the first time since he entered the study. 'Thank you,' he said, and releasing Lord Henry's hand, he crossed the large, oak-panelled study for the last time, opened the door and quietly left the room.

Outside he stopped and took a deep breath, more moved than he had realised. He took the cheque out of his pocket to tuck it safely into his wallet and dropped it clumsily onto the floor. His fingers were trembling. But as he bent and picked it up, he turned it over in his hands and saw that it was for double the amount he had saved. It was twice his pension. He swallowed hard and stood looking down at the cheque. Then he tucked it away and carried on through the house to the kitchen. That part of his life was over now and he had been properly paid for it.

The following morning he and Francesca left Motcom for good. They drove away in the pristine '63 Rover, John's belongings having preceded them, and headed down the long oak-lined drive of the park to the main road.

John glanced behind him before he pulled out into the

traffic and saw the full Georgian splendour of Motcom in the bright September morning. He smiled. No regrets, he thought, strange after so long. Then he indicated right, pulled away from the gates and accelerated off, leaving the house and park behind him.

Eighteen

Jesmond, Newcastle Upon Tyne

JOHN HAD FOUND A SMALL mid-Victorian terraced house in a residential area just outside Newcastle city centre. It was sandwiched between two larger houses, a rickety grey brick cottage with a white wooden Gothic porch over the front door and a rambling rose climbing over it, glorious in late-summer bloom. It was neglected and run-down but as soon as he saw it he fell in love with it. It was a rough-cut gem, bright and unique, just lying amongst the dull, smooth stones around it.

It had a garden at the front: twenty feet of tangled weeds and overgrown grass bounded by a fence with honeysuckle trailing over it, and a path, trodden through the rank vegetation to the front door. The sash windows were large, their wood slightly rotten from lack of care, and the front door was painted a garish turquoise.

Inside the rooms were small but adequate: one long, narrow room at the front, knocked through from two, and a kitchen out the back. The original fireplaces remained, along with a huge stone sink in the kitchen and racks and racks of oak wood shelves. Best of all, on the end wall was an old nineteen-fifties range, an oil-burning Aga.

Upstairs were two small bedrooms and a classic Edwardian bathroom that a previous owner had tried to rip out. It had obviously proved too much because he had given up halfway through and left the wide square sink and

bath with their curved chromium-plated taps and enough of the tiles for them to be able to match them. He had ripped up the floor, though, and lined the boards with a lurid patterned lino in shiny orange and black.

But it was home, and for John it was his first. Despite all the flaws and all the hard work he knew it would involve, he looked on it with elation and pride. It was his, his to share with Francesca, his own tiny piece of England.

They moved into the house two weeks after leaving Motcom Park. The legalities were a matter of course – Lord Henry's solicitor had rushed things through for them – and John collected the keys from the agent's on the third Monday in September. He held them in his hand and thought: fifty-five and my first home. Better late than never. And he stood outside the estate agent's and laughed. Who would have imagined that I would be doing this?

Francesca had not seen the house before they moved into it. John had wanted to keep it a secret, desperate not to disappoint her lest anything should go wrong. And, although her name was on the contract, she had merely signed where John indicated and thought no more about it.

She had been so tired since they left Motcom, her weight dropping and her energy drained, that John worried constantly about her. Every day to get up was an effort, and the hours she was awake she longed for the dark, heavy relief of sleep. Her mind was blank and he could see her existing in a sort of half-state, alive but not aware of the life she was living. He pinned all his hopes on the house. Father Angelo had told him that she had a fierce will to survive, and he could sense that she also had a tremendous strength, deep down inside her, to fight back. He was giving her the chance to live for something, to see a way out. He was offering her a future. He just prayed that she would take it.

The morning of the move he still did not tell her. Full of childish excitement, he wanted it to be a surprise. He arrived back from the agent's, took her by the hand and led her out to the car.

'I've got something to show you,' he said, opening the car door for her. 'Something important.' He started the engine, put the car in gear and Francesca sneaked a glance across at him, his face bright with enthusiasm. She was intrigued: something about his manner had pierced through her outer shell and she found herself smiling at the tuneless notes he unconsciously hummed. His glee was infectious.

He took her round the long way, through the tree-lined streets of Jesmond, past the pretty Victorian houses and the cricket ground, and finally to Marston Avenue, a long, wide road that ran down towards the Dene and the deep green expanse of park.

It was a warm Indian summer day, with the ever present north-eastern breeze blowing through the leafy green branches of the trees and scattering patterns of shadow across the road. The light was clear and bright and when John drew up in front of the house, it had lit the flame red of the roses on the grey brick and made their colour look like fire.

'Here,' he said as he drew in alongside the kerb and switched off the engine. He sat and stared up at their home. 'This is what I wanted to show you.'

'This house?'

'Yes, this house.'

Francesca climbed out of the car. She stood on the pavement in the sunlight and looked at the old grey stone cottage with its jumble of a garden and its bright turquoise front door. She smiled. Walking up to the wooden latch gate, she stood and snapped a small twig off the honey-

suckle that grew over the fence, putting it up to her nose and breathing in its sweet, heady scent.

'It's lovely,' she murmured. John placed a hand on her shoulder as he came up behind her. He stood and followed her gaze.

'It's yours, Francesca,' he said quietly. 'Your home.'

She spun round to face him. 'Mine?' For the first time in weeks her eyes seemed to come alive and the green of them deepened.

'Yes, it's yours, and mine, our home.' He looked down for a moment. 'Do you like it?'

And then he felt himself swept up on a wave of emotion as Francesca threw her arms around him and hugged him. He saw her face, that peculiar smile of hers that transformed it and made it beautiful, and her eyes, dazzling green, bright with excitement, their terrible blankness vanished.

'Is it really mine? Really? I mean my home?' She spoke so fast that she tripped over her accent. She stopped suddenly and took a deep breath. She could hardly believe John had done this for her. He had taken her in, helped her and cared for her. He given her the chance of a new life. 'It is really mine?'

'Yes, it is really yours, really, your home.' John laughed, but the relief in his heart made him want to cry. She had come to life again. 'You signed the papers, remember?'

She shook her head and then it dawned on her what he had been doing and she threw her arms around him again. 'It's really mine?' she whispered.

He held her tight. 'Uh-huh.'

'Thank you, John,' she said softly. 'I will try to make you so proud of me.' What was past was past, she would accept it and get on with her life. 'Thank you,' she whispered again.

John stood back, momentarily embarrassed by his own

emotion, and looked up at the cottage. 'You may not thank me in a week's time,' he said gloomily, 'when your hair is full of grit and grime and you haven't had a bath for days!' But she laughed and followed his gaze. 'Never!' she answered. 'This is the best thing . . .'

And then suddenly she stepped aside, moved past him and opened the gate. 'Oh my God!' she exclaimed from two steps inside the garden, her hands in the air in a typically Italian gesture. 'We had better get started right away!' She glanced over her shoulder at him, her look deadly serious. 'The first thing we must do is paint the front door.' And she pulled a face. 'Some people, really! What a truly horrible colour it is!'

And John, unable to help himself, let out a long, loud peal of laughter.

So they began work on the house by painting the front door. They filled the cracks in the wood, stripped back the layers of dirt and tarnish from the brass knocker and letter box and painted the door, a deep, dark glossy green. It was the first step.

Inside the house, they cleaned and sorted, swept and polished and it took only a matter of days before their home was habitable. Dora had sorted out a bundle of old linen which she sent up from Motcom and John had his picnic hamper to tide them over with cutlery and china. They had everything they needed and they settled in, warmed their house with a bottle of wine and started to lay the foundations of their new life.

The week after they settled, John began the long and arduous process of looking for a job. He had worked his finances out with great care. He had spent most of his savings on the house, but he knew that they could last a couple of months if they had to, providing they were careful. He

needed to find work though, as much for his own morale as for the money, and he set about it in the meticulous way he did everything, scouring the situations vacant columns in the local papers and borrowing a typewriter to type up his details.

He had gauged that it would probably take him several weeks to find something he liked but he was prepared to sit it out until he did. So he duly sent off letters to the local companies that interested him, answered the adverts that he liked, put his name down at the employment office and spent countless hours sorting through possible job opportunities.

Francesca watched him over the next two weeks with her heart full of hope. She had taken on the responsibility of the house and while John looked for work, she stripped walls and woodwork, sanded, cleaned, washed and painted. She toiled endlessly, finding relief in the physicality of the work, needing to bury herself in it.

She was determined to forget, to make John proud, and she tackled the work with gusto, labouring long into the night, searching out bargains, sewing, painting and pouring all the love she had to give into the rickety little house. She wanted to make it into the best house ever, into a home they could both be proud of.

And as she tried to do so, John found that she had an innate sense of style, painting the walls a clean, bright white and sanding the floorboards, polishing them up to a deep oak shine. At the windows she hung lengths of Victorian lace that she had found rummaging around in the local church jumble sale, and she scattered heaps of beautifully patterned cushions over the high old Chesterfield sofa she had picked up in a sale room. The kitchen she painted yellow. Finding a massed assortment of glass jars, she filled and arranged them on the oak shelves, then hung

up her strings of onions and garlic and her bunches of dried herbs.

Finally, for the bedrooms, she found a pair of Victorian brass bedsteads, probably from the servants' quarters in one of the large old houses, and she put one in each room, investing in feather pillows from Bainbridge and two blue and white striped, duck-down quilts. She covered small round tables in the same stripe and placed a square of white antique lace over the top. She blacked the iron fireplaces, polished the floors and lastly laid a rug in each room, faded, muted Indian carpets in blues and deep reds that she had cleaned and repaired after finding them abandoned, wet and dismal, in a skip behind Holly Avenue.

By the middle of October, the house was as finished as they could afford. It was comfortable, stylish, polished and clean. John had cut back the garden, ready for Francesca to plant, but the weather had turned very cold very quickly and the ground frost made it impossible to dig the earth. They decided to leave it until spring.

But there was also one other reason to postpone any more improvements: John had begun to worry about his finances. In all the time that Francesca spent on the house, John had searched relentlessly for work. His great plans to take only something that he was really keen on faded to something that he quite liked and eventually to anything he could get.

Time and time again he was told that they were looking for someone younger, that he did not have the right experience or that he was under-qualified for the job. Most of the time, however, the answers he received merely informed him that the position had already been filled.

No explanation and no hope.

He knew that they had enough money, but by now it was only just enough. He found his prospects becoming increas-

ingly bleak and their bright new future together began to look precarious. He told nothing of this to Francesca. He worried alone, the fear of failure gnawing away at him like a persistent, troubling ulcer.

Francesca was aware of everything he suffered, though – she was far more perceptive than he realised. She watched him, as she used to watch her father, silently and unseen, and she was anxious for him, she wanted to help. She knew that she had kept the business of living too distant for too long; burying herself in the work of the house, she had withdrawn from the world. She had done what she needed to, and the house had given her the strength to come through the pain, the will to survive. It was time to start her life again.

Without telling John, within a few days of finishing the house, Francesca made the decision to look for a job.

She had no idea what she wanted to do but she read through the local paper as John had done and on the last page found a small, elaborate advert for the 'Start-Right Employment Agency'. She made a note of the number, and the following morning, when John had gone to the library, she telephoned to make an appointment. She was told to come in later that afternoon.

Ringing off, she sat for a moment, dazed by such a quick response, then she jumped up, overwhelmed with nerves, and rushed upstairs to try to find something suitable to wear.

By the time John returned from the library it was lunch-time and Francesca was sitting at the kitchen table, dressed in her only skirt, one of the thick, checked Viyella shirts John had bought her for Scotland, thick black wool tights and her flat brown lace-up shoes. She looked like a respectable middle-aged spinster from Surrey, reading the free paper and drumming her fingers nervously on the

table-top. His black and brown tweed jacket hung over the back of the chair behind her with one of his bright silk handkerchiefs in the breast pocket.

'Goodness me! Are you going somewhere?' He crossed to her and kissed the top of her head before pulling out a chair opposite her. He forced back the smile that her rather old-fashioned appearance evoked. 'Yes, you may borrow my jacket.' He leaned over and readjusted the handker-chief. 'Come on then, tell me! I'm dying of curiosity here, where are you off to?'

Francesca bit her lip and then took a deep breath. 'I rang an agency this morning for a job and they asked me to come in this afternoon for an interview.' She had removed her hands from the table and picked anxiously at her nails. Then she looked up at him. 'Oh, John, I don't know why I did it! I wanted to help you and I thought it was such a good idea up until now. But what am I going to say? I really don't think I can go. Perhaps I can ring up and say I'm not very well?'

John reached out and placed his hand over hers, stop-ping the nervous agitation of it. He squeezed her fingers and smiled. 'No, you can't ring up and say that. You'll just have to go.'

She pulled her hand away and stood up. He could see he had upset her but he had to be firm. She had made a move to be independent and he was not going to let her back out halfway through. It was important, she was ready to start a life of her own, she just needed a little push.

'You'll be fine, Francesca,' he said gently. 'There is noth-ing to worry about, really. Come on, sit down and let's go through what you're likely to be asked. There won't be any-thing you can't cope with, I promise you.'

She frowned and he said again: 'Come on, I'll pretend to be the interviewer and ask the questions and you can answer them. OK?'

She nodded and reluctantly sat back down.

'Reeet!' he began in a high-pitched Scottish accent. He crossed his legs, toes pointed, touched his hair and pursed his lips. 'Exactly what sort tai job were ye after, Miss Camerooon?'

And Francesca suddenly laughed. She relaxed back in her chair, folded her arms and they continued in high spirits with the interview.

But, two hours later, as she waited in the glossy reception of the Start-Right Employment Agency, Francesca had forgotten everything she had rehearsed with John. She sat, once she had filled in the application forms, hands clenched in her lap, ankles neatly crossed the way she had seen in a magazine and a grim, set expression on her face. She had heard the girls on the desk snigger as she went through to sit down and was painfully aware that she wasn't dressed right, in her dull, unfashionable clothes.

She stared at a framed Cecil Beaton print on the wall opposite and gritted her teeth while her hopes of a job faded with every minute that ticked by.

'Hellooo! Miss Cameron?'

Francesca started and blinked rapidly several times to clear her vision. 'Yes.' She looked towards the door where a short, smartly dressed, middle-aged woman stood, holding a clipboard and smiling, the sort of smile that primary school teachers wear.

'I'm Marjorie Davidson,' the woman said Her glasses were perched on the tip of her nose and she peered over the top of them at Francesca. Oh my God, Marjorie thought, what on earth is the dear girl wearing? She smiled again to cover her distaste. 'Perhaps you'd like to follow me, would you, dear?' Her voice was modulated north-east, toned

down to suit the more executive client; she'd worked very hard on it.

Francesca stood, tried to pull up the wrinkles in her tights without being seen and crossed to the door, following the woman out into the corridor.

'I see here that you can speak Italian,' Ms Davidson said over her shoulder. '*Buon giorno!*' Her accent was so exaggerated that she rolled her R for several seconds before adding on the rest of the word.

'*Buon giorno. Come sta?*'

'Ah, yes, quite. Very nice, dear.' Ms Davidson's Italian stretched to good morning and Valpolicella only. 'Very nice indeed,' she said again and stopped at a door marked 'Interview Room'. She wrote something on the paper on her clipboard and opened the door, ushering Francesca inside.

'Do take a seat. Can I get you some tea? Coffee?' She waited for the briefest second. 'No? Oh good, I do hate wasting time.' She came in and closed the door behind her. 'Now, let's have a look at this form, shall we?' She sat down opposite Francesca, crossed her legs and touched her hair, just as John had imitated.

'Right, let me see . . .' She looked down at the clipboard. 'Hmmm,' she said, after a few minutes, and then, 'Uh-huh.' She tapped her toe on the floor and after what seemed like an hour to Francesca, but was in fact only a few minutes, she finally looked up again.

'So you've no recognisable qualifications then?'

Francesca swallowed and then shook her head. 'My father wanted me to leave school to help him run the shop,' she said, her voice tapering off at the end to just above a whisper.

'Pardon?' Ms Davidson readjusted her glasses and stared.

'I left school at fifteen, to help my father in the shop,'

Francesca said again, only a fraction louder.

'I see. And skills? Have you any commercial skills?'
Francesca shook her head.

'What about experience?' It was clear Ms Davidson was
beginning to lose her patience. 'You put down here, running
a shop, what exactly did that involve?'

Francesca had lost her nerve. She was completely intim-
idated by the whole interview and all she could do was
look fearfully at the smart, sophisticated woman and shrug.
All her knowledge of printing and design flew out of her
mind and all she could whisper was: 'I don't know, really.'
She looked away, hot and tearful with embarrassment. She
had made a terrible mistake, an awful, humiliating mistake.
She had nothing to offer. Nothing.

Ms Davidson waited for several minutes, the tap of her
toe sharp on the polished pine floor, then she decided to be
generous – it'd been a quiet afternoon anyway.

'We see all kinds of people here, you know, Francesca,
but they must have *something* to offer a prospective
employer. You do understand that?' She pursed her lips
and waited for Francesca to nod. 'Good. Now, is there anything you can think of that might interest one of our clients,
a talent perhaps, something you're good at, a skill, like
organising, for instance?' She knew she was being patronising, but really, the girl was a complete waste of time!

'Organising,' Francesca murmured faintly.

'Pardon? Do speak up, dear!'

'Organising.'

'Organising. Yes, quite.' She made a note of it.
'Organising.' Then, after only a few seconds, she looked
up. 'Look, to be quite honest with you, Francesca, there is
absolutely nothing I can offer you. I'm sorry.'

Francesca nodded.

She seems struck dumb, Marjorie thought briefly,

nodding like that all the time. 'Why don't you go away and think about what you want to do, and then maybe try to get on a training scheme? Hmmm? Or perhaps try for some qualifications. Hmmm? I really think that would be the most sensible thing to do, don't you?'

Once more Francesca nodded.

Oh, for goodness' sake, Marjorie thought, I really must get the girls on the desk to weed 'em out.

'I think perhaps it was a tiny bit premature to come in today, Francesca. If I were you, I should leave contacting any other agencies until you've got something behind you. That make sense?'

For the last time, Francesca nodded and Ms Davidson stood up, left the clipboard on the chair and began to move towards the door. Francesca followed, her tights hopelessly wrinkled and beyond rescue.

'Nice to meet you, Francesca.' She held out a long, slim hand with scarlet-tipped fingers and Francesca took it.

At least her handshake's firm, Marjorie thought. She couldn't stand wet, limp handshakes.

'Goodbye then,' she said quickly. 'And good luck.'

'Thank you.' Francesca went to turn the wrong way down the corridor. 'Goodbye.'

'It's to your left.'

'Oh, yes, thank you.' And blushing almost crimson, she headed off towards the reception and the way out.

Down on the pavement, the freezing air hit Francesca's face with sudden impact and cooled the burning of her cheeks. She stood for a moment, bit back the tears of humiliation and then turned up the collar on John's jacket and pulled it in tight around her. She headed off towards the bus stop and felt the first icy drops of rain on her face

*

Marjorie Davidson walked slowly back to her office counting, with quiet deliberation, from one to ten. She always did this when irritated.

She sat down in her leather swivel chair and looked at the pile of administration on her desk, which seemed to have grown in the past twenty-five minutes. What a hopeless case, she thought, a waste of my time and hers. She sighed heavily and stood, crossing to the window. Young people today haven't got a clue, they're all instant gratification – none of them have the staying power that I had at their age.

She looked out at the freezing grey drizzle and remembered herself at seventeen, determined, no, more than that, she thought, passionate to succeed. I had nothing to start with, nothing but poverty and ignorance; I lied my way into my first job, but boy oh boy, once I'd got it there was no stopping me.

She smiled and thought back twenty odd years. All she'd needed was a chance, that one opportunity, and from there on in, it had been clear, all the way to the winning post.

From her corner office in Ridly Place, Marjorie could see the main road and the empty space outside Luckies where great crowds of students gathered in the summer. She could see the cathedral and the traffic and the bustle of Newcastle city centre. She loved her view – it was right in the middle of things – and as she stood and surveyed it all, she felt as she always did, that she'd made it. And that was a bloody marvellous feeling.

Today it was crowded; Friday afternoon and everyone knocking off early. They stood at the bus stop with huge bags of shopping from the Green Market and something new to wear for tonight, a long queue of people who had trudged through the sleeting rain to work and back again.

She looked at them all from the warmth and comfort of

her office and thought how glad she was not to be out there. She surveyed all their miserable faces, peering through her glasses, and right at the end of the queue, she saw Francesca Cameron.

The girl was out, way beyond the shelter and the rain had soaked her through, making her look even more dull and drab. She was obviously shivering in the cold, the ridiculous outsize jacket pulled in tight around her, her hands tucked up the sleeves. Oh dear, Marjorie thought, she looks like a drowned rat. And then, quite suddenly, and for no reason at all, she remembered the very first interview she had attended, for a job in a shop down on Grey Street.

She had been caught in a shower on her way there, a really heavy downpour that had drenched her right through and made the dye on her cheap wool jacket run so that her hands were streaked with black and the cotton skirt she wore was ruined. She smiled. She remembered she had backcombed her hair and lacquered it heavily to keep it in place. By the time she arrived at the shop it looked like a bird's nest, all matted and sodden and smelling foul. She hadn't had the nerve to go in, she had simply looked at herself in the plate-glass window, turned round and gone back home. She cried all the way on the bus.

God, it was hard getting started, she thought. If it hadn't been for Tommy, giving me that first chance . . . She smiled again at the memory of her friend and then, in a sudden moment of impetuous decision, she crossed to the coat-rack in the corner of the room, pulled on her overcoat and grabbed an umbrella. She was out of the door of the office, down the stairs and into the street before she had a chance to question what she was doing.

*

Francesca had lost sensation in her toes. Her feet were so cold that it felt as if they were no longer there, just big clumps of icy flesh on the end of her legs. Her teeth were chattering and her head ached with the tension in her jaw. She stared down at the ground and tried to think of something warm.

'Francesca?'

She looked up, thinking she heard her name but immediately looked down again, she must have been imagining it.

'Francesca!'

She looked up a second time and felt a hand on her sleeve. She saw Ms Davidson from the agency standing in front of her, in a long, cerise, wool swing coat with a cerise and white umbrella over her head.

'Oh, I . . .' She didn't know what to say, the sight was so surprising and so dazzling against the drab grey of the wet street that all she could do was stare.

'Look, Francesca. I think I may have a job for you, or an interview at least.'

'Oh, er . . . really?' She was too taken aback to think straight.

'Yes, it's a sort of general assistant job, for a fashion studio on the Quayside. Would you be interested?'

'Oh, yes! Yes, I would!' Francesca clasped her hands together.

'Well, if you'll come back to my office for a few minutes, I'll tell you all about it. All right?'

'Yes, yes of course!' And then she smiled, for the first time since meeting Ms Davidson, and Marjorie saw her face light up and suddenly change to something really quite beautiful.

'Come on then,' Ms Davidson said. The rain continued to pour. 'Come under my umbrella, you must be freezing!'

Francesca stepped forward and the cerise was reflected onto her skin, making her feel instantly warmer.

'What a terrible day!' Marjorie commented as they made their way back to Ridly Place. But Francesca just shrugged. She didn't mind the rain at all. Not now, anyway.

THE MONDAY MORNING FOLLOWING HER interview with Marjorie Davidson, Francesca found herself at eight-thirty, bleary-eyed, and sick with nerves, on a bus that was headed for town. She had an appointment with David Yates at nine o'clock.

Getting off at the Odeon, she crossed into Grey Street, walked down past the Theatre Royal and onto Dean Street, the road that led down to the Quayside. She wore exactly what she had on Friday, the jacket smelling faintly from its soaking and her shoes half a size smaller, having shrunk in the rain. They pinched painfully as she walked.

Over and over as she strode, she repeated the answers that Marjorie had given her and tried to imagine what David Yates would look like. Marjorie had told her practically nothing but she had found some of his clothes in *Vogue* and fallen in love with them instantly. They were elegant and feminine, always simple but the line of them seemed to have a life of its own: it caressed the models in the photographs.

He must be terribly smart and sophisticated, she thought, conjuring up images of a tall, blond gentleman in a cream linen suit. She saw him with a panama hat in his hand, greeting her with a long, manicured hand, and giggled at the image. Minutes later she was at the corner of Dean Street and she followed the road round to the left, and then on into Queen Street, looking up at the buildings for the brass name-plate of the David Yates Studio.

She found it on the corner and saw that the windows overlooked the Tyne and the series of bridges over the river. It all looked so terribly glamorous that she was suddenly filled with overwhelming awe and excitement. She rang the buzzer, her heart pounding, said her name into the speaker panel and pushed the door open when she heard it unlock. She stepped inside, into a small square space about four foot by four, directly in front of a dark and narrow flight of steep stairs. She blinked to adjust her eyes to the lack of light.

'Come on up! First floor, pet!' The accent was broad Geordie, yelled against the buzz of music from the radio.

She began to climb, holding onto the wobbly banister and trying to avoid brushing John's jacket against the large patches of damp on the wall.

'There y' are. Go on thro', pet, Dave's waitin' fo' ya in the studio.' The girl on the desk smiled as she said this and motioned with her hand towards the door that Francesca should go through. As she did so the mass of bangles on her arms, the chandeliers of beads at her ears and the heavy silver necklace around her neck all jangled at once in a tinkling, chinking melody.

'Thank you,' Francesca said.

'Nee bother. Go on, but watch out fer yeselv – he's in a right bloody mood this morning!'

Francesca pushed open the double doors of the studio and walked into the room.

It was a massive space, like a warehouse, with a huge bank of windows along one side and a high, metal-beamed ceiling from which hung canopies of lights. Francesca blinked again, this time trying to adjust to the glare.

'Ah!' She heard a shout from the other end of the studio. 'You must be the girl from the agency.' She turned her head towards the voice and saw a tall, thin man with incredibly

long limbs and a wave of dark hair that receded slightly from his forehead and was brushed back into a short, glossy ponytail and tied with a leather thong. He wore khaki combat trousers with what seemed like hundreds of pockets all stuffed full, and enormous brown hiking boots laced up with purple laces. His shirt was checked, faded cotton and as he strode towards her, he pulled out a lime green baseball cap from one of his pockets and slipped it on.

'Don't like strangers looking at me bald patch.' he said with a north London accent on reaching her. 'Shall we go and sit somewhere?'

She nodded, completely amazed and utterly disappointed. No linen suit and certainly no panama.

'Here.' He removed a pile of fabric from a canvas director's chair and motioned for her to sit down. Pulling up a stool, he perched on the edge and looked her up and down, from top to toe.

'You're not into fashion then.' He reached across and felt the sleeve of her jacket. 'Nice fabric, though.'

'Yes.' She cleared her throat and tried again. 'Thank you.'

He smiled. 'Not at all. Now, what did the old dragon at the agency tell you? Nothing, probably. Still, I can't blame her. Where shall I start?' He pulled a torn and crumpled handkerchief out of another pocket and blew his nose before continuing. 'That's better. Now, where was I? Oh yes, I don't want any fashion groupies. I've had two already — they get bored with the nitty gritty and piss off without a word. They get in the bloody way as well! The job's not great, I won't lie to you, but the perks are good. You'll have to clear up, make tea, go out for pastries, clean the loo, all that kind of shit. The money's OK, seventy-five quid a week, plus bus fares, and you can have any odd bits of fabric lying around and some of the clothes the models don't want. That's about it, I think.' He folded his arms and

leaned back, staring at her again. After several minutes of scrutiny, he said; 'If you like the sound of it, you can start this morning. All right?' He began to stand up.

'But . . . I—'

'You'll need to change – you can't work in my studio dressed like that. There's a bin of odd stuff over there, you can help yourself.' Turning away from her, he suddenly remembered something and looked back over his shoulder. 'Marjorie told me all about you but she probably didn't say a word about me. I'm a pig to work for, so stay out of my way. All right?' He saw the look of alarm on Francesca's face and as he walked away, he had his first good laugh for days.

Still a little dazed, Francesca stood up and walked towards the huge cardboard box that David Yates had pointed to. She glanced behind her before she bent, and saw that the five or so people in the studio were all occupied and nobody was watching her. She knelt down, leaned into the box and began to have a good old rummage round.

Half an hour later, she had pressed the clothes she had chosen, changed into them and was heading out towards the reception to see if the girl on the desk knew what she should do next when she heard the unmistakable shout of David Yates.

'Oi! Girl from the agency?'

She turned and saw him in the corner of the studio that was occupied with two high drawing tables and surrounded with big screens covered in swatches of fabric and sheets of rough designs. He was beckoning to her.

She changed direction and began to walk across the huge space, noticing for the first time the ordered chaos that seemed to fill every square inch of the studio. She smiled at a couple of girls standing by a rack of clothes and squeezed past a long table where an elderly woman was cutting out

shapes from a roll of cloth. The floor was covered with scraps of material, pins, waste paper and general dirt and she bent to pick up a dressmaker's chalk that she had almost stepped on, slipping it into her pocket.

'There you are. Took your time, didn't you?' David Yates sat at his drawing table and scribbled colour onto a design with some thick felt-tipped pens. He finally looked up after finishing the sketch.

'Very nice. The ugly duckling emerges as a swan.'

Francesca looked down self-consciously at the tight black canvas jodhpurs she had chosen and the soft red wool shirt.

'You need some shoes, those brown things look ghastly. What size are you?' Dave could see that the girl he had just employed was a potential beauty and anything with style and grace pleased him. 'It doesn't matter, just ask Tilly on the desk to ring Cable and Co. for a pair of black cropped riding boots. Tell her your size and they'll send them over. All right?'

Francesca nodded. She could hardly believe this was happening to her.

'I forgot your name,' he said. He had started another drawing and spoke to her without looking at her. 'I can't keep calling you "girl from the agency".'

'Francesca.'

'Right. Francesca, go downstairs into the junk cupboard and bring up all the dummies down there. All right?' He didn't wait for her answer. 'You can get the key from Tilly.'

'Yes Mr—'

'Dave!' he barked and she jumped. 'The only person that calls me "Mr Yates" is my bank manager and he's an arsehole. All right?' He still didn't look at her; he was drawing the long line of a dress with a heavy black pen.

'Yes. Dave.'

'Good.'

And Francesca realised that seconds later he had completely forgotten she was there.

By the time the lunch-hour arrived Francesca's back ached, her legs ached and her feet were hot, sweaty and sore inside her new leather boots. She had walked up and down the stairs fourteen times carrying the dummies up to the studio and ten times carrying the ones he didn't want back down again. She had swept the floor twice, seeming never to be able to clear the dirt up completely, and had produced twenty-seven cups of coffee for six people, most of which had been only half drunk.

Dave had dismissed her for lunch at half past two, having forgotten that she existed up until then, and she had hurried out of the studio, down the dark narrow stairs and onto the street, relieved to be away from the shouting and the constant noise that the business of creation produced.

But the lunch-hour went too quickly and before she knew it Francesca was back in the studio. All afternoon she worked, cleaning the little kitchen that everyone used to cook and make drinks in until it gleamed, folding and tidying the piles of discarded fabric, making endless tea, running out for biscuits and sweeping the floor for the third time that day.

At the end of the afternoon, Francesca sat down for the first time that day and wondered just where the time had gone. It had rushed by in a flash. She glanced at the clock on the opposite wall, discovered it was after six and then realised that she hadn't eaten all day. She was ravenously hungry and felt a low, determined rumble in the pit of her stomach.

'Bye, Francesca!'

She looked up and saw Evelyn Wardly, the tailoress, leav-

ing with Tilly. She waved and smiled and realised that she was one of the last people left in the studio. She bent and rubbed her toes inside the new boots and wondered whether it would be all right if she left.

'Francesca!'

Jumping up quickly, she forgot the ache in her toes and hurried across the studio to where Dave was still working.

She spoke quietly in his presence, awed by him and even a touch afraid.

'You still here?' He kept his head down as he growled the question. Francesca swallowed hard.

'Yes . . . I—'

He looked up. 'You what?'

She shrugged, tongue-tied.

'You, me dear, should get yourself home, put your sore little feet in some hot water and mustard and tomorrow don't wait for me to remember that you're still here. All right? Just piss off when you've done the work.'

She nodded and hot with embarrassment, turned to leave.

'Oh, and Francesca?'

She glanced back.

'You were bloody marvellous today! Thanks.' And without a smile, he put his head down again and continued with his work. She crept across the studio, collected up her things and silently left the building.

Outside, in the cold night air, she gave a whoop of excitement and, despite the discomfort of her boots, ran all the way to the bus stop with a smile of pure elation on her face.

John was in the small yellow kitchen when she came in after seven. He had made a start on the supper.

'Hi.' She rushed into the room bringing in a breath of cold air with her and bent down to kiss him on the cheek.

'Hello!' He turned his head to look at her as she took off his jacket and neatly smoothed out its creases before hanging it in the under-stair cupboard.

'Come on! Don't keep me in suspense any longer! Sit down here and tell me all about it!' She had rung him at lunch-time to tell him she'd got the job and he could tell now, by the flush of excitement on her cheeks, that the first day had gone well.

'I want to know everything,' he said. 'Every little detail.'

She laughed and pulled out a chair, sitting down with him at the table.

'That's new!' He reached out and touched the red wool shirt and she beamed. 'So you got clothes as well as a job?'

'Oh yes! John, you wouldn't believe it! I nearly fell off my chair when he told me I'd got the job. He just said: if you like the sound of it you can start this morning! And I couldn't believe it! He never asked me any of the questions I thought he would and then he said if I worked there I would have to find something to wear and I chose what I've got on and then he said I should have some boots to go with it and Tilly, she's the girl on the desk, she's got masses of long blonde hair and she wears hundreds of beads and bracelets and things, well, Tilly rang this shop and they sent a pair over for me, in my size! Just like that!' She stopped, momentarily out of breath and bent to rub her aching toes inside her boots. 'Trouble is,' she said, without realising how comical it was, 'the boots are absolutely killing me.'

Later, after supper, when he had heard everything, John made a fire up for Francesca in the front room, sat her feet

in a bowl of steaming hot mustard water and stood alone in the kitchen finishing the washing up. He enjoyed the moment's peace after the nonstop chatter of the evening – it gave him chance to think.

As he meticulously dried and put away, however, he felt an odd sense of despondency, a nagging feeling that he had somehow failed. It depressed him and made him feel old. He supposed that it was because he had not yet found himself a job, although he was sure that he would. And yet, as he listened to the silence of the little house, he knew that it was probably more than that. He felt alone and, for the first time since he had left Motcom, he wondered if he had made the right decision.

Francesca has found her independence, he thought, and as she grows, she will no longer need me. I'll be a friend to her, of course, but I won't be essential. It is only right, I know that, and yet I just can't stop the terrible ache in my heart every time I think about it.

He dried his hands, folded the towel and wandered through to the sitting room to see if she was all right. He stopped at the door when he caught sight of her, feet still in the bowl, but her head dropped back, her eyes closed and fast asleep. He padded silently into the room, gently lifted her feet onto the towel, covered them and went to fetch a rug.

Minutes later, when he returned, she had curled herself up onto the sofa, crossed her arms around her and was breathing deeply and slowly, lost in a world of dreams. He tucked the blanket round her, removed the bowl and began to walk back to the kitchen.

'John?'

He stopped and turned. Francesca had opened her eyes and smiled at him, a crooked half-smile, half awake, half asleep.

'Thank you,' she murmured. She sighed and settled back down to sleep. 'Oh, and I love you, too.'

It was only a faint whisper but he heard it. He smiled and continued back to the kitchen, realising somehow that whatever he felt, it was the complications of life that made it worth living.

CHAPTER
Twenty

THINGS FOR JOHN AND FRANCESCA settled down over the next few weeks into a routine that seemed to suit them both.

Francesca worked hard at the studio – she was always up and out early, often in late – and John kept the house running in his efficient and ordered way. They managed on Francesca's money: their needs were simple and their expenses mostly food. They ate together every evening in the small, bright, warm kitchen, and afterwards Francesca would spend her time sitting at the old oak table drawing and designing, something she hadn't done for many months, while John struggled with the *Times* crossword. They talked and shared the day over these hobbies and their friendship strengthened and blossomed.

Each day Francesca rose at seven in order to be at the studio by eight. She made herself coffee, fiddled about with the odd assortment of clothes she had found at David Yates, in order to get the right look, and then dressed carefully, checking herself once briefly in the mirror before she left the house.

On the way to work she ate an apple and bought the *Daily Mail,* which she had taken to reading avidly. Once she arrived at the studio, she began her chores straight away. Alone and with the radio blaring, she would clean and sweep, tidy and fold, check everything was out that was needed for the day and finally make a huge pot of dark, steaming fresh coffee, that smelled delicious all the way

up the stairs and enticed people earlier and earlier into work.

'Yo, Francesca! How ya doing?'

It was the beginning of the week and Francesca had just finished mopping the floor when Matt, David Yates' textile designer, came tramping into the studio in wet, muddy baseball boots. He squelched all over the floor.

'Oh shit. Sorry.' He pulled a helpless face and then shrugged, continuing across the length of the studio to his drawing board and leaving a trail of mud behind him.

Francesca held her breath and counted to ten in Italian. It took her longer than in English now and gave her more of a chance to calm down. There was something she couldn't quite like about Matt Baker – he was very charming and all that but for some reason she just didn't trust him.

She looked up, startled out of her irritation as Tilly came rushing into the studio. Tilly rushed everywhere, bangles and beads jangling musically, her mane of teased gold hair flying out behind her and the scent of gardenia like a heavy cloud above her head.

'Oh my God! I canna believe it! I've gone an' forgotten to book the models for this afternoon! I only remembered on the bus on me way home last night, like. What the friggin' hell am I gonna do? He'll bloomin' kill us.' She said all this in a frenzied rush, full Geordie and hopping anxiously from one foot to the other. Her hair this morning looked even more dishevelled than it usually did, as if she had just literally got out of bed.

'Oh God, Francesca! He'll kill us!' she wailed again.

Francesca leaned on her mop and thought hard. Tilly was right about that one, Dave was likely to kill her when he found out. He was right in the middle of the collection for London Fashion Week and his stress level had gone

through the roof. All it took this past week was one small thing and he exploded like a volcano.

'I just don't know what I'm gonna do! You've gotta help us, Francesca.'

'Look, Tilly, calm down!' But Francesca had begun to panic herself – Tilly's mood was infectious. 'Have you tried all the agencies?'

'Yeah, I have. I've been on the phone since seven this morning!'

'OK. Well . . .' Francesca tried to think. Dave wanted six girls that afternoon for the first fitting of his designs. It didn't matter what they looked like from what she could gather, as long as they were the right shape. And that meant five-nine at least and not more than seven stone.

'Who else uses models round here? Anyone you can ring for help?'

Tilly shook her head. 'I can't think of anyone.'

'Oh God.'

'My sentiments exactly!' Tilly slumped down onto one of the odd chairs lying around and put her head in her hands. She looked like a schoolgirl in her grey tunic and black tights, desolately waiting outside the Headmaster's study.

'Schoolgirls!' Francesca suddenly said aloud.

'What?'

'Schoolgirls! We could try to find some girls in one of the local schools.' She was delighted with her flash of inspiration but to her amazement Tilly burst out laughing.

'Oh, Francesca! How many five-foot-nine schoolgirls am I gonna find by this afternoon?' She wiped her eyes on the back of her hand as she stopped laughing and Francesca realised she was perilously close to crying. 'Aw well, it was worth a try. Thanks, Francesca.' Tilly stood up and turned towards the reception desk.

'Hey, Tilly! You seen that number anywhere of the

student up at the college who came in yesterday?' Matt shouted above the din of the radio and Tilly shrugged. Then suddenly, she spun round, clapped her hands together and shrieked.

'You're bloody marvellous, you are!' She swamped Francesca in a fog of perfume and hair and hugged her tight. 'Bloody marvellous!'

'What? What have I said?'

'Schoolgirls! The fashion students up at the college have a list of 'em 'cause they can't afford models!' She looked across at Matt. 'I've got the number of the college on me desk, Matt! I'm just gonna ring 'em now. Any message?'

'Nah. Just pass the number on when you've finished.'

'Right, will do!' She looked back at Francesca. 'Thanks a lot, Francesca.' Then she smiled. 'That's a hell of a mouthful, ya know. I think I'll call ya Frankie.' She laughed gaily. 'After me hero, Frank Bruno!' And delighted with herself, she hurried back to her desk to ring the college, the hair and the trinkets all moving at the same time in one mass of noise and colour. Francesca watched, dazed by the speed and intensity of the encounter.

'Frankie,' she said aloud, and deciding she quite liked it, she put the mop in the bucket and began to tackle the mess Matt had left on the floor.

Mopping the floor was the last bit of sanity Francesca experienced that day. No sooner had she put her bucket away than the studio burst into life and she was hit with the full force of last-minute preparations for the first fittings of the collection. Everywhere, everyone seemed to be working twice their normal speed.

To begin with, the cutting tables were cleared, and great lengths of cloth were piled onto Francesca's outstretched arms so high that she could barely see over the top. She was

given six foot of space and had to measure each length, fold it neatly and then label it, stacking the newly made pile on one of the long racks of shelves against the back wall.

The floor was swept again, and the rails of half-finished clothes were wheeled into the centre of the studio where everyone could see them and take them to work on. Boxes of shoes were delivered from Freeze and Stable and Co., hats from Marian Dash, a new young designer who was showing with David Yates for the first time, and bags from Galeria 21. The once-cleared cutting tables were now crowded with all the accessories.

Next, Francesca collected the army of dummies that she had carried up that first day, fifteen in all, and each one heavier than the next. She gave them all names, to relieve the boredom of trudging up and down to the storeroom, and provided the one comic moment of the morning when she dumped Lorna-May on the studio floor and told her: 'Stay there, while I move these boxes out of the way.'

She had not noticed that the radio had been turned off for a minute while Dave was speaking and everyone in the studio heard her talking to the dummy. She got a tumultuous round of applause.

By midday, most of the preparations were over and the look of the first fitting was beginning to take shape. Tilly's name 'Frankie' had stuck and all morning Francesca had run round in all directions as 'Frankie' just seemed to roll off the tongue and was so easy to shout above the din of the radio. She hadn't stopped, no one had. Despite the intense work of the past few weeks there still seemed to be so much to do: last-minute alterations, re-cuts, trimming and hemming. Even though the clothes were still in the first stages, they had to look complete for Dave to be able to judge them properly.

At half past twelve, the morning was declared officially

over and Dave announced that everyone would be eating takeaway pizza for lunch, courtesy of David Yates. A cheer went up and Francesca collected orders, phoned them through and ran out to Marco Polo in Dean Street to pick up the eleven boxes.

There were six permanent staff altogether at David Yates: Tilly, who worked on the reception and did all the secretarial and admin; Evelyn and Cherry, the two tailors; Matt, the textile designer; Francesca, girl Friday; and Pete Walker, business manager. In the few short weeks that Francesca had worked there, however, she had only seen Pete Walker twice. She had no idea what he did exactly but whenever he was around he gave the air of being someone very important indeed.

For the first fitting of the collection there were also four extra people in the studio to help out, mainly students from the college who wanted the experience and didn't mind lending their services for an extremely cheap rate. Altogether this made eleven, extra large with all the toppings, pizzas to carry back and it was as much as Francesca could do to get them back in one piece.

Lunch over, the boxes were cleared away just in time for the models to arrive: six lanky, giggling schoolgirls aged between fourteen and sixteen and who looked about twenty-two. They shuffled in, momentarily embarrassed, and stood while Dave looked them over and decided who should try on what. Then he sent them over to the corner of the studio, screened to make a dressing room, and the rail of clothes was wheeled across. The afternoon's gruelling work began.

Francesca spent the next three hours behind the screens with Tilly, dressing and undressing the long, thin, undeveloped forms of the schoolgirl models. She styled hair, rummaged through boxes to find the right sort of shoe or

hat, put on jewellery, took it off, buttoned, zipped, unbut-toned, unzipped, squeezed, pinned, tucked, and tried, above all this, to catch some of what was going on on the other side of the screens. It was the most exciting and fas-cinating thing she had ever known.

Every now and then, in a momentary lull, she would peep round the screen and listen to Dave talking to Evelyn and Cherry about the cut of a coat or a jacket, drawing in chalk on it where he thought it should change, or pinning it to make the shape right, explaining what he meant by the design. She hung on every word he said to Matt about the prints, noting what colours he thought worked and how the pattern should fit in with the line and feel of the garment. She remembered her own designs at home, her own expe-rience of printing, and wished she could write it all down, just in case she forgot even one of the essential and inspir-ing comments.

Francesca totally lost track of time, so absorbed was she in the work. She hardly noticed the fatigue of constantly bending and straightening, of lifting and carrying or of the intense concentration it took to remove a garment that had been altered by Dave, so as not to move a pin or brush away any of the markings he'd made. By the time the last few items were seen, and finally removed from the girls, she managed to glance up at the clock on the wall and realised with a jolt that it was after six. The lights in the studio blazed and the sky outside wore a thick blanket of dark-ness, yet she had no recollection of just when the day had faded and the evening begun. It had all passed in a blur.

She helped the last two young girls dress – they were both stiff and aching from standing for so long – and then she stood and rubbed her own back, noticing for the first time that it really was quite sore.

'Frankie?'

She popped her head round the screen.

'Yes?'

'Christ! You look like the Punch and Judy show from behind there! Come out, for God's sake!'

She scurried round to where Dave was perched on the edge of the cutting table.

'That's better, now I can see you.' He smiled at the look of embarrassment on her face. 'It's all right, you're one of those women who were meant to be seen. Don't look so mortified by the idea!'

She nodded, wishing she could say something witty in reply.

'Look, Frankie, I know that you've worked unbelievably hard today and you must be knackered, but . . .' He shrugged apologetically. 'I'm going to have to ask you if you'd mind staying behind for a while tonight to clear up the debris of today and have it ready for us to start work on the alterations tomorrow.'

She felt a sinking feeling of disappointment at his request but she covered it as best she could.

'I know, it's a bummer! I'm sorry, but Matt has been banging on about starting straight away in the morning and I'm inclined to agree with him. If we don't clear tonight, most of tomorrow'll be gone by the time you get round everyone's mess and then we'll be a day out of sync. I just can't afford the time, I'm afraid, there's so much bloody alteration to do.' He reached out and patted her shoulder. 'I'm sorry, Frankie,' he said again and then he stood up, took his baseball cap off and rubbed his forehead. 'You don't mind too much, do you?'

She managed to shake her head convincingly.

'Good. I'd ask one or two of them to stay and help but I think I'd have a mutiny on my hands if I did.' He walked across the studio to his drawing table and picked up a pile

Contents

FOR MY PARENTS,
WITH LOVE

Acknowledgements

I would like to thank the following people:

Nancy Redfern, consultant anaesthetist at the RVI, Newcastle, for her medical advice, Rebecca Whitfield for her advice on fashion, Anthony Franzolin from the New York City Police Department, Andrew & Roz Joyner and the Lishman family for their friendship 300 miles from home, and finally Jules, for pretty much everything.

MB.

Dangerous Obsession

morning and even if she wouldn't, he would put an end to this ridiculous accusation once and for all.

Crossing the landing, he drew the curtains across the small stair window and stood on the top step, looking out at the cold grey sky and listening for the sound of Francesca sleeping. It was then that he heard the noises.

Hurrying over to the door of Francesca's room, he put his ear to it and listened more closely. The noises were of ripping paper, and he could smell something . . . He sniffed deeply. He could smell burning.

Turning the handle, he tried the door. It was locked.

'Francesca!' He tried again, rattling the handle. 'Francesca! What are you doing in there?' The smell increased. She was making a fire in the small Victorian grate. 'Francesca! That chimney hasn't been swept! Francesca! Open the door! Now!' He began to panic. The chimney for both bedrooms had not been swept for years; it could so easily catch light. In fact it was almost certain to.

'For God's sake, Francesca! Open the bloody door!' Losing patience and fuelled by his panic, John leaned his shoulder against the door and shoved hard, trying to budge the lock. Nothing happened. Standing back, he turned his shoulder towards the door again and this time pushed forward into it, using all his strength against it.

'Jesus!' His shoulder cracked against the door and suddenly it flew open. John was instantly propelled inside the room.

'Oh my God! Francesca!' He rushed over to her as she knelt in front of the small Victorian fireplace with a pile of her beautifully coloured designs and sketches, ripping them into tiny pieces, one by one, to add to the small fire she had made in the grate.

'Stop it! Francesca, stop it!' He pulled the pile away from her and grabbed the drawing already in her hands.

'Put it down,' he shouted. 'Stop being such a fool!'

She looked up at him, as if broken from a trance, and shook her head. He threw the drawings on the bed and ran out to the bathroom for water. Moments later he doused the fire and it sizzled and hissed, dying almost instantly, and a black, sooty smoke rose and billowed into the room. Francesca started to cough. As she spluttered her eyes watered, the tears streaming down her face, and she realised she was crying and how ridiculous it must all look. She let John take her hand and lead her out of the room onto the landing where she stood, weeping and watching the white and blue room fill with thick smoke.

John opened the windows in the bedroom and the bath-room and then on the stairs. He came back to her and watched as the room began to clear and the horrible smell died away. His heart was still pounding from the thought that the whole house might have gone up in flames.

Finally he turned to Francesca.

'I want you to get yourself dressed now, in the bath-room, while I wait here. All right?'

She nodded. She had been a fool, a complete idiot, she knew that, but laying in the dawn light, looking at the pieces of work that she had laboured over and loved, had filled her with such anger and frustration that she had had to destroy them. They were just another reminder of the happiness that had been snatched away from her.

Padding barefoot into the room, she glanced only once at the drawings while she picked up her clothes and then she walked through to the bathroom, closed the door and John heard the sound of her dressing. Minutes later she emerged washed and dressed and John took her downstairs.

'Sit down, Francesca.' They were in the long, narrow sitting room. The lamp was on and John had lit the small electric fire to take the chill off the room. Outside the sky

Dangerous Obsession

was leaden and grey, the wind swept down the road and the last of the autumn leaves blew with it, propelled along with little piles of dirt on each powerful gust.

Francesca sat on the edge of the sofa and picked at the corner of one of the tapestry cushions. She did not want to look at John.

'Francesca, I have something to say to you. It is something that I will only say once and something that perhaps I should have said a while ago. But . . .' He shrugged. 'I didn't want to interfere. Now, I feel I must.'

She kept her head down.

'Would you look at me please, Francesca?'

She tilted her face up and caught his eye.

'Thank you.' He took a breath. 'Francesca, I'm sorry but this can't go on. I have tried to be patient with you, I have tried to understand, but I have to admit that I don't, I don't understand and I don't sympathise. I know that the dismissal from David Yates was hard, I know that you must be upset, but you can't just hide away, take the blame for something you didn't do and accept it for no reason that I can see other than self-pity.' He stopped at this point; he knew he sounded hard but she needed a jolt.

She bit her lip but said nothing.

'Francesca, the world will always be tough, but you're strong and you can survive. What I want to know is when are you going to start fighting back? Hmmm? When will you learn to change what isn't right for you, what you find unacceptable? You can't just take everything that gets dealt out to you, and not even argue! It's not right. And it certainly isn't healthy.' He walked across to her and sat on the edge of the armchair facing her. 'Look at you, Francesca, you're tired, anxious, upset.' He took her hand. 'I hate to see you like this. You've got to learn to stand up for yourself, to do things like go to David Yates and tell him the truth. You can't always let everyone beat you, you mustn't.' He stroked her long, thin fingers with his own. 'I can't help feeling,' he said quietly, 'that you take it all as some kind of punishment, as if it was meant to happen.'

She pulled her hand away and turned her head so that he could not see the expression in her eyes. She had told him everything that night at Motcom, but she had not admitted her own feeling of guilt. She just couldn't, not then, not ever.

'You don't understand,' she said coldly.

'Yes! Yes, I do understand! Guilt and blame, that's what I understand!'

She looked back at him the moment he said those words.

'You see, I know. But I don't think it's right, to go on and on and on, blaming yourself, suffering for it.'

'How would you know?' She was angry now – he had touched the raw nerve. 'How would you know what it's like?'

'I don't,' he said simply. 'I am almost forty years older than you and I don't even pretend to know what it feels like, what you've suffered. I do know, though, that you cannot go on thinking that whatever happens to you is a punishment, some sort of bizarre sign from God. Guilt is very hard to live with, Francesca. It will destroy you if you let it.'

'Well, I won't let it!' She stood up and moved angrily away from him.

'Francesca, listen to me.' His voice was quieter now, softer. 'Please, just listen to me.' He looked at her back and saw her shoulders relax slightly. 'There are good things that come out of bad, you know, sometimes. Sometimes things that you never expected can happen, but you have to give them a chance. There is new life, even after disappointment and grief – if you fight for it, that is.'

She turned back to him. 'What if I don't want to fight?'

'Then you might as well give up now. You almost have anyway.' He saw her eyes flicker when he said that, he knew it hurt. He stood up and walked towards the door. Very quietly, he opened it and left the room. She didn't say a word to stop him.

For a long time Francesca stood at the window and looked out at the little piece of garden that was hers, its patch of newly dug earth, the bush she had planted last weekend, bought with the small amount of money she had saved from David Yates. She looked at the rickety fence, her fence, John's fence and the gate, not painted yet but primed, ready for its coat of deep, glossy green. Out of bad things come good, sometimes.

She thought about Giovanni, for the first time in many months, and then she thought about Patrick. From violence and murder had come love – no matter how brief, it was love. And out of deceit and disappointment had come this home and security and John. She blew on the glass and where it steamed up she drew a heart, her heart, and she was about to add the tear through the middle that she always did when she stopped and left it complete.

John was right. She had been happy, content at David Yates, she had begun to see a future. It was in her hands, she had the chance to change the situation if she wanted to. All she had to do was go and speak to him, explain what had happened. If he didn't believe her . . . She bit her lip anxiously. If he doesn't believe me, she thought determinedly, then at least I will have tried. Change what isn't right, John said, change what I can't accept. She turned away from the window and took a deep breath. Well, that's what I must do!

*

'John?' She stood at the door of the kitchen with her coat and beret on.

He turned, took off his reading glasses and looked at her.

'I'm going to see Dave,' she said. 'I think you're right, I should tell him what happened with Matt.'

John stood up. 'Shall I come with you?'

When he had woken this morning he had not expected to say what he had earlier and, just then, sitting alone in the kitchen, he wondered if he hadn't gone too far. Now he knew he had done right. 'Will you be all right on your own?'

'Yes, I'll be fine.' Her tone was strong and defiant. Then she smiled and added: 'I'm pretty scared, though.'

John smiled back. 'Don't be. I've every confidence in you.'

'Thanks.' She turned and her stomach lurched with nerves. She felt suddenly very sick.

'John you do think—?'

'Yes, I do. Go on now.' He walked her to the front door and opened it. 'Give 'em hell!' he said.

She nodded, tightened her coat around her, pulled her beret down over her ears and without thinking any further about it, stepped out into the thick, damp early-morning air and made her way down towards the bus stop.

Dave was curled up on a roll of very expensive cashmere and lambswool mix when he heard the persistent buzzer for the front door. But it took him quite some time to gain consciousness, remember where he was and finally to raise his head up and open his eyes. A painful and revolting ordeal.

'Ahhh, shit!' He put his hand up to his head and held his temples for a moment, which throbbed with a heavy, aching rhythm. 'Who the hell . . .?' He continued to hold his head as he sat fully upright but very slowly, his stomach inching up towards his mouth and threatening to spill out its contents. He groaned, stood, and immediately threw up into a smart black metallic wastepaper bin, retching for several minutes while the buzzing continued aggressively around him.

That over and feeling slightly better, he staggered over to the panel, carrying the bin, and released the main door, then staggered back across to the leather sofa in one corner of the studio and lay down on it, wondering why he hadn't done that last night. A vague memory of anger and frustration rose in his mind and then faded again, swamped by the terrible nausea in his stomach. He had no idea how he had got onto the roll of fabric on the cutting table; he was just thankful that he hadn't rolled off it and broken his back in the middle of the night.

He heard the doors of the studio open and he held up a hand to wave.

'Over here,' he warbled. The hand fell limply to his side again. Christ, he felt ill.

'Hello, Dave?' Francesca had crept over the floor of the studio, too nervous to allow her boots to make any noise. She stood looking down at Dave, his face unshaven, his hair frizzed and messy and his clothes crumpled and dirty. The whole place stank of booze. She knew the smell better than any other.

'Dave?' She said again, this time more quietly as her nerve began to fail her.

'Yeah?' He removed his arm from across his eyes and opened them slowly to look at whoever was interrupting his hangover. He saw Francesca, in her coat and black beret, and in an instant the whole of the previous night came back to him.

'Jesus frigging Christ!' He sat up suddenly and Francesca jumped back.

'Oh God, sorry! I didn't mean to—' He stood and clapped a hand over his mouth. ' 'Scuse me,' he mumbled and turning, leaning over the metallic bin at his side, he vomited once again.

'Urgh . . . Shit!' He wiped his mouth on the sleeve of his shirt and slumped down onto the sofa again. 'God, I'm sorry, it's disgusting!' He took a couple of deep breaths. 'Boy, am I glad to see you.' Resting his head against the back of the sofa, he closed his eyes for a moment, swallowing painfully. 'I owe you an apology, Francesca. Boy oh boy, do I owe you an apology! I've been one hell of an arsehole, I can tell you. An A1 frigging jerk!' He wiped his brow. 'I don't suppose you'd be kind enough to grab me something for my headache would you?'

She nodded.

'And a glass of water? My mouth tastes like a parrot's arse!'

Francesca returned five minutes later with the water, a cold damp cloth, the spare toothbrush she knew Dave kept in the kitchen drawer, pills, liver salts and a large black plastic bin liner to put over the offending wastepaper bin. One thing she certainly knew was how to deal with the results of a heavy night's drinking.

Dave had his eyes closed as she placed the things down on a chair in front of him. He opened one halfway and smiled.

'My God! Am I seeing things? I think it's an angel!'

She laughed.

'That sounds good, Frankie! I could use a little laughter.' He opened both eyes and sat forward, reaching for the toothbrush. She had even brought for him a bowl to rinse in. 'Were you ever a trainee nurse by any chance?'

'No . . . I . . .' She realised he was joking and looked away for a moment. Then she said: 'My father was an alcoholic.'

It sounded so simple put like that. Only she knew how much it took to admit.

'I'm sorry.'

'Yes, well . . .'

Dave got on with the business of cleaning his teeth and washing his face. He swallowed down three aspirins and fizzed up a large glass of liver salts before drinking them down in one.

'Urgh!' He shivered. 'The scourge of the masses! If I told you that I drink only once a year, on the anniversary of my Bar Mitzvah, then perhaps you'd know why I feel so bloody rough!' He put the glass down, rubbed his hand over his hair and looked directly at Francesca. 'Thanks, Frankie.'

She shrugged, embarrassed at his gaze.

'I suppose I'd better tell you what's been going on. It's a hell of a story, that's for sure! Oh, I forgot to ask, what are you doing here?'

She took a big breath. 'I, er, came to tell you about the night the drawings were stolen.' She sounded much more confident than she felt. 'I thought I should say something about—'

'About Matt. Yeah, I know. The little bastard stitched me up good and proper.' Dave took out his cigarettes and lit one up. The first drag made him shudder but the nicotine was good, he needed it. 'You know of course that I'm fin- ished! He laughed ironically. 'That raving little queen – in his first job as a textile designer – managed to bugger my business manager and run off with my collection. Pretty impressive, huh?'

Francesca sat stunned. 'What do you mean?'

'I mean, darling Frankie, that in the past year, Matt has been bumming round with my business manager, getting me to sign all sorts of things that I couldn't have given a toss about because I was too wrapped up in the sodding work, and then he runs off with Pete Walker, sets up his own label, his own fucking label, for Christ's sake! And uses all of my designs to launch it with! Ha! If I didn't want to kill the little shit I'd have to admire him for sheer bloody nerve.'

'But how can he do that? I thought the designs were yours?'

'Oh no, apparently not! I signed a little piece of paper that handed all creative rights over to my partner and business manager! I never even saw the bit of paper, let alone remember signing it!'

He stopped and stubbed the cigarette out, grinding it underfoot on the polished wood floor. Then he put his hands up to his face and ran them over the tired, sagging flesh. He looked up briefly at the beautiful teenage girl opposite him and saw all his failure in her bright young face. Years of work and sweat down the toilet! His collection was finished and in this climate he'd never recover.

'Frankie?' He removed his hands. 'D'you fancy a drink?'

But Francesca sat perfectly still and just stared at him. Somewhere in the pit of her stomach a knot had formed, like a fist, hard and strong inside her. Her mind was perfectly clear, strangely clear, and focused and determined.

'No,' she said. 'I don't want a drink, and nor do you.' She sat with her hands folded in her lap and continued to look at him. 'We're going to redesign your collection,' she went on, quite calmly, as if it were a simple statement of fact. 'We have, what, six weeks? If we take on an extra tailor and some-one to trim, it can be done. Not easily, but it can be done.'

He looked at her suddenly as if she had gone mad. 'You must be frigging joking!' he said and laughed. 'Frankie, I can't possibly turn out that kind of work in six weeks! And who's the "we" by the way?'

'It's me, and you, and everybody in the company. And I'm not joking.'

'Look, I'm really grateful for you being here and listening and all that, but Frankie, be serious! This isn't time for wild fantasies — what in God's name do you know about fashion — or textiles, for instance? I can't turn out a collection without a fabric designer – and printing? What about printing? Matt took care of all that shit, and his designs were magic, they—'

'They were never as good as you thought. You advised him, you told him what colours worked, what patterns looked best for what lines. Don't you remember?'

'Yeah, but—'

'But I know as much about printing as anyone. I've done it for years, in Italy! And I can design, I'll show you!' Francesca could hardly believe these words were coming out of her mouth. She couldn't stop herself, they poured out, along with all her fierce determination and strength.

'Just have a look at my designs,' she said. 'Just look at them, and if you don't like them, then maybe I was wrong about all this. It won't do any harm to look, will it?'

Dave watched her face as she spoke. Her eyes burned with passion – it was like the sun blazing into the green of an emerald – and she looked so full of hope. He took a breath. Maybe she was right, maybe he could do it. It wouldn't hurt him to have a look at her work anyway, and even if it wasn't any good, maybe she could help him sort the mess out here and he could get on with the work. She had a hell of a lot of spunk, that was for sure.

'Frankie,' he said. 'If you want me to look at your work, I'll look.' He saw her face light up with that peculiar smile of hers. 'I won't make any promises, though. Remember that, won't you?'

'Oh, yes, of course!'

'Look, can you ring round everyone and tell them the studios closed for the day? I need to go home and have a shower and a shave and then you can bring your stuff round. All right?'

'Yes, that's fine.'

'The numbers are in the book in Tilly's drawer and you'll have to do it now or else they'll all be on their way.' He stood, a little shakily, and smoothed back the wave of hair with his hand.

'I'll leave you in charge and expect you at my place about, what time? Eleven?'

She looked up at the clock, it was eight forty-five. 'Yes, eleven.' That should give her enough time to get home and collect up her stuff.

'My house is one of the mews houses in Brandling Village, past the school, number ten. Can you find it all right?'

'No problem.'

'Right!' He made a move towards the door and then on impulse turned back to her. 'Frankie? Have you had some sort of religious conversion? I've never seen you like this, ever?'

She laughed. 'No, I'm just taking the chance John told me about.'

'What?' He looked confused.

She shrugged and smiled. 'Nothing really.'

He felt too awful to pursue the matter. 'See you at eleven then,' he said, turning back to the doors and taking the offending wastepaper bin with him.

'Yes, see you!' She watched him go and then stood up and suddenly gave a yell of delight. Gathering up her coat and beret, she went through to Tilly's desk and found the book with all the numbers in. She sat down and began to dial the first one. She listened to the sound of the ringing tone and then the click of someone on the line. Out of bad comes good, sometimes, she thought.

John was amazed when, later that morning, Francesca ran into the house, calling out to him as she did so, then up to her room and down again in five minutes flat. She stood briefly in the doorway of the kitchen and he saw the clutch of drawings in her hand.

'I'm off to show Dave my work,' she said quickly. 'His house is in Brandling Village, I shouldn't be long!' She turned towards the front door and John called her back.

'What happened this morning?'

'Oh, John, it's so long I can't tell you now, Dave's expecting me at eleven. I'll come straight home and give you all the details when I'm finished.'

He looked at her. This was a different Francesca to the one that had gone out that morning. She seemed infinitely stronger, more confident.

'OK. Off you go! I'll see you later.'

She waved and hurried out of the front door, slamming it carelessly behind her in the rush. This was certainly a different Francesca, he decided, getting up to check she hadn't broken anything with the bang. Who knew what would happen next?

David Yates' house was a small mews house in one of the most exclusive parts of Newcastle. It was between two other houses, painted white with a glossy black front door and a bay tree outside it, in a dark Italian terracotta pot that Francesca noticed was discreetly chained to the wall. You couldn't leave your washing out in Newcastle.

She banged the heavy brass knocker and stood back waiting for the front door to open. She straightened her beret and turned the collar of her coat up. She wanted to look her best when he saw her.

'Oi! Frankie!' She looked behind her, confused for a moment.

'No! Up here!'

She glanced up. Dave was hanging out of the bathroom window, shivering at the cold rain against his bare chest.

'Here! Catch!' He threw a key down to her. 'Let yourself in, will you, I haven't finished in the shower yet.' She bent and picked up the key, then looked up at the window again. He had closed it tight and gone back inside. She let herself into the house and realised in the warmth just how wet she was. Pulling off her beret, she hung it on one of the brass coat hooks in the entrance porch and then took off her coat, placing that on top. She wandered into the hall and on through to the sitting room.

The house had been completely converted, she could see that at first glance. The small narrow facade outside gave no indication of the airy space within, with its light Scandinavian pine floors, cream walls and huge open sitting room. She stood just inside the door and thought, hmmmm, this is the house of a designer, and then smiled at how much she had learned since she started at David Yates.

The sitting room was sparsely furnished – just two big gold brocade sofas with high straight sides and huge feather cushions, a long dark wood Regency table along one wall that had a pile of antique books on it and a bronze figure, which she later found out was Art Deco by Ferdinand Preiss. The fireplace had no surround; it was simply a space carved in the chimneypiece, painted cream with a heavy black iron grate in the bottom. To one side of that was a collection of what looked like antique earthenware pots, all varying heights and shapes, perfectly arranged, and finally, on either side of the chimney in the alcove, sat a pair of

Regency mahogany sabre-legged chairs, both upholstered in a dark gold velvet.

'You like it?'

Francesca jumped. She had forgotten that Dave was upstairs and she had been staring quite intently at the room, taking in every last detail.

'Gosh, yes, I . . .' She stuttered with embarrassment.

'Go on in and sit down. D'you want a coffee?' She looked over her shoulder at him as he jumped down from the last stair, pulling his sweatshirt over his head. She noticed how brown the skin was on his stomach and how it stretched tightly over the muscle.

'Oh, yes, er, thanks.' She went into the room and perched nervously on the edge of the sofa. She was still clutching her work.

'That your work?' Dave came through the connecting archway from the kitchen.

'Yes.'

'Can I see?'

She suddenly felt ridiculous. Looking at this glorious room, its perfect shape and detail, she regretted that she had ever asked him to look at her designs. How could someone with this expert eye ever see anything in her pathetic little sketches? She kept hold of the drawings and looked down at the floor.

'Come on, let me have a look!' He smiled, recognising her sudden anxiety. 'I won't say anything too wicked, I promise.' He crossed to her and she held out the pile of work. 'Look, I'll take it into the kitchen, spread it out on the table there and have a glance through while I'm making the coffee. That way neither of us will be embarrassed. Right?'

She nodded. The confidence of that morning had completely deserted her.

'Put a CD on if you want. I won't be long.' He

273

disappeared with the pile of work and Francesca glanced about her for the stereo. 'It's out in the hall,' he shouted. 'In the under-stair cupboard.' She wondered if he could read her mind. 'I hate the sight of all things practical!' She stood up and went to see if she could find it.

Dave sat in the kitchen at the long marble-topped table with Francesca's pile of work spread out in front of him and an A4 drawing pad on his knee. Behind him the coffee pot on the hob bubbled and hissed away, the smell of burned coffee filling the air. He was completely oblivious to it. His mind buzzed and his fingers worked, quickly and deftly, the lines and shapes fitting together on the pages of his pad, as he scribbled endless variations, notes, ideas, and brilliant design after brilliant design.

The fabric designs he had before him were far better than anything he had seen for years and they outshone Matt by a million miles. They were breathtaking, real talent, the sort of talent that comes along once in a lifetime, and Dave sat mesmerised by them, filled with inspiration and the joyous knowledge that he had discovered something magnificent.

Meanwhile, Francesca remained in the sitting room, listening to the mellow, upbeat sound of Black Box and tapping her toe anxiously to the beat of the music. She didn't know what to do.

Dave had been in the kitchen for twenty minutes now and she could smell the coffee, its aroma becoming more and more acrid as it burned on the stove. He had not uttered a word. Several times she had decided to get up and go in to see what he thought, but her courage had faded as soon as she stood up and she'd sat back down again instantly, pretending to herself that she was involved in the music.

Finally, she could stand it no longer; the suspense was making her feel sick. She stood purposefully, bit her lip and strode across the sitting room to the arch. Just as she did so Dave was coming out of the kitchen and they collided head on.

'Ouch!'

'Oh, shit! Sorry!' He caught her as she was about to topple off the two steps down to the kitchen and they swayed precariously for a moment.

'Whoooa!' They regained their balance and Dave kept hold of her. He looked down at her face, young and eager and hopeful and terrified, all at once. 'You, my darling Frankie,' he said gently, 'are a star!' And then, unable to stop himself, he bent forward and kissed her, long and hard on the lips.

She pulled back suddenly, her cheeks hot and flushed. She didn't know whether to laugh or cry.

'You like my drawings?'

'No, I don't "like" your drawings, I absolutely frigging love your drawings! They are fantastic!' He bent and kissed her again. 'They are more than fantastic, they are incredible!' He started to laugh. 'Frankie, I'll be honest, I never even dreamed you could design like that, never in a million years! Never in a trillion, squillion years!' He took her hand and led her into the kitchen.

'Now, you, little Frank, are going to sit in there and tell me exactly what you know about printing and then we are going to work out just how we can get this thing off the ground.'

'What thing?' She had begun to feel dizzy. She wasn't sure whether it was the excitement or the shock of the kiss or the terrible smell of the coffee.

'The new David Yates collection! Here!' He pulled out a chair. 'Sit!'

She meekly did as she was told. 'Er, Dave?'

'Uh-huh?' He was leafing through the work again.

'There's just one thing before we start.' He glanced up.

'What's that?'

'Do you think you could turn that coffee off? I think it must be done by now.'

John looked at his watch for the fourth time that hour and wondered what he should do. He had called the studio twice, got no reply and then tried to find David Yates' number in the telephone directory – it was ex-directory.

He drummed his fingertips on the kitchen table where he was unsuccessfully trying to do the crossword and thought that perhaps he should try the studio one more time. It was beginning to grow dark and he was worried about Francesca.

It was just then that he heard the faint sound of voices at the front door and the sound of the key in the lock. He hurried through the hall to the front door.

'John!' A wet and smiling Francesca stood on the step and behind her was a tall, dark-haired man in an American baseball cap and a brown leather RAF flying jacket. 'John, this is Dave Yates.' She moved aside and John took in the full appearance of Francesca's former employer. They shook hands and John ushered them in. He was not impressed. As he took Dave's jacket, he noticed the scruffy ponytail at the back of his head and held down the disapproving tut that came automatically to his lips.

'Er, come in.' He led the way into the front room. 'Would you like a drink?'

Dave shook his head. 'Thanks all the same, but I had a bit too much last night.' He smiled but John only nodded, straight-faced. Dave sensed his hostility.

'Look, John, I'm sorry about barging in on you like this

but I wanted to talk to you about something.' Dave cleared his throat nervously. 'Apart from bringing Francesca home that is, of course.'

'Yes, of course.' John stood his ground, his lips in a tight line.

Dave thought: I must be frigging mad! He'll never agree, no matter what Francesca said. And then: Do I want him anyway, miserable old Scot?

Still he went on: 'I think I had better explain briefly what's been going on the last few days at my company and then I'll tell you why I'm here.'

John nodded.

'Firstly, the business of the drawings that were taken from my studio. I know how worrying it must have been for you and I can only apologise for the terrible mistake I made. I've explained it all to Francesca and I think she understands, but it wasn't until last night that I found out the truth, you see, and I'd been led to believe that Francesca was responsible. Anyway,' he took a deep breath, 'the drawings, if you can believe this, had been taken by my textile designer, as Francesca suspected, and he has, God knows how, managed to stitch me up, along with my so-called business manager, so that my whole collection is now completely out of my hands.'

John sat down. 'Oh dear, I'm sorry about that.'

'Yeah, well, so was I until this morning.' Dave glanced at Francesca at this point and she blushed. 'The thing is, I've decided to start all over again.'

John raised an eyebrow. 'That sounds like an awful lot of work!' Francesca mentioned to me what was involved the first time round.'

'It is!' Dave came forward and sat down opposite John. 'To most people, it probably sounds pretty impossible and I'd have thought so myself until Francesca showed me her work. But when I saw it, I knew I couldn't turn down this chance. She has a real talent, John! Her colour, feel of the fabric, design, pattern, everything, it's miles better than anyone out there already. With her on my team I'm sure this could be a major collection, and if not, it can only get better!'

He stopped, suddenly aware of John's silence. 'None of this is bullshit,' he said quietly. 'I can't afford to lose this collection, my whole company could go under if I did.' Then he stood up, moving to the fireplace. 'What I wanted to ask you, John, was if you would consider coming in with me and running the studio?' He paused for a moment but he did not look at John. He wasn't at all sure what his reaction would be. 'Part of the problem before, you see, was that I didn't have time to look after the admin. I let things get on top of me and that's how I lost so much, I guess.' Dave looked at John now. He could see the hostility had been dropped and it gave him confidence to go on.

'Francesca told me that you're used to running things, accounts, admin and staff. I need someone I can trust. I need someone who'll leave me free to do the work I'm good at. D'you understand?'

John returned Dave's direct stare. 'Yes, I understand. But I'm not at all sure that you are talking to the right person, Mr Yates—'

'Dave.'

'Dave. I know nothing about fashion design, or clothes or commerce, and to be quite frank, I really don't think that I would be suitable.'

'John!' Francesca burst out. 'You would be brilliant!'

'Francesca, please!'

'No, really, John, you would be!'

He smiled finally at her blind confidence in him and it broke the ice. Everyone smiled.

'Dave, perhaps you could tell me a little more about the business, about your suppliers, retail outlets, that kind of thing?'

'Yes, of course.' He grinned. 'Actually, I've got some of the business files in the car. I was rather hoping you might want to look at them. Shall I get them?'

John laughed. 'Yes, go on and get them.' He suddenly felt part of a great new scheme and his adrenaline began to flow. As Dave crossed to the door he said: 'I have the feeling that this is going to take quite some time. Am I right?'

Dave nodded.

'Well then, perhaps you would like to join us for supper, Dave?'

Dave nodded again and smiled. The miserable old Scot was beginning to cheer. He glanced at Francesca and she grinned, like a schoolgirl. 'Thank you, John,' he answered. 'I'd love to stay for supper.' And he went out to fetch the accounts.

Later, when dinner had been eaten and all the arguments raised and discussed, John finally lifted his glass to drink a toast to the new David Yates and Francesca Cameron collection, managed by John McBride. They drank to it.

It was the beginning of something new, a chance that had to be taken, and as she sipped the wine and looked over the top of her glass at John and Dave Yates discussing their future, Francesca knew that it had to be right. She was filled with a fierce determination to make it so, to put her heart and soul into it, and to prove that she could change her own life. Out of bad things come good, sometimes, John had said, and you have to give these things a chance. He was right. Out of bad things come good, sometimes – if you have the wisdom to look for them, that is.

CHAPTER

Twenty-two

THE FOLLOWING DAY WAS A Saturday but to Francesca,
John and Dave this made no absolutely difference – it was
business as usual. It was by now well into November and
there were just six weeks to go before everything had to be
ready. London Fashion Week was at the beginning of
February and the collection had to be ready for the end of
December. There was PR to organise: press packs, a photo
shoot, and Dave had already booked office space in Covent
Garden for the week after Olympia, so that buyers could
view the collection. It felt, waking up on that first morning,
as if there was not even a minute to waste.

Dave had ended up staying the night on Friday. They
had talked for hours, long and hard, discussing ideas and
making notes, all three fired by a zealous enthusiasm. By the
time John cleared away the coffee things, it was the early
hours of the morning and it seemed easiest to throw a blanket onto the couch for Dave, sleep for a few hours and then
start all over again in the morning. There was so much to be
done.

Francesca woke at eight, knowing she was the first up.
She padded downstairs in her robe and bare feet to make
the coffee, trying to be as quiet as she could but feeling the
whole time as if she could sing at the top of her voice,
shout, bang all the pots and pans, and laugh with excitement. She crept into the kitchen, though, silently drew back
the little patterned curtain and crossed to the sink to fill the
coffee pot, keeping the tap on trickle so as not to make any

noise. She turned to put the coffee into it, reaching out to switch on the ring of the electric hob, and, as she did so, she caught sight of Dave in the doorway, standing barechested, in a pair of checked boxer shorts, and watching her with a funny smile on his face.

'That's a very attractive dressing gown.'

'Oh! I . . . Dora gave it to me.' Francesca looked down at the huge, faded towelling robe. She had pulled it in tight with the belt but it was still heaps too big and made her look like a little old bag lady.

'Who, my darling Frank, is Dora? And does she not like you or something?'

Francesca smiled. 'You are horrible!'

'I told you so, the first day you came into my den.' He walked into the kitchen and came to stand by the Aga, which was giving out a steady heat. He folded his arms across his chest and leaned back against the front of it, warming his bottom.

Francesca looked away from him and tried to concentrate on the coffee. His body was long and lean, much more muscled than she had thought it would be, and his skin was nutty brown, not tanned as such, just dark, the colour of roasted almonds. He looked ruffled, slept in, his hair was loose and she realised it was thick and wavy, cut to just beneath his ears.

'Hurry up with that coffee, will you?' He was looking up at the rows of glass jars on the shelves when he said this and she glanced at him out of the corner of her eye. His comment irritated her and she frowned.

'The one thing you're going to have to get used to, working closely with me,' he continued, still looking up at the shelves, 'is that I can't stand waiting for anything?' She moved away from him and held down an angry retort. When she looked round a minute or so later, to find the cups, she saw him doubled over with silent laughter.

'God, Frankie,' he sniggered. 'You are so easy to wind up!' And, still convulsed, he staggered out of the kitchen to find his clothes.

The three of them had breakfast in the kitchen and then, leaving the mess for later, they left for the studio in Dave's car. There was a sort of unspoken agreement between them that for the next few days they would do everything together and the only thing that mattered was the work. By the time the team arrived on Monday morning, Dave wanted to be sure they all had something to look forward to, that David Yates had a future. He felt a tremendous loyalty to his staff and saving the company was as much for them as for himself.

Arriving at the studio, Dave parked down on the Quayside by Hanrahans and unlocked the main door of the building, answering John's questions about leases and property values in that area of town. He led them up the long and narrow staircase and John made a note of the damp patches in his book. Opening the door of the studio, Dave switched on the panel of lights and the huge warehouse space was instantly illuminated. John stood with Francesca in the doorway and looked at what lay before him. He was filled with pride. I will make this place run like clockwork, he thought; we will make David Yates into one of the best labels in the UK.

'Right! Come on in! John, we hang the coats over there, kitchen's on your left, lays on the right and the storeroom is down a flight.' Dave had already taken off his jacket and was walking across to his drawing table. 'Have a good poke around while I get myself sorted and find Frankie some space over there. Make a note of anything you want to ask and give us a shout when you've finished. All right?'

John nodded, took off his coat and went to hang it up.

Francesca trailed behind Dave to the drawing tables.

'Here, Frankie! Catch!' Dave threw her a baseball cap, purple with a white and gold golfing badge on it. 'Put it on.' She pulled a puzzled face and then slipped the cap onto her head.

'No! Pull it forward a bit, and adjust the peak.' She did as she was told.

'Great! Now at least you look the part.' He smiled. 'Come on over here and start clearing that arsehole's rubbish off the board, will you? It's yours now, to cover with anything you like, even pictures of Jason Donovan, if you want!'

At eleven, they took a coffee break. Francesca and Dave had been working steadily for two hours, both completely silent, totally absorbed in the drawings. They had agreed on a colourway before they started and Dave had given Francesca a short brief to stick to. He wanted designs for silk, daytime, informal, for a line that was loose but tailored. He was working along a completely new train of thought, classic-cut wool blazers with silk sarong skirts and loose pyjama trousers, pencil-cut wool trousers, with long silk tunics and turbans. It was the simple and the ornate, the clean cut and the flowing; both had to work, and both had to connect perfectly. Francesca knew exactly what he meant.

As he drew the lines, she filled in the forms. She designed great swirls of muted colour, in mauve and deep reds with black and indigo slashes. She drew intricate patterns of squares, reminiscent of Paul Klee, the colour as brilliantly matched as his, all seeming to glow individually and yet merge together to form a coherent whole. She focused in on one colour, a crimson or a gold, and she mixed shade after shade of this colour, each one just a fraction different until she had found a whole spectrum of hues within one tint. She worked almost nonstop from the moment they arrived and when it was time to take a break, Dave had to literally drag her away from her drawing board.

'So, John? What horrors did you find to torment me with?' Dave carried the bag of cappuccino coffees that had just been delivered from Marco Polo over to the sofa. He took out the steaming plastic cups and handed them round.

'All morning I've had this kind of dread that you'd find something nasty in the corner and walk out disgusted!' He laughed and poured two sachets of sugar into his coffee, stirring it with the end of the pencil he drew out from behind his ear.

'Well, actually I did!'

'No shit?'

'Yes, but I decided to stay.'

Dave laughed again. 'So, tell me what you found.'

'OK.' John opened his notebook. 'Firstly, the damp. I need to see a copy of the lease agreement, but I'm pretty sure the landlord has to fix that. If he doesn't then you can get a reduction on the rent, argue something like unfit working conditions. Second, I noticed when we came in that the heating was on full blast. Do you have some kind of timer switch?' Dave shrugged.

'OK. If not, we'll get one – it should save a lot of money on heating bills. Third, leftover fabric. What happens to it?'

Again Dave shrugged.

'Well, it could be measured and sold as remnants. Longer lengths can go to the college maybe, for the fashion depart- ment – it could bring in a fair amount. Fourthly, accessories. You should have some kind of promotional deal going with all the people who provide the accessories.'

'I do, they give them for free.'

'So they should! How many times have you been in one

284

of the fashion magazines in the past twelve months? Say *Vogue* or the *Face*?'

Francesca looked up at John's sudden knowledge of style and fashion and smiled.

'I dunno, six, maybe seven times.'

'Right! And every time you've used Marian Dash hats or Freeze shoes, it's free advertising for them. These people would normally pay through the nose for that kind of thing and they get it free off your back.'

'I never thought of it like that.'

'No, but I bet this Pete Walker chappie did! I wouldn't be surprised if there wasn't something going on that front straight into his pocket.' John smiled, pleased with himself. 'I'm pretty sure we can organise some kind of deal with several of the accessory suppliers – they use your garments in their adverts, that kind of thing, and probably a substantial sum as well.'

'Christ! That just never occurred to me.'

'No,' John said. 'Filthy . . .'

And so it went on. In thirty minutes John highlighted ten points that needed immediate action and Dave sat there dumbstruck. He was relieved that John was so thorough but he was also livid that he'd let himself be stitched up for so long just because of his own ignorance. He felt the pangs of self-pity at ever having come across bastards like Walker and Baker, and then he glanced across at Francesca and saw his future in her face. The self-pity evaporated and a steely determination took its place.

'All right then, if that's all, I think I'll get back to work.' He stood, his fingers itching to get back to the drawing board.

'There is one more thing.'

'Uh-huh?'

'I wanted your permission to ring my old employer for

the name of his solicitor. I think we need a good legal firm on our side right from the beginning.'

Dave was staring out of the window and John waited patiently for his reply.

'Dave?'

He looked back. 'Yeah? What? Oh, sorry.'

'The solicitor?'

'Yes, of course, John.' He turned and then looked over his shoulder. 'Look, you're in charge now, John,' he said. 'I trust your judgement. Do whatever you think is right.'

And he went back to his designs, leaving those words hanging in the air. For John, they were the best words he could have heard.

On Sunday evening, at eleven-fifteen, Francesca and Dave sat down together on the leather sofa and went over their work to finalise the details. In front of them, they had the first drafts of the collection.

John made what felt like the hundredth pot of coffee of the day, handed out the cups and sat opposite them on one of the directors' chairs, sipping and watching the two of them talk it through. He was exhausted himself, trying up all the loose ends, going over the accounts with a fine-tooth comb, analysing the expenditure for the coming months. It was going to be tight, he knew that, very tight, but he didn't want to say anything about that, not yet anyway. He would worry about the business while Dave and Francesca worried about the work. When everything was in place, though, if the collection worked, then David Yates could be back in the black by the third month of next year and from then on it would be head down and fast forward.

He looked across at Francesca and could see how tired she was. Her face was drained of colour and she had faint shadows under her eyes from lack of sleep. But he could also see how alive she was, how vibrant, and he could see how the work inspired her. She spoke about it with a confidence he never knew she possessed, with a knowledge and assurance, as if at last she had found out who she was and now felt certain and comfortable in this new identity.

Dave watched her too. He could see such a startling difference in her, from the shy, nervous girl who had walked into his studio just four weeks ago, into this sparkling, animated creature beside him who just made him glow just sitting near to her. The glimpses he had caught of her face when she smiled before, of its beauty and life, gave no real indication of how she looked now. She was radiant, her eyes burned, and the smile, so forceful in its loveliness, was there all the time, behind her eyes and on her lips. He was drawn to this passion, he wanted to touch her, to check she was real, and as he looked at the work she had produced in just twenty-four hours he wanted to kiss her, overwhelmed with the absolute enormity of her talent.

'Well, I think, my darling Frankie, that just about wraps it up!' He turned the last sketch over and stretched out his legs. 'I don't know about you two, but I am fucking knackered!'

John coughed.

'Sorry.' This had been the pattern of the past two days: every time Dave swore, John coughed or tutted and Dave apologised. It seemed to work quite well for both of them. 'You look tired, Frankie.' Dave reached out and brushed the lock of hair that had fallen over her forehead. She was growing it and it hung in varying lengths, getting in her way and not long enough yet to tie the back or style.

She nodded. 'Do you think we have everything ready for Evelyn and Cherry to start on tomorrow?' She turned back to one of Dave's designs.

'Yup. They'll get on with the paper patterns while you

start work on the printing. I've rung Charlie, by the way – he's the technician at the print studio – and told him to expect you tomorrow at eight.'

Francesca pulled a face.

'Oi-oi, not fed up with it already? It was your idea, you know.' Dave smiled and pulled his cap down the way Francesca was wearing hers. 'We can design the whole collection,' he said, *sotto voce*. 'Just you and me, in one afternoon!'

Francesca started to laugh and slapped him on the thigh.

'I'm just tired, that's all!'

'Of course you are. So get your things together and piss off home! And take that miserable old Scot with you as well.' John smiled. 'Come on, Francesca.' He couldn't bring himself to call her Frankie. 'He's right, let's get off now.'

She stood. She was nervous about the morning, a new studio to visit, different print equipment. She wasn't sure how she would cope. She hovered uneasily, wondering if she should say something.

'Charlie is a nice old bugger,' Dave said, getting to his feet and stretching. 'He'll show you how everything works and give you all the help you need. He's rather partial to attractive women, is our Charlie.'

Francesca smiled up at him. He always seemed to know what she was thinking.

'Go on, go home, Frankie and McBride.' Dave bent and kissed Francesca on the top of her head. 'Get some beauty sleep, not that you need it.' He turned to John. 'That was Francesca I was talking about, not you. You could use all the help you can get!' He laughed. 'Have you decided what you're going to say in the morning?'

'Pretty much. If you still think I should tell the staff, that is.'

'It's a good way to start, John – let them know who's in

charge right from the word go!' He held out his hand, suddenly serious. 'Thanks, John. I mean, for everything you've done.'

John was touched. Dave was tough on the outside but pretty decent underneath, if only he'd get himself a good haircut. He smiled. 'See you tomorrow then. Ready, Francesca?'

Francesca had collected up her drawings and was scrabbling around in her rucksack for the car keys John had given her. She found them and held them up. 'Ready,' she said, and linking his arm, she walked with John across the studio and out through the double doors to the staircase.

'I must ring that chap that Lord Henry recommended to me in the morning,' John said as they began to descend the stairs. 'Get something sorted about this damp.' He ran his finger over the damp patch and tutted.

'What chap was that?'

'He works for Lord Henry's legal firm and although Lord Henry hasn't used him, he has a good reputation, apparently.'

'Oh really? What's his name?'

John thought for a moment. He was tired and couldn't remember it offhand. 'Er, Bracken somebody,' he said. 'That's it, Richard Bracken.'

Francesca stopped. 'How odd,' she said. 'I don't know why but that name sounds terribly familiar.'

John shrugged. 'They're all called Richard or James or Michael, solicitors. It probably just sounds like something else you've heard.'

She smiled. 'Probably,' she answered, and letting it go out of her mind, she carried on down the stairs.

Francesca stood straight and lifted the length of fabric from the print table, gently holding it aloft to check the colour before taking it over to the drying rack and clipping it into place. She stepped back a pace and took a long, hard look at it, running her eye over the intricate shapes of the pattern, and peering closely at how the dye had taken to the fabric and how the colour was now beginning to match that of her design. Satisfied, she moved back to the print table and removed the screen ready for cleaning. This was the part of the job that most people hated but for Francesca there was satisfaction in it: the final chore of a day's work, it meant the completion of the task well done.

She doused the screen with turps, scrubbed off all the ink and wiped it clean. She repeated this several times until the mesh was spotless, then focused in on the table and did the same thing. It took nearly an hour, the smell was disgusting and by the time she had finished the bin was full of dirty, inky paper. She placed it with the others to be collected in the morning and took off her rubber gloves, breathing a sigh of relief. Moving back over to the drying rack, she took another look at the seven lengths of fabric that hung there, all in various stages of completion.

It was now Thursday and she had printed a different colour each day so far. For some of the designs, this meant they now had four colours and were starting to take shape; for others, the crimson she had been working with today was the first or second dye and they were still in their early stages. She was working systematically, printing all the base colours in the designs first and building on top of these. It was painstaking work, but she loved it. She spent every waking moment at the print studio and when she was there she was so absorbed in her work that Charlie had to practically drag her away to get her to eat.

Gazing up at the designs, her mind buzzing with ideas, Francesca stood, leaning back against the edge of the print table and rubbing her fingers thoughtfully back and forth

over her chin. She ran her hand through her hair, swept
back the persistent lock that kept falling forward into her
eyes and tutted irritably to herself. She was so preoccupied
with thought that she didn't hear Dave come into the studio, not had she any idea that he stood watching her, for
quite some time, before he made his presence known.

It was the first time Dave had seen Francesca for days
and once again he was fascinated by the change in her.
Even in his short separation from her she had grown. She
seemed more self-contained than shy now, more confident
and her face was even lovelier than he remembered. Her
body looked different too, fuller, more womanly, and she
held it differently – she stood straighter and looked taller.
He smiled to himself. If anyone could hear his thoughts,
they would say he was smitten, had a bad case of the hots.
Mind you, he thought, letting his eyes run the length of her,
no one could blame him if he had.

He walked right into the studio and silently came to
stand beside her, waiting for her to turn and spot him. He
glanced sidelong at her face and saw that where she had
rubbed her chin it was covered in ink and in brushing back
her hair she had plastered her forehead with it as well. He
burst out laughing.

'Oh! My goodness!' Francesca visibly jumped and put
her hand up to her pounding heart. 'You scared the hell out
of me!'

'Sorry,' he managed to say when he had stopped laughing. He pulled his face straight and saw that he really had
frightened her. 'Sorry,' he said again. 'Honestly, I didn't mean
to upset you.'

She shrugged and tried to calm the panic in her chest.

'It's all right,' she answered quietly.

'No, it's not all right. Here.' He took her hand and led her
over to the workbench. 'You've got ink all over your face.'

he said gently. 'Stand there and I'll get a hanky and clean it off for you.' He bent and found a box of tissues under the bench, then he went to the sink, filled a cup with water, picked up the soap and came back to her.

He smiled, still finding her appearance terribly funny. 'How on earth did you manage to get it all over your mush? Huh?' He sat her on the edge of the bench and leaned over her, dipping a tissue into the water, rubbing some soap onto it. He put it up to her cheek. She flinched.

'Hey! Hold still! I can't do it if you jog about all the time now, can I?' He buffed her skin and looked at the tissue. 'Ugh! It's everywhere! Here.' He wetted another tissue and tried the patch above her eye, by her hairline. He glanced down at her face as he did so and saw she had both eyes shut and was perched, rather impatiently and irritably, waiting to be cleaned, like a child with a dirty face. He stared at the shape of her face for a second and inadvertently his hand slipped and dug her in the eye.

'Ouch!' She leaped up in pain and put her hand to her eye. She caught him on the chin with the top of her head as she did so and their faces bumped together. Suddenly, without thinking what he was doing, Dave cupped her face with his hands and guided her lips to his own. He kissed her and held her still until he could feel her respond. He let her come up for air.

'Oh, I . . .'

He kissed the corner of her mouth. 'You what?'

'I don't know.' Francesca was disorientated, confused. She was surprised by the kiss and even more surprised at how nice it was. Her body was sending out strange signals and her face flushed with the frantic beat of her heart.

'Frankie?'

She pulled back and tilted her face up. 'What?'

He slipped his hands down her back and kissed her

again. 'Got you!' But this time the kiss was different. Parting her lips with his own, he darted his tongue inside and tasted the sweet warmth of her mouth. He heard her gasp and try to pull away but he held her firm. She relaxed, and moments later, kissed him back. Her head was swimming, it had disowned her body, and as his mouth travelled down her face to her neck and his fingers slipped inside the hem of her shirt she felt completely beyond control. She wanted to call out but he pressed against her and it felt so good that she was unable to utter a word. Within seconds, he had unfastened the buttons on her shirt and his lips had moved down to kiss the hollow of her neck. She gasped, loving the feel of the cool air on her skin, and her fingers were tangled in his hair. He lifted her onto the bench. Her shirt fell off her shoulders and her breasts were visible through the thin chiffon of her camisole, the nipples hard. She leaned back against the bench, her whole weight pressed back and the hard shape of her bag digging into her back. Seconds later, her rape alarm went off.

'Jesus! Fuck!' Dave sprung back and the piercing scream of the alarm enveloped them, deafening and shocking. He put his hands up to his ears and screamed at her. 'What the fucking hell is that!'

Francesca knew exactly what it was. John had bought it for her the day she started work. She leaped up and spun round, knowing that she must have set it off with her bottom. Reality hit her with a sudden blow and she scrabbled to pull her shirt together and find her bag. She had to get out of there! Jumping down off the bench, it took seconds for her to get herself together. She held her shirt with both hands, gripped the bag to her chest and with the alarm still screaming, she flew out of the studio.

Dave was left standing there, stunned and dazed with the

taste of her on his lips and the annoying problem of a rock-hard erection.

'God damn and shit!' He strode to the door but he knew she had gone. The noise had stopped and the pavement outside was deserted. She could run like hell, he thought, adjusting his shorts to accommodate his size.

'God damn and shit!' he said again, and stepped outside, slamming the door shut behind him.

Exactly the same expletives were uttered at exactly the same time but three hundred miles away, in a flat in Mayfair, by Lady Margaret Smith-Colyne. The only difference was, these words were uttered very faintly, under her breath, and Charles, concentrating only on himself, was completely oblivious to them. She couldn't afford to be interrupted, not the first time, so she let the telephone ring on.

'How about this then?' he said at last.

She glanced over her shoulder at him and saw that he had finally managed something reasonably impressive. She purred and smiled.

Standing, legs apart with her back to him, Lady Margaret presented him with the naked curve of her full, milky-skinned bottom. Since her thighs were encased in black shiny leather boots and her mid-section was laced into a black leather corset, it was the only part of her flesh that could be seen from the back.

At the front, however, her large, creamy breasts hung over the top of the corset and rubbed up against the marble of the fireplace where her hands were bound with the silk of Charles Hewitt's Old Etonian tie. She moved her hips provocatively and pretended to struggle with her bondage.

She heard Charles' breathing quicken.

'Come over here, darling,' she whispered.

He crossed the room and she saw his reflection in the

mirror above the mantelpiece. He was flushed and sweating and held his stomach in so that it didn't roll over the top of the leather jockstrap he wore. He slipped the pouch down and moved towards the swell of her rump.

'Hmmm, that's good . . . '

Suddenly, without warning, he took her and she gasped, mainly with surprise, but then managed to remember to moan loudly. She thought about where she was and caught a glimpse in the mirror of the face she had seen so often in the circles of power. Her excitement rose and, wriggling her hips, she leaned forward, closed her eyes and verbally gave it her all.

It was over in a matter of minutes and Lady Margaret breathed a sigh of relief. She felt Charles attempt a second go and for one tricky moment was unsure of quite what to do. Then, right on cue, the telephone rang for the second time. Thank God, she thought, raising her eyes upwards to heaven, saved by the bell.

Padding naked across to the side table, Lady Margaret wriggled her hands out of the silk tie and picked up the receiver, crooking it between her head and shoulder. Charles discreetly left the room to dress.

'Hello.'

'Margaret?'

'Yes.' She had begun to loosen the corset as she spoke and breathed a sigh when her chest was able to expand freely.

'Margaret, it's Richard.'

'Ah. Hello, Richard.' She was only just able to keep the irritation out of her voice. She had not called Richard Brachen for over a month – she had no use for him now. 'What can I do for you?' She remembered giving him the Mayfair number right back at the beginning and realised now it was a mistake. Charles would not like it at all.

'More what I can do for you, Lady M.' Richard could hear the slowed, throaty tone of her voice and knew what she'd been up to. He felt himself harden. 'I have rather an interesting snippet of information for you, involving your husband's man, John Mcbride. Remember him?'

'Yes.' She refused to give anything away. 'So?'

'So it also involves that young girl, what was her name? The beautiful Italian one who had that thing with Patrick. What was her name?'

'All right, you've made your point.' Anything about Francesca was useful, Richard knew that. He could see just as clearly as she did that Patrick wasn't paying enough attention to his sister, Penny. Perhaps a little information would act as an insurance policy. 'I'm interested in what you have to say. Do you want to meet?'

'Yes. At the Savoy, the American bar.'

She glanced over her shoulder at Charles as he came back into the room fully dressed. Richard never left after just one fuck.

'What time?' It was just after nine.

'Twenty minutes.'

'No, give me half an hour.' She needed to shower.

'All right, half an hour.'

'I'll see you then,' she said, lowering her voice to a whisper so that Charles couldn't hear. She went to hang up.

'Oh, Margaret?'

'Yes?'

'Don't bother to dress.' He laughed and the line went dead.

Exactly thirty minutes later, Lady Margaret walked into the American bar at the Savoy and the head waiter showed her to Richard's table. She had a long, pale fawn cashmere overcoat on, black stockings, high heels and a fawn and black

Hermès scarf at her throat. The waiter went to take her coat.

'No, thank you. I'll leave it on.'

Richard smiled.

'So what is this information?' She lit a cigarette as he poured her glass of champagne. 'Are we celebrating?'

'Sort of.'

'What, may I ask?'

He reached over and ran his finger along her cheek. 'The renewal of our relationship.'

'You're very confident.'

'Yes. John Mcbride rang me earlier this week and asked me if I would consider acting for him in a new business venture. Well, not new as such. He has gone into business with David Yates, the fashion designer.'

Lady Margaret sat back and looked at Richard. She knew he wasn't lying – he was too transparent to be able to lie well. 'And?' she asked.

'And, David Yates is designing a new collection with a partner. John wants me to take care of the legal side, copyright, et cetera. The partner is a young Italian girl, Francesca Cameron.' Richard smiled, he could not help himself. Lady Margaret's face had changed, literally in that second.

She eyed him suspiciously. 'What, do you suppose, a seventeen-year-old schoolgirl knows about fashion?'

He shrugged. 'No idea. Apparently something, though. David Yates has a good reputation; he wouldn't risk it on a no-hoper.'

Lady Margaret ground her cigarette out into the ashtray. 'Have you given your answer yet?'

'Well, that rather depends on you.'

And for the first time since she arrived, Lady Margaret smiled.

'Richard,' she said. 'I think I may have underestimated you.' She picked up her glass and took a sip. 'You will keep me informed about everything?' Whatever he could tell her would be serviceable. Information was power.

'Everything that I am party to, of course.'

'Of course.' She crossed her leg and the coat fell open. He could just see her stocking top. 'Shall we drink up and leave?'

He signalled to the waiter. 'There's no need to drink up. I'll have them send it up.' He stood and held out his hand. 'Come on.' He was rock-hard. 'One favour deserves another. Don't you think?'

She smiled and got to her feet.

'Absolutely,' she answered.

CHAPTER Twenty-three

OVER THE NEXT MONTH, WORK at the David Yates studio went on almost nonstop around the clock and everyone involved, even down to the new girl Friday John had hired, was passionate about the Cameron Yates collection. It was new, dynamic, and breathtaking; it was superb, they all knew it. And, as it began to take shape, after that first week when Francesca made her trial prints and Dave cut the paper patterns, each person in the company became more and more committed to the work. Spurred on by John, who somehow made the studio run like clockwork, they forgot Christmas, which sparkled around them, glittering in the shop windows and audible in the drinking crowds down on the Quayside, and they worked to ever tightening deadlines, knowing it had to be finished by the end of December. Somehow, this time round, nothing else mattered.

Once Francesca's prints had been made up and altered wherever needed, they were sent out to a big textile company over in Sunderland to be printed off on rolls of good quality Italian silk. She had finished ten designs but was still working on the last two by mid-December. She had sent off two per week to the factory to be fully printed off since she started; these were all back, only the final pair remained to be done. Her work had been never-ending: the trial screen prints, the altering of colours, shapes and patterns until the design was just right. Dave was amazed at her tenacity.

Wherever he felt a change was needed, he had bluntly

said so and Francesca had simply gone back to the drawing board, produced a variation and started work on it straight away. Most other designers would have argued and whined but she seemed to know instinctively what he meant. Each time she went away to make changes, she came back with something he would have chosen himself. It awed and inspired him and his own work flourished under her influence.

The designs that Dave produced for this collection, he knew, were amongst his best ever. Perhaps it was Francesca, perhaps it was knowing that his company depended on it, but whatever it was, he didn't analyse it, he just got on with the work, designing long and hard, working through the night and putting every ounce of his creativity into it. The wools arrived in great lengths from Scotland in a dazzling array of colours and he directed their cutting with a thrill and confidence he had not felt since his very first collection. He knew his line perfectly, he knew his shape and his look and he was convinced that when they put it all together for the first fitting it would work. It would do more than work, he thought, it would frigging make love.

As the third week in December began, and Christmas was just a few days away, the collection was in its final stages, ready for the first fitting. Everyone in the studio felt excited, anticipation seemed to hang in the air along with a wonderful feeling of exhilaration, as if they knew it would be good. This time, for the first fitting, everything had been organised properly: the models had been booked and John had insisted on a decent space in one of the huge, airy suites in the Swallow Hotel in the city centre. He had done a deal with the hotel, promised to do the final shoot for the press pack there if they lent him the space, and they were only too happy to do so. He wanted to make sure the studio was left untouched so that any work to be done could be tackled straight away and he felt it was important to see the clothes in the right setting.

He had organised with the management for a catwalk to be set up so the models could strut and turn, swirl and move the clothes. He reckoned that this way everyone could get some kind of feel for the final show in London, an idea of what music would fit, and of how the line-up should be organised. They were running out of time and the more they could do at once the better. But there was also one extra reason for booking the smart hotel space. The whole team would be present and John wanted to thank them for all their hard work.

He had ordered a Chinese feast of dim sum, chilli king prawns and sizzling chicken to be delivered from The Golden Goose in Stowell Street, along with several bottles of hot saki, chopsticks, and tiny china cups to drink out of. He had asked for a huge Norwegian Christmas tree to be set up and decorated with white candles and tartan ribbons and he went to the Body Shop and had baskets made up and tied with huge red bows, one for each member of the staff. John knew that morale was high at David Yates, but he also knew that if he was going to have to ask them to work over Christmas, and he thought he might, then he needed to make sure that everyone, even Elaine, their resident gofer, knew how much it was appreciated.

It was the Wednesday before the final fitting and Francesca was up early, sitting in bed looking at the last two swatches that the textile company had sent through the previous night. It was the first hour she had had to herself for weeks and she took her time going over the colours and the pattern, checking that it all matched, enjoying the solitude and the moment's peace. She could hear John moving around downstairs, sorting out his files and accounts for his meeting with the bank. He was tense, she could tell from his rushed movements. She wondered about it for a minute and then climbed out of bed, going over to the top of the stairs.

'John?' She heard him come out into the narrow hall. 'Are you all right? Can I get you some coffee or something?'

He smiled up at her. 'No, you go on back to your work, I'm fine.' He didn't want to say anything to anyone, not until he had met with the bank. It was his problem, anyway – he was supposed to be managing the business. 'I'm off now to the studio – I have to collect some files before I go to the bank. I'll see you later.'

She nodded, pulling her dressing gown in tighter. It was cold – the ground was frozen outside and the little house was chilly. 'Bye!' she called and went back into her room to dress. The luxury of being in bed was spoiled now because she was too cold to enjoy it.

Laying out her clothes, Francesca thought about what she would wear and tried several combinations before deciding on the outfit. Finally, she put on a short pleated tartan skirt, in bright blues, greens and black, with black opaque tights and one of David Yates' black knitted silk sweaters.

The jumper had a high neck and was tight fitting in the body and sleeves. It emphasised her slimness and the length of her body. She tried on a pair of black high heels but thought that they made her look too tall, so she changed them for a pair of black suede loafers, narrow-toed with a gold buckle, one of the promotion pairs from Freeze. She added gold earrings, a bright blue and green square of silk tied as a bandanna in her hair – one of her own prints – and she was ready. She looked at her face, newly washed and tingling, and brushed a sprinkling of translucent powder onto her cheeks. As she left the room, she wondered what

Dave would say this morning about her appearance.

The past two weeks, she had wondered this every morning as she laid out her clothes, brushed her hair or looked at her face in the mirror. Recently he had made her more aware of herself than she had ever been. She could sense him watching her as she worked, or looking at her as she crossed the studio. It unnerved her, but it also excited her; it made her body feel strong and powerful; it made her feel alive. They had never spoken about the night in the print studio, but they were both conscious of it – it was there between them, the energy of physical attraction, and it made their work connect, sizzle with excitement.

Leaving the house at her usual time, Francesca slung her bag over her shoulder and set off towards Osborne Road and the Metro, stopping at the newsagent's on the way to buy her morning paper. She picked up the *Mail*, tucked it under her arm without looking at it and paid, continuing on her way to the station. On the platform, she finally opened out the paper while she waited for the train and looked down at the front page. She glimpsed the photograph and a searing ache went through her. She closed her eyes, oblivious to everything but the pain.

'Are you all right, pet?'

She felt a hand at her elbow.

'Yes, yes I'm fine.' She opened her eyes and looked up at the lady in front of her. She felt disorientated, slightly sick and her hands were trembling.

'You look pretty pale to me. Would you like to sit down?'

'No, honestly, I'm fine.' She was abrupt; she couldn't think straight.

'All right, pet, whatever ya say.' The lady moved off and Francesca called after her: 'Thanks anyway!' The lady turned and smiled then continued down the platform.

Francesca reached down for the paper. In her confusion and shock she had dropped it on the ground. She saw the picture again, and the same pain went through her heart.

Looking up at her from the front page was the face of Patrick Devlin, smiling and waving at a crowd. The headline read: Leading Light In Tory By-Election.

She stared down at it, the memory of him so strong that just a photograph, black and white and slightly blurred, could evoke the touch of his mouth on her skin, the warmth of his smile, his laughter, so relaxed and spontaneous that it sounded like a boy's. She remembered everything about him and what she could not remember she had drawn: a sketch of him asleep, of him throwing Sophie up into the air, of him holding both children and smiling at the comfort of the embrace. She had captured every detail of him; she had the whole of him locked away in her heart, and bound up with her fears and her love. But now, at just a glimpse of him, of his life, it all came to the surface and it hurt more than she ever thought it could.

Blindly she staggered to a bench and sat down, clutching the paper, the image of his face fresh in her mind. She sat there for some time. The train came and went and she heard nothing but the words inside her own head. I am being stupid, she told herself. It is over, it is in the past. And yet, despite all she had done in the last few months and despite how she had grown and changed, just the sight of him made her want to weep. I should hate him, she thought angrily, but she didn't.

'Pull yourself together,' she muttered fiercely under her breath and then suddenly, she smiled. That was one of John's expressions. The thought of John made her feel instantly better. Getting to her feet, she took a deep breath and shook her head to try and clear her mind. It must just be the shock, she told herself, pushing back all the crowding emotions. It reminds me, that's all, it brings back bad memories. Then she folded the newspaper and dumped it aggressively in the nearest rubbish bin. Still not quite convinced, she held her head up and said to herself: I am my own woman; I will not let Patrick Devlin ruin my life!

And she stepped forward as the train approached, feeling the cold gust of air on her face as it blew down the tunnel, cooling her cheeks and sweeping into her mind, forcing back the shock of his image. Moments later, she climbed onto the train, took her seat and glanced at her reflection in the glass of the window opposite. Again she took a deep breath, calming herself and pulling the threads of her self-confidence together.

I have changed and I have grown, she said silently to the face in the glass. I will choose my own destiny, love whom I please, and be my own person. Isn't that what John said? Change what I can't accept? Nothing will interfere with that. 'Nothing,' she said quietly, thrusting everything that hurt deep down inside her. 'Nothing.'

Walking into the studio half an hour later, as always the first one there, Francesca crossed to her space and took off her coat, throwing it over the back of her chair. She was thirsty and before she did anything else, she needed a coffee. Going through to the kitchen, she filled the pot with water, added the coffee grinds and turned on the heat on the stove. She found herself a cup, put a big spoonful of sugar in the bottom and waited for the coffee to boil, flicking through a *Vogue* as she did so. When it was ready, she poured the thick black coffee into her cup and turned to leave the kitchen.

'It must have been a heavy night last night.' Dave blocked her path as he stood in the doorway. 'By the look of the coffee, that is.'

She shrugged and took a sip of the scalding liquid, looking at him over the rim of her cup. He was leaning against the doorframe. His hair was loose for once and she noticed he had had it cut. It was dark and glossy and as he ran his hand through it, sweeping it back off his face, she suddenly remembered her own fingers tangled in its length. She blushed.

'Wicked thoughts, Frankie?' He stood where he was, just smiling, and she wondered again if he could read her mind.

'Of course not!'

'Good. Can I have a sip of your coffee, by the way?'

She held out the cup and he took it. She noticed his lips briefly as he put the cup to his mouth and took a gulp. 'Hmmm. Delicious.' He held it out for her. 'Here.'

She took it back and swallowed another mouthful, aware of the faint, exciting smell of his cologne on the cup. She saw that he was watching her.

'Are you all right this morning?' He kept his eyes on her face as he asked.

'Yes.' She avoided his stare. 'Why?'

'Oh, I don't know, you look a bit . . .' He scratched his chin. 'A bit preoccupied. As if there were something on your mind.' He wanted to add: 'It's kind of sexy,' but he didn't dare.

'No! Of course not!' She laughed falsely and went to step past him. It was the first time they had been alone since the night in the print studio and she suddenly felt unnerved, excited, unsafe. I will love whom I please, she thought briefly. He touched her arm as she passed.

'Frankie, have dinner with me tonight?' He had no idea why he asked. He had told himself time and time again to leave well alone but it just slipped out. She looked so intense this morning, as if all the passion that she locked up had risen too close to the surface and she was struggling to hold it down. The thought of it gave him a raging hard-on. 'Will you?'

She glanced down at his fingers on her arm. They were strong and masculine and his scent was warm and heady. She wanted to choose, oh how she wanted to be free to choose. Of course she would go. She was young and independent and she found him very attractive.

'Yes,' she answered. 'I will have dinner with you.' Then she looked up at him and saw his tongue dart over his teeth; she could hear him breathing. 'Where?' she asked.

'My house? I'll cook.'

'Yes. I'd like that.' She could not believe she was saying these words. What have I got to lose? she thought.

The sound of Tilly in the studio broke the moment between them and Dave dropped his hand away from her arm. She squeezed past him. Halfway across the studio she turned back. 'What time?' she called.

He shrugged. 'Eight, eight-thirty? You can come straight from here if you like, I'll give you a lift.'

'OK.' She liked that idea better, it gave her less time to think about it. Turning away again, she carried on over to her space. She heard Dave shout at Tilly but she switched on the radio and his voice was drowned by the noise of the music.

John sat in the outer office of a suite belonging to Mr W. Ackroyd, the business development manager of Dave's bank, and stared up at the glossy photographs of manufacturing and commerce in progress, all funded by this particular division of the bank. His eye was constantly drawn to the photo of Dave, in the middle of a crowd, clutching the fashion award he had won four years ago and smiling beneath his name written up in lights: David Yates. This gave John hope. David Yates was one of the success stories, one of the bank's true protégés. Applied for funding in 1982, expanded 1985, award-winning 1987 and always in the public eye. Surely this would help? He tapped his toe lightly against the leg of his chair and continued to wait.

'Ah, Mr Mcbride. Sorry to have kept you waiting so long.' Ackroyd came into the room, carrying his file. 'Do come this way.' He led the way back into the inner office and John followed. He waited for Ackroyd to speak.

'Mr Mcbride, I have been on the phone all this time to our venture capital advisors down in London and unfortunately I have to tell you that we are unable to do much more for you. I'm sorry, truly I am, but with the current economic situation we have a much tighter loan policy operating and we simply cannot extend you any more credit.'

John was silent for a moment; he had been expecting this. They had already been through the whole argument but he felt he should give it one more try. He leaned forward in his chair and quietly said: 'Mr Ackroyd, I understand the bank's policy but it is hardly the fault of my company that two of our biggest retailers have gone under. Surely we cannot be held responsible for that? And we have the prospect of a brand new collection!'

'I know that, Mr Mcbride, but it's a fact of life that the chances of ever getting the money owed to you when a company has gone into receivership are very small. You are way down on that list of creditors and the bank has already done as much for you as we are able to. I'm sure this new collection is very good and I don't doubt the skills of Mr Yates, but it is just too much of a risk for us at the moment. I'm sorry. I wish you every success with the venture.'

John snorted and shook his head. Ackroyd could see his anger barely hidden beneath the surface.

'Look, let's be reasonable,' he said. 'I understand your

dilemma, Mr Mcbride, believe me I do. But we are up to our loan limit on your company and to be blunt, we simply cannot afford to keep giving out large sums of money, particularly to a new business manager, with no track record of this kind of venture, and an unknown, inexperienced designer.' He shrugged. 'It's a very depressed market out there. You must know as well as I do how fickle the fashion business is.'

John remained coldly silent.

Ackroyd tried to placate him. 'Banks are suffering in the recession too, you know.'

At this point John exploded. 'So what, Mr Ackroyd, am I supposed to do? You won't lend me the money and I cannot go any further without extra funding.'

Ackroyd fiddled awkwardly with his pen. 'There are other loan companies who would probably be in a position to help, or there is the option of remortgaging your property.'

'No, I can't do that.' John shook his head. He had no intention of putting the house up for collateral and he knew the type of loan sharks Ackroyd was talking about – no wonder he looked so shifty.

'Thank you all the same, Mr Ackroyd, but I don't think that sort of advice applies to a reputable company. I will try another bank.' John stood to leave. He was angry but he knew that Ackroyd had little to do with the decision: he was just the man on the dud end of the arrangement. 'Thank you for your time,' he said, picking up his files.

Ackroyd held out his hand and John took it.

'Good luck, Mr Mcbride. I'm sorry we can't help, truly I am.'

'Yes, thanks.' John turned and silently left the room. He walked out into the corridor and did something he rarely did: he swore.

'Shit!' he said aloud and then carried on down to the lifts.

Instead of going straight to the studio, as he would normally have done, John went home to Marston Avenue for some peace and quiet. He needed to think things through. Although he had told Ackroyd he would go to another bank, he was pretty sure that the answer would be the same whoever he chose to talk to. Ackroyd was right: he had no credibility in the business world; he was inexperienced and too old for the job – shame, he was damn good at it.

Sitting at the kitchen table with a cup of tea, John decided to ring Richard Brachen to discuss the situation with him. He didn't know if Brachen would be able to help but he had said to call any time John felt there was a problem that needed advice. Taking the telephone off the wall, John looked up Brachen's number in his diary and dialled London.

'Hello? Er, Richard Brachen, please. Er, yes, my name is Mcbride, John Mcbride. Thank you.' The switchboard put him through.

'Hello, Richard Brachen's secretary.'

'Ah, hello, is it possible to speak to Mr Brachen?'

'May I ask who's calling?'

'Yes, certainly. It's John Mcbride.'

'One moment, Mr Mcbride, he's on the other line at the moment, can I ask you to wait?'

'Of course.' The faintest of clicks sounded and John listened to the silence of an empty line.

Richard Brachen's secretary stood up and popped her head round the door of his office. 'Richard, there's a Mr Mcbride on line two for you.'

Richard Brachen nodded and she disappeared. He continued with his call on line one.

'Good Lord! He must be bloody psychic, that man!

D'you think he knows we were just talking about him?'

'Don't be ridiculous, Richard!' Lady Margaret laughed on the other end of the line. 'Call me back if it's anything interesting, will you?'

'Of course.' He pressed the button and Lady Margaret was instantly cut off. 'Put him through please, Sally.' John came on the line.

'John!'

'Hello, Richard.'

'What can I do for you?'

'Actually, Richard, I wonder if I might ask a little advice, regarding finance for the company?'

'Of course. Anything you like.'

And John told him the story of the failed retailers, the debt that had just come to light and the need for extra funding. He told him about the bank, about the urgency of the loan to fund the show at Olympia and about his inexperience as a business manager, as if Brachen didn't already know. All the way through his dialogue Brachen listened attentively and commented every now and then; all the way through he had a faint peculiar smile on his lips.

Minutes after he had put the phone down to John Mcbride, he redialled Motcom and waited for Lady Margaret to be called to the phone. His smile had widened.

'Margaret?'

'Yes? You sound pretty jolly!'

'I am. Listen, would you be able to raise sixty to eighty thousand pounds in cash in the next week?'

She laughed. 'That's a ludicrously large sum, Richard! Why, may I ask?'

'In return for a fair proportion of the collateral of David Yates, the fashion company.'

'Good Lord!'

'Exactly! I think I may just have done you a pretty big

favour, Margaret!' Richard sat back in his chair and drew pound signs on his blotter as he spoke. 'John Mcbride just rang me with a finance problem. It's a long story and I won't bore you with it – bankrupt creditors et cetera – but he needs funding, to the tune of sixty thou'. He can't proceed without it – the bank's refused to extend his loan facility and he has a collection to produce.'

'Are you sure?'

'Of course I'm sure, why would he lie to me, for God's sake? I'm his bloody solicitor!'

'But he'd never let me loan him money, Richard! He would be highly suspicious of my motives, after all the business with the Italian girl.' Lady Margaret found it very difficult to use Francesca's name.

'Are you surprised?' Richard smiled. 'What *are* your motives, Margaret?'

'None of your bloody business!' She only had one, and that was Patrick. He was on the way up and no one was going to ruin that for him. His pining for Francesca was pathetic; it was blocking the path to Penny Brachen, both she and Richard knew that. And marriage to Penny, in Lady Margaret's eyes, was an almost perfect match for Patrick. Penny was the ideal politician's wife, well connected, immensely rich and easily dominated. Yes, she thought, it was about time she upped her insurance, a stake in David Yates was worth an awful lot more than the sixty thousand she would be paying for it.

'You're quite right, Margaret,' Richard said, 'it is none of my business.' He could afford to be deferential. Richard knew exactly what Lady Margaret was up to, and with Patrick's recent, albeit rather forced, interest in Penny, anything she did to secure Devlin's future could only bode well for his sister. Richard wanted Penny married: she had big problems that only he knew about and he wasn't sure she could cope much longer on her own. 'Anyway, whatever your reasons, Margaret,' he continued, 'John wouldn't have to know anything about you. I'd tell him it was a consortium looking to make an investment through a nominee company.'

'Really? Would that work, d'you think? John is pretty shrewd, you know.'

'Not that shrewd!' She was so bloody patronising at times.

'OK. I think I could raise the money relatively easily – I've a number of shares I could get rid of without Henry knowing too much about it all. But do you really think it would work?' Control, that was what mattered. Patrick was on the brink of success and if she had a little power to play with . . .

'Yes, it would. In fact, John is all set to come down to see me this afternoon. I said I might be able to help and he said if I had anyone interested, he'd get the next train out of Newcastle.'

'Oh, Richard, you clever thing, you! Presumably I could leave you to work out all the details, make it look good?'

'Of course.'

'Excellent!' She smiled and knew that Richard could sense her pleasure. 'Looks like I might have to come down to London myself tonight. Doesn't it?'

'If you like.' He hated himself for reacting as he did but even the sound of her excitement over the telephone drove him mad.

'Oh, I like!' Her laugh fluttered down the line and he could hear her breathing. He imagined her mouth close to the receiver and reached down to his crotch. Seconds later, the line went dead. He started as his secretary came into the office.

'Richard, you have a client in reception, a Mr Frosome.'

'Oh God, yes!' She always did this to him – he forgot everything, it was as if he was obsessed. 'Tell him I'll be down in five minutes, will you, Sal? I've got to go to the loo.'

'Ye—' She stopped. He had zipped past her, out of the office and along the corridor to the Gents before she had time to reply. 'No problem, Richard. Thank you, Sally,' she finished and made her way down to the lifts.

But Richard Brachen was more than five minutes. He knew what pleasures he had in store that night if things went well with Mcbride and he needed to get rid of his excess excitement. Margaret certainly knew how to repay a favour and that required extraordinary staying power.

Later that evening, at the same time that John got on the train at King's Cross, after his meeting with Richard Brachen, Francesca slipped into the passenger seat of Dave's Golf GTi and fastened her seat belt. She waited for him to come round to the driver's side and fiddled with the stereo to find some music: he always had the most complicated of sound systems.

'It's here.' Dave leaned into the car and pressed a button on the dashboard, lighting up the stereo. INXS came blaring out of the speakers and Francesca jumped.

'Oops! Sorry!' He turned the volume down and slid into his seat. 'There's some tapes in the glove compartment if you don't like this.' He started the engine and Francesca rummaged through a pile of unboxed tapes to find something she liked. She picked out *Themes from Walt Disney*, held it up for him and he changed the tape. 'I'm the King of the Swingers' flooded into the car and they both smiled.

Pulling off, Dave headed up Dean Street and towards the A167 and Jesmond. 'D'you want to stop for a drink somewhere before we go home for supper?'

Francesca looked out at the late-night shoppers, struggling home with their packed carrier bags. 'No, I don't think so. It'll probably be packed in town.'

'OK.' They drove on in silence, and Dave whistled quietly to the tune on the tape. It was dark and warm in the car and he could see Francesca's face in shadow, lit every now and then by the lights from the street. She was staring ahead and again he could sense her intensity, just as he had that morning. It fascinated him; it was like a magnet that drew him to her and made his whole body tense with excitement.

'You all right?' He turned off the main road into Jesmond.

'Yes.' She wasn't lying, but she wasn't being exactly honest either. She was feeling confident and free and she was thinking: I know what I am doing, I know how I feel. And yet there was the tiniest of echoes in the very back of her mind that said: 'Oh no you don't!' She ignored it and turned to smile at him as they swung left into Brandling Village and pulled into the narrow side lane that led to his house. Dave stopped the car and switched off the engine. The music died instantly and she began to climb out of the car.

'Frankie.' He touched her shoulder.

'Yes?' She looked back at him and he bent his head to kiss her. It was a short kiss and she felt a tiny thrill in the pit of her stomach. But the echo sounded again and she thought for the briefest second: do I really know what I'm doing? She kissed him back, determined that she did.

'You taste wonderful,' he said and kissed the tip of her nose. He climbed out of the car, coming round to open the passenger door for her. 'Are you hungry?'

'Sort of.'

He held her hand and fumbled with his keys to open the front door. Finally managing it, he led her inside the house and pushed the door closed with his foot.

'Now, let me get you a drink. What would you like?'

'Water? Orange juice? Anything, really.'

'Ugh! I've got some wine, I'll get you a glass of that. OK?' He headed off to the kitchen, then called out: 'D'you want to have a shower?'

'No thanks.'

He came into the sitting room carrying a large globe of cut glass filled with a dark red wine. 'Mind if I do? I feel pretty shitty after a hard day at the office, dear.'

She smiled. 'No, of course not.'

'Good! If you sit here and drink your wine, I'll be ten minutes, and then I'll cook you the most delicious chicken chasseur.'

'You will?'

'Well, not actually cook it, just sort of warm it through. At least, that's what Cherry told me to do on the phone this afternoon. But I will make the salad. I am an expert at opening the Marks & Spencer's bag and shuffling it round in a bowl with some dressing!'

She laughed and took a sip of the wine.

'I'll be down before you finish the glass.' He walked across the room. 'See you in a minute,' and seconds later she was left alone.

For some time Francesca sat and sipped the wine, staring at the calm and ordered sequence of the room. Everything was in its place and was perfectly suited for that place; everything fitted together. She recognised the same quality in the room that she saw in Dave's work: it was classic, beautifully defined and yet there was a hint of quirkiness, always something unusual. Standing up and crossing the floor, she looked more closely at the prints on the far wall and, with a blush, suddenly realised that she had pin-pointed the touch of quirkiness in the room. From afar she had seen the small pictures as abstracts, moving shapes in grey and brown tones; nearer, she saw they were finely drawn erotic sketches, figures entwined, skin and hair tangled together. She took a large gulp of her wine and peered a little closer; the signature was D. Yates.

Standing back Francesca felt a strange excitement, she felt a warmth and intimacy with the figures. Images of a long, lithe body, dark-skinned and muscled, ran through her mind and she recognised the male torso in the drawings. She caught her breath, shocked at her response, and moved away from the wall. She turned and finished her wine in one swallow. The soft velvety taste of it made her shiver.

In the centre of the room, she stood for a moment, poised, holding her glass and running her fingers involuntarily along the long thick stem. She was not thinking; she was listening to the rhythm of her body, a body she wanted to control, to direct and to tell to love where she pleased. She felt suddenly confident, as if she could do anything, anything at all. And in that instant she rashly made her decision. She placed the glass carefully on the table by the sofa, slipped off her shoes and quietly climbed the stairs in her stockinged feet.

In the main bedroom she could hear the gush of the water in the shower and feel the dampness of the steam that crept underneath the door. She recognised the same warm, heady cologne she had smelled that morning. Silently, she pulled her sweater over her head, unfastened her skirt and slipped off her tights. The cotton body she wore underneath was already damp as she peeled it down over her chest and then her hips. She opened the bathroom door, all thought emptied from her mind, and crossed to the shower. Sliding back the glass panel, she stepped inside.

Dave felt her before he saw her. She seemed to step through the steam and he felt the shock of her body against his own, the firm, long line of her and the fullness of her breasts. His breath caught in the back of his throat and his arms went around her, pulling her close. He looked down through the torrent of water at her.

'Jesus, Frankie!' She silenced him with her mouth.

His own body was slippery from the soap and her hands slithered along his spine and down to his buttocks. Her lips opened his as the water poured down over their faces and into their mouths, in a glorious, hot stream. He edged her back against the wall and bent his head to her breasts, licking the wet skin, drinking the water as it flowed down over her nipples. He heard her moan as she reached for him. He lifted his head to hear her, the sound of her voice almost more exciting than the touch of her body.

Suddenly he leaped back.

'Patrick? Who the hell is that?' He yanked back the glass door and in an instant had stomped out of the shower. He grabbed a towel to cover his dying erection and stood, panting heavily. Francesca stumbled out after him, as if woken from a dream, and the water gushed down behind her.

'Who the hell is Patrick? he asked insistently, towering above her, his face like thunder.

'Oh my God! I . . . I can't believe it . . . I . . . .' Francesca stood wet and naked before him and in spite of his anger just the sight of her inflamed him.

'I . . . I don't know what . . .' Dave was almost menacing in his fury. 'I just don't know . . .' Suddenly she burst into tears. Sobbing, she ran past him out of the bathroom.

'Shit!' He heard her struggling with her clothes in the next room and crossed to the shower to turn off the water. He took a warm towel off the heated towel rail and followed her through to the bedroom.

'Frankie, here.' He moved over to her and put the towel around her. She was shivering and had put her hand through her tights in her hurry to get them on. Her jumper

was stuck on her head and she looked so young and ridiculous that he pulled her to him, hugged her and started to
laugh.

'Oh, Dave, I'm so sorry, I . . .'

'Ssssh.' He rubbed her back and then walked her over to
the bed and sat her down. 'Now, do you want to start
again?'

She shook her head. She couldn't, she didn't dare.

'Do you want to talk about it?' Again she shook her head.

'OK. I shall leave you to get dressed and go down and
start doing magical things with the supper.' He stood up.
'Seeing as I can't do magical things with you, that is.'

He smiled. His anger and frustration had vanished. I'm
probably better off not getting too close to her anyway, he
thought. He got the feeling that with Frankie it could so easily be more than just a damn good screw, and he didn't
want to take that kind of risk. Better just friends, he reckoned, far better that way.

'See you in a few minutes?' He grabbed his robe from the
back of the door and turned to leave.

'Dave?'

'Yup?' He looked at her from the doorway.

'It's nothing to do with you.' She stopped. She didn't
know what it was, why she couldn't get Patrick out of her
head. 'I mean . . . you made me feel really wonderful.' She
blushed.

'I should bloody well hope so,' he answered, grinning. 'I
have medals for this sport!' And he walked out, diplomati-
cally leaving her alone to dress.

Francesca sat on the bed, huddled in the thick white
towel and buried her head in her hands, desperate with
humiliation and shame. She had made the most terrible,
terrible fool of herself. She would never be able to face Dave
again.

Why, she thought miserably, why? I have tried so hard to forget Patrick. I have willed myself to forget him, forced him deep down into my heart, and yet somehow I cry out for him, my body yearns for him and unconsciously I need him, like a drug. Why, damn it, why?

She felt the warmth of her tears splash down onto her bare thigh and brushed them away. 'You thought you could change everything, Francesca,' she whispered bitterly. 'You changed nothing, not even the secrets of your own heart.'

Having thought better of leaving Francesca alone, a few moments later Dave came back to the bedroom and stood silently in the open doorway, watching her cry. He felt completely helpless, embarrassed by her grief, and thought that he would like to get hold of the bloke that had made her feel like this and kill him. He moved to leave, unsure of what to do, but she looked up and saw him standing there.

'I have made such a fool of myself,' she whispered. 'You must hate me.'

'Hey!' He crossed to her and sat on the bed. 'These things happen, Frankie,' he said gently. 'And I could never hate you – we're friends, remember?' He stopped, looked away for a moment and then continued: 'You know, sometimes we think we want one person when all the time it's someone else. It's like a safety valve, lets out all that emotion.' He picked up her hand and turned it over, running his finger across the palm. He saw for the first time the faint scars on her wrist where she usually wore her watch and turned away to hide his shock. 'You can't change some things, you know, Frankie,' he said gently, 'some of the things inside you, some of the scars. You just have to learn to accept them, to live with them.' He touched the marking on her wrist. 'Did he do this to you?'

She shook her head. 'No. All he did was love me. I think that hurts more.'

'Did you ever tell him about it?'

'No, there's no point. He knew, but I wasn't good enough for him, you see.' The way she said it made him want to hold her like a child, it was so simple and hopeless. 'I've tried to work it out and I think . . .' She paused and took a breath. 'I think he might have wanted me if I'd been different, if I'd been good enough.'

'Oh, Frankie.' He kissed her hand. 'You were good enough, you've always been good enough and you always will be. And as for now, you are about to be a star, my darling Frankie, shooting across the sky and blinding us all with your light.' He smiled. 'I shall look up at you in a few weeks' time and have stardust in my eyes!'

Finally she smiled back. 'Thank you, Dave.'

He shrugged. 'For what?'

'For . . .' She should have said, for making me see that perhaps I can't have it all my own way, that some things I can't change. But she didn't, she hadn't quite worked it all out yet. 'For being you,' she answered and he rolled his eyes, smiled and said: 'Fat lot of good it did me, huh?'

CHAPTER

Twenty-four

AS THE FINAL FEW WEEKS slipped away after Christmas and the first fitting was over with, the show at Olympia emerged out of the distance as much more of a reality and Dave's prophecy for Francesca seemed ever more likely. She was on her way to becoming a star. Everyone could see it: the collection was the best they had ever produced and her flair for colour, her feel for fabric and design showed the mark of a true artist. But she was totally oblivious to it.

The level of excitement rose day by day as the preparations for the show began in earnest. The photo shoot took place, with the best photographer John could afford, and the pictures were stunning. The press pack was designed, the releases were written and Francesca and Dave were photographed together for the front of the folder. They were laughing in the picture and they looked good together, an attractive and well-matched pair. The Cameron Yates collection looked set to succeed.

This was the general opinion and there was little to deter everyone from accepting it. John had secured his finance from Richard Brachen for twenty-five per cent of the shares in David Yates – a little over the odds, he privately thought, but who was he to argue? They needed the finance and they'd be sunk without it. Besides, Richard had organised a good deal for John. He told him he had written a release clause into the contract for David Yates, and negotiated a reasonable rate of interest on the loan. John could not have asked for more. With Richard explaining all the legal details to him personally, all he had to do was sign on the dotted line and not bother with pages of small print. With a collection to direct and produce, it was a great weight off his mind to know that he had someone he could trust.

For Francesca, those weeks after the night with Dave passed in a flurry of work, and through that, through their exchange of ideas and dedicated commitment, she coped with her shame and embarrassment and found, much to her surprise, that they actually drew closer together and became greater friends. The physical attraction between them was still there, only now they knew how to deal with it. Dave knew that Francesca needed more than he was capable of giving and that he wasn't the right person anyway. But nevertheless, he adored her. He could see the love and respect she had for John and found himself hoping, quite extraordinarily, that she might feel the same about him one day.

Finally, the morning of the departure to London arrived and the David Yates studio was in a frenzy of excited activity. Every inch of space in the studio was taken up with clothes in various stages of packing, with shoes, hats, and boxes of jewellery, and each person involved with the collection seemed to be running in all directions, fiddling, finishing and panicking in the usual fashionable way.

Francesca sat with Dave on the big black leather sofa and watched it all while he went over their schedule of interviews with the media the next day – who she would be seeing, what to expect and, most importantly, what she should say. She nodded and made the odd noise but her mind was focused on the clothes, checking how they were being packed, seeing that the right accessories were going in with them. She wasn't really interested in the promotional side of London Fashion Week; she just wanted to show the clothes, sell the collection and move on to the next one. Her fingers were already itching to get back to the drawing board.

Dave tapped her on the thigh and she jumped.

'Are you listening to me?' She smiled sheepishly. 'To be honest with you, no.'

'Frankie! We've got the most important interview first, bloody Sod's law, and you, my girl, have got to know what you're going to say. You won't have time to rehearse on some of the lesser trade mags; you have to be word-perfect first time round. I don't want us to fuck up here, Frankie! All right?'

She had never seen him so uptight; he was much worse than the last time round. 'All right,' she said. 'I'm sorry, what is it we have to say?'

'It's all here in note form, and I'll go over it again. This bloke at *Fashion Review* is pretty much queen bee, and also one hell of a bitch. He'll give you a right pasting, I guarantee, so try to listen this time.'

'Yes, OK! I'm listening!'

Dave went through the interview for the second time and began to feel a little more relaxed as Francesca reacted well to the questions he fired at her. After his coaching she was going to sound as good as she looked and he knew, as most designers did, how important it was to be the darling of the press.

By lunch-time, most of the clothes had been packed and the studio was beginning to look empty and slightly forlorn, with mounds of disused tissue paper and plastic wrappings all over the place and the remains of the last-minute work discarded on tables and chairs. Evelyn and Cherry had finished for the day, all the trimming and detail on the clothes was complete and only Tilly continued to work, finalising the packing and bossing the men who moved the great racks of clothes down the stairs and out to the van.

Elaine sat and waited for everyone to depart, then she would start to clear up the mess.

It was twelve-thirty when John called the team together. He was due to leave with Francesca and Dave on the two o'clock train from Newcastle Central and he wanted one final meeting before he left. He turned off the radio and shouted across the studio floor for everyone to pull up a chair over by the black sofa and then he went to his office area and picked up a file from his desk. He had agreed his idea with Dave a couple of days earlier and his last task for the show had been to put his thoughts into action.

'OK. Everyone present?' He looked around at Tilly, Evelyn, Cherry, Elaine, Francesca and Dave. 'Good,' he said and felt a surge of pride at his staff. He smiled.

'As you all know, the first showing of the new Cameron Yates collection will be in two days' time at Olympia.' Everyone groaned loudly at this obvious remark and John held up his hand to quieten them. 'All right, all right! Bunch of smart alecs! What you probably don't know, however, is that I have a small envelope for each of you to say how much we – Dave, Francesca and myself – appreciate your hard work in putting this collection together and how much we are indebted to you for its quality and finish.' He moved forward and handed round the small brown envelopes. Murmurs of thanks went through the group. 'What we have done hasn't been customary in this company before, but we felt it should be. You've all been involved in making the collection; you should have the chance to see it as everyone else does.'

'You what?' Tilly's voice was sharp with excitement as she tore open her envelope. 'I don't believe it!' She leaped up and threw her arms round John. He coughed back a mouthful of hair and she stood back laughing. 'Friggin' brilliant, this is, friggin' brilliant!'

'Oh, John!' Evelyn had opened her envelope. 'I've never been to London, I mean, not to stay in a posh hotel an' all.'

The rustling of paper continued and everyone found their train tickets and a glossy leaflet on one of the smaller THF hotels in London.

'We have organised an overnight stay in the hotel you see in the brochure,' John said. 'And you have complementary tickets for the show – out front, or in the back with the three of us, it's up to you.' He smiled. 'I hope you'll all be able to make it.'

'You bet!' Elaine's voice boomed and everyone burst out laughing.

'Good! That's settled then!'

Dave stood up and looked across at John. It was time they were moving.

'Well, I think it's time we made tracks, everybody,' John said.

Dave pulled Francesca to her feet and put his arm round her. 'Listen, everyone,' he said. 'I, er . . .' He paused self-consciously. 'I don't know how I would have survived all this without you.' He smiled. 'Francesca, John, Tilly, Evelyn, Cherry and Elaine. If this collection makes it, it's because of you.' His voice trembled momentarily and Tilly swallowed back a tear. 'You're the best, all of you. Thank you.' He shrugged and Tilly jumped up again, hugging both him and Francesca.

'Right! We're off!'

There was a general movement then and everyone wanted to kiss Dave and Francesca and hug them and wish them luck, and John embraced all the girls, feeling slightly ill at ease but smiling through it nevertheless.

'All right? Is that everyone kissed?' They all laughed. 'Come on then, let's get going!'

Dave, John and Francesca walked to the door, collecting coats and briefcases on the way, and the team moved with them, in a mass, all chattering about London and wishing them luck for the next day of interviews. The mood was high and full of emotion. Finally they were ready to leave and a last round of hugs was made with Tilly openly wiping away the tears.

'Goodbye all!' John called. He ushered Dave and Francesca down the stairs as the others stood in a small crowd at the top, waving and calling out.

'Good luck!' Tilly cried as they made it out of the door. Her voice was bright and clear. 'Good luck!' she called again and her cry, joyous and exhilarating, sent them on their way.

Later that afternoon, as they arrived at the hotel in London, Dave thought he could use a little of the luck Tilly had called out to them. He was feeling decidedly on edge.

Eddy Mars had called and left a message that he would have to cancel their meeting at *Fashion Review* as he had another designer to see urgently across town and could they meet later at the Ritz, in time for cocktails? Sure, Dave thought, pompous little jerk, and guess who'll be buying all the drinks at the bloody Ritz, for Christ's sake!

Even so, he called Paul Smith and asked for a suit to be sent over with a shirt and tie. He reckoned he could get away with his black desert boots at the Ritz, but only just. Whatever Eddy Mars asked, he thought, the designers did. He was not worth jerking around with, unless you were into that kind of thing, of course. Dave smiled.

'Anything we should know about?' John met him

halfway across the lobby of the hotel on his way back from the phones.

'What?'

'You were smiling.'

'Oh, no, nothing much.' Dave looked around him. 'Where's Frankie?'

'She's gone over to South Molton Street, to some place called Molton Browner, to have her hair done; styled or something, she said. She got a freebie from a magazine, I believe. And she wants to have a look at Browns' and just wander round a bit, I think. She's pretty nervous about this interview thing.'

'Snap!' Dave looked at his watch. 'I hope she's not too long, I don't want to be late for Mars.'

'Is it really that important, this interview?'

'Put it this way, John, I've known Eddy Mars wipe designers off the face of the earth because he didn't like the colour of their socks.'

John laughed.

'I'm not joking.' Dave walked across to the lifts. 'He's gay as well,' he called as the lift arrived. 'And I'm a hundred and ten per cent hetero. The two don't mix in my book.' Dave stepped inside the lift. 'I'm counting on Frankie to charm him,' he said as the lift doors closed. 'Ah, if only she were a boy!' He shrugged and disappeared from sight.

Francesca put her hand up to her hair as she crossed to the door of her room and wondered for the hundredth time if she had done the right thing. She glanced down at her clothes, flicked a speck of fluff off her skirt and pulled open the door. Dave was standing there, half turned away and chewing a fingernail.

'Frankie!' He spun round when he heard her and stopped dead. 'Oh shit, what have you done to your hair?'

'My hair?' Her hand fluttered nervously around her neck where the stylist's slick, geometric bob ended in a straight line held together with what looked like glue. It was parted and drawn horribly down one side of her face; it made her look like a particularly vicious vampire. 'Don't you like it?'

He stood where he was for a moment and stared hard at her head, then shook his head. Moving quickly forward, he grabbed her hand and strode past her into the bedroom, pulling her behind him. 'Don't say a word,' he muttered. 'Just let me deal with it.' He yanked her into the bathroom, turned on the shower full pelt and dunked her head under it. 'Shampoo?'

'It's on the side,' she answered, throwing a towel over her shoulders. She was near to tears and had to swallow hard while he scrubbed her scalp, rinsed and dumped a towel onto her head. He rubbed hard.

'Ouch!' Her eyes were watering.

'Be quiet.' He led her back to the bedroom and found the hairdryer in the drawer. 'Bend forward.'

She did as he asked and he turned the dryer on, running his fingers through her hair as he blasted it, scrunching the roots in his hand and pushing it back from her forehead. Five or so minutes later he was finished. 'OK. Stand straight and hand me the comb.' He walked round her, carefully combing through some of the top strands to give it a slightly more groomed effect. 'Right! Grab your coat and let's go. We're late!'

Francesca ran to the bed, picked up her jacket and managed to sneak a glance in the mirror on the way to the door. Her hair was almost back to normal, full and slightly wavy, swept back off her face and emphasising its shape. She took a second glance, relieved at what Dave had done, and then hurried out of the room to his waiting figure in the corridor.

'You look wonderful,' she said, looking at the suit and tie.

'Don't take the piss,' he growled and pushed her inside the lift.

Eddy Mars was already at the bar in the Ritz when Dave and Francesca arrived. He was on his second pink gin and not in good humour. He could not abide paying for his own drinks. Seeing Dave Yates come in, he jumped elegantly off his stool and waved at them to join him. He had trained with the Royal Ballet and every movement he made was long and graceful; the wafting of arms, the tilt of his head were all postured to a turn.

'Dave!' His handshake was quick and limp and he stood back to admire. 'You look wonderful! So masculine, darling! Hmmm.' He fingered Dave's lapel. 'Paul Smith. Divine colour.' He completely ignored Francesca.

'Thank you. Eddy, can I intro—'

'Hmm, definitely, but let you get me a drink first! I'm parched.' He motioned to the waiter. 'Two pink gins – you will drink gin, won't you, Dave? Not too effete for you? Hmmm?' He laughed, showing immaculate white teeth.

'Yes, and an orange juice please.' Dave spoke to the waiter directly while Eddy leaned back on the edge of his stool and turned away from Francesca. He pulled up a stool for Dave.

'Now, tell me all about this collection, darling.' Eddy took his gin, sipped and then ran his tongue over his teeth.

'Yeah, sure. Eddy, can I introduce Francesca Cameron? She's my new partner.' Dave found Francesca a seat.

Eddy Mars finally turned to Francesca. 'How nice,' he said and looked away to a face he recognised just coming into the bar. 'There's Tom Vance, from the Beeb.' He leaned closer to Dave. 'Came out of the closet last week. No wonder his suit looks so bloody crumpled!' He laughed loudly and Dave smiled politely. He'd heard the same joke the last time. He decided to get down to business.

'The collection was designed by Francesca and myself. Francesca was responsible for all the textile design.'

'Really?' Eddy glanced a little sneeringly at Francesca and pursed his lips. 'You think I'm going to buy that one, do you, Dave my sweet?' He turned away to ignore Francesca for the second time.

Dave tensed. 'Yes, obviously, or I wouldn't have said it.'

'Well, darling, you must have lost more than just a few designs when Matt walked out on you, that's all I can say. He tells me that your young lady here used to be general dogsbody before she became the greatest show on earth!'

'What the fuck is that supposed to mean?' Dave raised his voice and Francesca put her hand on his arm.

'Look, Dave sweetie, there's no need to get shirty! I have been generous enough to give you my time, for which you were late, I might add. The least you can do is cut the bullshit and tell it to me straight. Don't insult me, Dave sweetie – I've already had an interview with Matt Baker, so I know all the gossip and I'm here to see you, not some cheap little floozie you're sleeping with. Oh, divine collection by the way, Matt's, I had a sneak preview. Very like your own work, I'd say.'

'Oh yeah?'

'Yes, absolutely! Matt tells me you're all washed out, Dave, inspirationless. Hanging your hopes on your cock!' He smiled nastily. 'I didn't believe him, of course. I said: "Matt darling, I won't believe you till I've seen Dave myself! If he insults me by bringing a schoolgirl for drinks, well then I might just . . ." '

Dave kept his temper just long enough to stand up, position himself and then slam a right hook into Eddy Mars' face. He watched the fashion editor of *Fashion Review* topple backwards off the stool, a look of shock and horror on his face, and then slump down against the bar with the pink gin glass still in his hand and its contents spilled rather embarrassingly over the front of his crotch. Dave was so angry it didn't even register what he had done.

'Come on, Frankie!' He took Francesca's hand and pulled her away from the body, seething with rage. 'This man's an arsehole!' he shouted. And they left the bar, only five minutes after entering it, leaving Eddy Mars to pay for the drinks.

Outside on the pavement, the sharp, ice-cold February air hit Dave full in the face and brought him instantly round to his senses. He stopped dead, screwed his face up and put his hands to his head. 'Ahhhh . . . Jesus Christ! How the hell did I do that?'

Francesca stood and faced him. She was almost speechless. 'I don't know! After everything you've said about . . .'

'Yes, I know!' Dave snarled. He was livid with himself and was taking it out on her. 'I don't need you to tell me how important Eddy Mars is!' He began walking away from her towards the tube, striding ahead, angry and defiant. Francesca called out to him.

'Dave? Dave!' She ran to catch him up. 'There's no need to be horrible to me!' she said, hurrying alongside him, flushed and out of breath. He stopped and looked at her. 'Oh God! I'm sorry, Frankie. What a bloody fool I've made of myself!' He shook his head and sighed heavily, his breath forming a thin cloud of steam in the freezing air. 'I just don't know what came over me.' He shoved his hands deep down into his jacket pockets and looked down miserably at the ground. He knew exactly what had come over him – pride, idiotic foolish pride. He'd let himself be wound up by a jumped-up little jerk. He looked up. 'Trouble is,' he said

Dangerous Obsession

anxiously, 'I can't even begin to contemplate what damage I've done.'

The following morning, when Dave woke with a sore head and looked at the remains of his mini bar by the side of the bed, he somehow knew, instinctively, what damage he had done. He had a ghastly premonition of what was to come. Sitting up, he belched loudly and was heavingly sick.

'Oh shit!' The scene in the Ritz came back to him, as it had done all night, and he put his hands to his aching head wondering how the hell he could have been so bloody stupid. Whamming Eddy Mars was the most idiotic thing he had ever done. Whether the bastard deserved it or not was irrelevant. He knew, along with the rest of the fashion world, that nobody offended Eddy Mars, let alone smacked the bugger in the face! Racked with remorse, he looked at his watch and picked up the phone to dial the *Fashion Review* offices. The bloke was a jerk but an apology was in order, John was right about that, if they wanted to have any show left, that was. He dialled the number.

'Hello, Eddy Mars please. Thank you. Yes, Eddy Mars please. Oh, I see. When was this? Ah, right. No, no message, just wish him a speedy recovery.' Dave replaced the receiver and looked at his right fist. 'Oh shit,' he said again and slumped back on the pillows. That was it, he'd blown it! Mars was off sick with a suspected broken jaw and they might as well pack up the clothes and head back to Newcastle. There'd be no show after Mars got round the press; or rather, thought Dave ironically, there would be a show, probably the best of the week, but no one would turn up to it, not once the word was out. The phone went by the side of his bed and he rolled over to answer it.

'Dave, it's John.'

'OK. Give me the bad news.'

'It's worse than you thought actually. The *Face* called at eight this morning to cancel, *The Times* at eight-fifteen, and I just put the phone down to the *Mail*. You are being scrubbed out of diaries as quickly as BT can put the calls through.'

'Oh Jesus!'

'I have a feeling, Dave, that prayer could be the only way out.'

'Very funny!'

'It's not meant to be!' John was angry. 'You've got one more interview to go and I'll be amazed if they don't ring to cancel. You'd better start praying.'

'Fuck!'

'Exactly. If I wasn't so much of a gentleman I'd have said that myself!'

'Look, John, I told you last night, the bloke was insulting – rude, and bloody insulting! I admit it was pretty frigging stupid to hit him but I have to say he deserved it.'

'All right!' They had been over that ground last night. John was tired and worried and he couldn't be bothered with right and wrong this morning. 'It's done now anyway,' he said. 'I suggest you get yourself dressed and down here to reception and we'll go through who we can call to rustle up some support. Let's just try to remedy the situation instead of arguing about it, shall we?'

'Yeah. I'll be down in about ten minutes.' Dave hung up and climbed out of bed. He scooped the empty miniatures into the bin and went through to the bathroom. John was right. They would have to try and sort this mess out, and with a whole load of luck they could just do it! A few calls to some of Dave's old mates in the rag mag business might bring in some support – that was what friends were for, wasn't it? But Dave knew as well as anybody that the results would be pretty bloody paltry, particularly after the promise of all the press interest in his new prodigy, Francesca Cameron. He glanced at his pallid face in the mirror and it seemed to slump before his eyes. OK, it was paltry, he thought, but it was something. It was a hope, however small. And it was the only thing that kept them going through a miserable and desperate day.

By seven o'clock that evening, they had called everyone Dave knew and no one was available to interview them, or was even interested for that matter, in the story of the new Cameron Yates collection. All previously arranged appointments had been cancelled. In fact they had called everyone in the business and just two unknown trade magazines were vaguely interested – but only if they could think up an industrial slant to the story. The press had totally blocked them out.

Dave sat in the lobby of the hotel with Francesca and John and realised for the last time just how damn stupid he had been. Wasn't it him who'd been banging on about the importance of Eddy Mars for weeks? God! What a sodding joke! The man was malicious in the extreme and Dave had known it, more than anyone else, and still he had thumped him! He sat and stared down at the patterned carpet, counting the squares and diamonds and feeling more wretched than he had ever done in his life before.

'I suppose that's everyone on the list?' John said, interrupting the miserable silence. He folded the paper he held in his hand and chucked it onto the coffee table.

'Yup.'

'Well, there's nothing more we can do then.'

'Nope.'

'Oh, for God's sake, man! Stop acting so morose! It's done, and bloody moping won't help!'

Dave looked up, surprised at John's tone. He thought about arguing and saying it made him feel a whole lot better but he could see the strain on John's face and he knew that if he went down he took John and Frankie with him. It made him suddenly very humble and so he shrugged and said: 'I know, I'm sorry, John.' And then he smiled. He uncurled his long legs from the chair and tapped Francesca on the leg with his toe. She looked up from her sketchbook. 'I suggest we go out for a drink and something to eat and try to forget all about this shitty business. Frankie?'

'Yes, fine.' She was trying to keep as quiet and calm as she could. She trusted John and he had told her that he didn't think the situation was actually as bad as it looked today. He was lying, but he felt there was no point in adding to her worry and stress.

'John?'

'No, it was nicely put, but actually I don't really feel up to it tonight. I think I'll just get room service.'

'OK.' Dave stood up. 'Frankie, this isn't my part of town, being a norf London boy, but I'll see what I can do. Get your bag and we'll hit the nightspots of Pimlico. Let's get drunk, all right?'

Francesca got to her feet and stretched. 'Sure.' She ran her fingers through her hair and pushed the sleeves of her jacket up her arms. The silk suit she wore was crushed from sitting so long but it looked better that way, natural chic. She bent and picked up her bag.

'John, we'll see you later. We won't be long.'

'Yes, fine.' He looked up at Francesca and smiled, but the smile belied his frustration and worry. They had to succeed tomorrow, they just had to. The trouble was, he just couldn't think what the hell he could do now to make any difference. If the press didn't turn up tomorrow and the show wasn't reviewed, there would be no buyers and no finance. All the hard work and effort and inspiration and hope down the drain. All that, along with David Yates the company and David Yates the designer. It just wasn't fair!

'John? I said we'll be back around nine-ish.' Dave had his combat jacket on and was digging in the pockets for his handkerchief. He found it and blew his nose. 'See you later then.'

'Yes, fine. See you later.' He blew Francesca a kiss and watched them leave the hotel. They looked good together, he thought; they *were* good together, they made a superb team. He sighed and stood wearily. He was hoping against hope. It just wasn't fair.

Patrick Devlin sat in the saloon bar of the Dirty Duck in Vincent Square, one of the back streets of Westminster that bordered on Pimlico, and tucked into his pie and chips. He had been in the House all day and was in for a late-night sitting by the looks of things, so he'd taken an hour out to eat in one of the pubs not frequented by politicians. He had a copy of the *Lancet* propped up against an empty beer glass and read while he chewed, oblivious to the noise around him.

Francesca followed Dave into the pub they had finally managed to find, after walking for nearly an hour, and sat down on a bar stool, slipping off her suede loafers and rubbing her toes with her hand. She didn't bother to glance round the bar – all pubs looked the same to her – she just sat and squeezed some life back into her feet while Dave read the menu out loud and argued the merits of sausages over a Cornish pasty to her.

And that was how Patrick first saw her, her head bent, her thick, glossy hair falling over her face and one long, curved leg out straight on the bar stool opposite while she rubbed her foot with her hand. He had looked up briefly to attract the barmaid's attention and seen her. He started physically, recognising her instantly, despite how her hair had grown, and felt a hot rush of blood to his head. He sat for several minutes, not knowing what to do, the intensity of his emotions throwing him into confusion. He stared, unable to take his eyes off her, just the sight of her overwhelming him with acute memories and a suffocating sense of loss.

Then he stood, moved clumsily round his table and hurried across to the Gents. He needed air, some time to think. He pushed the door open and escaped out into the cold passage, holding onto the wall and feeling his heart pound against his chest, the throb so strong that it rose up into his throat and made him swallow painfully. Jesus, what was he doing? He had begun to sweat and he fumbled in his pocket for a handkerchief. He wiped his forehead, took a deep breath and stood straight, carrying on outside to the beer garden.

Out in the cold air, he again took several breaths and his body began to calm. It was dark, empty; the wet tables were piled to one side up against the fence and the chairs had been packed away. It was silent and cold after the noise and warmth of the pub and he sat down on an icy stone bench by the door, leaning his head wearily back against the chill brick wall. He closed his eyes. The shock of seeing her had brought it all back to him, all the stupidity of his action, the shame and guilt, the hopelessness and grief, and most of all the wretchedness at his own pathetic weakness. It made him feel sick to think of it.

He had known as soon as he left her that he had made a mistake. Oh God, what a mistake! But he had underestimated Margaret's strength, her domination and power. He had tried to look for Francesca, but Margaret had threatened, cajoled and blackmailed, and in the end he hadn't the strength to fight her any more. You'll forget her, she had said – he almost laughed out loud at the thought of it! Now, here he was, frightened to go back in and face the woman he loved. Jesus! Forget her? He felt the familiar ache in the pit of his stomach and almost welcomed it. Forget her!

He opened his eyes and looked around him. How could he forget when the very sight of her made him ache for her? And what did that say about the past five months, about Penny Brachen and Margaret's schemes? He knew in his heart that they no longer held any sense for him, that Penny had slipped from his consciousness: she had simply ceased to exist. His life, politics, Margaret, Penny, every part of it had vanished from view. All he could see was Francesca. Francesca. He said her name again and again in his mind. It was beautiful; it was the one word he said in his dreams. Francesca. She was more real to him now than anything he had ever known in his life before.

He stood up and swallowed hard. He would have to go to her, there was nothing else but that, not when his whole body told him the truth. He turned back towards the pub. Forget her? How could he ever have imagined he could do that, when one glimpse made everything in his world seem pointless without her?

Standing across the bar, Patrick watched her for a few minutes, the tilt of her head, her smile, the same natural grace that he had first noticed about her. He smiled when she laughed at something her friend had said, feeling the warmth of it from twenty yards across the room. He walked over to her, unable to stay away a moment longer, and stood behind her. He coughed and then he said her name. 'Francesca?' He wanted to reach out and touch her hair. He remembered its thick silkiness. 'Francesca?'

She turned.

She had heard his voice and known it was him before she saw him. She had felt it in her heart, that instant recognition of someone loved and cherished. For one split second she had sat perfectly still and the past five months – all the pain and humiliation – had disappeared; she was simply here, with him. And then suddenly the moment vanished and she remembered. She turned and saw his face and she remembered, everything. The hurt crowded her mind and the pain was as fresh and raw as if it had happened yesterday, filling her with rage. He saw her face, the anger in her eyes, and he went to touch her, not believing it, but she flinched and dropped her glass. It smashed down on the floor.

'Don't!' She slid off the stool and backed away from him. 'Don't touch me! Just . . .' She moved towards Dave for protection. 'Don't!'

'Francesca, please!' He reached out. God, he should have known, blundering up to her like that, insensitive fool. She backed away again, instinctively, like a frightened animal, and he grabbed hold of her arm impulsively, desperate to get through to her. 'Francesca, please!'

'Get off me!' she cried, yanking her arm free. She turned towards the door. She had to get away from him.

'No, Francesca!' Patrick went after her and caught her as she fled out into the street. All he knew was he had to hold her, speak to her. He gripped her arm tighter but it only incensed her further and she struggled against him, trying to pull free. She kicked him in the shin and he released him with the shock of the pain. 'Ouch! Shit!' She made a run for it. But he was quicker than she was. He seized her before she got very far and pulled her in close to him.

'Francesca!' She fought violently. 'Stop it! Francesca, for God's sake, stop it!' He held her tighter. She was almost hysterical. 'Stop it!' He grabbed her shoulders and shook her to her senses. Almost immediately she calmed and stopped struggling. She stood still, half in his embrace, and stared down at the ground, her eyes bright with tears.

'Listen to me, Francesca, please! Will you just listen?' He had his arms around her again and clutched her to him so that she couldn't move away. The feel of her body was so powerful that it made him almost dizzy. 'Francesca, I love you!' he said, over and over. 'I love you, please believe me, I love you.'

Dave had come out onto the pavement. The whole scene had happened so quickly that he'd not known what to do. He heard Patrick's words and turned to go back inside; he shouldn't be there, they hadn't even seen him. He disappeared back into the pub and watched from behind the glass to check she was all right.

'Francesca, will you just listen to me, please?' Patrick still held her even though she was still. He couldn't let her go. 'Please? Just listen, just talk to me. Please.'

Finally she nodded. She was in turmoil; it was easier to agree.

He let go his grip slightly and looked down at her face. He knew it so well; he had carried the memory of it in his mind for months. He put his finger under her chin and tilted it up. She flinched.

'I don't want to talk about what happened,' she said defiantly. 'Not now. I can't.'

'OK.' He could not see her eyes, the eyes that gave everything away. 'Shall we go inside?' He didn't care what happened now, he had her close to him, that was all that mattered. He felt alive again for the first time since she had gone.

'All right,' she answered wearily. He led her back into the pub and over to the bar. He did not touch her but the strength of her physical presence pulled him to her. They approached Dave and Patrick held out his hand.

'Patrick Devlin,' he said.

Dave started at the name. He knew, of course he knew, who else could it have been? 'Dave Yates,' he answered and looked closely at Patrick's face. The two men shook hands without much warmth and then Patrick turned back to Francesca. 'Do you live around here, Francesca?'

'No, we live in Newcastle.' She didn't qualify the 'we' and Patrick experienced a jolt of shock. He swallowed hard.

'Frankie and I work together.' Dave had picked up on his response – the emotion was so intense he could almost see it and he felt momentarily sorry for the bloke. 'We're in London to show a collection at London Fashion Week,' he said. 'Tomorrow, actually – that's if anyone turns up for it!'

'I see.' Patrick's relief was apparent. 'What do you mean, if anyone turns up for it?'

'Oh, we've had a bit of a problem with the press. I got into a ruckus with a right dickhead from *Fashion Review*, more bloody fool me, but the word's out to blackball us. Bleeding arsehole!' Dave took a sip of his pint and realised that Patrick wasn't really listening to him. He was watching Francesca.

'You work in fashion?' He had turned to her but still she wouldn't look at him. She just nodded and gazed away. Her heart and her head were spinning in opposite directions; she didn't know what to think or feel.

'She's only the most brilliant thing to hit the scene since Coco Chanel!' Dave interrupted. He could see Francesca's distress and squeezed her arm. He wondered if they should leave but Devlin seemed so desperate, so eager. 'Really, I mean that! I'm not just joking,' he continued, to cover the tense silence. 'That's why the whole thing pisses me off so much! This could be the best collection of the week and if no one bloody turns up to see it we've wasted our sodding time. We might just as well have stayed in Newcastle!' His voice had risen without him realising it and someone looked over. 'Sorry!' The face turned away again.

'Will they really not turn up? This "dickhead", does he have that much influence?'

'It's not so much that, it's more a case of him being in the know, if you see what I mean.' Patrick shook his head. 'Well, during London Fashion Week there are literally hundreds of designers all scrabbling round for a piece of the action from the press and even though I'm well known, I've never had the sort of clout of someone like . . . Conran, or Katherine Hamnett. The press turn up to all the big shows, see, and select the smaller ones by word of mouth recommendation. And that usually comes hotfoot from the doyen of fashion, our friend Eddy Mars!'

'Oh dear. I see.'

'Yeah, oh frigging dear all right! If Eddy Mars puts the word out that we're a bunch of crap then no one bothers with us. He had the first interview with us and he's obviously told them we're not worth the effort. No problem, they just slot in another designer for that time and we're forgotten.' He clicked his fingers in the air. 'Just like that! Fashion is a shitty business, Patrick – it's here today and gone tomorrow, that's the nature of the work.' Dave took a gulp of his beer, dry-mouthed after his rhetoric. 'Sorry,' he shrugged. 'I'm desperately hoping it's not as bad as I make out but it has been a bloody awful day!'

Patrick nodded. 'Sounds like it! Is there anything I can do to help?'

'Why? You're not a journalist, are you?'

'No, I'm in politics.'

Dave saw Francesca tense at this remark. Patrick said: 'I

used to be in medicine and I let my sister talk me into a political career. The opportunity arose and I took it. It was a mistake, really, I don't like it much.' He addressed the comment to Dave but it was clearly meant for Francesca.

Dave felt again that he shouldn't be there, that he was somehow intruding on something highly personal and emotional.

'I don't know what happened,' Patrick said quietly. He looked at Francesca and this time she met his eye. 'I don't know how I could have been so stupid, or why. I've never stop regretting that day, never, not one second since it happened.'

And Francesca looked down again for what seemed like ages, then she spoke. 'Dave, I want to go now.' Her voice was like a child's, all choked and high. She couldn't face any more. 'Please,' she said.

'Yes! Right, fine!' Dave hurriedly picked up his jacket and pulled it on. He moved quickly towards her, worried and concerned, but she didn't look up. He shrugged at Patrick – there didn't seem much more he could say – and Patrick stood aside. He knew he had to let her go – what else could he do?

Putting his arm round Francesca, Dave led her towards the door. All the time her face was averted from Patrick's gaze, her body held straight and tense. And when they stepped outside she just seemed to slump against him as if all her strength had gone. Dave swayed slightly as he tried to hold her steady. 'Whoa! It's all right, hold on.' He put both arms around her and his heart went out to her. All the times he had thought how old and wise and strong she was for her age, and now, she seemed more like a child to him than he could ever have imagined. Slowly they began to walk off. He dared not look at her, or back at the devastated face of the man in the bar. But he could feel the shudder of her sobs against his body and thought that he would never understand this extraordinary woman.

Patrick sat in his small office at the house and waited for his colleague to clear his desk and leave. The need to be alone was almost unbearable. He watched the second hand tick round on the clock, trying to focus on something other than the pain in his heart until finally the colleague left and the emptiness of the space surrounded him. He felt shocked and confused. Nothing mattered to him now, nothing but Francesca. His mind was blank, his relationship with Penny had ceased to exist, he could hardly remember it. All he could see was Franceesca. Every time he closed his eyes, Francesca.

How stupid he had been to imagine that he could walk back into her life and expect her to forgive him, to love him without question, or anger or recrimination. He had been a fool to think that she would even understand. Jesus, he wasn't sure he understood it himself! All that time wasted, all those futile months doing something he didn't believe in. And for what? For Margaret and the legacy of a drunken father, for trying to make up for the past. It didn't work, he knew that. The past is always with us.

He put his head in his hands and thought once again about what he had decided to do. He had to convince her, to show her that nothing else mattered, nothing but her. It was a good bargain, a fair exchange; a hefty piece of his life for Francesca's future. If it worked, that was.

Flicking through his address book, he found the number of an old schoolfriend and dialled the Kensington exchange. He waited for the ringing tone and then heard Suzie's voice on the line.

'Hello, Suzie? It's Patrick Devlin.'

'Paddy! How are you?'

'Fine, you?'

'Yes, very well. I read from Oli's paper that you've been gadding about with Richard Brachen's sister! Is she really as rich as they say she is?'

'Not really gadding, Suzie.' He felt instantly constricted by this conversation. He wanted to shout: 'It wasn't my idea, it was bloody Margaret!' But he just took a breath and thought: it'll all be out soon enough. 'Just a couple of evenings out, nothing more. Is Oli there?'

'Yes, of course.' She sounded surprised at his tone: usually he would enjoy a gossip with her. 'I'll just get him. Bye, Paddy.'

'Thanks. Bye.' He waited for Oliver Pearce to come to the phone. 'Oli. Hello, it's Patrick.'

'Patrick. How are you?'

'Fine. You? . . . Good! Look, Oli, it seems I've got a bit of business for you, if you're interested.'

'Oh yes? What sort of business?'

'Well, it's to do with the paper, really. I had one of your editors on the phone a few weeks back wanting an interview, an "exclusive", I think she called it, and well, I've rather changed my mind about doing it.'

'Oh really?' Oliver Pearce smiled on the other end of the line. 'And why do I get the feeling that it's not quite that simple? You could have rung her directly, you know.'

'Yes, I'm aware of that. It's just that what I've got to say is somewhat, how shall I put it . . . er . . . sensational, and I was hoping to get something in return for it. Strike a deal, so to speak.'

'Ah, I see. And what exactly is the "sensational" we're talking about, Patrick? Strictly confidentially, of course.'

'It's a love affair. Mine, to be exact.'

'Penny Brachen?'

'No, not Penny Brachen. A young girl, a fashion designer.'

'Oooh! Can you give me any more details? That sounds like quite a story!'

'It is. But no, no details, not until we've discussed the terms.'

'All right, Paddy, I'm interested. Terms? What's the fee?'

'There's no money involved, Oli. I'd like a favour. I'd like coverage of this girl's show tomorrow at Olympia.'

'Is that all? Aren't you selling yourself a bit short? If what you've got to say is that newsworthy?'

'No, I'd like you to organise as much support as you can. You have friends in the business and I'd like you to ring a few. I want a good review, from everyone.'

Oliver Pearce snorted. 'Come on, Paddy! Coverage I can arrange . . . maybe, but opinions? No way! You know I can't guarantee that sort of thing, at least not on any other paper. I have to say, that's rather an unreasonable demand.'

'All right. Coverage then. From all the press.'

'And?'

'That's it! That's what I want. Do we have a deal?'

Oliver looked at his watch. It was after eleven but he was interested – it could be a hell of a scoop! 'Paddy, I'm not entirely convinced. How about me coming to the House for a brief chat, in say, twenty minutes? I'd like to know a bit more.'

Patrick hesitated. What did he have to lose? He had nothing without her. 'All right,' he said. 'Twenty minutes.' And he hung up.

Standing, he felt in his pocket for his wallet and decided to go to the bar for a drink. He turned towards the door just as the telephone rang. He knew it would be Margaret – she always rang on a late-night sitting – and he waited, listening to the shrill bleep and then the click of his answerphone.

His own voice came on and he moved towards the door. He didn't want to speak to his sister; he didn't even want to hear the sound of her voice. Not now, not when he knew that what he was doing would destroy her. He stepped out into the passage and clicked the door shut behind him. I have to do it, he thought, I have to. But he really wasn't thinking straight; he was too much in love to realise just what and who he was taking on.

CHAPTER
Twenty-five

THE FOLLOWING MORNING JOHN WAS down in the hotel
lobby when he saw Francesca. He was checking the
arrangements for the team that night and turned from the
reception desk to see her come out of the lift.

'Hold on a moment please, miss.' He hurried across the
lobby towards her. 'Francesca!' He took her arm. 'What's the
matter, are you all right?' She was deathly pale and looked
unwell, as if she had not slept all night.

She nodded and managed to smile. She did not want to
tell John about last night, about seeing Patrick and all that
it meant for her: it would make him anxious and he had
enough to worry about. But she could not get it out of her
mind, the confusion and the hurt, all the betrayal and loneliness and yet, the strangest spark of joy, right down in the
pit of her stomach, at having seen him again. 'I'm a little
nervous,' she said to John. 'About today, that's all.'

He bent and kissed her cheek. 'It will be fine,' he told
her. 'And you will be wonderful.' He took her arm. He was
worried sick himself but she needed his confidence. 'Now,
you go on in and have some breakfast and I'll join you
when I've checked everything for tonight.' They walked
across the lobby together. 'Are you sure you're all right?'

He was so comforting and warm that she almost told
him then how frightened she was and how much just seeing Patrick had hurt her. But she merely smiled, brighter
this time, and said: 'I'm fine, really, John. Don't worry.' She
loved John and she knew him better than he realised. He

was anxious already and she could not add to it, no matter how troubled her own mind. 'See you in there,' she said and squeezed his hand, walking into the dining room alone.

The three of them ate breakfast together that morning, chatting to fill the void of excitement and anticipation, and trying to cover their intense nerves and expectation of disappointment. It was a quick meal. There were things to be done at Olympia, and they were up and out of the hotel by eight-thirty. They took a black cab across town to Kensington, loaded down with boxes of press packs and the emergency kit bag, stuffed full with scissors, threads, odd bits of trim, buttons, pins, tape, elastic and glue. If anything went wrong it could be mended or if needed, stuck into place.

The space they had booked for the show was already busy by the time they arrived, teeming with people and crammed with clothes. They met up with the three professional dressers John had hired and Dave started to go through the collection with them to make sure they knew what they were doing, while Francesca checked the racks of clothes and John ticked off his list of accessories. By the time that was finally sorted there were just two hours to go before the show.

The models arrived, along with the hairdresser and a couple of odd people who could only be described as hangers-on. Everyone was introduced and briefed, and the full preparations for the show ground into motion. Within fifteen minutes the whole scene was one of organised chaos and the Cameron Yates collection was underway.

By two o'clock, with only thirty minutes to go, the lights had been trained onto the catwalk, music was being played over the speakers and the chairs had been lined up, each one with a programme and press pack on top of it. The buzz backstage had increased as the dressers went over their clothes order again with Dave and the models began to psych themselves up to perform. The team had arrived and sat out the back watching and longing to interfere. Soon, there were just fifteen minutes to go.

'How does it look?' Dave glanced up at John as he came round from the front. He shrugged and Dave jumped up. 'Bad?' John nodded.

Dave walked out past the screens onto the catwalk and looked at the rows of empty chairs. He felt a moment of panic and utter despair, then the bitter ache of disappointment. I knew it was too good to be true, he thought, to find Frankie, to create so brilliantly, to have such a collection against all odds. Something had to go wrong, it had to. He put his hands in his pockets and turned back. I'll have to cancel, he decided; we can't show to nobody!

'Dave!' He turned.

'Everyone's leaving it a bit late, aren't they?' Sophie Enson from the *Telegraph* walked up to the catwalk and Dave hurried across to her. He crouched down and leaned forward to shake her hand.

'Good to see you, Sophie!'

He was grinning from ear to ear and shaking her hand vigorously in both of his. It must have been the most effusive greeting she had had in years.

They turned as two more reporters came in, one with a photographer. Sophie Enson smiled at one of them and looked back at Dave. 'I heard *Northern Life* are coming down with a camera crew. It must really be something, this show!' She laughed. 'Eddy will be livid when he finds out that he got it wrong!'

Dave laughed with her and mumbled something about everyone making mistakes, as he squatted down and watched the chairs fill up, almost miraculously. He spotted

Mariel Higson from *The Times* and a photographer from the *Mail*, and glimpsed the commotion outside caused by a cameraman and sound technician, barging through the queue with their equipment.

He jumped up. 'See you later, Sophie. Come on through when we've finished – I'd like you to meet my partner.'

'Love to.' She took her seat and opened the press pack as the noise out the front began to rise and Dave hurried through to the scene behind the screens.

'John! Frankie! John!' He found them both together stitching one of the models into a halter-neck top. John held it while Francesca sewed.

'Go and have a look out front! Go on! I'll do this, just go! Now!' He took the fabric out of John's hands and the needle from Francesca. They exchanged glances and Francesca followed John round the side to look at the gathering crowd. They were back in a few minutes.

'I don't bloody believe it! What the hell happened? There's even a camera crew out there!' John had started to laugh, his eyes filling with tears, and Francesca went across to hug him. 'Thank God for that, Francesca,' he murmured. 'Thank God for that.' He wiped his face with his handkerchief and then smiled at Dave. 'I suggest you find that terrible baggy suit you had on the other night, Dave my lad, because you're not going out front to take your cheers in that scruffy old thing!'

Dave burst into laughter and whacked John on the back. 'Let's just wait and see if they cheer, shall we?'

'Oh, they'll cheer,' John answered. 'I guarantee it. They'll cheer all night if we let 'em!'

And he was right. The first of the collection went out and the camera flashes went off, the music throbbed, the models spun and moved, creating a whirl of colour and shape, and the clothes trumpeted their splendour. The applause rang through the room. The second part of the collection went out as the first models came in and the dressers deftly stripped, redressed, rearranged, pinned and tucked, pushing the first models out with the third part of the collection as the second lot of models came in. The music changed, the lights altered and the clothes, layers and layers of colour, brilliant and strong, strutted up the catwalk. The applause thundered. And so it went on.

Journalists left for brief minutes to make calls to summon their photographers and the room began to pulse with excitement as the collection became more and more dazzling. People stood at the back, trying to inch into the room to catch a glimpse of the clothes, cameras juggled for space and the noise grew as the climax of the show approached.

The evening wear came on, swathes of velvet, perfectly cut and hung on the long shapes of the models and hand-painted with eighteenth-century designs, or embroidered in gold and silver thread. Then shifts of the finest silk chiffon, almost completely sheer, showing beautifully beaded corsets underneath and silk stockings held up with embroidered garters and diamanté suspenders. The crowd roared.

Finally the wedding dress. A single model walked out onto the catwalk, no groom, no attendants, no fuss. The lights cut and a single beam lit her from underneath. The music stopped and a gasp echoed in the silence.

She wore a long white silk chiffon dress that was threaded through with thin strands of silver and fell from her shoulders in one cascade of what looked like shimmering water. Her hair glistened with drops of silver, long and full, so pale it was almost white, and her feet were hidden in silver slippers, their long thongs of silver tied round her ankles and up her calves. She was motionless for half a minute with a wind machine rustling the folds of fabric, rebounding the light off it. And then suddenly the catwalk lit up and all hell was let loose.

Purcell's trumpet fanfare blasted out, a shower of white rose petals fell down over the bride and the crowd and the catwalk instantly filled with all the models from the show. The music changed again and everyone was bopping and moving on the catwalk when a cloud of multicoloured balloons floated down from the ceiling, all with the designers' tag on them and the address of the Covent Garden offices for that week. A great cheer went up.

'Whoa! Frankie! That's our cue!' Dave yelled above the cheer of the crowd and threw his arms round Francesca. She was laughing and crying with excitement as he pulled her forward and out from behind the screens. They walked out onto the catwalk and the cheer rose even louder. Surrounded by the models, they walked the length of the catwalk, camera lights flashing, and took a bow at the front. Dave swung Francesca round into the glare of a flashlight and said in her ear: 'That one's for Eddy Mars!' and hugged her tight, laughing all the time. He looked behind him and shouted for someone to go and get John but John would not come out without the team, and minutes later, they all stood there, Tilly, Evelyn, Cherry and Elaine, holding hands and laughing as the applause rang out. It was a hard-earned moment of glory and by their faces in the heat and glare of the spotlights, it was worth every exhausting second.

Patrick stood at the far end of the room and waited for the last of the crowd to wander away or out to the back to try to get an interview with Dave Yates and his new star Francesca Cameron. He caught glimpses of Francesca every now and then as the screens were moved away, her face alive with excitement, answering questions, or talking through some detail on an item with a journalist. He saw John also, in amongst a group of what he assumed to be buyers, and thought how much the man had changed, how much more assured he looked, how relaxed.

He was hidden in the back by the shadows of the lights on the catwalk, and he could see and hear undisturbed. He watched Francesca, and saw that she had grown, that her confidence shone and that Dave was right, she was truly talented. As she disappeared from view he thought: she deserves all the attention she gets; I was right to do what I did.

'Hello, Patrick.'

He glanced to his left suddenly and realised that he had been staring so hard for her figure in the distance that he had not seen her approach. She stood slightly away from him, as if wary of coming any closer, and fiddled with her fingers, looking down at her hands.

'I didn't think you could see me, from the glare of the lights.' He wanted to take her hands and quieten them, putting her fingers to his lips, but he dared not touch her. He remained quite still and kept his distance.

'Yes, I could see you.' She glanced up at him momentarily. His face was so painfully familiar to her that she looked away again.

'Congratulations,' he said to fill the silence. 'Dave was right. You're very talented; you deserve success.'

'Thank you.' This time she turned back and looked at him, meeting his gaze. 'I think you had something to do with this today. The press turning up. Did you?'

He shrugged. 'Why d'you ask?'

'Someone told Dave they'd had a call this morning from their editor. Orders from above.'

'No, I—' He stopped because she was smiling, her whole face lit up in that peculiar fashion, and his heart ached at

355

the sight of it. 'Thank you,' she said. 'We would have gone under without this.'

'I wanted to help.'

'Well, you did.' She began to turn away.

'Francesca?'

She stood with her back to him, desperate to turn round but unable to. From the first moment she had seen him she had experienced it, the awesome, smarting desire to run to him, to be in his arms, enveloped in that glorious feeling of love, even if just for a second, to have it once again. But she couldn't; she was too afraid of it. So she stood her ground, the pain of it forcing her back.

'Francesca, will you see me? Please?' She didn't answer. 'Please, just for an hour, for a walk in the park, anything, I don't care, but I have to talk to you. I have to explain, make you see how much I love you!' He moved towards her but she turned and he stopped. 'Please, Francesca?'

She looked at him and knew then that she could not refuse. How could she refuse when her whole body responded to him, to the sound of his voice? 'Yes, all right, tomorrow. Just for an hour.' She started to walk away before he could say any more.

'But what time? Where?'

She looked back. 'After breakfast. I'll meet you outside my hotel, in Warwick Square.' And then she continued to walk away. He had helped her, she owed it to him, just an hour, to give him the chance to speak.

But as she felt his eyes on her back she knew, deep in her heart, it would be more than that. Some things you can't change, Dave had said, some things deep inside. And despite the heat, she shivered and hugged her arms around her. That thought filled her with both terrible fear and joyous hope.

*

John kissed Francesca for the second time that morning in the hotel lobby and stood back to look closely at her face. It was flushed and her eyes were a bright, vibrant green, yet she was quiet and restrained, nervous about something. It bothered him. 'Are you sure you don't want to come to the offices?'

'I'm sure.' She longed to tell him why not, but she was afraid that he would question her and she would not be able to answer reasonably. Seeing Patrick was unwise, she knew that, but she could not stop herself.

'All right, I'll catch up with you later, then. Tell Dave I've already gone, will you?'

'Of course.'

'Where did he get to last night? He vanished after dinner.'

'I think he had a date with one of the models.'

'Ah.' John tried to cover his relief. He had long had a sneaking suspicion that Dave had designs on Francesca, and had feared that this might damage their working relationship. Furthermore, he was determined that she should not be hurt again. 'Well, tell him to meet me there when he gets up.' He picked up his briefcase. 'Wish me luck, Francesca!'

'You don't need it, John. But good luck anyway.' She smiled and he left the hotel, waving as he went. Minutes later Dave came in, still in the Paul Smith suit he had worn the night before.

'Hi, Frankie my love.' He hugged her. 'Is John all right? I just saw him on the pavement getting into a taxi and he gave me a very disapproving look.'

Francesca laughed. 'He doesn't really understand you. I think he's a bit shocked.'

'Hey!' Dave held both hands up. 'Cari is an old girlfriend, we go back a long way.'

Francesca kissed him on the cheek. 'You don't have to explain it to me.'

He shrugged. 'I saw Patrick Devlin walking into Warwick Square, by the way.'

'Oh.' She blushed and Dave looked down at her.

'It's all right,' he said. 'You don't have to explain it to me either.' He patted her arm. 'Be careful though, Frankie, hmmm? Politics is a tough game.'

She didn't really know what he meant by that and she resented his tone. 'I know what I'm doing,' she answered tartly.

'Yeah, sure.' He smiled, somewhat half-heartedly. 'Go on then, don't keep the man waiting.' And she waved and disappeared out of the double doors. Dave worried for a moment about her and wondered if he should tell John. Then he decided it was none of his business. Francesca was young, but she sometimes shocked him with her peculiar strength and wisdom. She probably did know what she was doing. She had done so far; why question it now?

Patrick was striding towards the hotel, the *Times* under his arm and his black cashmere overcoat buttoned through against the cold. It was a typical February day: the air was foggy and a chill wind whipped against his face. He saw Francesca come out of the glass doors and shiver in the freezing air before looking around her and seeing him along the pavement. She started towards him.

She was dressed in a long navy overcoat that was fitted to the waist and then flared out into a full swing skirt. It had brass buttons and a high neck and on her feet she wore low-heeled leather boots that laced up over her ankle to mid-calf, making her look almost Edwardian.

'Hello.' They met halfway down Warwick Square. He wanted to kiss her but she turned her face to look up at the grey sky.

'It's a terrible day,' she said.

'Yes. Shall we go to the park? Or would you rather have a coffee somewhere?'

'No, the park is fine.' She did not want to sit and face him in a restaurant, not yet. She needed time to find out how she felt.

'St James's?'

She nodded.

'Shall we get a taxi?'

'No, let's walk.'

'OK.'

So they turned and headed down to Belgrave Road, then through St George's Square and on towards the river. As they walked, they kept their distance, Francesca looking straight ahead most of the time while Patrick chatted casually and pointed things out to her along the Thames. He knew she was evaluating him; he knew he was being tested. He wanted to hold her and say that for him it was as if the past few months had never existed, that it was the same, that he knew from the first moment he saw her again that he loved her. But he didn't push her. She needed time and he had to give it to her. She would work it out for herself, he knew she would.

As they walked, Francesca thought how much she still liked the sound of his voice, how warm and gravelly it was, and how it hadn't changed, not at all. As he talked, managing to make even the most boring detail sound interesting, she found herself relaxing with him and laughing at his comments. She found herself looking at him every now and then, to check it was all real, and then meeting the warm gaze of his eyes and smiling in answer to his own smile. She found herself caught up in the embrace of love, its comfort and joy making the grey of the morning disappear, and flooding her heart with light. The pain of the past vanished and the elation of the present took hold.

Some way along the river, he took her hand and dug it into the warmth of his pocket. His fingers were just as she recalled them, long and slim, the skin on them fine and almost polished. She did not pull away. The action was so natural that it somehow felt right. Instead, she moved closer to him, leaning very slightly against his arm, and her hair brushed against his face when the wind blew from across the river. There was an ease about them; they were two people wrapped up in each other, in a private, radiant world of their own.

They walked on, up past Parliament Square, Patrick dropping her hand to point out his tiny office in the great Gothic government building, and on to Birdcage Walk on the edge of St James's Square. The traffic roared past them, the fog thickened and people hurried in both directions, emphasising their luxury of just strolling. They walked closely now, unable to stop their bodies from touching, and they talked more quietly, their heads bent together. They were oblivious to the world.

The women's editor of Oliver Pearce's paper came out of the stuffy office on Old Queen Street and took a great gulp of cold air. She was in a bad mood. The story she had been pursuing had amounted to nothing much and she had just wasted forty-five minutes of her valuable time. She looked across the road in both directions for a cab and then walked round the corner into Birdcage Walk. She stood on the edge of the pavement, ready to hail one when it arrived, and spotted what looked like a familiar figure in the distance.

She pulled her glasses out of her bag and slipped them on. She was an expert at recognising a face, even at a distance, and as the couple turned, she saw straight away who it was. Instantly her mood changed. Stepping back into a doorway, she took out her mobile phone and dialled the office, excitedly watching the couple in the distance. What bloody luck, she thought, the promise of a sensational scoop and photographs to go with it! What bloody luck!

She got through after several rings. 'Yeah, hi. It's me. Can you send Steve down to St James's Park right away? Tell him I may have a bit of a scoop and ask him to meet me in Birdcage Walk, at the entrance to the park. Yeah. What? OK.' She waited for a minute and then her secretary came back on the line. 'Of course tell him to bring his bloody camera! Why else would I need a photographer, for Christ's sake?' She clicked the button down on the phone and shoved it back in her bag. Jesus, that girl was an idiot! She lit up a cigarette and made her way up the street to the park entrance to wait for the photographer. Devlin and his woman had disappeared but they'd be in the park somewhere, probably feeding the ducks, she thought, sneeringly.

'So then what did he say?' Patrick held Francesca's hand across the table and squeezed it. He was grinning at her story of the birth of the Cameron Yates collection. They sat outside the café in the park, in the fog.

She laughed and told him and he said: 'My God, Francesca!' And thought how much she had grown. In a few short months she was hardly recognisable as the shy, timid girl he had met in Scotland. And yet she still retained her naivety and her innocence; she was a beguiling mixture, now more than ever, of the woman and the girl. He longed for both of them.

'Shall we go?' They had finished their coffee but she shrugged. He stood up and walked round to her, bending to hug her. She felt the same as he did, he could sense it.

'What shall we do now then?'

'I don't mind. Anything.'

He pulled her to her feet and close to him, tightening his hug and feeling the length of her body against his own.

'Oh, Francesca,' he whispered into her perfumed hair. 'I have missed you.' He squeezed her tight and then lifted her off her feet. She laughed and the echo of it cut through the fog. He lowered her face level with his own and found her mouth. Still holding her above the ground, he kissed her and her hair fell forward and covered their faces. He let her slide down his body until her feet were on the ground and then he tangled his fingers in her hair, pulled it back and kissed her face, moving his lips over her eyes, her cheeks, her mouth.

And from the edge of the café's garden area, hidden from view, the automatic lens of the Pentax clicked and whirred away.

Later on in the closing afternoon, Francesca sat inside the glass covering of a sightseeing boat and looked out at Patrick as he stood in the icy drizzle watching the banks of the Thames from the water. They were the only couple on the boat, along with a family of Americans, who shivered in their waterproofs and snapped hopelessly at the buildings through the misty rain.

She wondered at the extraordinary happiness she felt, at the completeness. She had no desire to question it. It engulfed her, filling her and making her see everything in a new, clearer light. It had brought her alive; the past had just slipped away, out of her reach, and she had no use for it. None of it mattered now; she could think only of him.

Patrick saw her and beckoned to her to join him. She stood and walked out into the freezing rain to the edge of the boat. He opened his coat and pulled her inside against the warmth of his body.

'You fit with me,' he said.

She put her arms around him and thought how right he was.

They were nearing Westminster Pier to dock and the reflection of the Houses of Parliament fell across the water. Patrick knew how worthless all that was for him; he knew there was no going back after today.

'Would you like to come and see my new house, Francesca? I think you'd like it.'

'OK.' She rested her head on his chest and her answer was muffled.

'Are you sure?' It pained him to think that she might not be interested. He wanted her to see everything about him, to know everything.

She glanced up, catching his tone. 'Of course.'

'Good.'

They wobbled slightly as the boat docked and then he led her off onto the Embankment. The lights had come on and an orange glow shone through the darkening mist. He held her hand as they walked up onto the road.

'We'll take a cab. I think it's going to pour any minute.'

'No, let's walk. I love walking through London.'

'Even in the rain?'

She smiled and her whole face was radiant. 'Yes, even in the rain.'

And that was exactly what they did. Halfway along Millbank, Patrick's forecast proved right and the fine drizzle turned into a steady downpour. They carried on walking. They followed the river along Grosvenor Road, the rain coming down at a steady pace, until they made it to the Chelsea part of the Embankment. Then it began to pelt down.

'Good God!' Patrick put his head down and held Francesca tightly. 'I live just up there on the right,' he shouted through the noise of the gushing water. 'Come on, let's run!'

Together they ran along the main road, the cars splashing up puddles of filthy water and the rain stinging their eyes. Patrick led her into Swan Walk and finally stopped outside a black glossed front door. He fumbled in his pocket for his keys while Francesca stood beside him. Finding them at last, he opened the door and pulled her inside, then banged the door shut behind him.

'My God! That was unbelievable!' They stood in the hall, dripping great pools of water over the floor. 'Here! Take off your coat, it's drenched.'

Francesca unfastened the buttons and opened the over-coat. Her clothes underneath – a knitted silk shirt and a short wool skirt – were wet through and clung to her body. Droplets of water ran down her neck to the open front of her shirt, and her hair was plastered to her head.

Patrick moved forward.

Within seconds, he had her face in his hands and was kissing her, his mouth open, caressing every inch of skin, his hands moving down over the wet clothes. He was senseless, overpowered by the incredible passion that rose up and swamped him. He pushed her back against the wall as she struggled to pull him free of his coat. She felt it too and was unable to stop her body; it ached for him. She found his shirt and her fingers ripped the buttons, needing to get to his skin. He had moved his mouth down over her breasts and his hands lifted her skirt, making her cry out when they touched the bare skin at the top of her stockings.

She had opened his shirt and was biting the skin on his neck while her hands unfastened his trousers. He moved away and knelt, putting his mouth to the top of her thighs, but she moaned and pulled him up by his hair so that he was against her. He pressed her back into the wall, undressed her with one hand, then lifted her hips, holding her secure with the weight of his body. Her head was thrown back and she was breathing in short gasps as she pushed her hips towards him. 'I love you,' he said fiercely and she cried out. 'I love you,' he said again. 'I love you, I love you.' And he kept on saying it, with the rhythm of their bodies, until he could no longer speak and their cries sounded out in the silence, together.

The hall seemed cold when they finally stopped breathing hard and their bodies calmed. Francesca had been carried out of time, oblivious to the world, but as her senses steadied, she gradually became aware of her surroundings.

They were in a long, Victorian entrance hall with a black and white marble floor and a round, highly polished, walnut William IV table in the centre. The wall light in the porch lit half the floor with its glow but the rest of the house was dark. What they had done suddenly seemed illicit. Patrick was smiling.

'What are you smiling at?'

'Nothing.' He kissed her. 'I need to get you into a bath and we should turn on some lights and make it feel as if I actually live here.' He released her, kissed her face gently and moved away. Francesca adjusted her clothes as he switched on some lights. He came back to her.

'Don't do that.'

'What?'

'Don't make it look as if nothing happened.' He pulled her shirt out as he kissed her mouth. 'You look glorious, all damp and messed up.'

'Patrick!'

He laughed. 'Come on upstairs. You need a bath, or you'll get cold.' He led her up the first flight of stairs to a bathroom at the end of the house, turning on the light in the passage but leaving the bathroom in shadow. He half closed the door, letting the light from outside just filter in, enough to see her, and then sat her on the edge of the bath, a huge white Victorian tub with high brass taps in the centre. He turned on the taps, sprinkling some oil from a Penhaligan's glass bottle into the bath, and hot water gushed out.

Francesca sat and watched him as he pulled his ripped shirt over his head and ran his fingers through his damp hair. He was beautiful, she thought, strong and powerful, warm and gentle. He was all things for her; he was complete.

'Francesca.' He bent and went to kiss her.

'No.' He stopped and looked at her.

'Go and sit down.'

He glanced behind him at the wicker chair and then back at her.

'Go on,' she said. Her voice was a soft whisper and yet it controlled him. He moved and sat down opposite her, his excitement flaring in that one moment.

She stood and, very slowly, unbuttoned her shirt, peeling it off her shoulders and leaving her lace bra underneath. She eased the straps down, watching his face, and then the fine lace of the bra, revealing her breasts, full and pink-tipped. She saw his face change. She unhooked it and it fell to the floor. Next she unzipped the back of her skirt, let it slide down over her hips and stood in just her black stockings and boots.

She ran her hands down over her breasts to her hips and then her thighs, the thrill of showing her body in this way, the slow revelation of it, making her movements more and more erotic. Patrick sat completely still and silent. Just the quickness of his breath revealed his desire.

Lastly, she put one foot up on the edge of the bath, leaned forward, her breasts touching her thigh, and unlaced her boot, kicking it gently off. She did the same with the other boot and then stood straight. She moved across to Patrick.

'My God, Francesca . . .' She bent her head and found his mouth. His hands went around her thighs, his fingers touching the silky film of stocking. He pulled her down onto his lap, wound his hands in her hair and watched her face as slowly she began to move.

'Thank God for big baths.' He still had his hands in her hair but his head was back against the chair and his body was limp. She lifted her head from his shoulder and smiled.

'Do you want to turn off the taps or shall I?'

'You can.' She moved and lifted her body up and off him. He eased himself out of the chair and across to the bath.

'There's a bathrobe in my bedroom,' he said over his shoulder. 'It's the second door along.' He was testing the water so she picked up his shirt, pulled it over her head and wandered out onto the landing and into the bedroom. She switched on the main light and looked around for the towelling robe.

The bedroom was big and had a masculine feel, decorated in yellow and cream stripes with Georgian mahogany furniture. She liked it – it was just as she would have imagined it to be. She saw a collection of photographs on the chest and curiously walked over to have a look. There was one of Patrick as a boy, one of Lady Margaret's wedding and a recent one, of what looked like a tennis party at Motcom. Patrick was standing next to a brown-haired girl and had his arm around her waist. They, and everyone else in the picture, were laughing, as if the photographer had just said something funny.

Francesca crossed to the bed. She could see another picture by the bedside in a large silver frame and she wanted to sneak a look at that as well. She picked it up. She caught her breath and thought for a moment that someone had suddenly turned out the light in the room. But then she blinked and the picture came into focus again. The grief of it doubled her over.

For that minute, as she stood crippled by pain, looking down into the smiling faces of the brown-haired girl and Patrick, she felt that time was suspended and that she hung there, locked into a black nightmare of realisation that shocked her to the core.

She was horrified but she could not take her eyes off the image, the smiling, happy, united image. It seemed to draw her in, like a whirlpool, pulling her down, her mind swirling in confusion, down and down in a spiral. The girl wore a ring, a large emerald with a cluster of diamonds around it, and it shone out, as radiant as her face. It was the only light Francesca could see, a flashing, spinning light.

Slumping down onto the bed, she covered her face with her trembling hands, desperate for the image to go away, but it burned there in her mind. The bright light shone out of the photograph and the smiles mocked her, sneering and malicious. She dropped the photograph to the floor and cried out.

'Francesca?' Patrick came into the room. 'What's wrong?' He was naked but for a towel round his waist and his body seemed to taunt her.

She stood up, unable to look at him. She felt violated, as if she had shown him her soul and he had laughed and scorned her for it. She felt dirty and used.

'Francesca?' Something about her frightened him. He could sense fear and pain. It was like a barrier across the room. 'Francesca, what is it?'

She wanted to sink to her knees and crawl pitifully from the room but her pride would not let her. She had to face him. Digging her nails into the palm of her clenched fist, she faced him and said: 'I must go now.'

The words came out cold and hard, and later, she wondered how that could have happened, knowing that she was so fragile at that moment, so frighteningly weak, that she should have screamed in pain, like a broken animal.

'What do you mean, you have to go now?' Patrick stayed across the room. The scent of her anger and fear was so strong it scared him.

'I've done what I came to do, and now it's over I have to go.' She saw his face, the flicker of pain in his eyes, and it gave her strength to know she could hurt him as he hurt her. He was a liar, a cheat, but she could lie too.

'Done what you—' He swallowed painfully. 'What you came to do?'

'Yes. You owed me one, Patrick, it was nothing more.' She glanced down at the picture on the floor. It sneered up at her. 'I had to know that it didn't mean anything but . . .' She shrugged.

'But what?' His voice was hoarse with emotion and anger.

'But fucking.'

He looked for a moment as if she had slapped him. Then he turned away. She moved across the room and tried to get past him.

'No!' He grabbed her arm and pulled her to him. 'No, Francesca! No!' She struggled. 'I don't believe you, I can't! I saw your eyes, I felt you!'

'Get off me!' she screamed. She yanked her arm back but he held onto it and pushed her up against the door-frame.

'Tell me,' he said fiercely. 'Tell me you don't love me!' His face was an inch from her own and she smelled the faint scent of sex on his skin. She saw the brown-haired girl in his eyes and his deceit made her feel sick.

'No,' she said. 'I don't love you!'

Suddenly he let her go. He slumped back against the wall and put his hands up to his face. The very charade of it angered her.

'I don't love you,' she said nastily, 'but you're a good fuck, Patrick!' She walked past him into the bathroom and pulled on her skirt and boots, gathering up the rest of her clothes in a bundle. The very thought of their sex disgusted her. His lies hung in the air around her and she had to get out. She came out onto the landing but she could not look at him – she was afraid to.

'I won't let you go,' he said as she went past him to the stairs. She said nothing. Lies, she thought, lies, lies, lies. He pulled her shoulder back. 'I won't let you go, damn it! I'll come after you, Francesca!'

She jerked herself free and made for the stairs. The faces in the picture flashed before her eyes and, not realising what she was doing, she started to run, desperate to get away from him. Frightened by the power of his deception.

'I'll come after you! I know you love me, Francesca!' he shouted behind her, the force of his voice making her weak.

She grabbed her coat from the hall and ran to the front door.

'I'll come for you! he yelled as she ran out into the street. 'I'll come after you! I won't let you go!'

She ran, as fast as she could, through the pelting rain, past the cars, the streetlamps, along the river, until the blood roared in her ears and her chest heaved with the effort. Finally she stopped, miles away from Patrick, and leaned against the cold brick of a building, her whole body shaking in reaction to the force of her emotion. She put her face up to the rain, closed her eyes and desperately began to sob.

CHAPTER
Twenty-six

LADY MARGARET AND LORD HENRY sat in the drawing room at Motcom on one of the rare evenings they were together and played a game of backgammon. The fire was beginning to die down in the grate as the game entered its final stages and Lord Henry was nearing the end of his nightcap. It was after ten and they played in companionable silence, relaxed and winding down ready for bed. The telephone rang.

'Good Lord! Who would be ringing at this time of night?' Lord Henry always associated late-night telephone calls with trouble. In his book people should only call after ten in the morning and before seven at night: any other time was a gross intrusion on one's private life.

'Don't worry, I'll get it.' Their new man had the night off so Lady Margaret stood up and walked out into the chill of the hall to answer the call.

'Lady Margaret?'

'Yes, speaking.'

'Good evening, it's Charles Hewitt.'

'Hello, Charles! How are you?'

'Not in particularly good humour, I'm afraid, Lady Margaret.'

'Oh? Why is that?' It really irritated her the way he insisted on using her title. It was prudent, she knew that, but it irritated her nevertheless. She wanted it to be seen that she was on first-name terms with the Foreign Secretary; she'd earned that honour.

'I've had a call from Chris O'Leary, the newspaper

magnate. Apparently your brother has been making deals with one of the tabloids. I've been on the phone to the editor of the paper involved for the past hour trying to put the whole ruddy mess right!'

'What do you mean, "making deals"?' She was confused. What the hell was Charles on about? Patrick hadn't said anything about it to her.

'Apparently, he promised them an exclusive on his relationship with a young girl called Francesca Cameron in return for the paper rallying round the troops to review this girl's fashion show. I gather that name will ring a few bells, Lady Margaret? Personally I think the idiot's taken leave of his bloody senses!'

Lady Margaret fumbled behind her for a chair. She slumped down onto it and sat stunned for several seconds. She was so angry she could hardly think.

'The situation at present is that I've managed to negotiate with the paper to scrap all ideas of a story and O'Leary put his word in. But that doesn't take care of Patrick. I don't know what the hell he's playing at, Lady Margaret, but I suggest that you find out pretty damn quick!'

'Yes, of course.' Her head was dizzy with rage.

'Didn't you tell me last time we met that Patrick had become engaged?'

'Well, sort of, yes.' She been pushing him for weeks to get a move on with Penny Brachen. She should have pushed harder. Jesus! Francesca Cameron!

'Well, the sooner an announcement is made, the better! The last thing the party needs is another scandal. I'd urge you to convince him of the advantages of a nice solid wife behind him, Lady Margaret, if he wants to stay in the job, that is!'

'Yes, of course.' She instantly felt panic. Was that a threat?

'And by the way, if anything should be said, I'd play up the thing about the family, the girl being an ex-employee. That way we pass off the connection reasonably neatly. Is that all right?'

Lady Margaret held the receiver very tightly. 'Yes, I . . .' She had never told Charles about Francesca Cameron's position with the family. His knowledge came from another source. Christ, what else did he know? 'Whatever you think, Charles,' she said quietly.

'I think you should keep a tight reign on your brother, Lady Margaret. We don't need a cock-happy MP!'

'No, Charles.' She glanced over her shoulder to check she had closed the sitting-room door. 'I'll come straight down to London to talk to him. Do you want to meet up for lunch tomorrow?'

'I can't, I'm afraid.'

'I see.' A sign of disapproval.

'Some other time, Lady Margaret.'

'Yes, some other time.'

And without another word, he rang off.

Lady Margaret remained in the hall by the telephone and tried to think rationally about what she had to do next. There was no time for games now. She would tell it to him straight and God damn it he would listen! She bloody well meant it this time, no idle threats! He might not care about ruining his career but she did! She would have her pound of flesh off Patrick – she'd paid for it and she would damn well have it! She stood and called out to Lord Henry.

'Darling, I'm afraid I have to go down to London tonight.' Charles had stopped the story for now but there was no time to waste. She heard Lord Henry groan as she went into the room.

He will have to be patient, she thought angrily, going to

the bureau for the car key, just like I have been all these years.

John was in his dressing gown when he received the call from reception. Patrick Devlin in the lobby? It must be some mistake. He hadn't seen or heard of Patrick Devlin for months, not since Motcom. No mistake, the girl assured him. Please could he come down to see Mr Devlin. He dressed hurriedly and left the room. The call had given him a sick feeling in the pit of his stomach.

'John!' Patrick crossed the lobby. They stood uncomfortably for several minutes and then shook hands, awkwardly.

Patrick was unsure where to start. 'Do you want to sit down?'

'No, thank you.' All the old feelings of protectiveness for Francesca rose in John's chest. He was still angry with Devlin and resented his appearance.

'What is it you want, Patrick?'

Patrick met John with the same bluntness. He saw no point in wasting time. 'I've come to talk to you about Francesca,' he said. 'About Francesca and me.'

John's face remained impassive but resentment overwhelmed him. 'You must be joking, Devlin! You get me out of bed to tell me that!' John snorted. 'What makes you think, after all these months, that she, or I, for that matter, would have anything to do with you?'

'I've seen her, John, today.' Patrick saw John's face alter. 'She didn't tell you?'

'No.' That fact made him even more angry. 'She is her own person, Patrick! She doesn't have to tell me everything!'

'I know, I know.' Patrick looked away. This was far harder than he had imagined. It had never occurred to him that he would have to face John's anger. 'John, I met Francesca the other night, in Pimlico, and then I came to the show. We met up again today.' He sighed. 'Look, I'm finding this very hard—'

'I bet you are!'

'I . . .' Patrick put his hand out and touched John's arm. 'John, will you just listen to me for a moment? I know you must dislike me, resent me, whatever, but I need to talk to you. Please, will you just listen to me?'

John looked down at the hand and then at Patrick's face. He could see the distress but it didn't soften him.

'All right,' he answered grudgingly. 'I'll give you five minutes.' They walked over to the seating area. 'What is it you want to say?'

Patrick took a breath and looked straight at John. 'Today has been one of the best days of my life, and one of the worst. I have realised today what an almighty mistake I made in Scotland this summer. I realised it as soon as I saw Francesca actually, and now I've got to tell her.' He hesitated for a moment and then continued. 'I love Francesca, and I think she loves me. She ran out on me tonight – it was a stupid misunderstanding – and I have to see her, I have to explain it to her. I thought, maybe . . .' He stopped. 'I thought maybe you might be able to help.'

John looked carefully again at Patrick's face in the harsh electric light of the hotel foyer and thought he looked haggard and old. More than that, he looked bereft.

'I don't think she had forgiven you, Patrick,' he said. His loyalty was to Francesca; he felt loath to say any more.

'Can you talk to her for me? Tell her that I love her?' Patrick was desperate.

'I don't know.'

'Will you at least think about it?'

John thought back for a moment to all the pain and anguish Francesca had suffered in her short lifetime before he answered. 'I will think about it, if you'll do something for me.' Patrick looked up hopefully. 'Anything!'

'Will you really think about how much you love her?'

'I—' John held up his hand to silence him.

'Yes, I know you have already thought about it but I want you to go home and think about it some more. Really think it through, Patrick. Think about how much you would be prepared to give up for this girl and what sort of difference she will make to your life. If, in the morning, the answer is everything, then come back and I will try to talk to her for you.'

Patrick remained silent.

'I don't want her to be hurt again, you see,' John said. 'I won't let her be hurt again.'

'No.' Patrick understood that. 'But I will be back in the morning.'

John shrugged. 'I hope so.' He held out his hand and they shook.

'Thank you,' Patrick said.

'Thank me tomorrow.' Patrick turned and left the hotel.

Lady Margaret swung the Range Rover into Swan Walk from Royal Hospital Road and pulled up slowly outside Patrick's house. She switched off the engine and sat for several minutes in the front seat of the car, illuminated by the light from the streetlamp, and let her body relax after the stress of the drive. It was two am. Then she collected up her jacket from the passenger seat, reached into the back for her bag and climbed out of the car. The house was dark but she had her key.

Ringing on the bell, she rummaged in her bag for the key and found it just as a light came on upstairs. She turned it in the lock and walked into the large, open hallway, switched on some lamps, then walked straight through to the kitchen to make some coffee. She heard Patrick upstairs and composed herself for him.

'Margaret! Good God! What are you doing here?' He stood in the doorway in his bathrobe and blinked at the bright light of the kitchen. 'Are you all right? Is something wrong at Motcom?'

'Yes, I'm fine and no, nothing is wrong at Motcom.' She crossed to him and kissed his cheek without much warmth. 'Go on into the sitting room, Patrick. I'll bring you some coffee in. We need to talk.'

'What do you mean, we need to talk?'

She had returned to the coffee and spoke to him over her shoulder. 'I had a call from Charles Hewitt earlier this evening. He suggested you and I talk a few things through.' She turned. 'Oh, do go and sit down, Patrick – you're making me nervous hovering around like that! I'll tell you what this is all about in a minute, but I need a drink first, it's been a long drive.'

Patrick went through to the sitting room and switched on one of the lamps. It was chilly in there and he suddenly resented the size of the room. Swan Walk had been Margaret's choice – somewhere you can entertain, she had said, somewhere closer to the House for you. She had decorated it and loaned him the money for it, but looking at it now, he didn't think it would suit Francesca. Perhaps, if he stayed in politics, they would move up to his constituency. She would probably like it in the country.

Lady Margaret came in with a tray and placed it on the coffee table. She poured milk into Patrick's cup, handed it across to him and then dealt with her own. She took a large gulp of dark, aromatic coffee and put the cup carefully by her feet.

'So?' Patrick watched her movements, slow and

deliberate, and waited for her to say what she had driven two hundred miles to say.

'So, what is the truth in the story you were planning to tell the *Mail*, about you and Francesca Cameron?'

'I beg your pardon?'

'The *Mail*, Patrick! It seems they were about to do an exclusive on you, photographs and all!'

'What the hell . . .'

'Exactly!' Lady Margaret pulled a long cigarette out of a box and lit it. She looked across at her brother. 'I'd like to know what the hell you think you're doing?'

'Christ!' Patrick was stunned. Free bloody press? The only person that knew was Oli and his women's page editor. 'Jesus Christ! How the hell did you find out?' He stood up and reached for Lady Margaret's cigarettes, lighting one up quickly and moving across the room to the window. He looked out, too angry to speak.

'I hardly think that's important!' Lady Margaret stared at his back. 'I asked you a question, Patrick, about Francesca. You didn't answer me!'

'I don't think it's any of your business!'

Lady Margaret stood up. 'Well unfortunately that's where you're wrong! It *is* my business, like it or not! When the Foreign Secretary rings me at ten o'clock at night to tell me to put you straight on a few things then I'd say it's pretty well as much my business as yours!' She stubbed out her cigarette, grinding it into the ashtray. 'Wouldn't you?'

Patrick turned. 'The answer is still no. My private life is my own affair.'

'Trouble is, it's not private, is it, Patrick? Not when you make stupid deals with old school chums in return for a national exclusive! It's not bloody private at all!' She threw up her hands. 'What in God's name were you thinking about? Answer me that! Are you really out to destroy everything we've worked for? Haven't you any pride?'

'Pride?' I think I've heard that word from you before, haven't I? Look where it got me last time! And in answer to your question, no, I'm not out to destroy everything you've worked for; I was thinking about the truth, that's all. I love Francesca, I want to marry her. I made a big mistake walking out on her, I know that now. I love her and she means more to me than anything else.'

Lady Margaret stood perfectly still and averted her eyes from Patrick's face. The very earnestness of his look made her feel sick. 'And tell me, what would you know about love and marriage, Patrick?' she asked coldly.

'As much as the next man!' He sighed wearily. 'Does it really matter? I love Francesca, it's right for us. Can't you understand that?'

'I'll tell you what I understand, Patrick!' Her voice rose suddenly in anger. 'I understand that you have a cheap little affair with a nubile eighteen-year-old and think it's love! It's quite pathetic, you lusting all over her like an old man and ready to throw in everything for it. You do realise that your career will be over if you continue this fairy tale? Who do you think will take you seriously? A man who can't think past his cock!'

'That's enough, Margaret!'

She shook her head. 'Oh no it isn't! I haven't finished yet! I've got a hell of a lot more to say before I'm finished!'

He began to walk towards the door.

'And you can bloody well stay and listen to it, Patrick! This time there won't be any kind words and pleading. This time I mean business!'

Unmoved by her anger, he stood and thought for a few moments. If he left now the rift would be so much harder to heal, but if he stayed then he would lose his temper and they would both say things that were better left unsaid.

'Sit down, Patrick! Sit down and listen!'

He stared at her. 'Don't order me around, Margaret,' he said icily. 'I'm not going to fight about this.'

And suddenly she nodded. 'You're right,' she answered. 'We don't have to fight.' She lit another cigarette. 'We fought about it once before and I told you that I was only doing what I thought was best for you.' She held the cigarette close to her face and the smoke curled up over her lips. 'Everything I have done has been for you. I hope you understand that.'

'I understand it, Margaret.' But he wasn't sure if he did, and he wasn't at all sure any more if she knew the difference between what was best for him and what was best for herself.

'Good, I'm glad you do.' She took a breath. 'Because I own a large percentage of the David Yates fashion company, not a controlling interest but one big enough to make things very difficult indeed for that company. And, if I felt it was necessary, that is exactly what I'd do! It would be a shame, wouldn't it? After such a well-reviewed show and particularly as they are struggling somewhat to survive in the current climate. I think it would be right to say that if I caused trouble, I could very probably finish them. A great shame, I'd say!'

Patrick stared at her in complete horror, momentarily confused with shock. He thought that maybe she had gone mad, but then he saw her eyes and saw that it wasn't madness at all, it was ambition, pure, unyielding ambition. She stared coldly at him.

'I wonder if Francesca Cameron would thank you for ruining what could be a truly glittering career, Patrick?' She took a last drag of the cigarette and stubbed it out. 'What do you think?' She blew the smoke out in a thick grey cloud. 'If the company were to fold due to an exorbitant rate on their loan, or constant stalling over decisions by a director, or even a takeover? Do you think Francesca would blame you if she knew you could have stopped all that but didn't?' Lady Margaret watched Patrick's face as a look of bitter disappointment came over it. She swallowed hard. She did not want him to hate her but she had to go on; she had to take that risk.

'Would your idyllic love survive disillusionment and resentment? Would Francesca forgive you, do you think?'

But Patrick could not find the strength to answer her. The enormity of her selfish ambition shocked him so deeply that he could hardly speak. 'Why?' he whispered. 'Why would you do this?' It was beyond his comprehension how anyone could hate so much, or scheme such evil. That it was his own sister made him want to weep.

'I don't want to, Paddy,' she said. 'I will only do what I have to.'

'But why?'

'Because I will not stand by and see you ruin your life,' she snapped. 'That's why! You have far too much to lose!'

'But I don't care, can't you see that? She is the only thing that's important. I would give up everything for her. Everything!'

Lady Margaret felt as if she'd been slapped in the face. After all her sacrifice, after everything she had done for him, everything, he would give it all up for that worthless trollop, in it for everything she could get? 'Over my dead body!' she muttered fiercely.

'What was that?'

'I said, over my dead body! You will give up nothing, Patrick! Do you hear me? Nothing!'

'I will do as I please! You just can't get that into your head, can you? That I'm a free agent, that I am old enough to make my own choices!'

'All right!' she shouted. 'Go ahead, make your own choices! But don't come running to me when it all collapses down around your ears, will you? She was livid at Patrick's stupidity. 'You can have that girl if that's what you really want, but mark my words, I will ruin her! I will do everything in my power to do it. Everything! You have a brilliant career ahead of you but if you want to throw it all away then there is nothing I can do to stop you. But you will throw me and the family away as well. I will not stand by and see you destroy your life!'

'But *why*? Why can I not have it all with Francesca?'

'With Francesca?' Lady Margaret laughed viciously. 'With a teenage bimbo in your constituency? A girl who came from nowhere, marked and bruised? She has a past, Patrick! A violent past, any fool could see that. Are you really naive enough to think that people won't pry? Oh, they'll pry all right! There's a can of worms just waiting to be opened and the gutter press will be falling over each other in the rush to prise off the lid! And what about Charles Hewitt? Do you think he'll back your career after you've embarrassed the government and yourself with this sordid little affair? Oh, for God's sake!' She snatched up her bag and dug into it for a tissue, tears of anger and frustration streaming down her cheeks.

'Margaret, please.' Patrick put his hand on her shoulder.

'No.' She shrugged him off. 'I won't listen to your whingeing and whining! You must make your choice!' She wiped her face. 'But if you choose Francesca, Patrick, then think very seriously about the consequences. I will be the first to find out what violent and terrible past she has hidden and mark my words, I will make her pay for it! I will never let it rest! Never!' She shoved the tissue back in the bag and turned to face him. 'It is not just your life any more; you owe too much to too many people. Think about that!' She walked past him to the door.

'Think about what you take on if you go with her, and then pray that you, and she, have the strength to endure it!' She spat the words at him and then left the room, slamming the door behind her.

Patrick stood up and drew back the curtains as the light broke over the city and the orange streetlamps flickered fleetingly, before going out. He looked up at the sky, heavy and thick with dirty rain as it lightened, almost imperceptibly, with the dawn, and then across the street at the parked car opposite with two men in it. They had been there all night.

He turned away and went over to the bureau, taking up several sheets of half-written paper and placing them in a large glass ashtray. He found Lady Margaret's lighter and clicked it open, holding the flame against the corner of the first sheet. It caught light instantly, then spread to the other sheets, and within seconds the fire had burned through the paper and the letters had gone. All that remained of his useless and wretched words of explanation to Francesca was a small shred of thick black ash.

He went upstairs and entered the guest bedroom. Lady Margaret was still awake.

'Margaret,' he said. 'Will you promise me that if I give up Francesca you will leave her alone?' There was no emotion in his voice he was numb and cold to the core.

She turned her head towards him. 'If you marry Penny Brachen, yes.'

He gripped the door handle. His whole body was suddenly filled with a terrible ache, the dull pain of loss. This was his lot, the price he had to pay to love Francesca, the price of her past and his future. He looked at his sister and she was more alien to him than he could ever have imagined possible.

'Give me your word that you will never harm her,' he said. 'Neither her nor the company, and . . . I'll do whatever you want.'

A smile hovered in her eyes but she kept it from her lips. 'You have my word,' she answered. 'But see her again and I will break her.' She turned away again and closed her eyes. Patrick walked silently from the room.

Exactly three weeks later John stood in the sitting room of the small terraced house in Marston Avenue, studying the handwritten white card. It had been addressed to him but the words in it were for Francesca. He did not know what to do. He gazed out of the window at the patch of front garden, newly dug and planted, and felt the force of her pain in the dark, churned earth. She had worked to the point of exhaustion, struggling with the ground as she struggled with her hurt and humiliation, tiring herself too much even to weep. She had wanted to batter her body, to numb it, but she could not escape the suffering, that he knew.

Now, as he waited for her to come home, he worried about her physical state. It seemed to him that she had no strength left, that something inside her had used up her spirit and left her weak and defenceless. She was drained; the shadow of what she felt hovered over her, like a dark angel. He turned as the front door slammed.

'Francesca?'

She came into the room. Her face was deathly pale but for two spots of high colour on her cheeks, like the flush of a fever, and her eyes burned unnaturally bright.

'Where have you been? I've been worried about you.' He tucked the card into his pocket.

'I had to go to the doctor's,' she answered. She fumbled

with the buttons on her coat for a moment and then looked up at him. 'John,' she said quietly, 'I'm pregnant.'

The stark honesty of the words stunned him. It took several minutes before they made sense and he stood, gazing blankly at her, not knowing what to say or do. Finally he walked across to her and held out his arms. She moved into his embrace and the comfort of his body was such a relief after the hours and days of lonely torment.

'What will you do?' he asked, still holding her.

She shook her head. It was a baby conceived in love, a child created through a passion and feeling so strong that the memory of it made her weak. Nothing, no deceit or lies, could take that away. 'I want to keep the baby,' she whispered.

He touched her hair. His life, so barren and useless, a life almost over, had suddenly found purpose, had begun again. She had done this for him and now she would give him the gift of a child. Not his, but a part of her, and in loving her as he did, thus a part of him. 'You must do whatever you feel is right,' he said. 'And I will support you.'

He thought of the card in his pocket and of Patrick's words, so simple and so desperate. I cannot love her without hurting her, he had said, and I would rather give my life than cause her any more pain. Tell her, if ever she should ask, to look at the words of Corinthians 13.7: Love bears all things, believes all things, hopes all things, endures all things. She lives on in my heart, and without her my life will never be complete.

Part II

Enzo – Rome 1990

CHAPTER

Twenty-seven

THE NIGHTMARE CAME AGAIN. IT was dark, black almost, and he was walking across the fields with the night sounds more eerie than he ever remembered them. He knew he was being followed. It was a sensation of fear, a slow, agonising fear, creeping up his spine, and he recognised it, he knew what would happen next. Suddenly an owl screamed and he spun round. A knife went up to his throat and the bulk of his brother overpowered him. His heart was pounding so fast he thought it would explode in his chest and as he opened his mouth to scream nothing came out, no words, no breath, nothing. He looked down and he was covered in blood, his own blood, flowing, full and thick and red, down over his chest to a pool on the floor.

'Giovanni . . . No!' He went to reach for his brother's hands but his strength had gone. 'No . . .!' he cried. 'God no . . . Francesca . . . Save me!'

He woke up.

'Ah! Jesus Christ! Shut the hell up, will you?'

'Shut it, for God's sake!'

The chorus of voices rang out into the still, putrid air of the room and he rolled over onto his side, curling his knees up, shivering and sweating. He thought he might be sick. Listening to the heavy breathing of the other men in the dosshouse, he stared at the black space, eyes wide open, afraid that if he shut them the nightmare would return.

So Enzo Mondello lay, locked in the terror of his

391

memories, and watched for the first signs of light at the boarded-up window and waited for the horror of the night to pass.

'Hey, Enzo! You want a cigarette?'

Enzo looked up from the pavement and leaned on his brush for a minute.

'I'll give you twenty for a piece of that tight little arse you got there!' A round of laughter rang out across the street and he put his head down to carry on sweeping.

'What's the matter, Enzo? Country boy doesn't like my jokes, huh?' The fat man in charge of the bins laughed and showed a mouth full of dirty, discoloured teeth but Enzo swept on and ignored him. The laughter finally died away and the men continued with their tasks.

Sweeping hard, Enzo felt the blisters on his hands, the coarse wood of the broom handle rubbing up against the sores, making them weep. They were painful to touch but he didn't care; he thought of nothing, cared for nothing. Not since Francesca left had he cared. He had sold the farm for a paltry sum just to be rid of it, to be free. Free to find her. That was all he wanted, to find her and to get her back. So, he did the work, his back ached and the grime and filth of the city seeped into his pores, into the creases of his skin and under his nails. He sweated, dirty, oily sweat, day after day, toiling for nothing but the few lire in his pocket, and he waited. He waited for the right time to move on, to find Francesca somehow.

Some time later, looking up a second time from the road, Enzo heard a commotion at the far end of the street and put his hand up to his eyes to shield them from the sun. All the men had stopped working and he followed their gaze in the direction of the brawl. He saw a car, casually parked on the pavement, and a young girl with a man beside it. She was

shouting and pulling at the man, not letting him get back
into the car, blocking his way and yelling abuse at him.
Some of the street workers had begun to laugh as she bullied him for more money and he pushed her away,
embarrassed by the scene.

The man, tiring of the argument, glanced behind him
briefly and saw that he was being watched by a crowd of
smiling street workers. He caught the arrogant sneer on
one of the men's faces and his attitude suddenly changed.
His temper snapped.

'Get off me, you stupid bitch!' he shouted. 'You've had all
you're worth!' He shoved the young girl violently away, and
she stumbled back, nearly losing her balance. Some of the
men watching jeered. She came back at him, arms flailing,
and hit him with both fists on his chest. Egged on by the
jeering, he grabbed one of her arms and wrenched it back,
making her scream with pain.

'Get off me, you filthy whore!' He pushed her again and
she fell. Turning away from him, she began to cry and it was
then that Enzo caught a glimpse of her face. He froze for a
split second and then he screamed.

'Francesca!' He dropped the broom and ran up the street.

Just as the man was about to get into his car, Enzo
pounced, his solid, muscled body powerful with anger. The
man stumbled back in shock. Enzo grabbed the man by the
throat, dragged him down onto the bonnet of the car and
hooked his arm in a stranglehold. The man began to choke
His body struggled wildly against Enzo's hold but he was no
match for the fit, tense body of a street worker. His face,
grotesque in agony, was crimson, swollen with the air forced
down inside his lungs, his eyes bulging with terror.

'Christ! Get him off the bastard!' Two men suddenly
dragged Enzo back and gripped his arms. His hold loosened.

'Jesus, he almost killed him!' Voices, everywhere, inside his head, on the street. He dropped his hands and put them up to his face. The man fell forward to the ground, panting and gasping for air.

'Stand back, give him some air!'

'Thank Christ, he's still breathing!'

Enzo slumped down beside the girl. Her weeping body was huddled on the ground; her arm hung painful and limp. He could see now that she wasn't Francesca and he dropped his head, a bitter disappointment stabbing his chest as he struggled for breath.

'You!' The man towered over Enzo, kneeling on the ground. 'You son of a bitch! You nearly killed me!'

Enzo did not look up; he had no life left inside him. It wasn't Francesca; that was all that mattered.

The man kicked him but he took the blow. 'I'll have you arrested! You bastard!' He went to kick again but Enzo moved suddenly and he hastened back. He ran to the car and pulled open the door.

'You filthy bastard!' he shouted from inside the car, starting up the engine and swearing blindly. He shook his fist at Enzo, revving the accelerator and yelling again out of the window. 'You filthy, dirty bastard!' He screeched off the pavement, narrowly missing Enzo and the girl, and roared off down the street. His engine screamed in the distance and then there was silence. A tense, uncomfortable silence. The men stood around for a few minutes, not knowing what to do, and then the fat man spoke: 'Leave him,' he said and the small crowd of workers backed away. He looked down at Enzo. 'You're fired!' He spat on the pavement and wiped his mouth on his sleeve. 'I don't want to see your miserable face again. Right?' And he turned and followed the others, who had started to move off down the street.

*

For some time Enzo knelt beside the girl. She was silent, rocking back and forth, her mouth clenched and her face ashen with pain. He could hear the faint whimper of her when the pain was too much, like a dog who'd been kicked and beaten, and he had the urge to hit her himself, his bitter disappointment having turned quickly to rage. Instead he tried to ignore her as she scrabbled for her bag.

'Here . . .' Her voice was no more than a hoarse whisper. She pushed the bag towards him with her good arm, every slight movement agony.

Enzo looked up.

'Take it . . .' She could hardly speak.

He pulled the bag towards him, opened it and found a wad of lire stuffed inside. He took it out to count it: it was more than he earned in a week. He glanced over at the girl. She was young, no more than fifteen, he reckoned, and she was pretty, but dirty from the scuffle and her features were blurred by pain. Her eyes were blank as she looked at him and he thought she was near to passing out. He took the wad of cash and pushed it down into his back pocket. 'Thanks,' he said. It would tide him over, at least until he found another job. He stood, and looked back at her, preparing to leave. Suddenly he felt guilty.

He moved across to her and attempted to lift her to her feet. 'Here, hold onto me.' He couldn't leave her there, much as he wanted to. He held her round the waist as she cradled her arm. 'What's your address?' She made no reply. Her legs were unsteady and she leaned against him for support. He bent and picked her up, carrying her across his arms.

'Eh! Signore?' He crossed to a paper seller just setting up for the evening editions. 'You know where this girl comes from?'

The newspaperman looked at Enzo and then at the

young prostitute he carried in his arms. He knew her – she was from a small brothel in the area. 'Take her to the Via Varese,' he said. 'It's off the Via Palestro, it's not far.'

Enzo nodded. He had been working round there the day before and he knew it vaguely. The girl murmured something unintelligible, looking up at him with blank eyes, and seconds later she passed out. The weight of her was like lead in his arms. He nodded to the newspaper seller to thank him and set off in the direction the man had pointed out.

Some time later, now holding the girl up as they walked, Enzo located the address she had given him. They stopped outside a three-storey dilapidated pink stone building on the Via Varese and he stepped forward to ring on the bell. The door was eventually opened by a tall, attractive woman, who came out of the house and took the girl from him, supporting her with both arms. She nodded to him silently in greeting and he nodded back. She turned to lead the girl inside the house and then glanced over her shoulder, looking Enzo up and down.

'Come inside, please,' she said. He was surprised at her voice – there was no trace of an accent. 'Perhaps you could wait until I have taken care of Sofia?'

'Sure.' Enzo pulled back his shoulders and as the woman turned again to the girl, he followed her through the heavy oak double doors.

'Carla, could you show Signore, er . . .'

'Mondello, Enzo Mondello.'

'Thank you, Signore Mondello to the reception rooms while I take Sofia upstairs to her room?'

Enzo found himself in a long, leafy courtyard with a vine-covered portico and several doors leading off it. One of the doors opened and a small, squat, elderly lady draped in the customary widow's black came out. She nodded in his direction and he stood and watched the younger woman lead the girl through another door and disappear out of sight.

'This way, please.' The old woman led him back through the door she had stepped out of, along a darkened passageway to a further door. He was amazed: the whole place seemed to be a labyrinth of passages and doors.

'In here, signore, please.' She swung open the last door and Enzo entered a long, darkened room, elaborately draped in reds and golds with high gilt mirrors, two or three low ornately padded and buttoned ottomans and a handful of chairs scattered around. It smelled musty, of old cigarette smoke and spirits; it also smelled very slightly of body odour, the distinctive scent of sex. With the door closing tightly behind him, Enzo stood in the centre of the room and took a good look round, fascinated by the seduction of the place. He must have stood there for more than ten minutes and he didn't hear the door open again.

'Signore Mondello?'

He started and looked round. The tall, attractive woman had entered and he eyed her suspiciously. She walked towards him, the silk of her dress swishing very slightly as she moved.

'Would you like a drink?' she asked coolly.

'No thanks.' He was embarrassed. His clothes were soiled and he knew he smelled of the dosshouse; he was out of place here and he couldn't wait to get away. He shifted his weight uneasily from foot to foot and waited.

'Perhaps you would like to sit down, Signore Mondello?' She gestured to a sofa and walked across to it herself. She sat and patted the space beside her, looking directly at Enzo. He could see she was sizing him up. He crossed to her, holding out his chest, and sat down awkwardly on the edge of the seat, again conscious of how filthy he was.

'Please, make yourself comfortable.' She smiled and he could see the straight white line of her teeth, expensive teeth, lips lined in crimson. She had a hard face, well made up, the lines expertly covered, but it was a cold, aging face, and her hair, swept back off it and twisted into a high chignon at the back of her head, emphasised this.

'Signore Mondello,' she said carefully, 'Sofia has told me what you did for her this afternoon and I am very grateful.' She paused. She had known the moment she saw him just how useful he could be; she had a sixth sense for this kind of thing. But she had to play it carefully, exactly the right balance between kindness and control. 'I realise that her money is missing and I presume she has paid you for your help?'

Enzo nodded. This one was no fool. He dug his hand warily down into his pocket and held the wad of lire.

'Good. I am afraid, Signore Mondello, that the young girls who work for me will still take their chances on the street every now and then.' She shrugged. 'Why, I don't know. I have a good establishment here, there is no need for them to . . .' She stopped, as if exasperated by the whole thing, and smoothed her skirt with her elegant fingers. 'Signore Mondello, Sofia has told me that you were, how shall I put it, quick and er, aggressive today in helping her.' She looked at him appraising his square shoulders, his heavy muscled frame. 'I can believe that.'

Enzo shuffled self-consciously on the sofa and she knew that she'd calculated him well. Not stupid, but malleable.

'I have a proposition to put to you, signore, if you would be so kind as to listen to me for a few minutes.'

The way she spoke was so controlled, confident and quietly aggressive that it unnerved him; he had never come across a woman like this before. But despite this he stayed seated. He had nothing to lose by listening, did he? He nodded again and she went on.

'Excellent. It is with regard to my business here.' She gestured with her hands to include the whole room. 'My entertainments business.'

Enzo kept quiet. He knew exactly what went on here but it wasn't like any whorehouse he had ever been in.

'I see we understand each other; I shall come straight to the point then. I am looking for a man to help out in my establishment, someone to look after the girls, to keep an eye on things for me.' She stopped. In truth she was looking for much more than that; she had ideas and it was as if Enzo Mondello had fallen into her lap, a gift from the gods. She licked the crimson lips. 'Enzo – I may call you Enzo?'

He nodded.

'Enzo, the work is easy, very low key. I need someone who could ensure that nothing gets out of hand at any point. Someone who could, how shall I phrase it? Who could protect my interests if the need arose. Do you understand that?'

Enzo was aware that all the time she spoke the woman was watching him closely. She did it in a very casual, understated way, but he knew and he found it vaguely exciting. Apart from the girls on the street, she was the first woman he had come into contact with since Francesca had left, the first real woman, not some hasty scuffle in the dark of a back alley. He was wary of her but already he didn't want to leave; she fascinated him.

'What sort of payment are we talking about?' he asked gruffly. He felt the need to assert himself, although he knew his self-control was slipping away. Just the closeness of her brought back a powerful ache, a sense of physical loss that no amount of cheap thrills could replace.

'Board and keep – I'd like you to live in. And, say, one hundred thousand lire a week, with a three-month trial period?'

Enzo pretended to think about it for a few minutes; he'd have stayed for much less. Besides, he had nothing to leave for, not yet, not until he'd found Francesca.

'I'd have to collect my things,' he said, thinking he needed to make one or two demands. 'And I don't know how long it would be for.'

The woman nodded. It would be for as long as he was useful to her. 'Of course. Understood.' She stood. 'We must get you some new clothes, Enzo, from the market in Via Sannio. You can take my card – most of them know me there and you'll be able to put some things on my credit.'

Quickly Enzo stood as well. He felt foolish sitting on the sofa while she towered above him.

'Well, that concludes our business, I think.' She held out her hand and Enzo hastily took it. He desperately wanted to touch her. 'I am sure we will have a good working relationship.'

He nodded and held her fingers a moment too long. He thought he saw a brief smile flicker in her eyes but it was gone before he had the chance to be sure.

'Details,' she said crisply, dropping her hand by her side. She had been in the business long enough to be able almost to smell sexual excitement. It amused her. Perhaps Enzo Mondello would prove useful in more ways than one . . .

'Some of the younger girls live with me here,' she explained quickly, 'but most of my girls arrive for work at six. We eat mid-afternoon – although some of my more regular customers occasionally like to use us in the daytime – and you will find that Carla has the meal ready after three. It is up to you whether you want to eat with us or not, but I would like you dressed and ready for work by five-thirty. We are mainly an evening establishment: we tend to entertain business clients after dinner, gentlemen wanting somewhere to drink late at night, that sort of thing.

Generally the hours begin around six or seven. Does this suit you?'

Enzo nodded.

'Good. I don't think I have anything else that I need to tell you. I will see you tonight then?'

'Yes, er . . .' Enzo tried to think of something to say, something to detain her a moment longer, but he couldn't.

'Carla will show you to one of the rooms on the top floor.'

'Yes.' He watched her walk towards the door. She held herself well, her body straight, her head tilted up, not haughty, just slightly aloof.

She paused at the door. 'By the way, my name is Isabella.' She smiled. 'Welcome to the Villa Isabella.' And without another word, just the soft rustle of silk, she left the room.

Enzo stood where he was for quite some time and stared after Isabella. He could smell her, the warm female smell he had longed for all these nights, and it made him dizzy. He put his hands up to his face and closed his eyes. He could see Francesca in his mind, naked, running in the warm sun towards the sea. It was the same image, over and over again, the same obsessive craving for her, the same violent need.

He snapped open his eyes and sniffed the air. Isabella's perfume hung, heavy and cloying in the musty atmosphere of the room, and Enzo inhaled deeply, breathing it in. It excited him, reminded him of his own power. Of how he had had Francesca and could have her again. It filled him with strength.

Looking up sharply as the door opened, he saw the old woman Carla and nodded as she gesticulated for him to follow her. All thoughts of Francesca disappeared; his mind was clear. He took one last glance round the room and walked across, stepping out into the darkened passage behind Carla. He stood a little taller and squared his shoulders.

Enzo had no idea how long he was going to stay here – that all depended on Francesca – but he did know that for the time being he had landed on his feet. He sniffed at Isabella's perfume again – it seemed to be everywhere – and slowly followed Carla up to his new room.

Twenty-eight

ENZO SAT IN THE SMALL dark space behind the two-way mirror and stared blankly at the scene in the next room for a few moments. A girl was stripping slowly and carefully to a small audience of men, her body swaying in time to the music, its rounded curves lit by the dull orange glow of the lamps.

Other girls sat around, several of them in just underwear and silk robes, some quite ornately dressed, but all with clients, all paid for. In the corner, on the chaise, the initial rustling and murmuring of sex had begun but Enzo wasn't interested; he'd seen it all the night before and the night before that. The novelty had worn off.

As he sat, he pared away at a piece of wood with his knife, skinning the bark off, gently shaping it with the small, swift movements of his hand. It was an anxious pastime, his eyes flicking rapidly from the scene behind the mirror to the motion of his fingers and then back again. He was on edge. He had been there too long, locked up for the past three days in the Villa Isabella, and his mind burned with images of Francesca. He needed to be free; he needed to be out on the streets where he had some hope of finding her. The constant buzz of women and sex was beginning to drive him insane.

Isabella walked along the darkened corridor towards the small room where Enzo sat, her mind made up. She had watched him carefully the past few days, seen his anxiety, his obsessive paranoia around the girls, and she knew she could use it. Isabella had been in the game for far too long not to know a secret when she saw one and Enzo Mondello had a secret, of that she was certain. What it was she hadn't the slightest inkling, but she would find out; tonight she'd find out. She couldn't keep Carlotti waiting for his answer any longer; she wanted in on the deal and she needed to confirm it. Enzo was her man but she had to have a tool to control him with. That was another thing she'd learned over the years: no one did anything for nothing. She needed something to manipulate him with.

Reaching the small space where Enzo sat, Isabella opened the door and motioned to him to leave and join her in the corridor. She waited in the semi-darkness for him and then turned on her heel as he came out. He followed her along the corridor and into one of the private entertainment rooms, a lavishly furnished bedroom hung with mirrors on the walls and ceiling and a large blank cinema screen opposite the bed. She stood and waited for Enzo to enter, then she shut the door and turned to him. She noticed a flicker of excitement in his eyes and it made her want to smile. Perhaps it was going to be much easier than she thought.

'Enzo, you can take the rest of the night off,' she said. 'I'm sure you must have things you want to do and I apologise for not being able to spare you the past few nights.' She shrugged. 'We've been so busy.' She watched his face as she spoke and saw a keenness there that she hadn't seen before, a different kind of excitement. 'There's not much else for you to do so why don't you go now?'

Enzo nodded. He was still holding the piece of wood and the knife and he glanced down for a moment before shoving them both into his pocket; Isabella made him very aware of himself and he was embarrassed at what he'd been doing to pass the time. He turned, catching sight of her reflection in one of the mirrors as he did so, and felt a sudden hardening of his body. He flushed and lengthened his stride. At the door he looked over his shoulder.

'I don't know what time I'll be back,' he said. 'I may be out all night.'

She shrugged. 'As long as you're here for work tomorrow night.'

He nodded, hesitated for a moment, then left the room. He liked the smell of her, the feminine scent, and yet he couldn't wait to get away from her. It confused him, unsettled him. It made him want Francesca all the more.

Hurrying along the passage, Enzo found his way out into the courtyard and went up to his room for some money. He checked his belongings, the small bag with his wash things, his odd bits of clothes and the envelope containing his photographs and his press cutting. He also checked his wallet: the money was all there. He knew it was stupid, this constant checking, but he trusted no one. Satisfied that everything was in order, he grabbed his new jacket off the bed and walked down to the courtyard again.

It was a clear night, the warmth of spring was in the air and the sky was stagelit by a full moon. Enzo made his way out of the building, conscious that he hadn't been seen, and headed up the street. It felt good to be out, to be on his own again. He took a deep breath and looked up at the sky. Somewhere under the same sky Francesca was waiting for him, somewhere. For nearly a year he'd been looking for her but he would find her, he knew that he would find her. She belonged to him, she was part of him, in his mind, in his body; she was his. And Enzo knew that no matter how long it took, he would find her.

Isabella watched him go from a darkened window at the top

of the house. She saw him stride off purposefully and followed his figure under the streetlamps until it disappeared from view. Then she moved away, walked out of the attic room and made her way to Enzo's bedroom. She was looking for a way to keep him there, a way to get him to work for her, and she was sure that she was going to find it.

Entering his room, Isabella left her key in the lock and switched on the overhead light. She was surprised at how neat it was. The only things visible were a shabby pile of folded clothes, a wash bag and the two new shirts he had bought for work. She crossed to the bedside table and pulled open the drawer. Sitting down on the bed, she took out a small brown envelope and emptied its contents in front of her. Two photographs fell out, a worn piece of newsprint and some sketches. She leafed through what was there, picked up the photographs and saw a pretty young girl in a blue cotton dress and a family snap of what looked like three brothers. Next she glanced at the sketches, both finely drawn, one of a young boy, the other of a house; both looked to be pages ripped from a book. Finally she read the scrap of newspaper and almost instantly the other bits of paper took on a whole new meaning. She smiled, gathered everything up and stood, smoothing the cover on the bed where she'd sat. Isabella was pleased; she had her secret.

Leaving the room as immaculate as she'd found it, Isabella locked the door behind her, still clutching the envelope, and made her way down to her sitting room and the small, secret safe that only she knew was hidden behind a mirror. She placed Enzo's history inside and closed it, turning the dial to lock it. Now all she had to do was wait. It didn't matter what time Enzo came back, she was in no hurry, not now she knew she had him. But the one thing she did have to do was call Carlotti. She wanted him to know that she had her man and that the real business could start any time he was ready. She was in the big time now and before too long she would be making enough money to retire on.

It was just light by the time Enzo made his way back to the Villa Isabella. He had kept to his habit of waiting for the early-morning papers and had scoured them for any news of Francesca. Disappointed, as usual, he had drunk two or three brandies in an all-night café and swallowed back some coffee before he was able to face returning. At least he could get some sleep at the brothel, not like working the streets where he'd have to go straight out again, dog tired and frustrated, angry at another wasted night.

He walked up the Via Varese to the three-storeyed building and entered the courtyard. It was silent, the business for the night over and the girls sleeping it off. He stopped and listened to the sound of the birds, high up on the roofs of the city, and then started across to his corridor. It had turned chill and he shivered.

'Enzo?'

He turned; Isabella was standing in the entrance to her private apartment and she beckoned to him. 'Can we talk?'

His pulse suddenly quickened and he nodded. She went inside and he followed, sniffing the air for her lingering perfume.

Inside her small sitting room, she moved across to a sofa and sat, waiting for him to join her. She was calm, in control; she had to be. For the past few hours Isabella had thought the whole thing through and she knew exactly what she wanted from Enzo Mondello. She wanted more than just the business; she wanted him. Enzo was right for her, for the moment anyway, and she needed the sex. It had been too long; she was always so careful. But now she had it all under one roof; she had him cornered and she was going to use him. She was going to squeeze him dry.

As Enzo sat next to her she could smell him, his response to her, his need of a woman, and it made her feel good. She put her hand on his thigh and a sharp spasm shot through the muscle. She smiled.

'Enzo, I have a little business proposition to put to you,' she said coolly. 'It's something I've been thinking of for some time.' She looked at him. 'Only I haven't been able to find the right person to manage it.'

He kept quiet. He was tired and just the closeness of her was making him ache. He was frustrated, angry with Francesca, with another futile night, and his whole body was tense.

'Enzo, I am moving into the drugs business with my associates,' she said quietly. 'And you are going to work for me.'

Enzo sat up straight. 'Wait a minute . . . I—' He stopped as her hand moved along his thigh up towards his groin. He had hardened. 'No, Isabella, I . . .' He edged away, despite the sudden heat in his veins. He wasn't stupid. Drugs in this city were run by the Mafia, everybody knew that. He wasn't going to get involved in that one, no way! He knew how drug runners ended up. Shit, he read the newspapers! Standing, he backed away from Isabella. 'I'm sorry,' he said, 'but I don't do drugs. It's too dangerous.'

Isabella shrugged. 'I think you'll do them for me, Enzo.'

He narrowed his eyes, suddenly suspicious. 'Oh yeah?' Isabella crossed her legs and the split in her dress revealed the top of her thigh. 'I went up to your room while you were out. I have your little brown envelope in my safe, Enzo, in case you want to know where it is.'

Enzo froze.

'I don't know the full story yet,' she went on, watching his face. 'But I will. It was some sort of family trauma, was it? A murder? Rape?' She ran her tongue over the crimson lips and smiled. 'You were in love with the girl, I'm sure of that. I wonder what happened to her? With her husband dead I'd have thought . . .'

Isabella gasped at the force of Enzo's grip, momentarily taken by surprise. But she was no stranger to violence. Bringing her knee up, she jabbed him in the groin and watched as he fell back, dropping to the floor in agony. She stood, rubbing her shoulder where he had held her and looking down at him as he groaned.

'Don't you ever' – she tapped him with the sharp point of her shoe – '*ever* touch me like that again. Now get up!'

Enzo rolled over and stared up at her, his eyes glazed. It took some time before he could focus properly, then he struggled to his knees and faced her. 'You have nothing on me,' he said hoarsely. 'Nothing.'

She raised an eyebrow but didn't answer. Slowly, Enzo got to his feet, still slightly bent from the pain in his groin, and Isabella put her hand out to touch his face. He flinched.

'The job isn't difficult,' she said gently. 'You pick up the drugs, you distribute them to my contacts.' She shrugged. 'That's all. Nothing more.' Her hand was still close to his face and she trailed a finger along his cheek, down to the solid muscle of his neck. He knew that he could have grabbed the hand and crushed it in his fingers; he could have ripped her arm from its socket, made her scream under his force. But he did nothing. There was something so powerful, so mesmerising in her touch, that it rendered him helpless.

'Come here,' she murmured.

Instinctively he moved towards her. The hand on his neck inched caressingly down over his chest to his waist and he drew in his breath. She ran her finger inside the waist of his trousers and then slipped it down to touch him. He shuddered. It had been too long, too long without that feeling, that deep, physical ache, and his mind was filled with a desire so strong that it overwhelmed all other thoughts.

Isabella moved closer. The tips of her nails touched his hard, smooth flesh as she put her other hand up to his hair. Dragging his face towards her own, she parted her mouth and darted her tongue over the hard, dry line of his lips. Then she kissed him. She felt the involuntary convulsion that ran through his whole body and she knew that he was hers. She had been right. It was all so much easier than she had originally thought.

Twenty-nine

ROME WAS HOT. IT WAS mid-July and the streets were baking, the stone of the buildings warm to touch, night and day. There was no wind; the air was still and choked with the fumes of a thousand cars. Everyone sweated.

The windows of the house on the Via Varese were constantly closed, the shutters tightly shut. The rooms remained dim and in shadow but nothing seemed to beat the stifling heat. In the day the girls lolled around the courtyard sunbathing or in the shade of the leafy vines that climbed the portico leading off it; at night they worked lethargically, their make-up running and dark stains of sweat showing through on their clothes. No one slept for long. The nights were hot and close; the mosquitoes bit and sucked and all the dawn brought was the rising of another fiery red sun.

It was the end of a Sunday night, Monday morning really, and Enzo walked the rooms of the house checking that things were in order. He had picked up the drugs as Isabella had told him to, put them in the safe, and now he wandered from room to room in the dark, close air; anything to avoid having to go up to Isabella, to go to her bed.

He knew he couldn't sleep. He rarely had the last few weeks – the nightmares had returned. For the first few months he had been with Isabella he thought he had escaped: there had been no dreams, his mind blank and numb in sleep. But not now. It was the heat. It reminded him and he woke, sweating and afraid, wanting Francesca so much that it hurt.

Switching off the lights as he went, Enzo finished his tour of the house and strayed out into the courtyard where he stood for a while, hating himself, hating his pitiful situation and dreading going up to Isabella. It was silent everywhere and the air smelled warm and dirty, clinging to his skin.

Finally, he crossed to Isabella's part of the house. Making his way up to her room, he unbuttoned his shirt and stopped outside to take off his new suede loafers. He left them by the door and walked quietly into the bedroom.

'Where've you been?' The room was dark and Enzo could just make out the shape of Isabella in the bed, her naked body only half covered by the sheet.

'Checking.' He had hoped she would be asleep. He was tired; he couldn't face her. Every time he touched her now it repulsed him. She was suffocating him with her dominating, controlling lust. He couldn't stand it; it was driving him insane. 'Go to sleep,' he said. 'I'll be a while.'

He crossed to the small sofa and sat down, taking up a magazine. He could feel her eyes on him but he switched on a dim reading light, opened the journal and started to read.

'Did you pick up the stuff?'

He didn't look up. 'Yes, it's in the safe.' He heard her sigh and turn over. He had done what she wanted; perhaps she'd leave him alone for tonight. Minutes later, the regular deep breathing of sleep was audible and he switched off the lamp, relieved. He put his feet up on the sofa and closed his eyes. He knew he wouldn't sleep but he needed to rest. He needed to think about how to get away.

The room was light. The morning sun had found its way in through the gaps in the shutters and the air was warm, fusty. Enzo opened his eyes and realised he must have slept. He could hear Isabella in the bathroom.

Swinging his legs down onto the floor, he put his head in his hands and rubbed his face. He felt sick and tired, the sweat damp on the back of his neck. His eyes stayed open, fixed onto the floor, the sound of Isabella behind him almost painful. Finally, he stood up.

Crossing to the bed, he took his wallet from the side table and shoved it into his pocket. He saw the small vial of amyl nitrite by the side of the bed and swallowed down the bile that rose in the back of his throat. She had wanted him last night – drugged and frenzied, she would have taunted him, goaded him to a climax. Thank God he had escaped it. Silently he walked out of the room, down the stairs and across the courtyard. He was out into the street before Isabella even knew he was awake.

He rolled up the sleeves of his new white silk shirt, dug his hands in his pockets and wandered off in the direction of the Via Palestro. He needed time to think, to calm himself before going back to Isabella, and walking the streets early in the morning was the best way for him to do it.

At the corner of Via Vincenza he turned and walked up to the main road. The air was already warm, still and noiseless. There was hardly any traffic, just the odd car and scooter that broke the silence with a piercing whine. He walked on.

He had thought, months ago when Isabella first took him, that he could forget, that he could escape the torment of the past few years. But now he knew that Francesca was inside his head again and he couldn't escape it. She was a part of him, deep down in his subconscious, and she kept on and on and on, invading his dreams, shattering his thoughts, torturing him. Every way he turned she was there – her image, her voice; even the air seemed to have the caress of her touch.

But he was doing all right. For the first time in his life, Enzo Mondello was doing all right. Even though Isabella used him he had managed to make himself a bit of money off the back of her little deals, from drugs and girls off the premises. If Isabella knew . . . He shuddered and dismissed the thought. She wouldn't find out; she couldn't control all of him. Enzo still had his mind, and his mind was free of her; his mind belonged to Francesca.

Walking on towards the café, Enzo let all the images he kept inside his head pass before his eyes. He didn't see the grimy pavement or the dilapidated, faded buildings; he saw Francesca, always naked, always free, sometimes hard and writhing under him, sometimes soft and pliable on top of him. He wrapped himself up in his warped obsession, and where he was, what he was doing were nothing to him, not compared to what he would do when he found her.

And he would find her. That was the only certainty in his life. He had no idea how, or when, but he knew he would find her. 'Wherever she is,' he murmured, 'I will find her.' The thought of that left him weak with desperation.

He stopped at the café; he needed a drink. He sat at the long, marble-topped bar and read a paper while Marco poured him a large measure of brandy and prepared the coffee filter. The clatter of cups and glasses and the whir of the machine were the only noises in the deserted café. Marco's was open all hours, but it was often empty in the early hours except for Enzo and a few shift workers. He liked that; it meant he could have some privacy .

'*Ciao*, Enzo!'

Enzo looked up as a young man slapped him on the back. He glanced over his shoulder.

'Pepe. *Come sta?*' Pepe was a desk clerk at one of Rome's

most expensive hotels; he brought the odd bit of private business Enzo's way. Mainly drugs.

'Yeah, good Enzo! Pretty good!' He sat on a stool next to Enzo. 'A coffee please, Marco.'

Enzo drank half of his small black coffee and turned to Pepe. 'Just finished work?'

'Yeah.' Pepe took out his cigarettes and offered one to Enzo. 'I came straight over; I thought I might find you here. I've got some business for you, Enzo.'

'Oh yeah?' Enzo glanced uneasily over his shoulder and then slid off the stool. Everyone knew Isabella; he couldn't be too careful. 'Let's move to somewhere more comfortable, shall we?' He led the way to a small table and pulled up a chair. Pepe did the same.

'It's an American. Loaded.' Pepe grinned. 'Pretty weird too. A woman – she wants two girls and a gram.'

Enzo looked across at Marco who was drying glasses and lowered his voice. 'Coke?' Isabella had it in the household safe and he could probably make a bit of money for himself here.

'Yup. No shit, though, she'll pay over the odds.'

'OK.' This was a good deal, too good to pass up. Enzo reckoned he might just be able to do it; tell Isabella one gram, take one and a half. If the American was greedy he would sell her the lot and pocket the extra profit. And from what Pepe said, Enzo guessed she could well be greedy. 'You told her tonight?'

'Yeah, she wants it about eleven, after dinner.'

'What room is she?'

'Fifteen.'

Enzo noted down the number on an old slip of paper from his wallet. 'You got a deposit?'

'Yeah. 120 thou. Here.' Pepe took a plastic bag out of his top pocket and pulled the wad of notes out, peeling off

Enzo's advance. 'I'm on duty tonight. Come in the back entrance, through the service doors. One of my boys will meet you there at eleven. OK?'

Enzo nodded. 'You told her the rate?'

'It's all taken care of, Enzo!' Pepe was cocky. Enzo's wariness irritated him. He stood up and drained his cup. 'See you later.'

'Yeah, *ciao*.' Enzo watched Pepe leave the bar and then glanced over at Marco again before he went back to the paper. Pepe could be careless – he was too young – but this was a good deal. He could charge over the odds for the girls, keep the change and with half a gram of coke lifted from Isabella as well Enzo would have a nice little packet to put away. Something for Francesca, he thought, as he finished his brandy and stood up to leave.

He didn't want to stay away from the house too long now. He couldn't afford to put Isabella in a bad mood.

Isabella looked up from her paper as Enzo walked into the bedroom. She was back in bed, propped up by several plump pillows, naked to the waist with the sheet covering her lower half and the newspaper on her lap. The shutters were half open and the room was lit by a bedside lamp.

'Where have you been?' She placed the paper on the bed beside her and studied Enzo for a few moments. He had been easier to dominate than she had ever anticipated, far, far easier. And yet in the past few weeks she had sensed that he had begun to slip away from her. She didn't like that. She did not want to lose him. He had been much more useful than she'd imagined. He dealt drugs for her, did the picking up and the carrying, all the dirty work, while she grabbed the big fat profits. And it was all from an arm's length. No, she didn't want to lose Enzo Mondello; he was a valuable asset.

'I went for a walk,' he answered. 'Stopped at the café.'

She watched him as he took off his shirt and dropped it on the floor. He took care of her other needs as well, and the sight of his hard, lean body started a familiar ache in her groin.

'Come here,' she said.

He turned and swallowed, avoiding her gaze. 'I have to shower first,' he replied, walking towards the bathroom.

'No, you don't.'

Enzo stopped. He could hear the thickened tone of her voice, heavy with desire. He glanced over his shoulder at her. 'Isabella, we have some business tonight. Over at the Hotel Romani. An American, wants two girls and a gram of coke.'

She raised an eyebrow and moved her leg so that the sheet fell away. 'So?'

'So I'll deliver,' he said.

She nodded and he breathed a sigh of relief. He walked back to the bed, knowing that it would be foolish to upset her now. He sat and watched as she picked up the amyl nitrite vial and fingered it. 'Take off your trousers,' she said, running a sharp red nail the length of his torso to his belt. 'It would be a shame to waste this, wouldn't it?'

He nodded and stood. He could see the hard look of control in her eyes and it sickened him. Still he unfastened his trousers and let her pull his hips towards her mouth, watching her face. He had to watch her face. If he let her go out of his vision for even one moment he would be tormented by Francesca. And only he knew the pain of that vision, the terrible exquisite pain.

At eleven that night Enzo tapped on the service entrance door and waited for one of Pepe's boys. He was always careful at the Hotel Romani. The place was hot on rules, security men everywhere. Several minutes later, the door was opened by a boy in a smart dark green uniform, no more than fourteen and already on the make. Enzo slipped him twenty thousand lire and ushered his girls inside.

'You know the suite number?' The boy tucked the money hastily away.

'Yes, it's the penthouse.'

'Use the service lift, then. It brings you out on the back staircase.'

'I know, I know, I've been here before!' The boy's calm authority irritated Enzo. 'Come on.' He led the girls along the passageway to the lift and pressed the call button. 'Cocky little shit!' One of the girls smiled.

On the seventh floor they stepped out onto the back staircase and turned towards the double doors that led into the corridor. Enzo pushed them open, checked it was clear and walked through. The girls followed him. He found the suite and knocked lightly on the door.

'Yeah?' The voice called out from behind the door, a bored, lazy voice.

'Room service.'

'It's open, come on in!'

Enzo turned the handle and opened the door. He found himself in a suite overlooking the whole city and it took him several moments to adjust to the size of the room. The curtains were open and the panoramic view over Rome, lit up against the thick black night sky, was incredible.

'You like the view, huh?'

He tore his gaze away from the window and took in a tall, thin woman, sitting at a small table draped with a white linen cloth, holding a half-eaten langoustine in her fingers. She was watching his face closely. Marianne Hart had been waiting for Enzo Mondello. She had paid a good deposit for him and she damn well hoped he was up to Pepe's recommendation. Biting into the pink flesh of the prawn, she dropped the shell onto her plate and motioned to him to enter. 'Come in,' she said through a mouthful of food. 'Have a closer look.' Her Italian was understandable but the accent drawled with the characteristic American twang.

'Do you speak English?'

Enzo shrugged. 'A little. I prefer Italian.'

'Yeah, sweetie, don't we all.' She said this in English and smiled at Enzo's lack of understanding. Enzo resented the private joke. 'OK. Italian it is.' She took up another langoustine and began to crack the shell with long, sharp red nails. 'Bring the girls in. D'you have the stuff?'

'Yes.' Enzo looked behind him and nodded; the girls came into the room. He closed the door.

Marianne stood, licked her fingers and looked at Enzo. She didn't seem interested at all in the girls. 'Sit down,' she said. 'D'you want a drink?'

'No. The girls only drink champagne.'

'Oh yeah? A small racket going with Pepe, huh?' She smiled. 'If you want champagne, phone down for it. I couldn't give a shit what you drink. But I prefer my coke on its own. Order me up some mineral water as well, will you?'

Enzo nodded to one of the girls and she went to the phone.

'So?' The woman came over to the sofa where Enzo and Sofia were sitting. She sat on the arm of a Louis IV reproduction chair and crossed her legs. Enzo took a good look at her.

She was in her early thirties, he guessed, not much younger than Isabella, but it was difficult to tell. She was classic looking, timeless, with her long, straight blonde hair and thin, lean limbs. Her face was flawless, with high cheekbones, a long, sculpted nose, even lips and immaculate white teeth. The perfect American specimen: cool, rich and arrogant.

'You think I look very American,' she said. 'And very rich.'

Enzo started. She continued to watch him with cold, slightly watery eyes and it unnerved him. How the hell did she know what he was thinking?

'It's OK. I'm psychic,' she said, almost in answer to his thoughts. He narrowed his eyes. 'I know all about you,' she continued. This much was true. Pepe had passed on his sparse knowledge of Enzo, gossip mainly, but he had told her just enough. He had told her how easily the woman at the brothel dominated him, how he had some kind of secret that she held him with. Enzo was Marianne's perfect man; she was really going to enjoy herself tonight.

'Enzo Mondello, from southern Italy. That right?'

Enzo laughed to cover his anxiety. Jesus, this one was really strange! He glanced away as Etta came back to the sofa and said: 'The drink's on its way.'

'Good.' The woman flicked a long strand of hair coolly over her shoulder and Enzo realised that he had an erection. He was shocked by it.

'Are you going to stay, Enzo?' Again she watched for his reaction. One of Marianne's pastimes was playing mind games, but it was always with people she reckoned she could control. She loved to tease and manipulate, coaxing out small secrets, fears and anxieties, and then taunting and torturing with her knowledge. It was a glorious, heady sensation of power and she could tell at a glance that Enzo was ripe for her game.

'How did you know my name?' Enzo was guarded. This was beginning to piss him off.

'I told you, I'm psychic.' Marianne could see she was easing into a stronger position. It reminded her of a game of chess. 'I know everything about you,' she said. Sofia giggled but Enzo pinched her arm and she shut up. He ignored the earlier question. The thought of staying excited him but he wasn't for sale.

'Well, are you staying?' Marianne's eyes flicked down to his erection, obvious in his trousers, and then back to his face.

'No,' he answered sharply, suddenly angered by her arrogance. 'I'm not part of the arrangement.'

'Oh?' She raised an eyebrow and moved over to the window. She stood with her back to him. 'I thought you were.' The dress she wore was tight, black cotton lycra, which clung to the shape of her muscled arse. She looked back at Enzo over her shoulder. It was as if the girls were no longer in the room. 'I would have thought it would make a change to fuck for some hard cash, instead of bed and board at the whorehouse.' She laughed, a knowing, taunting laugh, and it rang in his ears. She was psychic; she knew his mind. Suddenly confused, he stood up. She had disorientated him with her knowing comments and her sneering look.

'I have to go,' he mumbled. He had to get away. God, this woman was mad! She was playing with his head.

She turned. 'Back to earn your keep?' Again she laughed, a loud, tormenting laugh. 'Is that what you came to Rome for, Enzo? Huh? Is that what you wanted? To play pimp in a two-bit brothel?' She had moved another piece – she was going in for the kill. She wanted him rough; she wanted him angry and wound up: that was the way she liked it. 'Is it? Huh?' she taunted. She could feel she had him.

He shook his head, more confused. 'No!' he hissed. He didn't understand – what did she know? He was so used to being dominated that he was no longer sure of his own mind. He swung dangerously between reality and fantasy, images of Francesca dancing before his eyes. Could she see into his mind? He looked across at her, trying to make sense of what she was saying. Her face blurred and became something else, and all the time she laughed. He could hear her voice – taunting him, goading him. Push, push, push. What the hell did she know?

'I know why you came to Rome, Enzo baby, and it wasn't to end up in Isabella's bed, was it?'

Suddenly he snapped.

'Stop it! Stop it!' He rushed at her and grasped her shoulders, shaking her hard, rattling her thin frame. He had to shut her up! Still she laughed. Then he slapped her with the palm of his hand across her cheek and knocked her back.

'Enzo? Enzo?'

He spun round and knocked Etta away. 'Get out! Go on! Get out, leave us alone!'

She scrambled back and grabbed Sofia by the arm. They ran out of the room, slamming the door behind them. All he could see was red, the red in his nightmare and the laughter driving through his brain. He slapped her again. 'Shut up! Shut up!'

'Come on,' she muttered fiercely. 'Come on, make me!' He suddenly heard Francesca's voice. It was like with Isabella, only this time it felt real, painfully real.

'Make me!' she moaned. 'Come on!' She had begun to quiver with excitement. 'Come on, Enzo, give it to me! Make me quiet!' The heat flowed between her legs at his violence. 'Come on,' she urged.

It was Francesca's voice, the laughter, the words, the red blood, all spinning in his mind. He had to have her. He lost control.

Gripping her neck, he ripped the top of her dress down over her shoulders with one hand, pushing her down onto the floor, stumbling down on top of her. He fumbled with his flies, desperate to have her, his whole body raging with anger and lust. He forced her open.

'Come on,' she cried, Francesca's voice. 'Come on! Do it! As hard as you can, baby! I know you need it!' He thrust into her and she screamed. His mind went blank and his body took possession of his soul.

'Jesus Christ!' The woman lay panting on the carpet as Enzo rolled off her. He was breathing hard and the sweat ran down his face. She was sated. He was an animal and she loved it. Looking over at him she said: 'I remind you of her, don't I?'

The image before his eyes vanished. They changed, became veiled, then he turned away. 'Who?' He suddenly realised where he was and felt sick and confused, as if his mind was playing horrible tricks on him. 'I don't know who you mean.' He inched away from her, frightened by the intensity of the images he had just seen. She glimpsed that fear.

She had heard the name under his breath, through his clenched teeth as he rammed into her. 'Francesca,' she said. She knew she had stumbled on something really strange, something much deeper and more intense than the normal petty human fears. It fascinated her, excited her and intrigued her. She wanted more. 'Francesca,' she said again.

Enzo glanced nervously back. Just the sound of her name unnerved him.

'It's all right,' Marianne soothed. 'I know everything. I can feel it.' Sometimes she forgot all the digging and poking around, the scheming and manipulating. Sometimes she really did believe she knew it all, believed that she felt it. 'Same as I knew about you in that brothel,' she lied.

Enzo pulled up his pants. 'Yeah?' She scared him and he felt weird. Scared, but excited and relieved, all at once. Did she really know? He stood up and walked across to the table where the food was. What else did she know? He picked up a langoustine and pulled the head off, biting the flesh.

Marianne sat up. 'Where's the coke?'

'In my jacket pocket.'

'Get it, will you?' She was looking down at the marks Enzo had made on her breasts. 'There's a razor blade in the bathroom, and a mirror.' She had no embarrassment about telling him what to do. She was so cool, so much in control. She looked up. 'Now, please.'

Not surprisingly, he did as she asked; he was used to being told what to do. He brought the things from the bathroom and laid them out on the coffee table. His head was spinning and he found it difficult to see straight.

'Do the coke, will you? I have to go and change.' She stood up and covered her chest with the torn dress. She stepped past Enzo to the bedroom. 'Give me a shout when it's ready.' He watched her go and then he spread out a small amount of cocaine on the glass and meticulously began to cut it with the razor blade.

Five minutes later, he had finished and there was no sign of her. He stood up, wandered through to the bedroom and saw her lying on the bed, reading *Vanity Fair*. She didn't even look up as he entered.

'I've done the coke,' he said. He wanted her to look at him, to acknowledge him.

'Sure, fine. Bring it in, will you?' Still she didn't look up.

His temper sparked. He stood angrily by the door, unsure of whether to do as she said or just walk out. But he couldn't forget what had just happened. Images of the past burned inside him. He went and fetched the cocaine.

'My name's Marianne.' The woman had cleared a space on the bedside table for the mirror. 'I don't like to snort without being introduced.' She waited for Enzo to put the glass down and then climbed off the bed and knelt down with her face just above the table-top. She took a hundred-dollar bill out of the drawer and rolled it up tightly.

'Cheers,' she said and bent her head to draw up the drug.

Seconds later she sat back and sniffed furiously. 'Yours.' She moved away from the table as Enzo took her place. He had never done cocaine. Isabella used amyl nitrite to heighten her climax but she didn't waste expensive drugs. Enzo bent his head and sniffed through the rolled hundred-dollar bill.

'Whoa!' Marianne sat back on the floor against the bed. 'That's good stuff.' Her nose and eyes had reddened and she blinked continuously.

Enzo sat back on his heels and drew breath in through his nose. The rush hit him almost instantly; he had never experienced anything like it. 'Jesus! Shit!' Marianne laughed.

He turned to her and her face was sneering. He felt suddenly unbalanced and confused. She laughed even louder. He could see her in front of him and yet she didn't seem to exist. It was like a nightmare – the laughter, the tormenting laughter.

'Francesca,' she murmured. She could tell Enzo wasn't used to the high and she knew how to play it. She wanted to pick at the sore she'd found, make it bleed. 'Francesca . . .' She watched his face and felt a thrill at the change in it, at her power to do this. She felt huge, larger than life, as if she could control everything and everyone. She moved towards him and whispered in his ear. 'I know all about you and Francesca,' she said. The shiver in his body was like a thrill up her spine. 'I know because I *am* Francesca.'

She gasped as his hand caught her hair and wrenched her head forward. His eyes were manic, altered and clouded, unseeing. He covered her mouth with his own and pulled her violently down onto him. She was Francesca; she had changed him, incensed him, overpowered him. She laughed with the thrill of her control, wrapped her fingers tightly in his hair and maliciously dug her nails hard into his scalp. The feeling of power was exquisite.

Enzo woke up with the dawn. He was in the bed, covered by the counterpane, and he was alone, still half dressed. He sat up and looked around the room. Marianne was nowhere to be seen. Climbing out, he stretched and looked around for his trousers, buttoning his shirt as he did so. He felt good, sore and stiff but good. He had slept, a deep, blank and numbing sleep, and the anger had gone. Walking through to the bathroom, he splashed some cold water on his face and rinsed his mouth. He looked up at the sound of Marianne's voice from behind him.

'You sleep all right?'

'Yeah.' He saw her reflection in the mirror. She was as immaculate as the moment he had entered the room the previous night. She made him feel dirty and insignificant.

'Some friends of mine are going up into the hills today for a picnic. You want to come?' She picked at her nail as she spoke, only half interested in his answer.

Her coldness inflamed him. He wanted to take her there and then, make her moan for him to go with her. But he reached for a towel to dry his face. 'Maybe,' he said.

'Please yourself. If you come, can you bring some more stuff?' She turned and walked out of the bathroom.

'What time are you leaving?' He followed her and hung behind her, waiting for her answer.

She smiled. 'Midday. Come here first if you want.'

He nodded and she went through to the sitting room. Again Enzo followed. 'There's some money in the drawer. Take it if you want.' She lay down on the sofa and Enzo saw that only one thin line of coke was left on the glass. He went to the drawer, found the money and slipped it into his pocket. He wanted to count it but he knew she would sneer at him for doing so.

'I might see you later.' He crossed to the door and waited, for what he didn't know.

'Yeah, whenever.' She had crossed her arm over her eyes and he knew he was dismissed. Quietly, he opened the door and stepped out into the corridor.

Pepe rapped lightly on the door of room fifteen and waited for Marianne to call out to him. He had rung five minutes earlier and been told to come straight up.

'Come in!'

He opened the door and walked into the suite.

'I'm in the bedroom.'

Checking the sitting room quickly, he saw the remaining few grains of coke on the mirror and the discarded hundred-dollar bill. He crossed to the table and pocketed it. Then he went through to the bedroom. Marianne was on the bed.

'You did well, Pepe,' she said. He could tell she was still high as a kite. 'My bit of Italian rough was everything you said he'd be!' She laughed and crossed her long, thin legs. She wore a short silk shift and with her knees bent he could see right between her legs. She knew he could. 'In fact, I've taken quite a fancy to him! He's a tiny bit deeper than your ordinary meat loaf!' She flicked her hair back. 'He kept it up for hours.'

Pepe laughed; the woman was mad. 'So where's my tip?'

'Your tip?' She stretched her arms above her head.

'Yeah, my tip?' He was smiling at her and laughed again when she brought a tight roll of hundred-dollar bills out from behind her head.

'Is three enough?'

'Three is fine, thanks.'

'Good.' She held the roll in her fingers and then brought her hand down between her legs and smiled. 'Come and get them,' she said and relaxed back as Pepe moved towards her, the smile fixed grimly on his face.

Enzo walked into Isabella's bedroom and switched on the main lights, regardless of her sleeping form on the bed; he didn't want to scrabble around in the dark to find his clothes. In the last six hours he had changed – he no longer cared what she said, what she did. In the last six hours Isabella had lost her control. Someone else had it.

He heard her moan at the brightness of the lights as she opened her eyes, then she sat up abruptly. 'Where the hell have you been?' Her voice was tight with anger; she knew exactly where he had been. The girls had told her everything.

'Mind your own business,' he answered, pulling a shirt off its hanger. He found a clean pair of trousers and some underwear and made for the bathroom. He went inside and slammed the door behind him. Isabella jumped out of bed, furious at his behaviour, and ran across to the door, banging violently on it with her fist.

'Enzo, come out of there!' she shouted. 'Don't think you can just come and go as you like!' She banged harder. 'Don't think that you can humiliate me in front of my girls!' She kicked the door with fury and stood back, her chest heaving. 'I know all about you, Enzo Mondello! All your grimy little secrets, and I won't let you treat me like this!'

Suddenly Enzo swung the door open and grabbed her arm, yanking her forward. The violence of the action shocked her into silence for a moment.

'You don't know anything about me!' he roared. 'Nothing! D'you hear me?' He let go of her and shoved her back. The thought of her knowing about Francesca, know-

428

ing about what had just happened, incensed him. He had at last found someone who understood, who knew, and that was sacred to him.

Isabella stumbled and knocked herself on the dressing table. She saw Enzo's face change and was suddenly frightened; she remembered the newspaper cuttings. Hastily, she backed away, realising that she might be about to lose him. It brought things into sharp focus. 'Look, Enzo, I don't mind where you go, darling,' she said softly, 'or what you do, as long as I know.' She edged forward to him. 'All right? Hmmm?' She put a finger up to his cheek. 'Hmmm?'

Suddenly Enzo grabbed her wrist and held it, twisting it painfully. He wanted no more of her. In the drug-warped state of his mind all he could see was Francesca, Marianne's face blurring with hers into one erotic vision. He dropped Isabella's arm abruptly.

'I'm leaving,' he said. 'Moving on.'

Isabella caught her breath. 'But you can't!' she cried. 'I know too much about . . .'

The slap was hard and sharp as it cut across her mouth and cheek. She staggered under the force of it for a moment, then looked up, horrified. 'Jesus! You bastard!' She slumped back, clutching her face. 'Go on, go then!' she screamed. 'Go back on the streets!' She turned away and tasted the blood in her mouth. 'You'll never find her,' she hissed viciously. 'Never!'

Enzo walked across the room, leaving her hunched over, her lip already beginning to swell. He gathered up his things, the few items of clothing she had bought him, and stuffed them into a bag. He felt strong, stronger than he had done for months, aching to get back to Marianne, to Francesca. He was desperate for another taste of the drug that had made him come alive.

Pulling open the door, he stepped out into Isabella's

private corridor then stopped. He glanced back. 'The keys to your safe,' he demanded. 'Where are they?'

Isabella ignored him.

He looked at the bedside table and saw the drawer where she kept all her valuables. Dropping his bag, he strode over to it just as Isabella, realising what he was doing, lunged forward to stop him. They collided and he knocked her out of the way.

'Get . . .!' He raised his hand and she cowered on the floor. Yanking open the drawer, he took out the keys and stuffed them into his pocket. He didn't look down at her again. He was out of the room and into the silence of the early-morning courtyard before she had found the strength to raise herself up and call for help. By the time Carla reached her, Enzo had emptied both safes and was gone.

CHAPTER
Thirty

TWO WEEKS LATER, ENZO WALKED along the Via Sistina towards the Spanish Steps and the Hotel Romani, carelessly knocking shoulders with the crowds of tourists on the pavements as he went. Several shouted at him but he couldn't care less; he hardly felt the knocks. He had been out roaming the streets, unaware of what he was doing. He was tired, down; he needed another hit.

In the past two days, the weather had cooled slightly, down six or seven degrees from the high nineties, and a breeze blew through the city clearing the air and dispersing the clouds of bilious fumes that hung over certain areas. Enzo walked with his jacket on, for the first time in weeks. He felt neither hot nor cold, just shivery, as he began to come down from his high. He wanted to get back – to Marianne, to his drug and to his visions of Francesca.

He had been with Marianne only two weeks but it felt like forever. He could hardly remember what it was like without her. It was weird – he was disorientated the whole time, his mind moving through the past and present, never knowing what was real or imagined. He was either high, gloriously, powerfully high, or down, tired, angry and violent, desperate only to get back up again. But whatever his state of mind, she controlled him. He had simply given up one mistress for another.

Only Marianne was a different kind of mistress, far more sinister and dangerous than Isabella had ever been, because Marianne controlled his mind. She whispered things to him, while he slept, insinuated things while he lay with her, fed him cocaine, day after day, night after night. And all the time he thought about Francesca, dreamed about her, wild, frightening, beautiful dreams. She was within his reach, he knew it, Marianne could feel it. The waiting would soon be over, of that he was certain, because Marianne had told him so.

Climbing the Spanish Steps up to the entrance of the hotel, Enzo stopped for a moment, suddenly short of breath. He slumped down onto a step and sat for a while with his head in his hands. He had a horrible sense of confusion, of not knowing what he was doing. He felt in his pocket for the small cellophane packet. It was still there; he had nothing to worry about. Trying to relax, he looked up and suddenly the panic hit him.

Standing, he turned towards the hotel and began to run up the steps. He had to get back, to Marianne, to safety. His head spun and his mouth was painfully dry, but he knew he had to get back. Knocking a young child out of the way, he stumbled to the top of the steps, followed by screams and protests, and ran round to the back entrance of the hotel. He yanked the door open and fell inside, slamming it behind him and leaning up against it, his heart pounding, the blood roaring in his ears. The panic swept through his body and he stood, shaking and sick, seeing and hearing nothing, only the images inside his own head.

His chest heaved and he coughed up the phlegm in his lungs, spitting it out into the palm of his hand and fumbling in his pocket for a scrap to wipe it on. Slowly his body began to calm. After some time, he managed to stand straight and turn towards the back staircase, the panic now only coming in waves. Finally, he made his way up to the second floor.

He had no key to the room, but it was rarely locked

when she was there. Enzo tried the handle and it turned. He walked into Marianne's suite and began to unbutton his stained shirt as he walked towards the bedroom. He felt much better, secure and safe. He stopped halfway across the room.

'Marianne?' The suite was strangely empty. There were no clothes discarded over the furniture, no magazines; the carrier bags from the Piazza di Spagna had gone. He hurried through to the bedroom. 'Marianne?' All visible signs of occupation had gone from there too. He ran into the bathroom. 'Marianne?' He was shouting now, his voice high and tight. He flung open the cupboards to look for her things. They were empty.

'Jesus! Marianne!' He ran back to the bedroom and began frantically pulling open drawers, cupboards, flinging his own clothes around desperately.

'Enzo?'

He spun round.

'What the hell . . .?'

The next thing Pepe knew he was choking. Enzo held him in a grip up against the wall, his hands like a vice round his throat. 'Where is she?' he shouted. 'Where is she?' Pepe struggled to breathe, feeling the heat explode in his lungs. His eyes bulged as he tried to struggle against Enzo's rage. Then suddenly Enzo let go and he slumped down the wall to the floor. He gasped for breath.

'Jesus Christ!' He could hardly speak. 'Enzo . . . I . . .'

But Enzo had turned away and was wringing his hands. It was as if Pepe didn't exist. It took several minutes for Pepe to gain control of his breathing; his throat was bruised and raw. Finally he got up onto his knees and then his feet, holding onto the wall for support.

'You're fucking crazy, Enzo!' He held his neck as he spoke. 'You're fucking paranoid, that's what you are, fucking paranoid!' He leaned back against the wall. 'She's down in the lobby, waiting for you.'

Enzo looked up. His eyes were red, drawn down into the hollows of his face, and Pepe saw the confusion of cocaine in them. Enzo didn't know what was happening. Thank Christ, Pepe thought, that I escaped that mad American bitch. He backed out of the room, his eyes on Enzo.

'That coke's eating your head, man!' He spoke from the safety of the next room. 'That and the American.'

Enzo looked across at him. Pepe's words hadn't even registered. 'Tell her I have to change,' he said. 'I'll be there in five minutes.'

Pepe nodded, and without turning, he backed out of the suite and closed the door on Enzo Mondello. He'd tell her to wait, and as far as he was concerned, the two crazies deserved each other.

Enzo had taken a line, then showered and thrown his things into a bag. He felt a whole lot better. Walking out of the suite, he turned towards the back staircase and then suddenly changed his mind. He walked to the main lifts, called them and went down to the lobby as if he were a paying guest. He saw Marianne's Vuitton luggage and walked towards it but there was no sign of her.

'Enzo?'

He looked in the direction of the voice. It was Marianne's voice.

'Enzo, over here.'

A woman came towards him, a woman with long, thick dark hair, hair the colour of Francesca's; she was tall too, and long-limbed like Francesca. Enzo blinked and tried to refocus his eyes. The woman kissed him and he flinched.

'Oh, my darling! You don't recognise me!' Marianne ran

her hand down over Enzo's back to his bottom and began to laugh. 'Don't you like my wig?'

Enzo shook his head. The image of Francesca was coming and going in surges in his mind. Her laughter was making him dizzy. She took his arm.

'Come on now, darling, we have to go.'

He was dazed, confused. 'Where are we going?'

Marianne leaned close to him and put her mouth to his ear. She loved the tease of it all, he was so deliciously easy to tease. 'Do you have your passport?'

He nodded.

'Then we're going to America, to find Francesca.'

She felt him shiver when she whispered the name, as he always did, and it thrilled her. 'Francesca,' she whispered over and over. 'We are going to find Francesca.' This was better than all the money she could spend. He had told her everything; high as a kite, he had let it all go. She would play this game long and hard; it would take months for her to tire of it. 'Francesca is waiting for you there,' she murmured. And, taking his hand, she led him out to the waiting taxi.

Patrick – 1992

CHAPTER
Thirty-one

THE NEWLY APPOINTED JUNIOR MINISTER in the Foreign Office sat in the study of his constituency house in Little Horsely, West Sussex with a copy of his wife's *Vogue* magazine in front of him on the desk. It was open at page thirty-nine, and an article on the rising success of Francesca Cameron and David Yates stared up at him, with glossy colour photographs of the designers by Terry O'Neill, groomed, chic images. He ran his finger over the face of Francesca Cameron and traced the outline of it, then he stood up and walked across to the bureau to take out his file. He brought it to the desk. Sitting down, he gazed at the picture again, unable to take his eyes off her face. For Patrick Devlin it was almost too much to bear.

It wasn't the first time he had seen pictures of her. He had a file for the cuttings he had collected over the past two years. It gave him some consolation to know that she was so successful, to know that achievement and acknowledgement of her talent came out of his pain and grief. But it was small consolation for the days and nights that he had longed for her, for the terrible effort of trying to love Penny and for the bitter hopelessness of what his marriage had become. Small consolation indeed.

Not a day had passed in the previous two years that Patrick had not thought of Francesca, had not wondered where she was, or what she was doing. And despite the work, despite the acute pressure of his own meteoric rise to success, the memories of her did not fade: the touch of her skin, the feel of her hair against his cheek and the sound of her voice. There was not a day when he had not wanted to talk to her, to tell her about Penny, to unburden himself and have her forgiveness and understanding. Not one single day.

Sometimes he wondered if it was his own sorrow that made his time with her seem so intense, so heightened an emotional experience. But then he would take out the file and look at her, the soft features of her face, the brilliant green of her eyes, and he would manage to feel close to her, even through the false and distant medium of a photograph. He would feel so close that he could imagine exactly what she would say and how she would humble him with her wisdom. My father was an alcoholic, she had told him, and I had to try to love him more because of it, not less. And yet with all his education, experience and knowledge he had not been able to achieve that sort of wisdom. He did not love Penny and he had not been able to do anything but live the lie he had created for himself, pretending to a woman who veered dangerously from one emotional abyss to another, and making a sham of his life.

Looking up from the photograph, Patrick noticed how sunny it was outside and the brightness of the light cheered him. He reached for his scissors and carefully cut out the pages of the article on Francesca. He slipped the sheets into the file with the other cuttings and closed the magazine. Enough, he thought, enough of my self-pity for one day. He stood and replaced the file in the bureau, locking the drawer, and then pulled open the door to the study. Holding the magazine he crossed the hall to the sitting room and slipped the *Vogue* back into its place in the pile. He walked over to the window and looked out at the garden, its long, profuse and leafy greenness dappled with sunlight. He saw Penny down at the bottom cutting roses, her hands covered with outsize cotton gardening gloves, and a trug by her feet. She was absorbed in what she was doing and looked completely content. He sighed. She wasn't, of course, but he didn't want to think of that today; coping with her was only possible by living each day as it came.

He was about to turn away when she glanced up and caught him watching her. She stood straight, rubbed her back and then waved at him, taking off her gardening gloves and placing her hands on her swollen belly. She started across the garden towards him and he thought how serene her face was and how pregnancy suited her; it only made him more bitter about the way she really was.

He had tried, God knew how he had tried. That first night he had found her, drunk and bitter, violently abusive, he had tried to understand, tried to help, tried so hard to love her more, as Francesca would have done. But in the end the abuse, the violence and the hysteria had worn him right down, exhausted what little feeling he had for her and left nothing, except guilt that he was not capable of giving more. Pity, yes, he was capable of that, and care and nursing, but not love. Love was for someone else and he hated Margaret bitterly for that fact.

Opening the French windows, Patrick stepped out onto the patio and walked down the slope of lawn to meet Penny halfway. She was seven and a half months pregnant and so far it had been a struggle all through. There had been no pills and no drink, she promised him that, but her only emotional crutch had been him and there were times when she had used and abused him so desperately that he felt as if he had no strength left to go on. But the thought of their baby kept him alive in hope; that baby made it all worthwhile. With new life come new beginnings, he thought, a chance to live again.

'Darling!' Penny reached out her hands and Patrick took them. 'Have you finished your work so soon?'

He smiled. 'Not quite. I saw the sunshine and thought I'd have a break for a few minutes.'

She laughed, the same light, carefree laugh that had so deceived him in the early days. 'You will never be a proper minister if you don't do your homework, Paddy!'

How lighthearted her conversation is when she is well, he thought; how little I really knew when I married her.

'You look awfully cross all of a sudden, darling.' She reached up and touched his cheek with her finger and then let her hand drop away, as if she had lost interest in the action. 'Here, do you like my roses?' She held out the trug which she carried over her arm and glanced fleetingly up at his face. It was one of her habits, changing the subject when she felt like it, unable to focus for any length of time.

'Yes, wonderful.'

'They're for tonight, for the table.'

'Lovely.'

'I am a good wife to you, aren't I, Paddy?' Her face was suddenly serious, her voice slightly agitated.

'Yes.' He smiled, a safe, reassuring smile.

'I try to be.'

'I know you do.' He bent and kissed her forehead.

'I think I might go up for my rest now. I feel quite tired, I think it's the warmth.'

'Have you finished the roses?'

'Finished?'

'Yes, do you have enough for the table?'

'Oh, I don't know.' She glanced over her shoulder. 'I'll ask Mrs Dunn to arrange them for me – she'll know if there's enough. I really am quite tired.'

'Yes, I'm sure you are. Here, let me.' He took the trug from her and she smiled.

'Do you want to come up for my rest?'

'No, I . . .' He saw the flicker of anguish in her eyes and stopped. She had been reasonably balanced for some time now, and he was trying to do everything he could to keep her that way. 'Oh well, why not? I'm sure I can afford to take half an hour off my parliamentary duties!'

She laughed, the anguish completely vanished. He just couldn't tell which way she would go next. 'I'll ask Mrs Dunn to hold all your calls then.'

'No. I mean, don't do that, someone might have to get through.' He needed the interruption of calls. Just lying and comforting her stifled him.

'They can wait.'

'What if someone has to cancel tonight?'

'Oh God! They can't! I . . .' She instantly panicked.

'Penny! Please.' He held her shoulders. 'I'm sure they won't, please, don't panic, it's just a bare possibility.'

'Oh, I . . .'

'I'll tell Mrs Dunn to hold the calls. You're right, they can wait.' He saw the relief in her eyes and silently cursed his sister. She had bullied Penny into this dinner tonight and he knew she couldn't cope. There seemed to be no end to Margaret's malice; she would sacrifice anyone for her own gains. 'I'm sure everything will be just great tonight, honestly. We'll go up and rest now and you're not to think about it again. OK?'

Penny nodded.

'Good. You go on up, and I'll join you in a few minutes.' He dropped his hands and she turned towards the French windows. He watched her go and waved as she glanced back from the house. Then he let out a heavy, irritated sigh and walked down to the rose bushes to collect up her things.

*

Around six o'clock Patrick got up from his desk and wandered through from his study to the dining room. He saw that Mrs Dunn had finished off what Penny had started earlier that day and the table was set, the flowers arranged and the wine laid out on the sideboard ready for him to decant. He took in the details of the room and then crossed to the table to check the name cards were in the right order.

'Is everything all right, Mr Devlin?'

He turned and saw the housekeeper in the doorway. 'Oh, yes thank you, Mrs Dunn, it all looks very nice indeed.'

She smiled her acknowledgement. 'Is Mrs Devlin still sleeping?'

'Yes.' He had left Penny to rest after only ten minutes with her. She slept very heavily in the afternoons and didn't even stir as he closed the door behind him and went on down to his study. 'I suppose I had better wake her. Could you make some tea for us, please?'

'Of course.' Mrs Dunn turned immediately and left as silently as she had arrived, her soft-soled shoes noiseless on the stone floors. Patrick left the dining room and made his way upstairs to the main bedroom where Penny slept.

'Oh, hello! I thought you were still asleep.' Patrick came into the room and looked across at Penny who sat, in her bra and slip, staring at her reflection in her dressing-table mirror. The bed was littered with clothes, carelessly flung down, and the floor with umpteen pairs of shoes. It looked a mess, an aggressive, bad-tempered chaos.

'Penny?' He walked further in, closing the door behind him. She didn't answer. 'Penny? Are you all right?'

In front of her on the dressing table was a pile of discarded jewellery, and the contents of her make-up bag were dumped in a heap, lipsticks, powders, pencils, all messy and spilt onto the warm, highly polished Regency walnut table.

'Penny?' He crossed to her, his pulse quickening. 'What is it? Penny?'

Suddenly she jumped up and spun round, knocking the small stool she had been sitting on over and kicking it out of the way.

'Nothing fits!' she cried. 'Nothing!' Her eyes were wild and her face crumpled in rage and misery. 'I'm a fat cow!' she shouted. 'A fat, ugly cow!' She started to weep, with harsh, angry sobs. 'I hate this baby! Look at me!' Her voice had risen to screaming pitch and the tears coursed down her face, red and swollen with frustration. 'I hate this baby! Do you hear me? I hate it! Hate it!' She began to punch her stomach, her mouth shrivelled up in pain. 'I hate it!' She punched harder. 'I HATE it!'

'PENNY!' Patrick was across the room and had grabbed her arms, pinning them back hard before he realised what he was doing. She cried out in pain but he held her fast, his nails digging into her skin, so tight was his grip. 'DON'T! For God's sake!' He was breathing fast, the blood rushing in his ears and his whole body pulsing with fear. 'Penny! Don't!' He swallowed painfully and tried to calm himself. He could feel her confusion but stronger than that he could feel his own fear, the tight, paralysing fear for his child. He took several deep breaths as Penny sobbed in front of him. He didn't know what to do, his mind veering violently between fury and pity. Finally, after several minutes, he dropped her arms and let her go. She slumped down onto her knees and continued to sob.

'Oh God, no!' He looked down at her and the fury evaporated. He bent. 'Penny, here. Please. Come on, let me help you up.' He lifted her to her feet and steered her towards the bed. He sat her down and tried to comfort her, placing his arm uneasily round her shoulder. 'Please, Penny, don't,' he murmured.

She shrugged him off. 'I know that you find me repulsive,' she said through her tears. 'I know you do . . .' Her sobs had quietened and she was no longer angry, just childlike and pathetic. 'I'm disgusting. That's why you won't sleep with me, isn't it?'

He sighed and sat down beside her, taking her hand and holding it, despite her efforts to pull it back. 'Penny, we've talked about this before,' he began. 'You asked me if you were keeping me awake and I said yes. It was you who suggested I sleep in the other room.' She had stopped weeping and her body was calmer. 'And you don't look disgusting; you look lovely. I've told you a hundred times how beautiful you look now, haven't I?'

She kept her head down, the odd tear splashing onto the thin nylon of her slip.

'Penny, listen to me now.' He turned to her and tilted her face up so that he could see her eyes. Her skin was red and blotchy, swollen around her eyes and mouth, and she tried to put her hand up to cover her face. He eased it away.

'Penny, the most important thing in our life right now is that baby. You do understand that, don't you? It's your responsibility and we must try to bring it into the world unharmed.' Even as he talked he could feel the fear rising in his chest again. He was pretty sure that she hadn't done any damage with her punches of fury but just the thought of what she might have done made him feel physically sick. 'Penny, you must never hit yourself like that, no matter how frustrated you might feel.' He heard his voice rise and harden and he cursed himself; he was unable to keep the anger out of it. Quietly she began to sob again.

'Penny, I'm not trying to tell you off, really I'm not. I'm just trying to help.'

'No you're not! You don't understand! How can you?'

'I do, honestly.'

'You don't! It's me that has to carry this horrible lump around all day and all night; it's me that feels sick and disgusting all the time, it's me that . . .' She stood up and moved away from him, still crying. From the window, she turned and said: 'You don't even want to touch me any more!'

Patrick stood up and walked over to her. Gently, he put his arms around her.

'Come on now, Penny, sssh.' He stroked her back. 'That's just not true,' he murmured, 'you know it isn't.' He felt her relax, and after a while the crying ceased. It always ended like this, always. She had never enjoyed making love with him, lying unresponsive and cold under him, but she needed it for her security and self-esteem. She was like an ill person enduring treatment in the knowledge that it would make her feel better. She looked up at him and he kissed her tenderly on the lips.

'You do still want me, don't you?' she whispered.

'Of course I do,' he lied. He felt for her hand and then led her over to the bed. She sat and waited for him to undress her. 'Of course I do,' he said again as he held her. 'Of course I do.' Another guilty lie.

Halfway through the dinner that night, Patrick glanced across the table at Penny and saw the flush of excitement on her cheeks. She was involved in a conversation with the new Health Minister and Charles Hewitt and her voice was clear and confident as she argued a point. He looked away again before he caught her eye; he did not want to be drawn into their circle. It was extraordinary, he thought, how well and normal she could appear, even bright and sparkling, and ironic how quick her recovery had been from the trauma of the early evening. He glanced back briefly and checked her glass. Mineral water; at least that was consistent.

Catching Mrs Dunn's eye, Patrick could see that she was ready to serve the coffee. Penny was not very adept at those sorts of things so he nodded to her and announced that coffee would be served in the sitting room. Then he stood and excused himself to fetch his cigars. The general conversation continued around the table as he left the room.

Crossing the hall to the study, Patrick realised in the sudden quietness that he was really quite tired. He was glad to be free of the chatter of politics, the gossip and backbiting, for a few minutes. He listened to the odd comfortable creak of his wonderful old house and went on through to his study, relieved to be alone. He poured himself a whisky from a bottle he kept locked in the bureau, and sat down at his desk. No one should miss him for at least ten minutes or so.

Lady Margaret walked across the hall to her brother's study and stopped Mrs Dunn on the way.

'Hold the coffee for a few minutes, will you, Mrs Dunn?'

'But Mr Devlin said to—'

'I know what Mr Devlin said, only I think it would be better if you held it back for ten minutes. All right?' Lady Margaret's voice was sharp; she was irritated. Patrick really had no idea, she thought as she carried on to the study. Serving coffee straight after dinner; everyone would have violent indigestion!

Pushing open the door to the study, she didn't bother to knock and walked straight into the room. She stopped short.

'Excuse me?' Patrick glared across at her. 'Weren't we

always brought up to knock before we enter a room?'

'Don't be sarcastic, Paddy!' Lady Margaret crossed to the desk and glanced at the bottle. 'May I?'

'If you insist.' He let her find a glass and pour her own drink, continuing to sip his in silence. She pulled up a chair and sat down.

'Paddy,' she began softly, 'I think we need to talk.'

He looked at her. 'Oh yes?' Swallowing his drink down in one, he reached over and poured himself another. Her presence annoyed him and he made no pretence of covering that fact.

'How is Penny?' Lady Margaret decided to change the subject, to start on something neutral.

'She's coping. Just.'

'She looks well tonight.'

'That's what you think!'

Lady Margaret sighed heavily. 'Look, Paddy, can't we stop all this? Can't we sit down and just talk for once, like we used to?'

'What about?' He was deliberately antagonistic, refusing to give her an inch.

'About anything, I don't know! There's no friendship between us any more, no companionship.'

Patrick stood up. 'Are you really surprised?' He began to make his way to the door. She had ruined his peace; he might as well get back to the dinner.

'Paddy, wait!' She turned to look at him. 'Yes! Yes, I am surprised. Why?'

He spun round. 'God, Margaret, you really are a joke! Why? You're actually surprised and you want to know why?' His voice was bitter and sneering. 'Any trace of feeling I had for you died a long time ago. As to why, I think you can work that one out for yourself, can't you? After all that's been said between us?'

'But Paddy . . .'

'But what? I'm civil to you; I jump when you say jump, and I've got you the kind of powerful friends you always wanted. There are no buts, Margaret.' He shrugged. The bitterness had gone; his voice was now resigned and sad. He turned back to the door. 'Switch the light off when you've finished,' he said, and silently left the room.

Penny reached the bottom stair without wobbling, her step faltering only slightly when her foot touched the floor. She gripped the banister and straightened herself. Breathing into her hand, she sniffed to check her breath and then crossed the hall to Patrick's study, her nightdress sweeping the floor as she went. She knocked lightly and waited for him to call out, then she entered.

'Penny! I thought you were in bed!'

She stood in the doorway. 'No, I . . .' She smiled tentatively. 'I thought you might want to come up with me.'

He stood up. 'Come on in, sit down, you'll get cold in just that thin thing.'

'No, I'm fine. Are you coming up? I've sent Mrs Dunn home to bed.'

'Good, she looks tired. Penny, you go on up, I'll be with you a bit later. I've still got some work to do.'

She held onto the doorframe, feeling slightly dizzy. 'Can't you do it in the morning?'

He needed some time alone. He couldn't face another forced love scene. 'If I do it now,' he said, trying to placate her, 'I'll have more free time tomorrow to spend with you.' He smiled. 'Sound fair?'

She nodded. 'Yes, fine.' It sounded like another excuse to her. She looked down at the big fat lump. 'I'll see you in the morning then.' She waited for him to come across to kiss her but he stayed where he was. 'Good night.'

He smiled. 'Good night, Penny.'

She could hear the relief in his voice. Closing the door behind her, she padded across the hall and held on tight to the banister to make it up the stairs.

Back in her bedroom, she locked the door and sat down on the bed, lying back against the pillows and putting her feet up. She knew that Patrick would sleep in the spare room tonight and that she was alone. She reached across to the bedside table and picked up the bottle of mineral water, unscrewing the cap and putting it to her lips. She took a big gulp and felt the warm, consoling sensation of the vodka in her stomach. The bottle dropped onto her lap.

Closing her eyes, she imagined herself slim and beautiful, in black velvet, her hair piled up on her head and the Brachen diamonds at her throat. She was laughing, spinning round and round and everyone was clapping as she danced. She took another swig. It was Patrick she was dancing with; no, it was her father or maybe even Richard. Whoever it was, he loved her, and she felt warm and secure and loved by everyone. She smiled and took another gulp.

Mineral water, she thought, looking at the label on the bottle, how clever of me! She was feeling drunk now, warm and relaxed for the first time that night, and she began to giggle as she read the words. But her vision was blurred – she had been drinking all night. After only a minute or so, she gave up and took another gulp, letting the bottle drop onto the bed beside her. She was sleepy, languid and content, locked safe and secure in her room. Funny this baby doesn't kick, she thought, closing her eyes again and letting her mind drift away. She pulled the counterpane around her and turned over onto her side. Perhaps it can't be bothered, she thought, just like me.

She shut her eyes tighter to try to block out the image of Patrick that had suddenly come into her mind, then a deep, heavy blackness swamped her brain and the smiling, pitying face of her husband disappeared. Instantly she lost consciousness and seconds later, she was enveloped in a heavy, drunken sleep, an all-cleansing, all-embracing nothingness.

CHAPTER
Thirty-two

THE GLORIOUS JULY WEATHER HAD lasted about two days into Patrick's summer recess and then the rain set in, chilling the air and making everything damp and clammy to the touch. It poured, in long, drenching bouts, the sky thick and grey, huge gusts of wind moving the great plains of cloud slowly across the country, soaking the land. August, and the English summer had properly arrived.

Patrick drove up the gravel drive of Long Wind House and parked in front of the garage. He rushed into the house, covering his head with his briefcase, then took off his Barbour in the hall, shaking the rain from it and calling out to Penny. There was no response, so he walked through to the kitchen and found Mrs Dunn there alone and preparing the lunch.

'Hello! Where's Mrs Devlin?'

She turned from the sink. 'Ah, hello, Mr Devlin. Mrs Devlin has gone out to lunch with a friend. She said she'd be back this afternoon about four-ish. Would you like some lunch?'

'Yes, please, whatever there is.' He crossed to the fridge and took out a carton of orange juice. 'D'you want some?'

Mrs Dunn smiled. 'Yes, thank you.'

Patrick poured two glasses, handed one to Mrs Dunn and pulled out a chair to sit at the table. He felt the need to talk, and Mrs Dunn was always quite content to listen, unlike Penny.

'You know, this hospital closure is really going to take up much more of my time than I'd thought.' He sighed. 'There are a lot of very angry people out there. The problem is that we have a cottage hospital here that is really just that, I'm afraid. All right, it serves the basic needs of the local community, but it's a constant drain on the District Health Authority's finances and it simply doesn't have the resources to cope with emergencies, or the staff, for that matter.' He shrugged. 'It's very hard to argue one way or another, though. I can see how much people rely on the hospital but I can also see that anything major has to be sent over to Crawley General because the Morton just can't cope – and that's not good enough. What a situation!' He swallowed down his orange juice. 'Did Penny say who she was going out with, by the way?'

'No, I'm sorry, she didn't.'

Patrick nodded. 'Oh well.' He stood up. 'I think I might go and start some letters on this before lunch. Do you think you could bring me something through on a tray seeing as I'm eating alone?'

Mrs Dunn smiled. 'Of course. It should be ready in about ten minutes.'

'Good.' He walked to the kitchen door. He was strangely restless today. Perhaps it was the meeting that had upset him – local feeling was running high on the issue, but he felt on edge, not quite sure whether he wanted to stay and talk to Mrs Dunn, or go to his study. 'Were there any messages for me this morning?' he asked, hanging around to waste time.

'Oh my! I completely forgot! A delivery came from John Lewis earlier this morning. I sent the packages upstairs to the small bedroom. I'm sorry, I meant to tell you when you came in. I hope that's all right?'

'Yes, that's fine.' Patrick felt an immediate lifting of his spirits. 'In fact, it's great!' It had to be the things they'd ordered for the nursery. He beamed at Mrs Dunn, unable to conceal his excitement. 'Can I change that request to something upstairs?'

'Of course!' Mrs Dunn smiled back. She found Patrick Devlin's delight in the preparations for his first child really most endearing. 'Go on up and I'll bring it to you when it's ready.'

'Thanks.' And with all thoughts of the hospital, all worries about local feeling suddenly much less important, he hurried out into the hall and ran up the stairs, two at a time, and along to the back bedroom and the boxes from John Lewis, the first real things they had bought for their child.

Inside the small nursery the three large cardboard packages sat in the middle of the floor, wrapped and tied with the traditional green and white JLP paper. The cot had arrived, flat packed and stood up against the wall, ready to be assembled. Patrick tore off the paper and pulled out the leaflet and instructions, sinking down onto the floor to read them, and glancing up briefly to count the packs, making sure everything had arrived. Then he checked the delivery notes on the other three boxes and went along to his bedroom to find a penknife. He cut carefully down the lengths of tape, pulled open the top of each box and took out the contents, spreading them out over the floor and laughing at himself, thirty-five years old and acting like a teenager. He surveyed everything they had bought and decided there and then how he was going to spend the rest of the day. He would get the nursery ready and surprise Penny when she came home.

Looking up at the clean white walls of the nursery, he tried to imagine the border, along with the pictures and all the shapes in bright primary colours they had bought. He sized up the room, decided on the border first, pictures and shapes next and finally the cot. He walked out of the room, carrying the tub of glue, reading the instructions as he went and leaving the nursery floor littered with discarded packaging and all the bits and pieces. He would change, eat some lunch and then get started. He smiled and felt all the earlier restlessness disappear; preparing the house for their baby filled him with an enormous sense of pleasure and purpose.

Standing in the centre of the bedroom he occasionally shared with Penny, Patrick suddenly realised that he had no idea where he had put his old trousers and sweater after the move to Long Wind House and that he would probably have to scrabble around in the backs of wardrobes to try to find them. He dropped the pot of fixative down onto the bed and decided to start with their joint cupboard in the bedroom. If they weren't there, he would no doubt have to search everywhere, as Penny had the oddest habit of putting things in places one would never expect them to be. He crossed to the wardrobe, pulled back the rail of clothes and began to hunt.

Some fifteen minutes later, he still hadn't found them. He had been through the joint wardrobe, his own, Penny's, the wardrobe in the spare bedroom and was now about to tackle the small cupboard built under the stairs on the first-floor landing. Mrs Dunn had brought his lunch up on a tray but Patrick was so irritated by the search that he had forgotten it and left it to go cold and congeal nastily on the plate, while he muttered furiously to himself and ransacked the cupboards.

Kneeling on the floor, he opened the last small cupboard door and shined his torch inside the dark narrow space. He bent his head and peered inside, following the beam of light, and saw a large box, a plastic bag and a bundle of what looked like clothes. At last, he thought. God knows why she put them in here!

He pulled out the box, rattling its contents as he did so, and dragged it onto the carpet in order to get a better look at the bundle of clothes. It was then that he heard the distinctive chink of glass. Puzzled, he sat back, opened the top of the box and looked inside. Vodka. A case of vodka, four full bottles, seven empties. An alcoholic's supply.

He stared uncomprehendingly at the bottles and then suddenly the terrible reality of what they meant hit him. The evidence of what she had done to their baby almost doubled him over with grief. He turned away, unable to look any more, sickened to the heart. He experienced a pain of bitter disappointment, of guilt, and then a huge and violent fury. A fury so strong and powerful that he thought for a few minutes it would choke him. How could she? The bitch, he kept repeating, again and again, the stupid, stupid bitch!

He felt crushed by this anger, as if it pressed out every last ounce of life he had inside him. He knew what alcoholism did to the foetus. Taking a deep breath, he willed himself to be calm, fighting down the rage, wanting to hit out at something. And yet all the time he knew she couldn't help it, he knew she was ill.

Over and over he kept trying to calm himself, to think straight. How long had it been going on? How much of it had she drunk? When? Why? His mind spun with unanswered questions and a voice cried out, echoing round and round in his brain, desperate to be heard. My baby, it said, my baby, my baby.

Finally, through a wall of fear and pain, he managed to bring himself round, to scramble to his feet and make it to the bathroom. There, he was violently sick.

Slumping down onto the floor and resting his aching head against the cold enamel of the bath, Patrick tried to think back, to decipher when and how it had happened. He remembered certain things, the heaviness of her sleep, an almost coma-like state in the afternoons, her inability to concentrate on anything, the rages, the days of blankness and lethargy. He remembered the vast amount of time he had left her on her own, or just ignored her because the very thought of her exhausted him. He remembered his need to work, to bury himself and to try to forget, and he knew then how and when and why. He remembered it all, and felt, with an awful, guilty clarity, that it was as much his own fault as hers.

He pulled himself up and bent over the sink, running the cold water tap and splashing his face over and over until he felt some feeling and sense come back. Then he dried himself and walked slowly back to the bedroom, sitting down on the big double bed that they so rarely shared. He picked up a photograph in a silver frame, laid it on his lap and looked down at it. He unscrewed the top on the bottle of mineral water and took a big thirsty gulp.

'Ugh! Shit!'

The shock of the burning liquid in his throat make him choke it up instantly and he spat out a mouthful of vodka, the rest searing the back of his throat and burning down into his stomach, making his eyes water and his throat constrict. He coughed violently, spluttering for several minutes and struggling for breath. Finally he managed to recover himself, wiping his face with his handkerchief. He stood up and the photograph crashed to the floor.

'Stupid, fucking bitch!' he shouted, his voice hoarse with tears. He grabbed the glass bottle and flung it across the room, smashing it on the wall opposite. The splinters of glass sprayed out for several yards and the clear, lethal liquid ran down the expensive wallpaper. He swallowed hard, fighting back the rage and tears, then turned and left the room, the stench of alcohol sickeningly strong in his nostrils.

Penny drove along the narrow, winding road towards Little Horsley with her headlamps on full beam and the rain pelting down onto the windscreen, making visibility almost impossible. She leaned forward in the driver's seat and tried to concentrate, the fuzz of several late-afternoon vodkas heavy in her head and the dark shadows of the road deceiving. She felt a little dizzy again, and short of breath. She needed to lie down and the sooner she got home the better.

She had lunched with a couple of old schoolfriends, carefully lacing her drinks throughout the afternoon, making sure she averted her breath every time she spoke and refusing to kiss anyone when she left, feigning a cold. She hated lunching out and only went when she absolutely had to. She had grown used to eating alone – food on a tray in her room, the radio for company and the afternoons warm and secure, a few drinks and a comforting sleep. She had drunk far too much this afternoon, she knew that, but she had felt bored and left out, and it was her only consolation. Just a few more miles, she thought with relief, and I'll be home in my room, tucked up under the covers, safe and warm with my own special brand of mineral water. She put her foot down on the accelerator and increased her speed.

Patrick heard the sharp scream of brakes and the long drag of rubber on tarmac as Penny screeched the car to a halt and then yanked it into reverse, having overshot the drive. He ran to the bedroom window to see that she was all right and saw her lose her balance ever so slightly as she climbed out of the car to pull open the gates. The anger he had been trying to control all afternoon suddenly rose to the surface and he turned away disgusted. He walked down the stairs and into the hall, switching on the overhead lights as well as the lamps and leaned against the wall, waiting for her to come in. He wanted to be in a position to see her face properly. He heard her fumble with the lock and then the door swung open.

'Oh! Hello!' Penny stood in the doorway and blinked at the bright light. 'I thought you were Mrs Dunn, clearing up or something.' She came on into the house and avoided Patrick by crossing to the cupboard and taking off her coat, her movements careful and controlled. 'What are all these lights on for, Patrick?' She finished putting her coat away and turned. 'It's a terrible waste of electricity.' She went to the switch and clicked the overhead light off. 'That's better.' She smiled nervously, feeling a little more at ease in the dimmer light. 'I think I might go straight up for my rest, darling, if you don't mind. I'm awfully tired, it's been rather a long day.' She walked towards the stairs concentrating hard on keeping her movements steady.

'Penny?'

She stopped, not wanting to turn, simply eager to get upstairs to her room.

'Penny, come here please.'

She looked back over her shoulder; Patrick's face was grim and she suddenly felt frightened. 'Why?' she asked, trying to sound light. She cleared her throat. 'It really is time for my rest, you know.'

'Yes, I know, but just for once it can wait.' His voice was cool, much, much cooler than usual. The fear deepened. 'Penny, I need to talk to you.' He was keeping a tight rein on his emotions, sure that if he let them slip he might lose control completely. 'Let's go into the sitting room, please.'

She faced him now and saw that his eyes were dark and cold. She shivered. 'No, I'm going up to my room.' She couldn't face him; she didn't have the strength. She turned and continued on to the stairs.

'There's nothing to drink up there, Penny,' he said quietly. 'I've cleared the house.'

She stopped. Instinctively her hand went to the wall for support and she sagged, as if someone had taken the air out of her. She looked down at the floor and the blood rushed in her ears. She wasn't sure if it was the shock of being found out or the terrible need for a drink that made her feel so dizzy, so desperate. She held onto the solid wall and swallowed hard. 'You had no right to . . .' she whispered.

'I had every right to! God damn it, Penny! What the hell—?' He broke off. He was trembling and he had to clasp his hands together to control them. She won't understand, he kept thinking, you must try to be kind, you must try to help her. He moved forward a pace. 'Penny? Look at me, please.'

She lifted her head.

'Penny, you have to stop, you need help. You have to think of the baby.'

Suddenly her head jerked back. 'The baby!' she cried. 'The baby, the baby, the baby! That's it, isn't it? Fuck me, fuck Penny! It's the baby you want! It's all you've ever wanted! This!' She punched her stomach. 'This . . . this thing in here!' She was crying now, and shouting. 'You've never wanted me! Never! All you want is this!' Again she punched herself and Patrick lunged forward towards her.

'Get off me!' she screamed. She ran up the stairs. 'I know! I know about her!' She lost her footing slightly and gripped the wall. Patrick's whole body froze with fear. She turned halfway up to look at him. She was sobbing uncontrollably. 'I've always known! Always! All those things hidden in your study, magazines and pictures . . . and Richard said . . .' She broke off, momentarily unable to go on, and Patrick

461

watched helplessly. Then she carried on: 'You've never loved me . . . I was second-best . . . I had the money!' And she put her hands up to her face as her body heaved with great wracking sobs. Patrick inched forward and held out his hand to her.

'Penny, please. Please, don't.' All his anger had vanished; he was frightened as he looked up at her. She swayed precariously on the stairs, sobbing desperately. He stretched his fingers to touch her. If only I can touch her, he thought, to get through. He felt the cold, clammy skin of her leg through her thin tights.

'Don't! Don't you . . .!' She dropped her hands and yelled at him as she felt his touch. 'Don't!' She kicked out violently. Suddenly she lost her balance and screamed. The next moment she fell.

She was half a flight of steep steps above him and he had no chance to catch her. She fell awkwardly, plummeting forward onto her stomach, tumbling down, her body like a rag doll. She hit the wall with her arms, knocking her face on the banister. He put out both arms to try to grab her but he couldn't. He watched helplessly as she smashed to the ground and lay, shocked, eyes wide open looking up at him.

Then she began to whimper.

He ran to her and knelt by her side. 'Oh God, Penny!'

She was crying, in a small, terrified way, the sound half strangled in her throat. Her eyes remained wide open, staring, blank with pain.

'Where's the pain? Penny?'

He took her wrist and felt the pulse, then he slipped his hands down between her legs. She was bleeding.

'Penny, it's all right now, come on, it's all right.' He took off his sweater and covered her with it and then ran to the study for a rug. He tucked it round her and bent his head to her face. He kissed her, holding her hand. 'I'm going to take you into hospital. You mustn't panic, OK? Try to breathe deeply.'

Her whole body shuddered with a contraction and she cried out.

'Penny, darling, the baby is on its way. You've given it a jolt, that's all. Now remember your breathing. Come on now.' He glanced at his watch. The contraction had lasted just over a minute so far. 'Come on, Penny, hold onto me.' Again she cried out, and then it passed. Breathless, she closed her eyes.

'Oh Paddy,' she whispered. 'I'm scared. I'm bleeding.'

'I know,' he said gently. 'I know. It's all right, I'm going to get you to the hospital.'

He kissed her hand and then stood up, grabbing his car keys off the hall table. He ran out of the house and started the engine. Moments later he was back.

'OK, Penny, come on now. I'm going to pick you up and carry you out. Try to relax now, all right?'

He knelt, slipped his hands under her body and lifted her up, struggling to his feet. He carried her out, holding the rug tight round her, and gently placed her in the car. She had begun to shake. Running round the other side, he jumped in, spun the car round and drove off.

'It's all right, lovey. Here we go. Up onto here. There we are!' The nurse turned to Patrick.

'One- to two-minute contractions, you say? Every ten minutes?'

'Yes, that's right.' They followed the trolley as the porters hurried it into the hospital and down into one of the labour rooms.

'The obstetrician's been bleeped, he'll be on his way.'

'Yes, thanks.' Patrick watched Penny's face, ashen and creased with pain. His mind was blank.

'Mr Devlin?'

'I'm sorry, what did you say?'

'I said I think you know the obstetrician on call. He's from Bart's. Michael Tremayne.'

'Oh, yes, I do.'

A midwife hurried into the room. 'Hello. Mrs Devlin, is that right?'

Penny nodded as the midwife crossed to her. 'I'm just going to take your blood pressure and listen to the baby's heart rate, all right, dear? Lift up a minute . . . that's fine. I'm just going to clip this monitor onto the belt. Good. Be still now and try to relax. Is there any bleeding?'

'Yes, vaginal bleeding, not much. Regular contractions.'

The midwife nodded as the nurse answered her. All her actions were quick but controlled, emergency without the panic. Patrick had seen it so many times.

'Ah, Dr Tremayne!'

The obstetrician entered the room.

'Patrick!'

'Hello, Michael.'

'I thought it might be you when they said Devlin.' He strode across the room to the bed as he spoke. There was no time for pleasantries. 'Hello, Penny.' He looked across at the midwife.

'Blood pressure normal and here's the trace,' she said, glancing at the monitor. 'It's ninety to ninety-five between contractions, seventy to seventy-five during.'

'Right.' Tremayne looked up at Patrick; they both knew the signs of severe foetal distress. 'Penny, this baby looks as if it's on its way now. I'm going to take you straight into theatre. All right? Try not to worry.'

Patrick squeezed Penny's hand.

'Can you get a drip up, Mary? Organise theatre one. Also we'll need to call Crawley General, alert the Paeds.'

'Right.' The midwife moved away from the bed. She unfolded a gown and shook it out. 'Let's get you into this, shall we?'

'I'll do it,' Patrick said.

'Fine.' She handed him the garment and quickly left the room.

'Right, now, Penny, I'm going to get changed. There's nothing to be nervous about, OK?' Tremayne patted her hand, before moving towards the door.

'Michael?' Tremayne stopped at the sound of Patrick's voice. 'I want to be in theatre with Penny.'

Tremayne shook his head. 'I can't allow that, Patrick, I'm sorry.'

'Michael, I'm a qualified paediatrician – you may need me there!'

Tremayne thought quickly. Devlin knew what he was doing, although he'd been out of it for a couple of years. This was a small hospital and there might be complications; he had no choice. 'All right, Patrick. Come and change when you've organised Penny.' He turned, and not wanting to waste any more time, hurriedly left the room.

'Sorry about this funny angle, dear. We have to just get you onto the table here. That's it! Good. Now could you just drink this? Good girl!' The midwife turned to the anaesthetist. 'All yours.'

'Hello, Penny. I'm going to put a mask over your face to give you some oxygen. Try to breathe normally. That's it.' The anaesthetist slipped the sucker under Penny's head and turned away to get the syringe. He saw Michael Tremayne and Patrick come in and start scrubbing up.

'I'm going to send you to sleep now, Penny. I'm just injecting the drugs now . . . There. Good girl. When you wake up it'll all be over.' Her body twitched as the muscles relaxed and he opened her mouth, inserting the laryngoscope.

'All right, it's in,' he said to the midwife, 'go ahead.'

The midwife pressed her fingers down onto the central part of Penny's neck. 'It feels funny,' she said quickly. 'I don't seem to know where I am. Am I . . .?'

'Shit! She's throwing up! Here! . . . Right, seems to be clear now. I can see, give me the tube, let's get it in! OK!' He looked up briefly. 'Let's attach her to the ventilator.'

Michael Tremayne was at the table. 'Can I start?'

'Yes. She's quite stiff to ventilate. Is she asthmatic?'

'Not on the records,' Tremayne said. 'Patrick?'

Patrick wasn't thinking. He was too involved to think straight. 'No,' he answered automatically. Suddenly he looked up. 'Michael! She's an alcoholic!'

'Oh Jesus!' Tremayne looked across at the anaesthetist.

'You'll have to go ahead, there's no time . . .'

Tremayne nodded and the first incision was made, horizontal across the abdomen. He separated the muscle with his hands. 'Forceps!' He lifted the tissues. 'Peritoneum . . . Knife!'

'I still can't get her properly oxygenated!' There was alarm in the anaesthetist's voice. 'I'm going to give her some ventolin.'

Patrick felt his stomach contract with fear. He watched the brief fumble with the ampoule and saw the look of tension on the anaesthetist's face. He turned back to Michael.

'I'm into the uterus. I'm going to deliver her now.' He held his hands out. 'Retractor!'

'I'm having real problems here, Michael!' The anaesthetist's voice pierced the concentrated silence. 'Something's pretty wrong!'

'I've got a foot! Here it comes! Clamp.' Tremayne pulled out the tiny body, slippery and bloody.

Again the anaesthetist's voice, sharp and tense. 'Michael,

I can't resuscitate the baby – I can't leave here.'

Tremayne nodded. 'Here we are, little girl . . .' They were losing precious seconds. 'Patrick?'

'Christ . . . I don't . . .'

There was no time to panic. 'Patrick!' he said again.

'All right . . .' Patrick's voice broke as he took the feeble, struggling infant in his hands. The midwife followed him with the baby over to the resuscitaire. 'I've got you, baby, it's OK,' he whispered. Laying his daughter on the bed, he slipped the oxygen mask over her face and began to hand ventilate it, his vision blurred with tears. 'Come on, baby, come on.' He waited a few more seconds. 'I'm going to intubate her,' he shouted hoarsely. He took the mask away and fumbled momentarily with the laryngoscope before inserting it. He slipped the tube down.

'Jesus! Blood pressure's going down! I'm not sure I can hold her . . .'

'All right, I'm nearly there. Scissors.'

'I'm losing it . . .!'

Tremayne finished sewing the cut. 'OK. I'm nearly . . .'

'Oh Jesus! Michael, she's slipping . . . Cardiomyopathy, almost certain! Jesus Christ!' The anaesthetist shook his head and looked up, alarmed. 'She'll have to go to intensive.'

'Right!'

'Alert the General, we need an ambulance!'

Tremayne turned away from the table as the midwife ran from the theatre; there was nothing more he could do. He crossed to Patrick.

'Patrick?' He saw the blue, emaciated face of the baby, struggling to oxygenate. He touched Patrick's shoulder and felt him flinch.

'We'll get them to intensive,' he said. Patrick nodded.

'It'll be all . . .' He stopped. There was no point in false hope. 'I'm sorry,' he said simply, and quietly moved away.

It was after midnight, and Patrick sat in the canteen at the General Hospital, Crawley, drinking a lukewarm cup of coffee from the machine. The place was empty and the silence was punctuated only by the futile whir of the electric heaters. He held the plastic cup in both hands in an attempt to warm them, his whole body cold and numb.

'Patrick?'

He looked up as Tremayne walked towards his table. 'Want another coffee?'

'No thanks.'

Tremayne pulled out a chair and sat down. 'I'm sorry, Patrick,' he said. 'Really I am.' He paused and looked away. 'There was just no chance.'

Patrick didn't answer; he couldn't. The baby was dead and he had no words left.

'I've come to see if you want to go back to Penny.'

'Is she . . .?'

'Yes.'

'How long?'

'I don't know. A few hours maybe, not much more. I'm sorry, Patrick. But being an alcoholic . . .' he broke off for a moment, 'her heart just can't cope.' She was too weak – there was nothing they could do.

Patrick dropped his head down and felt Tremayne's hand on his arm. He swallowed and looked up. 'Let's go,' he said quietly.

They stood together and walked silently out of the canteen.

In the intensive care unit Penny looked so small and frail amongst the bank of machines, her body punctured with drips and tubes. She looked like a child, peaceful for once, sleeping.

Patrick sat down by the side of the bed and took her hand in his own, pressing it gently to his lips.

'Penny,' he whispered. 'I'm sorry.' He closed his eyes and saw the image of her pain, her desperate wracking sobs, her accusing eyes. 'I loved you as much as I could.'

Leaning forward, he stroked her brow, cool and smooth under his fingers, and then kissed the top of her head.

'I'm so, so sorry,' he whispered again. 'Forgive me.'

And he sat with her until the early hours of the morning when the dawn broke and her heart finally stopped beating.

CHAPTER

Thirty-three

PATRICK STOOD IN THE ENTRANCE porch of Long Wind House and waved goodbye to the last of the mourners – sober-faced people in dark clothes who had come out of respect, not feeling, and who had remained dry-eyed, speaking in hushed tones of a tragedy they knew very little about. He held up his hand, smiled soberly and then turned his back on them. Friendship should be for the living, he thought, not for the dead. Penny could have used a couple of friends.

Inside the hall, he noticed the house was cold and went to the radiator to check it was on. He had felt cold all the time recently; it was a numbness that seemed to go right through him. The heat was on, so he warmed his hands on the radiator and tried to summon up the strength to go back through and face his sister and Richard Brachen. All wanted to do was go to bed, shut it all out and sleep, sleep forever.

'Patrick?'

He turned. 'Oh, Margaret.'

'Good Lord! You're frozen! Come on into the kitchen and let me make you some tea. You need to stand by the Aga, warm up a bit.'

'It's OK, thanks. I'm fine.'

'No you're not! Come on.'

Lady Margaret walked through to the kitchen and he could hear her filling the kettle. He rubbed his hands together to get some feeling back into them and then followed her. She had been very good the past few days. He had needed her help.

'Well, I don't know what's happened to the British summer!' she said as he came into the kitchen. 'One minute it's here and the next we've all got the bloody heating on! Give me global warming any day! I can't stand it when it's like this, all cold and drizzly.' She shivered and then reached up to get the teapot and some cups down from the cupboard. 'You know, you really ought to make some kind of statement to the press,' she said with her back to him. 'It would be sensible.' She turned. 'Don't you think?'

'No. I don't think.' He looked away. 'My personal life is private, it's my business.'

'Is it?' She continued with the tea, trying to sound casual. 'You're very popular, you know, people want to know how you feel.'

'Crap! You never miss a press opportunity, do you Maggie?' Patrick shook his head. 'It's almost laughable! You're more ambitious than any of the men I've met in politics.'

She carefully put down a cup and turned to face him. 'There's no need for that! I am merely trying to think of your best interests.' His mood had been so changeable the past few days that she was constantly on her guard. She was trying not to bully but there were things to be done.

'Oh yes?'

'Yes.' She paused for a moment. 'In fact, I've been thinking that you should get away, right away. You need a break, a change of scene.'

He softened slightly. 'Yeah, maybe.'

Laying out the tray she said: 'Charles's trip to New York for the United Nations Summit on Eastern Europe is definitely on. Perhaps you should think about the invitation to go with him; it doesn't look good to refuse.'

'No. I'm not ready for anything like that. I need time.'

'Patrick, you've had some time!' Lady Margaret suddenly lost patience. Now she'd mentioned it she would have to push it hard. This was an opportunity that a junior minister couldn't afford to miss. 'You have to think about getting on with your life again, Patrick, really you do! How much time do you need?'

'Good God!' Patrick exploded. 'How much time do I need? I've had ten days! My wife and my baby have been dead for ten days and you're telling me to forget it and get on with my life?'

'Yes! If you want to put it like that! Yes, that's exactly what I'm telling you!' Now she'd started, her bile was up and she couldn't stop herself.

'You are the coldest, most calculating bitch I have ever known!' He laughed bitterly. 'As if I didn't know it already.'

'No. I'm just honest. Penny was a burden to you. She was an alcoholic who had a heart attack while under anaesthetic. That baby had foetal alcohol syndrome and no chance of recovery . . .'

'All right! That's enough! I know all the details!'

'Do you? *Do* you? She would have ruined your life, Patrick! You are better off shot of her and all you insist on doing is wallowing around in self-pity!' Lady Margaret's voice was low and hard so as not to be heard by anyone else and she almost spat the words at him. 'It was a mistake, Paddy, a bloody great mistake, I'll admit it even if you won't! And thank God you're out of it now!'

'A mistake, eh? Try telling that to Penny!' he shouted. He moved menacingly forward, his face close to hers. 'I thought a long time ago that you could never do anything more to shock and hurt me. I was wrong. You sicken me!' He punched his breast. 'Here! Right to the heart!' Then he turned and stormed out of the room.

Lady Margaret leaned back against the wall unit, her heart pounding at the shock of the confrontation. She looked down at her hands and saw that they were trembling. Why? Why wouldn't he listen? She only wanted the best for him.

'Well, well, well. Hardly a picture of familial love, now, is it?' Richard Brachen walked in through the back door of the kitchen. Mrs Dunn had left it open and Lady Margaret realised he had heard every word.

'It's none of your business,' she said angrily. She straightened up, smoothing her skirt. 'What the hell were you doing skulking around outside anyway?'

'I wanted a cigarette, and some fresh air,' he answered coolly. 'Besides, I'm never quite comfortable with your husband, Margaret. I always have the urge to tell him what a great fuck you are.'

'Don't you. . . .'

'Don't I what?' He smiled insolently and Lady Margaret caught a hint of malice in it. 'Don't I dare? Is that what you were going to say?' He laughed. 'Don't worry, Margaret, I wouldn't dream of telling him.' Spite was far better calculated.

'Do you care about anything, Margaret?'

'Oh please!' She put the kettle back on the Aga to reboil. 'I really don't need this. Go and play your silly little psychological games somewhere else!'

'I'm just interested, that's all.' He kept his voice even, controlled. What he'd heard outside hadn't shocked him, it had just hardened his resolve. He had always acknowledged the evil in Lady Margaret. At times it had excited him. But Penny wasn't responsible for her own death, he knew that. An eye for an eye, he thought, a tooth for a tooth. It was only right.

'Interested enough when you thought you might profit.

Is that it, Richard?' She took the kettle off the hob and filled the pot. 'You knew Penny was bordering on alcoholism when Patrick married her, didn't you?'

'We pays our money and takes our choice, lady,' he answered. '*You* were the instigator of that match, Margaret, not me.' He moved across the kitchen towards her. He stopped, only inches away from her. 'What is it you *really* want?' He leaned forward. 'Is it power? To see Patrick as a cabinet minister?' He put his finger up to her cheek and trailed it over the perfect white Irish skin. 'Maybe even leader of the party?' he whispered.

'What else?' She moved her face away. 'What else would you expect?' she said coldly.

'Nothing.' He dropped his hand and stepped back. 'You will get what you deserve, Margaret,' he said.

She shrugged. 'I hope so.'

And suddenly Richard smiled back. 'Oh, I know so,' he answered. 'I know so.'

Penny was dead and buried and the only break in the terrible weather in the whole month of August was the few days before Patrick left for New York. The sun shone brilliantly then, and on the one day that a couple from London came round to view Long Wind House the light was perfect and it sat, nestled in green, the warmth of the stone reflected in the afternoon sun. Patrick was glad. It was a beautiful house and he wanted them to see it at its best. Long Wind House deserved more than the unhappiness he had filled it with.

He showed them round the garden first. Old and established, it was in full bloom, a spectrum of colour and light. Then he took them through the stone-floored house, not saying much, letting them decide for themselves.

Upstairs they viewed all the rooms and left the small white-walled back bedroom until last. Patrick hadn't been in it since the Adoption Society had come to take all the baby's things, and even now he found it hard to swing open the door and not see all his pain in that small, empty space.

'Well, this is the last room up here,' he said. He opened the door and let them go in, standing slightly outside himself.

'Oh yes, this is perfect,' the young woman said. She was slight, with pale blonde hair; pretty in a delicate, understated way. 'I think it would make a wonderful nursery, don't you, darling?' She turned to her husband and caught the look of utter embarrassment on his face, then she put her hand up to her throat and blushed deeply. 'Oh, my, I am sorry, I . . . I just didn't think!'

The young husband looked at Patrick. 'Sorry.'

Patrick shrugged. 'Please,' he said. 'Don't be embarrassed.' His story was public property; of course they knew. 'It doesn't matter, really.' He tried to smile. 'Look, why don't I leave you to wander round?' he suggested. 'Come and find me in the garden when you've finished.'

'Yes, we will. Thanks.'

He saw the young man take his wife's hand to reassure her as he left and that one small, insignificant gesture made him feel suddenly very alone. I am glad to be going away, he thought. Margaret, for all the wrong reasons, was right about this. He walked out through the French doors to the garden and on down the sloping lawn to the rose bushes at the bottom.

Yes, he thought, looking down at the roses and bending to smell their perfume, in that ruthless, callous way of hers, Margaret at least spoke the truth. I never loved Penny and I have to face up to that. I can't blame myself for her death but I can make sure that I won't ever do anything again that's dishonest. I will never live another lie.

He turned as the young man called out to him from the

top of the lawn and realised he had lost track of time. I think too much, he decided, I always have; now it is time to act. He began to make his way back up to the house.

'Mr Devlin, the agents said you're away for a couple of weeks, is that right?' The young man spoke quickly, excited about the house. 'We're very keen on the house, you see.'

'Good, I'm pleased to hear that.' Patrick smiled. 'I'm in New York for a week and then I'm off to Bosnia.'

'Oh really? Is it a UN thing?'

'Yes. I'm off to argue for more refugees to be allowed into Britain. I don't think I'm going to be very popular with the government for it, but . . .' He shrugged. He was doing what he believed was right for once. It wasn't much, but it was a start.

'Oh, I agree with you,' the young woman said. 'I think it's awful, separating families, shunting people from pillar to post!' She spoke rather forcefully and then blushed again when she'd finished.

Patrick smiled. 'At least I've got one supporter then.' They all laughed.

'When are you leaving, Mr Devlin?' the young man asked, keen to get things settled.

'At the end of the week. You can call me any time up till Thursday, then I'm going to London. I've a house there to sell as well.' He had decided that was the right thing to do – buy something much smaller, with his own money this time.

'What we'd like to do is speak to the bank and then, if things work out, make you an offer.'

'That sounds just fine. I'll ask the agents to hold off viewing until I hear from you, shall I?'

'Would you?'

'I don't see why not.'

'That's terribly kind of you, Mr Devlin.' The couple

exchanged a look that implied they couldn't believe their luck. Patrick wanted to laugh.

'We'll go straight to the bank this afternoon and try to get back to you by the end of the week. Is that OK?'

'Of course.'

'Oh great!' The young man beamed and again took his wife's hand. 'Thanks a lot, Mr Devlin.'

'Yes, thank you.' The young woman's skin was slightly flushed with excitement.

'No problem. Would you like a cup of tea?'

'Yes, I'm sure we would.'

And Patrick led them inside the house, noticing the unspoken warmth between them. They will suit this home, he decided, and for the first time in weeks he felt the briefest glimmer of hope.

Richard Brachen drummed his fingertips on the desk top and glanced out of the window as he waited for Mcbride to come back on the line. Things were beginning to fall into place.

'Hello, Richard? Are you still there?'

'Yes, John, still here.'

'Good. I've got Jamie's birth certificate here, along with the other details I mentioned. There're several letters, both our wills, guardianship details, and I believe you've got all the documents for the company, haven't you?'

'Yup. Right in front of me. You want everything in the safe, do you?'

'Yes, everything. I've been meaning to do it for ages, you know how it is. What with this trip to New York, I'm much happier with everything safe and in one place.'

'Quite right. When are you off?'

'I'm off at the end of the week but Francesca isn't joining us until Tuesday. She's bringing Jamie out then. She thinks a week in New York is quite long enough for a small child and she won't leave him behind.'

'Understandable.'

'Well, he's only young still.' John sighed. If the truth were known, he was more fretful about leaving him than anyone else. 'So, I'll send all this by registered post this morning. And you'll ring me when you've received it?'

'Fine. It should be on my desk tomorrow morning.'

'I hope so.'

'Don't worry, John, people lodge confidential documents with their solicitors all the time. It's all quite safe.'

'That's what Paddy Ashdown's solicitor said!'

Richard laughed, perhaps a little too enthusiastically.

'Have a bit of trust, John.'

'Of course. Thank you, Richard. We'll talk tomorrow then?'

'Yes. Goodbye, John.'

'Goodbye.'

The line went dead.

Richard waited for a minute or so and then buzzed through to his secretary. 'Sally? Why don't you break for lunch now? I've a meeting at two and I'd like you back by then.'

'OK. No problem, I'll be back before then.'

He sat and waited for her to leave the outer office. Then he picked up the receiver and redialled. He knew the number off by heart. Nothing written down meant no evidence: it was always best to play it safe. The line connected and he waited for the voice to answer.

'Hello, it's me,' he said. The call was expected.

'Mr Brachen. You have all the details?'

'Yes. Everything will be in place by the beginning of next week.' He was out of the country on business as of Sunday. It was important to be as far away from the scene of the crime as possible. 'You know the workings of my office, and you've got the list of contacts?'

'Yes.'

'Good. I want everything in the safe cleared out. All the documents, all the photographs. Everything, all right?'

'Yes, Mr Brachen. Presumably you want a good price for it?'

'I've told you before, that's nothing to do with me!' Richard felt a momentary jolt of panic. He was taking a hell of a risk. 'What I'm paying for is the job on the safe. The rest doesn't concern me. You do understand that, don't you?' The last thing he wanted was any links with a pay-out from the newspaper. They could publish the photos he'd bought from the *Mail's* photographer, they could do anything they liked with them, as long as he wasn't implicated.

'Yes. I understand, don't worry.'

'Good. I'll leave it up to you then. The money will be left as arranged when the job is complete.'

'OK.'

There was nothing more to say. Richard Brachen hung up. By this time next week, he thought, Patrick Devlin will be exposed. He'll be smeared over every newspaper in the country in a scandal that will ruin him. The very idea of it made Richard feel better and he smiled tensely. Margaret will be able to do nothing at all about it, he thought. For all her scheming and manipulating there's a price, and this time she will be the one to pay it.

Francesca –1992

Thirty-four

FRANCESCA WOKE WITH THE SOFT patter of rain against the glass and the strange light of the sun piercing through the cloud. She opened her eyes and reached a hand out of the duvet to look at her watch. It was six-thirty am. Stretching and yawning, she rolled onto her back and looked up through the skylight, gazing dreamily at the gauze of cloud filtering the sunlight and transforming it, then she sat up and listened hard for sounds in the next bedroom. She heard a movement and smiled, then swung her legs over the side of the bed, stood up and padded barefoot through to her son's room.

'Good morning, sweetheart.' She bent and lifted Jamie out of the cot and up into her arms. He rubbed his eyes sleepily and she kissed the top of his head. 'Hmmm, you smell all sleepy. Did you have nice dreams?' Every morning, as she lifted her son into her arms, she could hardly believe the intensity of the love she had for him. It almost overwhelmed her and she held him close to her for a few seconds, awed at just how precious he was. Then, smiling at his half-asleep, grumpy face, she carried him along the narrow landing to the bathroom, sat him on the carpet, washed her hands and face, cleaned her teeth, and then turned her attention to him.

Ten minutes later, she carried him down the stairs, thinking how heavy he was getting, and knocked gently on John's door before carrying on down the second flight to the ground floor. She went into the small yellow kitchen, put

Jamie down on his feet next to his basket of toys and set about the business of making his breakfast and some hot fresh coffee for her and John.

'Good morning!'

'Hello, John. Did you sleep well?'

'Not really.' He smiled – she knew how nervous he was about flying – then he crouched down and spoke face to face to Jamie.

'So, what have we here, young Jamie?' He took the book that Jamie held out to him and looked at the cover, moulding his face into an expression of surprise. 'Well, well, if it isn't the *Where's Spot* book!'

Jamie smiled. 'Spot!'

'Would you like to read it?'

Francesca glanced over her shoulder at John and pulled a face. 'For the six hundredth time this week, I should think!'

John laughed. 'It gets better every time, you know, Frankie! There's a lot of hidden meaning in Spot! Did you not know?'

'No, I didn't! I was rather hoping you might be able to slip S.P.O.T. into your case this morning!'

'And deprive you of the pleasure of reading it to your son? No way!' John stood up and pulled out a chair. 'Come on JC, let's sit down and read then, shall we?' He sat and lifted Jamie onto his lap. Seconds later there was a thump out in the hall as the paper came through the letter box. 'Whoa!' Jamie scrambled down off John's lap and ran out into the hall. He toddled back a few minutes later with the paper.

'Here ye' are.' He spoke with John's Scottish accent and handed it solemnly over.

'Thank you, Jamie.' John exchanged smiles with Francesca. Jamie's accent thoroughly amused them. 'Shall we have a look through it?' But Jamie's attention had been caught by the cat, which had just come in through the flap in the door. 'No. All right then.' Jamie followed the cat out into the hall and John watched him settle down on the carpet before opening the paper.

'Is there much in it this morning?' Francesca placed a coffee mug down on the table and carried on preparing Jamie's breakfast. 'I never get the chance to look through the paper nowadays. If it wasn't for you, I wouldn't have a clue about what's happening in the world, apart from fashion, that is!'

John had turned to the political page and hurriedly read the article on the UN before going back to the front page. He made a mental note of the date of Devlin's arrival in New York and then glanced up at Francesca.

'No,' he answered. 'There's not much in it today.'

She carried on mixing muesli and he watched her, wondering once again if he was doing the right thing in keeping the news of Patrick's presence in New York from her. He didn't want her to meet Devlin – the last thing they needed was that complication.

Francesca has grown, he thought, my God, how she has grown. There was hardly a trace of the fragile young girl he had first known; the scars had all but healed over. She was confident, successful and happy. So, for that matter, was John. He had not told her about Devlin's wife. The papers had been full of it a couple of weeks ago, but now it had died down. There had been no need to unbalance her, no need to tell. He had decided then that if she heard it from somewhere else, or read it herself, then of course they would discuss it, but she hadn't and so he had simply ignored the story and let her get on with her life. If it is meant to be, it will be, he thought – but the very idea of losing her and of losing the child he looked on as his son filled him with absolute terror.

'I said, have you got everything packed?'

'Oh, I'm sorry, I was engrossed in the paper.'

'I know.' Francesca smiled. 'What will I do without your sparkling conversation in the mornings?'

'Very funny! In answer to your question, Miss Sarcastic, my case is ready and I've just got to bring it down.'

'Good.' She walked across to him, placed her hands on his shoulders and kissed the top of his head from behind. 'We'll miss you, John.'

'Oh, it's only a few days.' He patted her hand and looked out into the hall at Jamie. 'I shall miss you too.'

Francesca beeped the horn while John climbed out of the front seat to ring on Dave's doorbell. She looked behind her at Jamie and smiled, reaching back and tickling his toes. He giggled.

'Ah, here's Dave!'

Dave Yates slammed the front door of his mews house and walked round the car to the boot with his suit bag and his black Mulberry Company suitcase. He slung them in, then climbed in beside Jamie's car seat and reached forward to kiss Francesca's cheek.

'Hello.'

'Hi!'

'And here's me old mate JC.' He shook Jamie's leg. 'Oi! Where's your cap, Jamie?' He looked behind him and found the bright red baseball cap he had designed for Jamie, and slipped it onto his head. 'Right! That's a whole lot better. Now we can go.' He took his own cap out of his pocket and also put it on. 'Onward, driver!'

John shook his head. 'Oh God, I've got eight hours of transatlantic flight with this loony!'

'Not if the hostesses are up to much, you haven't!'

They all laughed and Francesca put the car into gear, reversed it round and, still smiling, drove off.

They arrived at Newcastle airport with not much time to spare and Francesca parked while John and Dave checked in. Carrying Jamie, she hurried along from the car park to see them both off.

'Have you got everything?' John was checking his documents and glanced up at Dave.

Dave rolled his eyes. 'Of course I've bloody got everything. Please!'

This kind of banter between the two men went on every day, and Francesca smiled. They were each dressed in character. John wore a Dior suit, dark grey wool, double-breasted, and carried his track-suit bottoms and sweatshirt for the journey in a smart black leather handcase. Dave was in loose-fit Levis, rolled up at the hem, Timberland walking boots, his flying jacket and his baseball cap. He carried an Indian rucksack and a four-pack of lager.

'I hope your seats aren't too close together.'

'We might not make it if they are!' Dave bent and scooped Jamie up. 'Now, little man, you look after your mother, all right? And we'll see you in a few days. Are you looking forward to going on the aeroplane?'

Jamie looked at his face and nodded seriously. Dave pulled his cap up and kissed his nose. 'Ugh!' he said as he handed Jamie over to John, 'That was big girls' stuff!'

John hugged Jamie tightly and the little boy put his arms around his neck. 'You be good now,' he said gently. He kissed Jamie's cheek and handed him back to Francesca.

'We'll see you in New York then,' he said.

Francesca hugged him and they stood for a moment, the two of them with Jamie in the middle. Finally she moved away.

'Good luck with all the buyers and ring me, let me know what's happening, how the arrangements for the show are going.'

'We will.' John picked up his bag and Dave kissed her.

'Bye, Frankie. Be good.'

She stood back a pace and they walked through to departures, standing for a moment at the security check-point to wave. She waved back and so did Jamie. Seconds later they had gone.

'Well,' she said, feeling suddenly very alone. Then she smiled at her son. 'Let's go and look at the planes!'

Later that morning, after settling Jamie with Shauna, his nanny, Francesca swung the Mercedes into a parking space on King Street. She climbed out, locked the car, and walked towards the office. Once inside, she climbed the staircase, newly decorated and hung with some of the large framed copies of the glossy Cameron-Yates media coverage from *Vogue*, *Marie Claire*, *Elle* and *Tatler*. She went on up to the second floor where the old studio still remained.

'Tilly! Morning! Could you come up and see me when you have a minute?'

'Hi! Yeah, no bother.'

Francesca waved at Evelyn and touched her hair. 'The new haircut's really nice!' she called, and Evelyn smiled.

Closing the door, she picked up the post and carried on up to the next floor, half of which they had converted the previous year into a large design space and an office for John. She walked over to her drawing board, dropped the letters down and then crossed to the small kitchen to put the coffee on.

'Frankie?'

'In here, Tilly. Would you like some coffee?'

'Yeah, great.' Tilly stood in the doorway and watched Francesca. 'Did they get off OK?'

'Yes, the plane took off on time and they should be at Heathrow now. The BA flight takes off at eleven.' She finished making the coffee and poured it into two small cups, then carried them across to her space. She placed them on the table and pulled out two chairs.

'Schedules,' she said and picked up her case. 'We need to talk about timings, and I've got a few last-minute alterations that I've been working on.'

Tilly pulled a face.

'I know, I know.' Francesca shrugged. 'I'm sorry, but I discussed it with Dave last night and I really do think these will look better.'

'If you say so. Hand 'em over then.' Tilly took the drawings that Francesca had pulled out of her case.

'We've changed the linings on those two long jackets to the reverse colours of the print in the skirt and Dave has lengthened the waistcoats. I'll come down and talk that through with Evelyn and Cherry myself if you like.'

Tilly was looking through the sketches. 'I think the linings are much better,' she said. 'Will you roll the sleeves up and open out the jackets?'

'Yes, maybe even take them off. What do you think?'

'Yeah, take them off.' She looked up and smiled, running her fingers through her hair. She had cut it all off the previous summer to a chic, boyish style. It suited her, as did the change of dress which went with the hair. The bangles no longer jingled and jangled, being replaced by a plain gold men's watch on a leather strap, and the clothes no longer flowed. Nowadays Tilly wore tight cropped trousers with long suede waistcoats and washed silk shirts. She was smart and tailored and, although Francesca didn't realise it, she had modelled herself on her boss.

'Yes, perhaps you're right. We'll be able to see it properly when we've done it. On to timings then.'

'Fire away!'

Francesca stood up and turned to her board. Dave had pinned a rough copy of their schedule on it and she stretched up to reach for it. Tilly thought how lithe and graceful she was as she did so and briefly envied her long, slim legs. Even in faded Levis and a black polo-neck sweater she managed to look elegant. Francesca turned back and handed Tilly the piece of paper.

'The clothes will be travelling out on Sunday with DHL and John is meeting them at JFK on Monday morning. That means we need everything finished by tomorrow night at the latest. DHL is due to pick up the collection first thing on Saturday to take it down to Heathrow. Does that sound all right?'

'Should be. Hopefully these alterations shouldn't take more than half a day. There's a lot of finishing to do, though.'

'I'll come down and do some myself later. Can you remember what time this interview is?'

'Half past twelve. It's lunch.'

'Oh God! I'd completely forgotten! Can I get out of it, d'you think?'

'No. The *Chronicle* has been very good to us and they want first shot at the launch in New York. It wouldn't be fair to cancel.'

Francesca sighed. 'Where shall I take them?' She was uneasy about doing this without Dave's support – she had never been interviewed on her own.

'Have lunch here. I'll order something from the deli, show them round, the studio in action, like, and then let them take a few pics. It'll be a breeze! No bother.'

'Oh, Tilly, are you sure?'

'Yeah, honestly!'

Francesca suddenly smiled. Tilly was so like Dave in certain ways that she felt instantly better. Then she looked down at her jeans and sweater.

'Oh dear, what should I wear, should I change, do you think? I don't even know what I've got. I've had everything dry-cleaned and laid out in our spare room ready for New York and I haven't even thought what to take . . . I don't think I've anything here . . . Oh God!'

'Hey! Calm down! Just stay as you are, all right? There's a long printed silk shirt that Evelyn has just finished – try that over the top of what you've got on and we'll get a big black suede belt that'll match your loafers over from Freeze to wear through your jeans. There! No sweat!'

Francesca laughed. 'Oh, Tilly, you don't want to do the interview for me as well, do you?'

'No chance! What about New York? Do you want me to come round tonight and help you sort some things out?'

'Oh, would you mind? It's just that I don't seem to have had the time to think about it at all, what with the last-minute panic on the collection and . . .'

'As usual!'

'Yes, as usual.' Francesca smiled. 'I think it's quite important, what with meeting our American backers for the first time and all the interviews we've got.'

'Yeah, Dave had me choosing his wardrobe until the early hours of . . .' Tilly broke off and suddenly blushed deeply.

Francesca widened her eyes. 'Until the early hours of . . . Go on!'

But Tilly drank her coffee down in one gulp and stood up quickly. 'I think I really ought to get going on these alterations.'

'Tilly!' Francesca was grinning broadly. 'You didn't finish!' She touched Tilly's arm. 'How long has this been going on?' she said gently.

Tilly shrugged. 'Oh, for me, about two years!' Then she smiled. 'But Dave seems to have finally noticed me and we've been going out for the past . . .' She made a small calculation on her fingers. 'Four weeks, two days and fourteen hours!' She laughed.

'Well, I think that's marvellous!' Francesca said and caught a glimmer of pure happiness in Tilly's eyes. 'Really, I do!'

Tilly shrugged. 'Me too,' she answered self-consciously. Then she turned towards the door. 'I'll ring the deli and then bring the shirt up for you. And I'll get Elaine to call Freeze.'

'Thank you, Tilly.' Francesca watched her walk towards the door. 'See you later.' She picked up the small pile of post as Tilly left the office and began to slit the envelopes open with her paper-knife. She was delighted for Tilly but it somehow made her a feel just a little less content than she had been earlier.

It was after five when Francesca finally got away from the office, rushing out of the door, shouting out her goodbyes and promising to be in early the following morning to put the finishing touches to the collection. She ran down the stairs, jumped into her car and swung out of the parking space, racing up Dean Street and right onto the motorway. She had said she would be home by five-thirty at the latest as Shauna had a big date that evening.

She made it with minutes to spare. Shauna and Jamie were waiting for her outside the house as she pulled up, and she piled them into the car and sped off for Kingston Park and Shauna's home.

Once that was done, she took Jamie on home for their few hours of peace together, bathed him, gave him his tea and read to him until he fell asleep. The day finished at seven-thirty and she finally poured herself a large glass of wine to celebrate. Taking it upstairs, she checked on Jamie in his loft room, then went into her bedroom next door. She placed her glass of wine on the dressing table and sat down in front of the mirror. The room they had made last year out of the roof was lit by the very last of the daylight streaming in through the skylights. She looked back at her reflection in the mirror, switching on the table lamp to see her face more clearly.

In the past two years she had grown her hair. It was now down to her shoulders, dark and glossy, brushed off her face and cut neatly, all the same length. Her face looked different too: softened, more lived in. The faint lines of worry and pain around her eyes were still noticeable in harsh, bright light, but she smiled so often and laughed so freely these days, that the whole way she looked had changed. She was beautiful now, not just suddenly, when a moment of happiness lit up her face, but all the time – the kind of beauty that attracts, not classic and aloof but warm and sensuous, alluring.

Francesca sat and stared at her reflection. She took off her sweater and chemise and looked at her half-naked body, the full shape of her breasts and the smooth unmarked skin of her stomach. Her body had changed too. It was slightly fuller, more womanly. She had lost her thin, boyish shape and her slim limbs were curved. Producing and feeding another body had given life to her own. She closed her eyes and thought about his touch, about the smell of him and the sound of his voice, low and whispered. She opened them again and sighed wearily.

She knew why Tilly's happiness made her sad and she knew why being without John and Dave and the frenzied bustle of work made her feel alone. She loved him. Not intensely, not with the terrible painful ache that she had first felt, but with a gentler, more enduring feeling, a love that just remained, deep inside her, and came back to her every living moment she shared with their son. She still felt betrayed but the anger had softened and she seemed to remember only the good things about him, not the pain and agony of the lies and deceit. Perhaps because of Jamie, perhaps because of her success, she didn't know why, but she had finally come to terms with the way she felt about him. It would probably never change. It would not grow or develop as it should, it would simply be, a knowledge that she had loved him in a way she would never love again. She sighed once more and put it from her mind.

Standing up, she reached for her bathrobe, slipped it on and took a gulp of wine. She took off her jeans and underwear and picked up her glass and her paperback. Tilly was arriving at eight-thirty and she wanted to be ready on time, with the table laid for their supper. Quietly, she closed the bedroom door behind her, checked on Jamie one more time and went downstairs for her bath.

Thirty-five

'GOOD AFTERNOON, LADIES AND GENTLEMEN. This is Flight Captain Willis speaking. We will shortly be starting our descent into John F. Kennedy Airport, New York. Our estimated time of landing is one thirty-five and the flight time has been approximately seven hours, thirty minutes. The weather in New York is hot, currently around thirty-five degrees with sixty-five per cent air humidity, and there is some low cloud cover. I hope you have enjoyed your flight with us here on British Airways and myself and the crew would like to wish you a safe on-going journey. Thank you.'

Francesca leaned forward and refastened her seat belt, did the same for Jamie and made sure he had a sweet in his mouth.

'Cabin crew to landing positions.'

'Hold on tight to Mummy's hand,' she whispered but Jamie wasn't interested; he was making faces at the lady in the seat across the aisle. Francesca closed her eyes and held on tightly to the arms of her seat as the plane began to lose height, her ears popping uncomfortably and her stomach churning. She was in a window seat and as she felt the plane circle, she suddenly relaxed and opened her eyes to take a good look out of the window at the Big Apple. Her spirits soared with excitement. I'm here, she thought, to show in New York, and she felt a powerful burst of pride and achievement.

*

'Frankie! Frankie!'

Francesca looked through the sea of faces to try and find Dave. She could hear him but she couldn't see him.

'Oi! Over here!' he shouted.

She glanced all round again and finally saw him. He was standing a little apart from the crowd, up on a trolley and waving a small Stars and Stripes flag frantically in the air.

'Hi!' She held Jamie's hand and they ran towards him. He jumped down, 'Whoa!', scooped her into his arms and twirled her round, then picked up Jamie and gave him a giant bear hug. 'Hey! You feel wonderful!' He placed the child back on his feet and then stood away to admire Francesca. 'Gee, it's great to see ya, kid,' he drawled.

'Oh God!' She shook her head. 'That's got to be the worst American accent I've ever heard!'

'Hey! Gimme a break will ya?'

'Ugh!' She went to her trolley and wheeled it over to him. 'Where's John?'

'Oh, he had a meeting.' Dave saw Francesca's face fall and took her arm. 'He couldn't get out of it. It's absolutely unbelievable here! We've had breakfast meetings, lunches, dinner meetings – they never stop, these Americans. And when they're not in the office, they're on the golf course talking business over a round of golf or making deals on the squash court. I'd get frigging knackered just changing in and out of me sports kit every five minutes!'

Francesca smiled. 'When will I see him?'

'When we get to the hotel. Oh yeah, and wait till you see the bloody hotel. Only the best! With a bed the size of a football pitch! I'd score a few there, I can tell you!'

Francesca had started to laugh. 'What on earth do the Americans make of you, Dave?'

He stopped dead. 'I have no idea. But come to think of it, they've started asking for John every time they ring us now.'

He led her out into the fray and to a waiting black stretch limo, courtesy of their American backers.

'My God, I can hardly believe this!' Francesca stared out of the car window and bent her head to see the tops of the buildings as they cruised down Fifth Avenue. Jamie was asleep on her lap, despite the noise and the crowds and the buzz of the city that could be felt even from inside the car. 'Here I am, swanning down Fifth Avenue in my limousine! I feel like a movie star!' She giggled and Dave flipped down a panel in the seat in front of them to reveal a small television screen.

'What do you fancy? A game show? They're hot on game shows over here.'

Francesca peered forward. 'I don't believe it!'

'That's the second time you've said that.' Dave grinned. 'Watch this!' He pressed a button and another panel slid down, revealing a drinks cabinet, fully stocked and with Waterford cut glasses. 'And this!' A side compartment in the door concealed a make-up mirror and a light came on overhead to illuminate her face.

She was giggling hopelessly now, completely overwhelmed.

'Excuse me, sir?' A voice came into their part of the car and Francesca instantly stopped laughing and sat up straight. Dave thought that was the funniest thing of all.

'It's all right, Frankie,' he whispered. 'He can't see us unless I put the panel down.'

'Oh!' She blushed. He pressed the speak button. 'Yes?'

'We are just approaching the hotel now, sir.'

'Right, thank you.'

The car slowed and Francesca turned again to the window.

'Oh my . . .'

The car stopped and she was cut off mid-sentence as the door was opened. A uniformed, smiling young man stood there, waiting and ready to help her out. He leaned into the car and plucked the sleeping child out of her arms, holding him carefully.

Thank goodness I changed on the plane, she thought with relief, and then swung her long slim legs out of the car. Another young man was ready with a helping hand, and she took it and stood up, smoothing her skirt. What lovely white teeth he has, she noted.

'Frankie, we'll go on in and someone will bring your luggage.' Dave nodded to another uniformed man and the limousine boot was opened. He took Jamie from the doorman, held him close, and kissed the top of his head. Then he glanced affectionately at Francesca.

'Well, if you feel as good as you look, Miss Cameron,' he said quietly as he led the way into the hotel, 'you must be walking on air!' He kissed her cheek, noticing that she had caught the attention of most of the hotel lobby.

Up in the suite, Francesca opened the door for the third time in five minutes and took the basket of fruit from the bellboy, handing him five dollars and telling him that she would try very hard to have a nice day.

'Fruit!' she shouted to Dave, who was in the bathroom. 'That's two flowers, one champagne and now one fruit!' She carried the gift into the sitting-room area and placed it on the coffee table next to all the others. 'This one's from . . .' She read the card. 'From the designer room at Saks!' She started to laugh. 'They've all sent something and every time I open the door the gift is larger and more extravagant than the last one!'

Dave walked back into the room. 'Of course!' he answered. 'We're quite a commodity, don't you know?' He crossed to the basket of fruit and stuck his fingers through the cellophane, peeling it back and taking out a kiwi fruit. 'Saks gets my vote, though. At least they've sent something edible.' He took out his Swiss Army knife and cut the fruit in two. 'Yum, yum, yum!'

Just as he bit into it, the door was flung open and John came hurrying into the room. The pale green flesh dribbled down Dave's chin as he looked up and John rolled his eyes.

'Oh God! Just don't eat one of those at dinner tonight! All right?'

'Sorry . . .' Dave mumbled with his mouth full but John didn't hear him: he had seen Francesca. He rushed over to her and swept her into his arms.

'Frankie!' He hugged her tightly then stood back to look at her. He no longer found it hard to touch Francesca. Having Jamie had taught him affection and he delighted in hugging the people he loved. 'How was the flight? Did everything go all right? How did Jamie cope, did he sleep? Where is he by the way?'

'Gosh! Slow down!' She held both of his hands in hers as she smiled up at his face. 'The flight was fine. Jamie loved it, I mean *loved* it! Yes, he slept and he made great friends with the lady across the aisle who gave him her business card!'

John laughed. 'The little devil! It seems like ages since I've seen him. Where the hell is he?'

'He's asleep. Jet lagged.'

'I'll go through and have a peep.' John hugged Francesca again. 'God, I'm glad you're here!'

'Sick to death of me, you mean!' Dave had finished his kiwi fruit and was unwrapping the foil on the bottle of champagne. 'Go on, look at the boy and then let's celebrate!'

John walked through to the bedroom and Francesca put

out some glasses. 'I'm sorry I wasn't there to pick you up,' John said as he came back. 'I've been up to my eyes in business.' He smiled. 'I have a feeling that this launch could be the best thing that's ever happened to Cameron Yates.'

'Whoa!' The cork exploded out of the bottle and flew up into the air. Dave reached for the glasses, spraying the white froth all over the carpet, and John and Francesca clapped. The bottle settled, he poured and then handed them both a glass.

'The clothes have arrived, the venue is set, rehearsals and interviews are tomorrow, we've had presents from all the buyers, we show on Wednesday and then we sit and wait for the orders.' Dave held up his glass. 'To New York!' He toasted. They all clinked.

'To success!' John said.

'And to happiness,' Francesca added. 'Oh, by the way, Dave, Tilly sends her love.' And for the first time ever, she saw him blush.

Later that evening, lying in the bath, Francesca thought about the coming few days and about just how far Cameron Yates had come in the past two years. This was the first time she had been away from the studio for more than the few days it took to show in London and now she was here: America, New York, and one of the biggest markets in the world! She could hardly believe it. They'd worked hard enough for it, but even so, it was still a surprise when it happened.

She thought back to when she had first heard about Will O'Connall. John had been staggered when the 'American Fashion Entrepreneur', as he called him, had bought up half the autumn wear collection at London Fashion Week. She smiled at the memory of John coming home after a day's negotiations, a look of stricken panic on his face and a suitcase full of dollars handcuffed to his wrist. But O'Connall's hunch had paid off. The Americans loved the collection and the clothes had been so successful that he came back two months later and asked them to design a winter collection specifically for the American market. And that was exactly what they had done.

They had tailored the collection to more of a ready-to-wear designation, less formal and using all English fabrics, silks, wools and tartans. The look was half English country, using the fabrics they had, and half relaxed American chic. She wondered at times how they'd managed it, designing for a market they had no experience of. But they had, and Dave had been inspirational. His whole house filled with things American, he had worked, eaten and slept the United States. The clothes were good, she thought, glancing up at a suit on its hanger above the bath to steam out its creases. No, they were more than that, she decided, analysing its cut – they were brilliant!

Climbing out of the bath, she realised for the first time how tired she was; it seemed at times that she did nothing but work. But, she thought, drying herself and wrapping a thick white bathrobe round her, this was a hell of a chance, and if it was successful, then next year London Fashion Week would be followed directly by Paris and New York. If they captured the American market, then Europe would almost automatically follow.

She walked across to the mirror and unwrapped her hair from the towel. She ran a comb through it and picked up the dryer, looking at herself in the mirror. Francesca had never expected success, and deep in her heart the guilt still told her she did not deserve it. She did not know why, but thinking about it too much somehow made her decidedly uneasy.

*

'Frankie!'

Walking into the sitting room of the suite, Francesca smiled as Dave and John turned to look at her.

'A suit from our evening collection, I think,' Dave said.

She twirled. She wore a fine wool crêpe skirt, cut short and perfectly straight. The jacket was long and tailored, with a black velvet mandarin collar and black velvet cuffs. Her legs were in sheer black stockings and she wore low-heeled black suede shoes. But it was the shirt that finished it off. It was fine crimson silk chiffon, overprinted with her own leaf design in a darker red. It was almost transparent but for the design and underneath she wore a red lace bustier, the top of which could be glimpsed provocatively where the shirt was unbuttoned. Her hair was loose and she wore no jewellery. The look was distinctly and perfectly Cameron Yates.

'My goodness!' John stood up and took her hands. 'Mr O'Connall is going to love you!'

'I hope so.'

'Frankie, you look every inch the star I said you were going to be nearly three years ago.' Dave pulled on his jacket and stood to leave. 'Let's go get 'em!' He crossed to the door, taking another long look at Francesca. 'Will said he would meet us in the restaurant. Wait till you see the Dining House, Frankie. You need half a million just to go for a piss there!'

John opened the door. 'I think he's trying to tell you it's a top-class restaurant,' he said and Francesca laughed.

'OK. Has everyone said good night to Jamie?' Both men nodded. 'And the sitting service is on?' Again they both nodded. 'And they have our number if . . .' Dave took one arm, John took the other. 'Do come on, Frankie. Please!' Together and laughing they chivvied her out of the suite and along the corridor to the lifts.

Down in the sweltering street the black stretch limo was waiting to take them to the Rockefeller Center with a chilled bottle of champagne in the drinks cabinet and three cut-glass flutes on ice.

Patrick Devlin stood tensely in one of the outer offices on the sixteenth floor of the United Nations Headquarters on the corner of First Avenue and Forty-seventh Street. He was waiting for Charles Hewitt to finish his call to London. The Prime Minister had been informed and what happened next was up to him. Patrick didn't expect much. Hewitt was in a flaming rage and a whole crowd of government flunkies had been rushing round all afternoon sending out memos, talking to the press, trying to backtrack on his comments. He had done what he came for. He had no idea of the diplomatic storm it would cause but now it was done, there was no point in grovelling to put it right. If you have to go, Paddy boy, he thought, go with dignity. He looked up as one of the flunkies called him.

'The Minister will see you now, Mr Devlin.'

'Thank you.'

He walked through two more outer offices and into the huge windowed office that Charles Hewitt had occupied all afternoon.

'Charles.'

Hewitt turned from the window. 'Sit down, Patrick!'

'I'd prefer to stand if you don't mind.'

'I don't give a fuck whether you sit, stand or jump out of the window.' He stopped. 'But apparently the Prime Minister does. So sit!'

Patrick breathed a sigh of relief. He pulled out a chair and sat, waiting for Hewitt to go on.

'Have you any idea of the row you have caused with our European friends this afternoon?'

'No . . . I didn't think . . .'

'You're damn right you didn't think! You raise an issue that is not on the agenda, that's not even being discussed, and put forward a British view on that issue that is the exact opposite of current government policy! What the hell did you think you were playing at, Patrick?'

'The Germans . . .'

'Of course the Germans backed you up! They've got so many bloody Eastern European political refugees they don't know what to do with them! They want to get shot of them; they were almost standing on their chairs applauding you! Jesus!' Hewitt stopped and took a breath. 'You haven't answered my question! What the hell were you doing?'

Patrick knew it was impossible to try and argue his point. He had embarrassed the British government and Hewitt in particular. He shrugged. 'I'm sorry.'

The apology took Hewitt by surprise. 'Yes, well . . .' He came over to the desk and sat down. 'The Prime Minister is willing to acknowledge that a junior minister with no diplomatic experience could be liable to make mistakes. I think that is extremely generous of him.'

'Yes, sir.'

'He is prepared, after much private negotiation with the French and Italians I might add, to overlook the matter.'

Patrick looked down. 'Thank you.'

'Frankly, Patrick, if it were up to me I would have sacked you immediately, but it is not up to me.' Hewitt leaned forward in his chair. 'You are officially being warned, though. From this moment on, if you put so much as a foot wrong, you'll find yourself down on the back benches before you know what's hit you. Do I make myself quite clear?'

'Yes, sir.'

'Embarrass me or the government again and you're out!' Hewitt snapped his fingers. 'Just like that!'

'Yes, sir.'

'Good. That'll be all, Patrick.'

'Yes. Thank you, Charles.' Patrick stood as Hewitt opened a file and bent his head to read. He left the room silently.

Out in the corridor he leaned against the wall and took a deep breath to calm himself. He noticed one of the diplomatic staff staring so he stood straight, smoothed his jacket and walked away. I'd do it again, he thought, heading down to the lifts, if it meant being heard. He called the lift, stepped inside and tried to put it out of his mind. He had dinner with an old schoolfriend to look forward to. He was being taken out to the Dining House, a restaurant way out of his league, and he was determined to enjoy it.

Stepping out at the ground floor, Patrick checked his reflection in the huge mirrored wall behind reception and straightened his tie. He was late and didn't have time to change. Hurrying out of the building, he whistled with two fingers in his mouth and managed to flag down a taxi.

'The Rockefeller Center,' he said.

'OK!' The driver set the meter, pulled off and Patrick sat back and felt himself relax for the first time all day.

Enzo stood in front of a heavy French gilt mirror in the hall of Marianne's Park Avenue apartment and neatly tightened the knot on his Hugo Boss tie. He ran his fingers over his hair, sleekly gelled back, and then checked his teeth. He sniffed twice to clear his nose, which was constantly swollen and sore nowadays from the coke, and tapped the breast pocket of his suit. Two grams of coke for Mr Robetti, some dickhead friend of Marianne's. It was easy money and about time too! The bitch had kept him short for too long this time; it was beginning to really piss him off. He pulled open the drawer in the Sheraton hall table and took out his key.

The naked body of Marianne's latest pick-up caught his eye in the mirror and he glanced over his shoulder at the heavy, muscled black buttocks as they strode through the sitting room to the kitchen.

'You like what you see, Enzo baby?'

He turned and saw Marianne along the hall. She stood in the doorway to her bedroom, wearing only her shoes, and fingered her nipples. 'We can do three up if you like?'

Enzo's nostrils flared but he said nothing. It was a whole lot easier if he kept his mouth shut.

'I have to go out,' he said. The fragile high from only the one line he'd taken was beginning to deflate. 'I'm sorry, I've got business.' He was eager to get away. The sight of her nakedness repulsed him.

'What about *my* business?' she drawled. Her voice was as rich and smooth as syrup but he could feel the malice beneath. She knew exactly where he was going but it'd be the last time – she'd seen to that.

'I'll be back as soon as I can.'

She walked towards him and he felt himself tense. She stopped just in front of him.

'You had better be, Enzo.' She could smell his tension and it excited her. She never tired of the game of power she played with him. She had prised all sorts of secrets out of her 'case study', as her friends called him. He told her everything when he was high, everything! It was really quite pathetic but it did mean she knew exactly how far she could push. 'If you aren't, you know what will happen, don't you?' She moved her hand up to his breast pocket and touched the silk handkerchief, smiling slightly. 'One little phone call to the feds, baby.' She looked up at him. 'Remember what you told me about Giovanni? All that blood!' She shivered. 'Litres and litres of blood . . .'

'Shut it, Marianne!' He grabbed her hand and gripped

the wrist. 'Fucking shut it!' he hissed. But she continued to smile. She liked him rough and she had him; she knew it and he knew it. She was in control of the game.

'Oh, baby . . .' she whispered. 'You still want it, don't you?' Enzo dropped her wrist and she saw the young black boy out of the corner of her eye. 'Larson,' she purred, 'come here and show Enzo what you've got for me.' The boy smiled but his eyes were cold and hard. He walked into the hall and Marianne put her hands over his erection. 'See,' she said. 'I'll save some for you, Enzo baby.'

Enzo swallowed down the bile that rose in the back of his throat and Marianne turned to put her hands up on the wall, bending forward slightly. 'Enzo might want to watch,' she said over her shoulder as the black boy took his position behind her. 'Do you, Enzo baby? Wanna see what we're going to do later?'

He stood, weirdly fascinated for a moment, and watched her face. It was always the same, it was dirty and sick but it fascinated him. He didn't understand it.

'Don't be too long, Enzo,' she murmured. Then she cried out as the boy entered her and laughed at Enzo's look of disgust. She was still laughing as he picked up his key, walked down the hall and out of the apartment, slamming the door behind him. Then, free of her, he ran all the way down the stairs and reached the lobby sweating heavily, the excited laughter still ringing in his ears. He stopped, leaned against the wall and tried to catch his breath. The blood rushed in his head and he lost his balance slightly.

'Bitch,' he muttered. He took out an expensive linen handkerchief bought by Marianne and wiped his face. He began to feel better. Christ, he needed another line! He'd have himself one courtesy of Robetti, then maybe score something to mellow out on, a couple of quaaludes, some grass maybe. If Marianne was playing games tonight he'd need to be out of his head – it was the only way he could play.

He stood straight and wiped his face again. He knew Marianne controlled him, but there was no way out, no choice. He'd told her too much, he needed his drugs and he was living here illegally. So that was it. He'd dug himself into a hole, a stinking, filthy hole, but it was papered with money and when he was out of his head he couldn't care what he did, he never remembered much anyway. He shook his head. He'd come here for Francesca – what a joke! Another of Marianne's little games.

Enzo smoothed his jacket and began to walk towards the entrance to the building. The taxi he had ordered was already waiting outside on the pavement. If he met Robetti at eight, he could have scored by eight-thirty; all he had to do was get to the Dining House on time. He pulled open the door and stepped out onto the hot pavement, beginning to sweat again in the warm, damp air. He gave the driver the name of the restaurant and slipped into the back seat of the cab.

CHAPTER

Thirty-six

ENZO'S TAXI PULLED UP OUTSIDE the Rockefeller Center on Fifth Avenue, Forty-ninth Street, and he climbed out. The driver had the account number and he didn't offer a tip; Marianne habitually kept him short of cash. He took the elevator up to the sixty-second floor and stepped out into the entrance of the Dining House. Nodding to the doorman, he walked through to the bar and saw Robetti straight away.

'You got my stuff?' Robetti was Ivy League, a Eurobond dealer for Goldman Sachs. He didn't like to waste niceties on low-life like Mondello. It beat him why Marianne hung out with the guy anyway, except that Marianne had weird tastes. He was welcome to her. 'I'll order you a drink while you go to the john,' he said. 'Leave it in the usual place.' He turned towards the bar as Enzo walked away, glancing nervously around the restaurant as he did so. Robetti was well known here but the deal still made Enzo uneasy.

He stepped through the doors into the Gents and moved across to the first cubicle, locking the door behind him. He bent and took a brown envelope out from behind the bowl, felt it for the cash and then slipped his own package back in its place. He had kept an unnoticeable amount for himself. Flushing, he came out and rinsed his hands, drying them thoroughly on a towel as a diner came into the washroom. He nodded to the guy and walked back out into the restaurant. He had begun to sweat again.

'Here's your drink.' Robetti passed him a heavy crystal glass with a measure of bourbon in it. Enzo knew the score.

He picked up the glass and swallowed back the liquid in one gulp. Robetti wouldn't waste time drinking with him – he was to drink up and leave.

'You'll letta me know if you wanna any more?' Enzo spoke American now but his accent was still thick. He saw Robetti sneer slightly and it angered him.

'I'll let you know.'

Enzo nodded. 'Thanks for the drink,' he said. He turned towards the door. He had the money and he knew Robetti was a dickhead, so why worry? But Robetti was worse than usual tonight, brusque, more dismissive. It bugged Enzo, it didn't feel right. Stepping into the elevator, he pressed the button and slipped his hand inside his pocket for the envelope. Suspiciously he took it out, and pulled out the wad of money. It was all one-dollar bills, twenty-four of them. They should have been tens. 'Fucking arsehole!' he spat, and stuffed the money back into his pocket. He stopped the lift, directed it back up several floors and stepped out, striding back to the restaurant. He was furious; nobody cheated Mondello!

'Robetti!'

The young Ivy League man at the bar turned as Enzo called out to him and his face changed. 'Get out of here, Mondello!' His voice was low to avoid a scene. 'What the hell do you want?'

'I want my money!' Enzo snarled. Robetti pulled him aside. 'I haven't got your money!' he hissed. 'Keep your voice down! You wanna get us both arrested?'

'Where is it? You owe me, Robetti!'

'Marianne told me not to pay you. She heard about the deals we've been doing and she told me not to . . .'

'She *what*?' Enzo felt every nerve in his body tense up. He moved towards Robetti. 'She fucking *what*?'

'Look, Enzo, cool it man . . .! I . . .' Enzo grabbed the

expensive lapels of Robetti's jacket. 'Get the hell off me!' Robetti's voice was high-pitched and the barman moved instantly round the bar. Enzo dropped his hands. 'Jesus Christ! You speak to Marianne . . . I just did what she told me to, man!' He backed away from Enzo 'It's not my problem! Just go ask Marianne!' The barman stood threateningly by Robetti and Enzo moved away.

He could hardly think straight. Robetti had cheated him. He'd scored for him and he'd cheated him; Marianne had told him to. Christ, he'd kill her! He glanced across at Robetti, who was smoothing his jacket. 'I'll get you,' he growled. Then he spat on the floor between them and turned heel, striding out of the bar.

At the entrance to the restaurant, he swung through the double glass doors and smacked hard into someone just coming in. He moved rapidly out of sight, into the lift, and the doors slid shut. Minutes later, he was out on the street and he began to run, an overwhelming anger pounding through his body, the blood rushing in his ears.

This time he'd had enough of her sly, dominating games; he'd had enough of her shit. This time he really would make her sorry for trying to make him look an arsehole. He saw her face as he ran, laughing at him, lying to him, and he saw the dark, evil glint of her eye. This time Marianne would be sorry.

'Jesus! Who was that?' The Maître d' stepped forward and helped Patrick into the lobby. He had been thrown off balance by the lunatic just leaving.

'Pardon me, sir, I believe one of our patrons had a disagreement with a gentleman in the bar. Here, allow me.' The man took Patrick's case while he straightened himself out. 'I do apologise. Are you all right now?' Patrick nodded. 'Good. Shall I put this away for you, sir?'

'Yes, please.' Patrick let him keep the case. 'I'm meeting some friends here. A Mr Bill Penchard?'

'Ah yes, of course, sir, it's Mr Devlin, isn't it? Follow me please. Mr and Mrs Penchard are already at their table.' He handed Patrick's briefcase to a hat check girl and led the way. Patrick saw Bill stand up and wave across the restaurant. Their table was almost entirely hidden from general view by the window and Patrick smiled at their thoughtfulness.

'Paddy!'

He shook hands with Bill and bent and kissed Liz on the cheek. She held his hand and squeezed it.

'Paddy. How are you?'

He shrugged. 'All right.'

Bill pulled out a chair for him. 'Come on, sit down and let's have a drink. We've been worried, thought you might not come.'

'I know, I'm sorry. I had a meeting with Charles Hewitt.' He pulled a face and then smiled. 'There was never any question of my not coming.' He put his hand out over Liz's and patted it. 'I need my friends. I feel as if I've been alone for too long.'

Dave leaned forward on the seat and tapped the glass panel that separated them from the driver.

'Is there any way out of this?' They were halfway up Fifth Avenue and the traffic had ground to a halt. The driver turned. 'I don't think so, sir. The RCA Building is about three hundred yards up on the left on Forty-ninth Street, if you'd like to walk. It might be a better idea.'

'Oh right! Yeah, I think we'll do that.' He glanced across at John and Francesca. 'OK with you two?'

'Better than being late,' John said and leaned forward to open the car door.

'We'll get out here then,' Dave called to the driver. John had already climbed out and was helping Francesca down from the car. 'You say it's just up on the left?' Dave asked before he followed.

'That's right, sir, straight up, you can't miss it!'

'Thanks.' He joined John and Francesca on the pavement and closed the car door. 'God it's humid out here,' he said. 'I'll be one big dollop of sweat by the time we get there!'

Francesca laughed and took his arm. 'Come on then, let's go! But if you drip on my suit, Dave, I shall never forgive you.'

'Marianne! Marianne!' Enzo hadn't stopped running all the way. His lungs heaved with the physical effort and the nausea rose in his throat. 'Marianne!' he screamed, flinging the doors open. 'You bitch! Where are you?' He stopped in the long dimly lit sitting room when he saw her. She was lying on the sofa, wearing her silk robe, a sneering smile on her lips. She had a copy of *Vanity Fair* open on her lap.

'So you know?' She lifted her eyes up to Enzo's face. They were cold and hard, watery, red, unseeing eyes and they mocked him, as they always did. She was as high as a kite. 'You should have guessed that I'd find you out sooner or later, Enzo baby,' she drawled, smiling. 'You're not half as clever as you think.' Her teeth seemed vicious, sharp and pointed, like a rat's.

'Shut it, Marianne! I'll show you who's fucking clever!' He moved towards her.

'Oh really? So clever that you knew about this? Huh?' She held up her magazine for him to see the full colour picture on the page, a photograph of Francesca Cameron. Then she began to laugh.

Enzo's whole body froze. 'How the hell . . .' He stood

motionless, unable to breathe, unable to think. He stared, and for that one perfect moment he was not there. He was in Italy, high up on the cliff, watching the girl move down on the beach below, imagining the long, graceful curve of her thighs wrapped naked and tight round his body. He groaned aloud as a deep physical spasm shot though his body, and in the next instant the image had gone. Marianne remained, laughing at him, sneering at him.

He stood completely still and waited for the pain to pass. And, when it did, he was filled with a vast and overpowering anger. It welled up inside him, huge and unstoppable, and then washed over him, drenching his mind with thick, dark blood.

'Bit of a shock, Enzo baby? Huh?' She was thrilled with his reaction, it was so much more desperate than she had dared hope and his pain was her exquisite pleasure. 'You're wondering how I knew, aren't you? Enzo the clever drug dealer!' She had seen an article, the picture matched up with Enzo's newspaper cutting, with his old photographs. The similarity was there and she had dug around, nosed and ferreted. She had been waiting for this. It was a moment of triumph for her, her climax. 'I've always known, baby . . .' Her voice trailed away. 'Always,' she whispered. 'She's staying at the Asprey, in suite seventeen, she asked me to tell . . .'

In a split second Enzo had moved across the room. He pulled Marianne up by the neck, both his hands around her throat. Her eyes stared wide and excited as he began to shake her, but still they mocked him. He staggered with her thin body for a moment and then stumbled and fell, his weight crushing her underneath him. On the floor he tightened his grip on her throat, yanked her head up and then smashed it down hard onto the sharp edge of the glass table. Blood erupted from the burst vein in her temple, spurting fountain-like over his hands as he lifted her head and cracked it down again. Again and again and again and again.

Suddenly he let her go.

Marianne's body slumped lifeless onto the red-stained carpet, her skull smashed, the blood seeping from it, slow and thick, like treacle. Enzo moved away.

On the floor, splattered with her blood, lay the *Vanity Fair* magazine, the picture of Francesca disfigured with the ugly red-black stain. Picking it up Enzo covered his face with it, and, smearing Marianne's blood over his lips, he kissed the face he had waited for for so long. Then he ripped the page out and placed it on Marianne's chest. She had paid for her sins.

An hour later he finished ransacking the flat and left the building by the back entrance, turning on the answerphone and double-locking the door. He headed downtown to Park Avenue, Forty-ninth Street.

Patrick finished the last of his coffee in silence. He could see that Bill and Liz were uncomfortable with the truth about Penny and he knew how they felt. It wasn't easy to understand – he wasn't sure if he even understood it himself. But it was the truth, at least he had come that far.

'Will you excuse me for a few minutes?' he said. He thought they needed a few moments to themselves. He stood up to go across to the washroom.

'Paddy?' He turned back. 'You all right?' Bill asked. He shrugged. 'Of course.' And he left the table, making his way through the other tables to the far end of the restaurant.

'Patrick! Hellooo! Patrick?' Halfway across the floor, he stopped and looked up as he heard his name being called. At a small table near the Gents he spotted one of life's more persistent journalists, something Brett – he couldn't remember his full name. He nodded and tried to continue on but the fellow waved again and remained standing. He had no choice but to go over. Halfway to the table he noticed that several of the diners had turned and his eyes skimmed their faces confidently, refusing to be embarrassed by some over-exuberant journo – until the last face he saw. And then he stopped dead in his tracks and met the deep green gaze, steady and knowing, and felt for one split second as if he had never left her. The colour drained from his face and he swallowed hard before walking on to her table.

'Hello, Patrick.' She had turned her head to see what the commotion was and had seen him some time before he noticed her. She too had felt that feeling, as if all the pain had suddenly ceased to exist, but she had had time to control it. She looked at him now with all the poise and composure she could muster.

'Hello.'

Her voice has changed, he thought, but her face is still so lovely. He managed to smile. 'How are you?'

'I'm fine.' She too smiled, a guarded, polite smile. 'What are you doing in New York?'

'Business, politics.' He shrugged. God, this was banal. He wanted to pull her up and hold her tight to him; he wanted to touch her hair, kiss her. 'You?'

She laughed lightly. 'Business, fashion.'

John had turned from his conversation and he looked up at Patrick. 'Patrick. How are you?' he asked coolly.

'Fine, John, thank you.' He nodded to Dave, who had stood to introduce Will O'Connall. Patrick shook hands with the American.

'Would you like to join us?' O'Connall asked. There was a short, embarrassed silence at the table and Patrick declined politely.

He glanced briefly at Francesca. 'Where are you staying?'

She hesitated and O'Connall said loudly: 'I've put them up in the Asprey!' He smiled. 'I like to look after my business associates.'

'You certainly do, Will!' Dave exclaimed. 'I've never seen anything like it!' They all smiled, a little tensely, and Patrick took the moment to excuse himself.

'Very nice to meet you, Will.' He shook hands all round and then took a final look at Francesca. He could see John watching him out of the corner of his eye. 'Goodbye, Francesca.' She met his gaze and the green in her eyes seemed deeper and more intense than he could ever remember it. 'Goodbye, Patrick,' she answered softly. He nodded and strode away from the table.

'Wow! Who was that beauty?' The journalist who had called Patrick over was still staring at Francesca.

'An old friend,' Patrick answered.

The journo looked back at him. 'Francesca Cameron, of Cameron Yates, I think.' He smiled, a yellow, nicotine-stained smile, and slapped Patrick on the back. 'Good to see you, Patrick! You look well, particularly after all that shocking business with your wife.'

'Yes.' Patrick was offended by the man's over-familiar manner. He inched away from his embrace.

'Thought I'd give you my number, Patrick. I'm in New York for a few days and I thought we could get together for dinner one night. Talk about things? Chew the cud?'

Patrick suddenly remembered the man's first name: Peter Brett, one of the up and coming tabloid stars. 'I don't think so,' he replied coldly. He couldn't think straight; he kept looking back to Francesca.

'Come on, Paddy! We're old mates. No one really knows the story of what happened with Penny, but there's a lot of speculation, you can't deny that. It could be a chance for you to put the record straight.'

'I don't want to "put the record straight". There is nothing to "put straight"! Sorry!' He started to move away. The man was beginning to annoy him; he hated pushers.

'Come on, Paddy! You can talk to me. She had a few problems, your poor wife, or so I'm led to believe. Was there someone else perhaps?'

That was it – Patrick had had it. He focused all his attention on Brett. The man was more than slightly drunk and his breath smelled. 'Listen, Peter, a word of advice.' He leaned in close. 'If I wanted to talk about my personal life I can guarantee you that I'd pick someone with a little more integrity than a scumbag like you!' His face was only inches away. 'So fuck off! Got it?' He moved back a pace, smiled politely and turned to go back to his table. Brett stood stunned for less than five seconds and then he made his way over to the Maître d'.

'I want to make an international call. Where are the phones?' The Maître d' pointed to a discreetly hidden booth and Brett walked off. He had an idea in his head and he needed to check it out. If he could get the paper to lay some groundwork, put some feelers out in the UK, then he could fabricate a nice little story about the junior cabinet minister and his fashion designer girlfriend in New York. Not necessarily true, admittedly, but as long as there was enough evidence to point the finger, who cared? He dialled his paper and waited for the line to connect. Nobody told Peter Brett to fuck off!

He was through in a matter of seconds. 'Hello? Bob? It's Peter Brett. Yeah, fine! No, I'm in New York still. Yeah, it's all right.' He lit a cigarette and dropped the match on the floor. 'Listen, Bob, I think I might have a bit of a story for you, it's about Patrick Devlin . . . yeah, that's the one!' He smiled briefly. Everyone knew the good-looking, charming Patrick Devlin. 'What? Yeah, he is. I just met him as a matter of fact. *What?* You're joking! When did this happen? Jesus!' Brett dropped the half-finished butt of his cigarette on the floor and ground it out under the heel of his shoe. His blood pressure had gone through the roof. 'So let me get this straight! Cameron Yates' solicitor was burgled and the contents of the safe included documents on an affair between Devlin and Francesca Cameron? He's the father of her child? Jesus! And Lady Margaret Smith-Colyne owns a huge percentage of the company under a false name?' Brett started to laugh. 'This is absolutely bloody fantastic! When does the story break? . . . Shit, tomorrow?' He thought quickly. 'No, listen, Bob! Can you hold off putting it to bed for say . . . a couple of hours or so?' He moved agitatedly inside the booth. 'You can? Brilliant! If I can get hold of CBN News, and a couple of photographers, I can be over at Cameron's hotel in fifteen minutes.' He felt in his pocket for his address book. 'Listen, I'll ring in again with my copy in about an hour, personal interview, photos if we're lucky, maybe even some tape! Let's say an hour and a half at the latest . . . What?' Again he laughed. 'No less than his resignation, I think, don't you? Arrogant little git!' And with that he hung up, slapped the counter with the palm of his hand and, smiling, hurried across to the Maître d' to pay his bill and cancel his dinner appointment.

Out on the sidewalk, in front of the building, Patrick kissed Liz and she hugged him close for a few moments. 'Are you sure you won't come back with us for coffee?' She was worried. He looked shaken and had wanted to leave the restaurant so abruptly that they'd simply paid up and departed without another word.

He shook his head. 'Thanks, Liz, but no. I'm pretty tired and I need some air.' He turned to Bill and they shook hands. 'Thank you for dinner.'

'A pleasure, Paddy. Are you sure you're all right?'

'Yup. Sure.'

'You'll take care now, won't you? Don't walk too far.'

Patrick smiled. 'No, Liz, I won't. I'll probably hang around here for a while, look at the center maybe, see Radio City Music Hall.' He shrugged, but he knew exactly what he was going to do.

'OK. If you're sure.'

'Yes, thanks, I'm sure.' He kissed Liz again and she tutted maternally. 'Bye, bye. I'll ring you.'

'All right. Bye, Paddy.'

Bill took her arm. 'Goodbye, Patrick. Speak to you anon.'

He watched them walk away and Moira turned before Bill hailed a taxi, and waved a last time. When they had driven off Patrick whistled for his own cab.

'Asprey, please,' he said and climbed in. The car pulled away. He didn't know if she would speak to him, but after seeing her again, he knew he had to try. It was time for the truth, and loving her, as he knew he still did, nothing else would ever do.

The young man on the desk at the Asprey was new to the job, but he had met Marianne Hart and her Italian gigolo; they were legendary in the hotel for the huge amounts of cash they spent. He'd heard that they dealt drugs – only to a select few of course, friends and such – and he knew the score. If something was going down he had been told to discreetly give out the room number they wanted and then turn a blind eye. With clients like Marianne Hart, who never tipped less than a hundred, you more or less gave them carte blanche and you certainly never asked questions. Money talks, or so he'd been told, and she had enough to keep everyone quiet.

He saw Enzo Mondello enter the hotel lobby and recognised him immediately. He nodded in his direction and sent the bellboy over for the room number. Writing the number of the Cameron Yates suite down on a piece of paper, he handed it to the bellboy and expected to see Marianne Hart come into the hotel after Mondello. He glanced over to the doors, surprised not to see her, and then turned back to Mondello.

That's odd, he thought. Mondello had already disappeared, without the customary tip and with no sign of his girlfriend. What the hell? The desk clerk shrugged; it was none of his business anyway.

Enzo took the back stairs up to the fourth floor, walked along the corridor to the suite and slipped his skeleton key into the door handle, silently turning it and unlocking the door. He eased it open and stepped inside the room. He was completely in control.

Walking through the sitting room, he looked around him at the pile of drawings on the table, the open magazines, a discarded jacket, then he stopped to leaf through the small pile of photographs on the sofa table. He picked up the first one and Jamie Cameron smiled up at him. He held the snapshot for several minutes, shocked and confused. It didn't make sense to him. The child, dark-haired and olive-skinned, who was he? He shook his head. Then he saw the eyes, the deep green eyes, and he understood. He crushed the smiling image in his hand, screwed it into a tight ball and cracked his fist hard against the wall. 'Jesus . . .!' He let out a strangled cry. She had deceived him, sullied herself, dirtied herself. He swallowed back the anger, and, walking across the room, he opened the bedroom door and stepped inside. There he saw the child asleep.

Switching off the small speaker that was the baby-sitting device, he crossed to the cot and crouched down to look at the innocent, sleeping face through the wooden bars. The face of her child. He could smell the clean sweetness of the baby's skin and, as he listened to the quiet, regular breathing of tiny lungs, he pressed his head against the side of the infant's bed and silently began to cry.

Francesca climbed out of the taxi while John paid the driver. She waited for him on the sidewalk outside the hotel.

'I'm sorry, John, you sure you don't mind leaving the dinner early?'

He took her arm. 'Will you just stop apologising? Hmmm? You know I don't like nightclubs and besides, Will's got his work cut out for him with Dave in tow!'

She tried to smile at his joke but her heart wasn't in it. John turned to face her. Damn bloody Patrick Devlin, he thought, damn the bastard to hell! But he couldn't let her see his impotent rage. Quietly he said: 'I'm happier back with Jamie anyway.' Which was the truth. 'I don't trust those baby-sitting services.' He placed both his hands on her shoulders. He'd known from the moment he saw her eyes on Devlin how she felt.

Francesca looked up at his face and shook her head. 'Poor John,' she said. 'I am sorry, I've ruined your evening.'

And suddenly he had to say something; he had to tell her, before it was too late. 'You've never ruined anything for me, Francesca,' he answered quietly. 'You made my life, my darling girl; you've given me more than I had ever dreamed of.' He looked away and felt the warmth of her breath on his cheek.

'And you me,' she whispered. Then she stood back and

laughed at the tears in her eyes. 'What a sentimental pair we are!' she said and took his hand. Together they walked into the hotel.

Patrick was waiting for her in the lobby. He was standing near the entrance, having told the desk clerk who he was and what he was doing there, and as he saw her walk in with John he stepped forward and they looked at each other for a long moment. She turned to John.

'I have to speak to him,' she said and he nodded.

He knew that, and he let her go. 'Don't be too long.'

She shook her head. She had wanted to say: 'I love you, John, I always will.' But she didn't want to embarrass him. So she just squeezed his hand and smiled at him as he walked towards the lift. In years to come she would remember it as the saddest moment of her life.

John tried not to think of anything as he walked along to the suite, except Jamie. He would look in on him, watch him sleeping for a while. The sight always calmed him, reassured him of the hope in life. Stopping outside the suite, he dug in his pocket for the key and went to put it in the lock. The door was already open.

His first thought was that someone from the baby-sitting service was in there. He never suspected any danger. He walked in and called out, crossing to Francesca's room where Jamie was asleep. It gave Enzo just enough time to move behind the door.

'Hello?' John carefully opened the door and peered into the room. 'Who's there?' It was lit by a dull red night-light and he looked across to the cot and Jamie, who, wide awake, smiled when he saw him. 'Hello, my boy!' he said gently.

The cut was quick and sudden.

Enzo grabbed him from behind and sliced the length of his throat with his knife, shutting off life almost instantly. The last thing John knew was the sound of Jamie's voice as he called out 'Dada!' to him and the smile on the little boy's face. He died with a searing joy in his heart.

The child began to scream.

Enzo moved quickly. He let John's body slump to the floor and ran to the cot, pulling the child up and cupping his bloody hand over the his mouth to silence the screaming. Grabbing a blanket from the cot, he held tightly onto the infant and ran out of the room. He didn't have time to think. Knowing the hotel as he did, he ran down the back stairs, through the laundry rooms and out onto Forty-ninth Street East. He covered the child with the blanket, keeping his hand roughly over his mouth, and made off in the direction of Forty-second street and Grand Central Station.

Patrick looked down at his watch. 'Ten minutes. It wasn't very long.' It was all she would agree to and he had hardly been able to say anything, only the bare facts about Penny and the baby. He wanted more; he wanted a lifetime, but Francesca just shrugged and said: 'I'm sorry. I need time.'

'Of course.' He looked away. Why did he feel as if they didn't have it? 'I understand.' He knew he didn't have any right to expect more. He stood up with her. 'You'll let me see you tomorrow?'

She hesitated. 'I don't know, I . . .' She hadn't told him about Jamie, not yet, maybe not ever. 'I'll call you.' He nodded – what else could he do? She began to walk across to the lifts.

'Francesca?' She turned back to him. He wanted to see her eyes. They had the same intense brilliance that he remembered and he felt a moment of hope. 'Is there anyone else?' He had to ask; he couldn't stop himself.

'No,' she said, 'there never has been.' And she carried on to the lifts. He watched her disappear before turning back towards the bar. He needed another drink.

It was only five minutes later that he heard the piercing, terrifying howl of the sirens. The lobby was suddenly filled with people: paramedics, police. Some were running, others stood with service revolvers drawn, and tape was being placed at the entrance to the hotel. He jumped down from the bar stool and elbowed his way out into the fray. It took only seconds to pick up on what had happened and then he ran, shoving his way through the small crowd, ignoring the shouts behind him, up the stairs to the fourth floor, his body throbbing with fear. As he made it to the corridor he opened the fire door and instantly he heard her screams.

Wild, desperate, animal screams.

CHAPTER
Thirty-seven

ENZO'S LUNGS WERE BURNING. HE coughed up more phlegm and spat it over the child's head. He was sweating, a heavy, pulsing sweat. He gripped the child more tightly and edged out of the shadowed doorway, then walked quickly down Fortieth Street East, cutting past the library, then up onto Forty-second Street. He made it into Times Square and merged in with the theatre crowd. The child was silent, wide-eyed and terrified.

Enzo wasn't thinking, he knew that. He'd panicked, seen the patrol car and freaked. They'd covered the station – it was crawling. He looked down at the child. Jesus fuck! He stopped in a doorway again, breathing hard. Jesus fuck!

'Over there on the right! Next to McDonald's. See it? Whadda ya think?' Both policemen had the man's description from the desk clerk at the Waldorf.

'Yup, got him!' Weller picked up the radio and switched it on. 'Looks like our guy.' The car swung sharp right to turn. 'Suspect spotted . . . Times Square, doorway of . . .'

'Shit! He's seen us!'

'Suspect moving off in the direction of . . . Jesus! Where the fuck's he gone?'

'Headed down the Deuce . . .'

'Pursuing suspect . . . east down Forty-second Street.' The lights went on and the siren wailed. 'Get out the fucking way, arsehole!' Weller shouted at a driver. 'Ah Jesus! He's gone! Way outta sight!'

*

Enzo slipped down an alleyway off Broadway and waited in the dark. A garish orange light advertising a twenty-five cent peepshow lit the grimy grey walls every five seconds and the stench was disgusting. He coughed up more phlegm and put his hand up to his throat. It burned like hell. Seconds later he spotted a cab pulling up alongside the alley. Holding onto the dead weight of the child, he ran to the car and pulled open the door.

'Whoa! What's the hurry, man? Take it easy, don't ruin my cab!'

Enzo slammed the door and leaned forward to the driver. He put the blade of his knife up against his neck and nicked the skin to draw blood.

'Drive!' he hissed.

'Shit! Jesus! OK! Where to, man? Just tell me where to?' The driver's voice was high with fear. He inched his thigh up to his fog light switch.

'I don't know! Just drive!' The car moved off and Enzo kept his knife tight to the man's throat. He still held the child to his body. He didn't know what to do; he could feel himself losing control. He was scared, for the first time in years, he was shit scared.

'Cab nineteen-twenty-one. I'm mid-town, heading west. I've just seen four-seven-twelve with fog light on. Can you put out a nine-eleven call? Looks like he's in trouble.'

'Gotcha, nineteen-twenty-one. Will do.'

Weller took the call from the radio dispatcher.

'Sounds like our guy again, hijacked a cab round the back of the Deuce.'

'Let's go! Hold on tight!' The patrol car did a twenty-mile-an-hour U-turn and set up pursuit. They radioed for assistance as they headed downtown towards Tenth Street East and New York City's low-life.

'Miss Cameron?'

Francesca looked up blankly. The room was full of people. She was completely silent but the screams went on inside her head. On and on.

'Miss Cameron?'

'Sorry?' Patrick squeezed her hand.

'Detective Sergeant Macey, Miss Cameron. We think we've located the suspect.' Francesca flinched and the policewoman felt for her – she had children of her own.

'Where is he? Has he got Jamie?' Her voice was high with panic.

'We think so.' Again Francesca flinched. 'Look, I'm sorry, but we need to know if there's any connection to you at all or if this is simply a drug-related crime.'

'What do you mean, simply?' It came out as a scream and Francesca felt Patrick's hand restrain her.

'I'm sorry, I didn't mean that. Francesca, we have a description from the desk clerk of an Italian man seen earlier in the hotel asking for your room number. We checked his address and found the body of his girlfriend; she's been murdered. Look, I'm sorry to have to put you through this, but do you know, or have you ever heard of a man called Enzo Mondello? We have reason to believe he's our sus . . .'

For a split second Francesca felt the ground slip from under her and her legs gave way. She toppled and Patrick caught her just in time. She swallowed back the screams in her head. 'Yes,' she whispered. 'I know him.' She spoke almost like a child and then moments later, looked up. Her whole face had changed, hardened.

'It's not my son he wants,' she said. 'It's me.'

Detective Sergeant Macey looked hard at the young

528

woman in front of her and made the sort of intuitive decision that had won her her promotion.

'OK,' she said. 'We think we know where he is.' She handed Francesca a vest. 'Let's go!'

Patrick stood next to Francesca in the lift down to the lobby but she kept her distance. He wasn't part of her life and he knew she could not turn to him for support. Yet Jamie was his child! He was shocked, it was almost too much to take in. What he had learned in the last half-hour had changed his life forever but still he felt the gulf between them and his helplessness overwhelmed him. The lift stopped and he stood back a pace to let her out first, the automatic doors sliding open with an electronic ping. It was the last second of silence they had.

'There he is!' 'Over there!' 'They're together!'

'Hey! Miss Cameron? Patrick? Hey! Over here!' The flash of the cameras exploded in their faces and the rush of noise hit them head on. The lobby was packed with a mob of reporters who flanked them either side, pushing and jostling, shouting for attention.

'Is it true, Patrick?' 'Have you any comment to make?' 'Did your wife know about your affair with Francesca? Did she know about the child?' Patrick's arm went automatically around Francesca's shoulder but her body was stiff and tense, her face ashen with shock.

'Did your affair have anything to do with her alcoholism?' The shouts grew louder, more insistent and aggressive. Francesca began to shake.

'Tell them it isn't true,' she whispered. 'Please, don't ruin your life . . .' But Patrick had her hand in his and he gripped her fingers so hard that the pain made her wince. He said nothing. Scanning the crowd for one particular face, he tugged her forward, following close behind the policeman, and trying in vain to shield her from the horror. At the end of the lobby he saw Peter Brett. The man was smiling.

'Brett!' He spotted the camera crew from CBN with Brett but it didn't stop him. 'Brett!' he shouted. The smile disappeared from Brett's face and a harsh triumphant look came over it. The crew made a rush towards Patrick.

'What the   .?' Francesca turned to him. 'Patrick, no! Please   .' Her face was stricken with fear. 'You mustn't say anything, please   ' She moved away to try and distance herself from him. 'You can deny it . . . you must!'

Brett shoved his way through the crowd, only feet away. 'No,' Patrick said. 'No more lies.' And he called out again to Brett. 'You want a story, Brett?' The camera loomed in on him, its huge sound mike just under his nose. 'Here it is. Our son has been abducted! The man is armed and dangerous, and he's somewhere on the loose in this city. For God's sake, find him! Put his picture out across the screen, tell everyone. Just please . . .' His voice broke. '. . . Find my son!' Pulling Francesca close to him, he moved past the camera and on through the crowd to the entrance of the lobby. The noise had quietened for the few seconds that Patrick spoke but now it erupted. Everywhere around them the screaming, frantic howl of the crowd could be heard as they clamoured for the story, and it followed them out onto the street. Peter Brett shook hands with the reporter from CBN News and then headed along to the row of telephone booths just past the reception desk to call the UK and file his story.

Enzo had ditched the cab at the back of St Mark's Church. He was being hounded. He ran, holding the child with both hands, his knife tucked inside the waistband of his trousers. He had to keep hold of the child. She'd come for the child, he knew that. She'd come for the boy.

The landscape changed as he ran on, deeper into the housing projects, the streets littered with garbage, the walls filthy with graffiti. He passed a derelict car and someone spat at him. He looked down at the mucus on his jacket but he didn't stop. All around him he could hear the wail of sirens and he knew he didn't have much time.

On Ninth Street, on the edge of Tomkins Square Park, he ran into an alley and stopped. He dropped the child down onto the ground and bent double with the effort of trying to breathe. The pain was terrible. The heat in his lungs had spread up his throat, and it burned, dry and red hot as he gasped for air. He was dizzy with the lack of oxygen. He closed his eyes for a second and when he opened them again the intensity of the light blinded him. He blinked twice in the glare of the headlamps, heard the engine noise and yanked the child up onto his hip. He backed against the wall of a tenement block, holding his knife up to the child's throat. There was no way out.

As the car edged closer, he glanced behind him and in an instant started to climb the fire escape.

Weller was out of the car, revolver drawn, and his partner was positioned on the other side. They waited for the back-up.

'What the fuck's he doing?'

'He knows we won't fire with the kid up there.'

'Bastard!' Weller was sweating.

Minutes later two more cars pulled up, all lights and sirens off. This wasn't an area to attract attention in. Detective Sergeant Macey jumped out of the car and went towards Weller. 'How long's he been up there?'

'Three, maybe five minutes.' Weller kept his eyes on the suspect.

'How's he looking?'

'Shit scared. Dangerous!'

She turned round for Francesca but the car was empty.

'What the . . .?' She moved over to the car. 'Jesus, that's all we need! Where is she? Where's Devlin?' The officer nodded towards the building. Francesca was walking in the direct light of the car headlamps towards Enzo. Her eyes were fixed on his face and he looked down at her, as he had done a million times in his dreams.

'Oh fuck!' Macey grabbed the radio to call for medical assistance. The next thing she knew she saw Devlin on the roof of the building. 'Jesus fucking Christ! I don't believe it. What do these fucking Brits think this is? A fucking cop movie?' The officer next to her moved round the car into a better cover position. She motioned to Weller. 'Get over to the left,' she hissed. 'Cover him that side. For God's sake, don't fucking shoot, not unless . . .' Her voice trailed away as Francesca reached the tenement block. She held her breath.

'Enzo?' Francesca was right underneath him now and she could see the ashen face of her son. She kept her eyes on Enzo, Patrick's shadow moving up above him.

'Francesca. I knew you'd come.'

'Of course I'd come for you, Enzo.' She could just see his eyes, blank and distant. 'You still want me then?'

He shivered and his whole body was filled with a deep ache for her. 'Yeah,' he said. 'I still want you.'

She sensed the change in him, saw his fingers relaxing their grip. She moved back slightly to where he had to strain forward to see her and began to unbutton her shirt.

'Remember, Enzo, how you used to watch me undress?' Her voice had softened, calmed, and she willed him to relax. The shirt fell open and she slipped it off her shoulders.

'Do you, Enzo?' Her eyes shone and he was drawn to the

light in them. She slipped the straps of her bodice down and he felt the lick of fire in his groin, the burning lust for her. He dropped his hand down to his crotch.

'NOW!'

Patrick lunged forward and grabbed his son's arm with every ounce of strength he had in his body. He pulled, yanking the child free, felt his balance waver and then his leg slip, crashing his spine down sharply onto the ironwork of the fire escape. He had Jamie in his arms and as he cried out, he hugged his son to him and held him with the force of his whole body. They fell against the building, together, crashing back. But they were safe.

The gunfire was instant.

Enzo plummeted forward, his body already limp in death, and fell five floors. Francesca screamed as his form smashed on the iron stairs and broke itself, crashing onto the concrete, the blood of his shattered skull splattering the cold grey surface of the street.

She ran forward.

Running up the fire escape, she called out to her son, to Patrick, stumbling, shaking with fear and relief. She fell several times and cut her legs but she didn't stop. She made it to the fifth landing and knelt before Patrick, surrounding him with her arms and holding both her son and his father to her heart. She began to sob.

Weller and his fellow officers began to move forward to the fire escape.

'Leave them!' Macey said sharply. The men stopped. 'They don't need us.' She looked away and swallowed hard. 'They need each other.'

And she turned and went back to the car.

CHAPTER Thirty-eight

PETER BRETT'S STORY WAS PRINTED in one of the biggest tabloid newspapers in the UK alongside the exclusive revelation of the true life of the Junior Foreign Minister, Patrick Devlin. The paper carried stills from the live coverage at CBN News in New York, photostats of the documents stolen from the Cameron Yates solicitor and the photographs that the *Mail* photographer had taken of Francesca and Patrick years ago in London. It hit the breakfast tables in Britain at approximately the same time as Patrick Devlin was transferred to the Mount Sinai Hospital in New York. He had the woman he loved and his son by his side.

Lady Margaret sat in the morning room at Motcom Park, a copy of the paper open in front of her and the tears of anger and humiliation wet on her face. It was all there, in black and white, the story of her brother's passionate love affair and her own shoddy involvement in trying to keep him from it. The paper had speculated, of course it had, in order to piece the whole thing together. But they'd done a pretty good job; the whole thing was as near to the truth as it could be. There wasn't much they had left out.

Hearing Lord Henry outside in the passage, Lady Margaret wiped her cheek with the back of her hand and folded the paper away. She stood and walked across to the fireplace where she'd left her cigarettes. She was opening the box when Lord Henry came into the room. She paused for a moment and looked over at him, saying nothing.

'I see you've read the paper then?' he said. His face was closed and she dropped the box with shock.

'I . . . er . . .' She bent to pick it up and he stood by the door watching her. She glanced up. 'Yes, I have.' Straightening, she pulled out a cigarette and lit it. She did not look at him again.

'Then I would hope, Margaret, that this will be an end to the whole thing.' He stayed by the door. 'And I do mean the *whole thing*!'

She turned now and faced him. 'Meaning?' her voice was cool, challenging.

'Meaning Richard Brachen, Charles Hewitt, politics, ambition and . . .' He stopped. Her face had suddenly lost its habitual hauteur and seemed to collapse before his eyes. 'And trying to make up for the mistakes you made in the past. It's over, Margaret, all of it, and I think it's about time you realised that.'

She had started to cry and put her hands up to her face, ashamed to be seen in such weakness.

'It became an obsession, Margaret,' Lord Henry said, more to himself than to her, 'and I didn't know how to stop it all. I am as much to blame as you, really.' He walked across to her and put his hands on her shoulders. 'There are some things we just can't change, Maggie my love, and the past is one of them. Let it go.' He took out his handkerchief and gently wiped her face. 'I think we've all suffered enough, don't you?'

Warner now offers an exciting range of quality titles by both established and new authors. All of the books in this series are available from:
Little, Brown and Company (UK) Limited,
P.O. Box 11,
Falmouth,
Cornwall TR10 9EN.

Alternatively you may fax your order to the above address. Fax No. 0326 376423.

Payments can be made as follows: Cheque, postal order (payable to Little, Brown and Company) or by credit cards, Visa/Access. Do not send cash or currency. UK customers: and B.F.P.O.: please send a cheque or postal order (no currency) and allow £1.00 for postage and packing for the first book, plus 50p for the second book, plus 30p for each additional book up to a maximum charge of £3.00 (7 books plus).

Overseas customers including Ireland, please allow £2.00 for postage and packing for the first book, plus £1.00 for the second book, plus 50p for each additional book.

NAME (Block Letters) ....

ADDRESS...

....

☐ I enclose my remittance for _____

☐ I wish to pay by Access/Visa Card

Number ☐☐☐☐☐☐☐☐☐☐☐☐☐☐☐☐☐☐☐

Card Expiry Date ☐☐☐☐